A GARRISON CHASE THRILLER

THE BAJA DIRECTIVE

CRAIG N. HOOPER

"But these few are the salt of the earth; without them, human life would become a stagnant pool."

— JOHN STUART MILL

CHAPTER ONE

THE PRESIDENTIAL MOTORCADE turned left off Highway One and barreled east down my mile-long gravel driveway. From my front porch, I sipped coffee and watched five Chevy Suburbans blow by the small Private Drive sign attached to my mailbox post.

Apparently, I needed a bigger sign.

Moments ago I was throwing my dog, Ranger, a slobbery tennis ball and waiting for the exact moment the sun peeked over the rolling hills behind my house. Since I had a peekaboo view of the ocean, it was a beautiful sight when the sun's early-morning rays cascaded across the blue water. Right now, however, my slim view of the Pacific was obliterated by a thickening dust cloud kicked up by the vehicles.

The three black SUVs at the rear of the convoy stopped suddenly about a quarter mile from my humble abode.

"Easy, boy," I said, grasping Ranger's collar and holding the German shepherd back.

The front two Suburbans, which were the route car and pilot car, continued their advance. They'd sweep in first, check things out, then radio the lead vehicle once they'd determined no immediate threats were in the area. Years back, when I was with the Bureau, I had a colleague who'd worked as a secret service agent. He'd spent four years on motorcade duty and talked my ear off about his time with the organization, so I was familiar with their procedures.

As the two Suburbans approached, they showed no signs of slowing. The deep, throaty burble of their engines echoed across my land. When they got closer, the cracking and popping of gravel underneath their tires sent Ranger into a tizzy.

"Easy, boy," I repeated.

Ranger didn't obey. He kept straining against his collar. Being a German shepherd, you'd think he was champing at the bit to charge these cars. Not so. All Ranger wanted to do was scamper off. He was a traumatized war dog I'd been unsuccessfully trying to rehabilitate for some time.

After a few strokes behind his ear, I let go of his collar. He stayed for a moment. But when the SUVs skidded to a stop in front of my porch, he bolted to the left and scrambled around the corner of my house in a desperate attempt to get to Mom's place. Mom lived in a granny unit behind the main house and Ranger often took refuge from visitors there. Currently, she was in Morro Bay at Dolly's Donuts with my son, Simon. Every Saturday morning she took him there for some sugary delights.

Two men from each vehicle quickly exited. Not surprisingly, they wore dark suits, and each man had an earpiece in his left ear. Sort of surprising was the fact that they paid zero attention to me. Not even a hello or a nod in my direction. I sat calmly, kept sipping my black coffee, and watched them work. Two agents circled my house in opposite directions. The other two kept their eyes glued to the horizon.

Naturally, I was surprised to experience an impromptu visit from the president of the United States. But, if I was being honest, it wasn't completely shocking since I had a history with POTUS. And yesterday I read in the local paper she was in California to bolster support from her top donors. She held a fundraising event last night for her reelection campaign at a Pebble Beach golf course, which was a couple of hours north of my place in Cayucos. Since the motorcade turned left onto my property, that meant the convoy came from the north. Perhaps the president wanted to see the beautiful stretch of Big Sur coastline on her way south through the state. But if she left from Monterey this morning, it would've been dark, and she would've missed the views.

Why come that windy, long route in the dark? And why stop here?

Once the agents reconvened at their vehicles and determined there were no imminent threats in the area, one of them radioed back. Within seconds of the call, the remaining three vehicles proceeded toward my place. The SUVs parked single file on the left side of my driveway.

President Henrietta Valenzuela exited the middle of the three vehicles. She held a leather valise in her left hand and wore a navy blue tweed coat that extended to her knees. A gray skirt poked out just below the coat's hem. Her dark heels were probably three inches high and had some girth to them. They weren't pencil-thin, night-on-the-town type heels. They were sensible and practical, just like she was.

Two agents swept in and spoke with her. Their backs were toward me, so I couldn't hear what they were saying. The president shook her head and waved them off, then proceeded toward my porch. The agents rushed alongside her, imploring her to stop.

She didn't. POTUS maintained her pace and glanced in my direction, giving me an exasperated look. Her long chestnut-brown hair bobbed with each step. The president had a dark complexion, a courtesy of her Mexican heritage. Though the woman was in her early sixties, she looked ten years younger. Easily.

Aside from her captivating green eyes, the president's other features were quite plain. The way she carried herself, however, with such strength and confidence, added a layer of attractiveness to her persona. I had always thought she was a striking woman, and that was now confirmed in person.

The secret service agents tried one last time to stop her approach, one of them even hurrying in front to block her from moving forward. I could hear them now.

The agent to her left said, "Madam President, we haven't secured inside the house yet. Please, wait here. Let us do our jobs."

"Hurry it up then." She stopped her forward march, looked at me, and mouthed, "Sorry about this."

As an agent rushed onto my porch, I did the polite thing and opened the door for him.

The president addressed the other agent. "We'll stay outside. All right with you, Mr. Chase"—she glanced over—"if we sit on your porch and chat? It is a fabulous morning after all."

"Sure thing," I said.

"All right with you?" the president said to her agent.

The agent was reluctant to respond, so she pushed past him.

"Madam President," he said, "I'll need to pat down Mr. Chase at least."

"Mr. Chase isn't a threat." She smiled at me. "Clearly."

The president had that right. I wore flip-flops and black sweatpants, and my royal-blue Golden State Warriors hoodie had a coffee stain on the left side of the chest area.

"It's okay, Madam President," I said as the agent hustled toward me. "Not a problem."

While he thoroughly frisked me, the other agent exited my house and conferred with the president that all was safe. Once both agents were by their vehicle, Henrietta Valenzuela stepped onto the porch with her hand extended.

I subtly pressed my right palm against my sweats to dry off the Ranger slobber, then shook her hand.

"Nice to finally meet you, Mr. Chase." She had soft hands but a firm shake.

"Likewise," I replied. "But please, call me Garrison." Though I preferred being called Chase, I thought it would be weird to tell the president to refer to me by my last name.

Before I had a chance to offer her a seat, the president grabbed one of the two Adirondack chairs on my porch and scraped it close to the one I'd been using. She stared at me with piercing green eyes. A large, infectious grin spread across her face. "So sorry this is the first time we're meeting, Garrison. I mean, you arguably put me in this job."

"Madam President, I was just doing my duty. My involvement in how things transpired in the presidential election was"—I paused to think of the right word—"inadvertent, ma'am. Totally inadvertent. An unintended consequence."

Three years back, just after the presidential primaries, I brought down her chief opponent. The opponent and his wife were into some serious treasonous business, which I uncovered during an intense FBI investigation. After the conspiracy was exposed, she was a shoo-in for the presidency since she ran virtually unopposed.

"First off," the president said, "we're in private here, and I must insist you call me Henrietta."

I was about to object, but she held up her right hand.

"I know that's difficult for you, Garrison, being in the military all those years ago, not to mention being a former operative and federal agent. Chain of command is in your blood, I get that. I certainly do. But, please, I have to insist."

"Since that's a direct order from my commander in chief, then Henrietta it is."

"Good," she said, nodding. "Now, listen, you did our country an incredible service, for which I'm eternally grateful. Again, I should've visited you in person earlier, but at the time it may have been construed as gloating or congratulatory or just simply inappropriate. You know, the optics of it all—"

"Totally understand, Madam Pres—I mean—Henrietta. Didn't expect a personal visit. Didn't think twice about it. And the letter you sent was lovely."

Good thing we hadn't gone inside. The president may have scanned my walls for the letter she'd written. And she wouldn't have found it. Mom was so enthralled by the note that I gave it to her. She framed it and kept it on the piano in her living room.

"That's kind of you to say, Garrison, but a letter doesn't quite encapsulate my gratitude. I've been meaning to reach out and connect, but time has certainly gotten away from me."

"You are the leader of the free world, so I'll cut you some slack."

She laughed, then reached out and tapped my knee.

"And besides," I continued, "you're here now, and that took some real effort. I can't imagine what you went through to get a small motorcade here." I motioned toward the vehicles. "That's probably half your usual fleet, isn't it? Plus, no sweepers or rear guard." I pointed in the air. "And no overwatch either. My guess is nobody knows you're here."

She pulled her hand away and settled into the Adirondack chair. "Look at that. A simple, well-built wooden chair is more comfortable than my seat in the Oval Office. I'll be. That's something." She patted the armrests, admired the chair for a moment, then looked up. "You're absolutely right. Most of my team is baffled about this impromptu deviation, and it certainly took some convincing. The rest of the presidential motorcade is currently proceeding south on the 101, with all the usual pomp and circumstance."

"And you're not with them," I added. "You're here, after a long and convoluted route down Highway One in the pitch-darkness." I leaned forward. "This can't be about meeting me in person to express your gratitude."

She shifted toward me and placed her right palm on my forearm and held it there. The president was way more touchy-feely than I would've guessed.

"That obvious?" she asked.

I nodded.

She kept her eyes on me. "You know, Garrison, since taking office, I've been following your career. From a distance, of course."

I scoffed. "My career? Some career. Spellbinding, right?"

"Seriously," she said, giving my forearm a subtle squeeze. "Where you ended up, as an independent security contractor, totally makes sense to me. Especially given your skills and . . ."

When she didn't continue, I prodded. "And what?"

"And demeanor." She paused for a moment, then said, "Makeup would probably be a better word."

Before I could ask what she meant, the president said, "I know you're not a licensed private investigator and that you detest being mislabeled as one. Isn't that right?"

She's done her due diligence at least. I nodded.

"Being the type of person you are," she continued, "your line of work fits. Totally makes sense."

I furrowed my brow. "And what type of person is that?"

"Someone with a strong sense of justice," she replied, not missing a beat. "A man who won't be encumbered by rules, not when they don't line up with what is right. It's no surprise—at least not to me—that you didn't last with the Bureau. Not with all their politicking and rule-following. A man like you thrives on his own; answers only to himself and his conscience."

Oh boy. I ran my right hand over my stubbled head. *Where is this butter-up going?*

"I need your help, Garrison. I need someone like you, now more than ever. And I need your absolute discretion, especially considering the ask. You're no longer a federal employee so your security clearances have been revoked, but that doesn't matter since this is extremely risky for me and so far off the books that..." She sighed and didn't finish her sentence.

"Henrietta, you said you know the kind of man I am. So, whatever happens here, whatever is communicated, stays between us. You have my word."

She nodded. "I know. That's why I'm here."

When she didn't continue, I said, "What do you need my help with?"

Henrietta glanced at her agents, who were standing by the Suburbans. Their eyes scanned the horizon and paid no attention to us. She spoke in a soft tone. "I need your help with a situation."

When she paused to lean in, I pushed her. "What kind of situation, ma'am?"

Still in a soft tone, she said, "Well, it's more of a person than a situation really."

"Okay, who then? And what do you want with this particular person?"

Her eyes locked on mine and took on a steely resolve. "I want you to . . ." The president paused and took a deep breath. After exhaling, she blurted, "Take care of them, Garrison. I want you to take care of this particular person."

I coughed into my arm, then looked back to see if she was serious.

Her expression hadn't changed.

"Madam President," I said, clearing my throat. "Are you asking me to kill someone?"

CHAPTER TWO

You'd think a seasoned politician like Henrietta Valenzuela would shy away from answering that question directly. Not this president. She was a straight shooter that embraced honesty.

"Yes, I am," she replied while maintaining her stare. "That's exactly what I'm asking."

I swallowed.

She continued. "Certainly once you get all the facts about this particular person and their circumstances, if you can think of something better, perhaps a more creative idea that doesn't end in termination, then I'm open to that. But from where I'm standing, and from what I know, that's what must happen. And I think you're just the man for the job."

I avoided her stare.

"Hear me out. I know it's a crazy, desperate ask, Garrison. If you want to categorically reject my proposition, fine. Just hear the situation first and what I'm up against, then decide. Like you said, you'll be discreet about this. And after hearing everything, if your decision is a no, then this conversation never happened. I'll have to insist on that. A very strong insistence, in fact."

For some reason, I envisioned scenes from the movie *Men in Black* where Will Smith and Tommy Lee Jones wiped memories clean by a flash from their fancy Neuralyzers.

Is that what her secret service agents will do to me if I say no?

"Garrison, are you still with me?"

I snapped out of it. "Sure, you just caught me off guard."

"Understandable," she replied. "Now you and your partner, Hans, operate a security firm, and your main clientele are members of Congress, so I assume you're up to speed on the current political climate."

Henrietta was correct about the security firm and our clientele, but she was wrong about us being partners. I simply worked for my buddy Hans—aka Slim—as an independent contractor. I took all his West Coast jobs. She was also wrong about me being up to speed on politics. That was Slim's specialty, not mine.

"What I'm getting at, Garrison, is I'm sure you know all about the political hell I've been going through, and what I'm currently up against."

She waited for me to answer. I didn't follow her political career too closely, but I didn't want to admit that and look like a dufus in front of POTUS, so I nodded.

"Originally, I'd commissioned a black-ops team for this mission. They were supposed to take out the target last week in Northern Baja. But everything started falling apart about a month ago, when that ATF raid in Nogales went haywire. I mean, that couldn't have gone worse, am I right?"

Though I didn't know specific details about the raid, I'd heard about it. Everyone had since the failed operation was all over the news for the past month. The president was in serious political hot water because she'd authorized a mission against Mexican cartel members that went south. Six American soldiers were ambushed and killed in the Nogales operation and Mexico was irate that they weren't consulted about the mission.

I nodded again and said, "It was bad; you're right."

Henrietta shook her head in exasperation and looked away, but she kept talking. "Because of the fallout from that botched mission, there was no way we could eliminate the current target, not on Mexican soil, anyway. And it's not like this man will ever set foot in America. So…" She tapped her fingers on the armrest.

"You want me to eliminate the target," I said. "You're here to hire my services, I suppose. Though killing isn't exactly a service listed on our website."

She grabbed my forearm again. "If there was another way, believe me, I'd take it. If there was another person, believe me, I'd ask them. But there's no one else I trust except you. If there was anything—"

"With all due respect, Henrietta," I interrupted, "I'm aware of the discreet black-ops teams you have at your disposal. Very aware. I mean, I was in The Activity a lifetime ago, and this job would be perfect for them. Beyond ideal, in fact."

"You're right," she replied, sighing. "It would be. The original plan was a sea-to-land mission, so I needed a naval team. That was why I had a SEAL Team Six ready to go and not The Activity. But with all the scrutiny and outrage from the botched Nogales operation, I can't risk using a black-ops team. I need a lone operative from outside the government. My administration can't be tied to this in any fashion, not even a rumor or a whiff of a rumor that we're involved. It's far too risky. Not only that, but it would also threaten everything we're trying to accomplish at the border. It would ruin my administration's revolutionary immigration policy."

I straightened in my seat. "Wait, is this a political legacy thing? Now that you're—sorry to say, Henrietta—maybe on your way out. Is that what this is all about?"

She hardened her gaze. "No, it most certainly is not. It's not about me or my legacy or shaping the history books in my favor. My legacy is forever tarnished from the botched Nogales mission and dead American soldiers. I'll likely be one of the few presidents to have just one term. I hope it doesn't play out that way, but it likely will, and I'll live with that. What I want is change—enduring change—Garrison. We absolutely must stop the illegal human trafficking that occurs between our country and Mexico. And we need to secure a reasonable path to citizenship for the Mexican workers. We're there. We're so close to making it happen." She peeled her gaze away. "We've worked so hard to get all the appropriate parties on board, so many concessions on both sides, but this one man . . ."

I watched her make a fist with her right hand and gently pound the armrest.

I settled back in my chair. "Okay, tell me about him. I want to hear it."

Her fist relaxed. She closed her eyes, only to open them a moment later. "Thank you for hearing me out. It means the world to me." Once again, she leaned over and touched my forearm. "What do you know about Operation Crossroads?"

Again, I didn't know much about her operations, especially that one, but I kept that nugget of information to myself.

"Enough," I said.

"Good," she replied. "We discovered damning information that stems from the Mexican employment agency my administration has been working closely with. The CEO of that agency, a man named Alejandro Ortiz, took on a silent partner to help bolster his financial situation. Ortiz knew this smooth-talking man from his past. Though the man had a somewhat questionable past, Ortiz believed he'd changed. He was wrong. The silent partner was still corrupt. Beyond corrupt, to say the least." The president looked up to the sky and shook her head in disgust.

"What was his partner doing?" I asked.

She shook her head again, then looked over. "This agency we work with recruits, hires, and trains Mexican employees. They pull workers from areas of Mexico where large Northern California agriculture companies also have their winter-time operations. They coordinate the workforce and bring the workers back and forth over the border, all legally, of course. The workers spend half the year in Northern California during their harvest season and the other half back home in Mexico during winter, which eliminates a lot of the historic problems between the Mexican workers and California employers. As these workers stay in the Crossroads program and build trust with their respective companies, they receive credit toward earning American citizenship. Citizenship isn't automatic, but it is a clear path toward that end goal. So, basically, it's an expansion on the H-2A visa program that already exists."

"Got it," I said. "So what about his partner?"

"Turns out Alejandro's partner is skimming some trainees—beautiful young women, that is—from the operation. Approximately two hundred of them."

"Two hundred?" I took a moment to digest that, then said, "With all due respect, ma'am, how'd you miss that?"

"The operation consists of 20,000 employees, Garrison, so two hundred amounts to just one percent of the total workforce. Not an excuse, it's simply a matter of workers slipping through the cracks of a very large operation."

"Or just bad oversight," I added.

"Point taken," she replied. "I delegated oversight and shouldn't have. At any rate, Alejandro's partner is doing everything to these women that we're trying to prevent. Everything we're dead set on eradicating, Garrison. Which, of course, is…" The president couldn't bring herself to say it.

So I did. "Sex trafficking and drug muling?"

As she slowly nodded, now I was the one pounding the armrest.

"When we found this out," she continued, "we immediately suspended the program, citing some administration snafus until we could figure out a solution."

"Why not just shut it down permanently?"

"Because the lives of two hundred women are at stake."

"How so?"

"Ortiz's partner, a man named Juan Manuel Delgado, is so deeply connected within the Mexican government and the Sinaloa cartel that the moment an accusation is leveled his way, even a rumor of an accusation, he'll use his considerable resources and connections to not only deny the accusation, but also to rid any evidence of wrongdoing."

"And by ridding evidence, I gather you mean these women?"

She sighed. "I do, unfortunately. Delgado has taken over a training facility in Northern Baja. Over the last year, he's brought in his own 'trainers,' which Alejandro believes are cartel members. These men won't hesitate to burn the facility to the ground and kill the women inside with just one call from the boss. Currently, the women at the facility are in the middle of a three-month training program. And I use the word 'training' loosely since they're brainwashed, drug-induced prisoners. I have a video I'll leave with you that shows exactly what's going on there. It's horrific, Garrison. The video will make your skin crawl."

My mind raced. "Tell me again why you won't use one of your discreet teams to take out Delgado? There must be more to it than you not wanting to use an in-house team."

"You're right," she said, nodding, "there is. Nogales failed because of a leak within that operation. I still don't know if that leak was limited to a single team member or if it went higher in the chain of command. Until I figure that out, I'm fearful the same thing will happen if I use one of my teams for the Delgado operation. That's why I have no choice but to use you, Garrison. Or at least someone like you who has the necessary skills and operates outside my channels."

I thought for a moment, then nodded. "Okay, so the fact that you originally greenlit the SEAL Team Six operation and now you're handing me a burn notice on this Delgado character means you've exhausted all other options on stopping this man. Is that fair to assume?"

"It is. We've explored all options, and now time is of the essence. Alejandro has been discreetly collecting evidence against his partner, but he's terrified to give us what he has or go public with it until Delgado is dead. Basically, Alejandro's not only fearful for these women's lives, but for his as well."

I smoothed out the tiny stubble on my head. "So Delgado dies, and Alejandro then feels safe enough to turn everything over. That's the deal?"

"Yes, that's right. After the hit, Alejandro will sell the plausible story that it was a rival cartel hit on Delgado; that two cartels were warring over control of Delgado's trafficking operation."

Plausible, I thought.

"SEAL Team Six," she continued, "was going to use a Mexican rifle commonly used by the rival cartel for the hit and leave it at the scene. As icing on the cake." She slid her leather valise onto her lap, then pulled out a thick, padded twelve-by-sixteen-inch envelope. "You can read about the mission plan inside here." She tapped the package. "If you agree to do this, you can adapt the plan accordingly, of course. You may even feel necessary to bring your partner into this, which is your judgment call. Unfortunately, I don't have a rifle for you to leave behind. But Alejandro doesn't need the rifle to sell the story. It sells itself. You must be invisible, leave absolutely no trace of your involvement. None whatsoever."

I blew out a breath and settled into the chair.

The president gave me a moment. Eventually, I said, "If I do agree to this, how do we explain this rendezvous between us? We're not exactly starting out under the radar." I motioned at the motorcade. "How many people are you traveling with?"

She reached into the padded envelope and pulled out a beautiful leather-covered box.

"What's that?" I said, furrowing my brow.

"Something you earned," the president replied. "And it's also our cover story, to explain what I'm doing here, and how I convinced secret service to approve this detour."

The crinkle in my brow must have deepened because she said, "Just open it, Garrison."

I did. Looking inside, I couldn't speak.

"From your silence and expression," the president said, "I can't tell if you're in shock or just don't know what you're looking at it."

I swallowed. "I definitely know what I'm looking at."

I didn't elaborate further, however, just continued to stare at the contents. Inside the box was a medal with a blue ribbon around it. The medal's prominent feature was a large white star with thirteen smaller gold stars encircling it.

"Are you sure, Garrison?"

I peeled my eyes from the medal and looked at Henrietta.

"It's the Medal of Freedom, Madam President, the highest award a civilian can earn."

CHAPTER THREE

POTUS DIDN'T GIVE me a second to process the award in my hand. She launched right into her story.

"What I'll do," she said, "is drape the medal around your neck right here on the porch. I'll have Willy Blanco, my chief of staff, take a picture for the official record, just in case anyone questions why I stopped here."

I held out the medal. "This is basically for show then?"

"Heavens no, Garrison." She quickly corrected herself. "Well, yes and no, I suppose." Before I could ask what that meant, she elaborated. "You've certainly earned this award with how you foiled that senators' killer plot last year. The Medal of Freedom is awarded to a civilian who makes an especially meritorious contribution to national security. Which, of course, you certainly did."

A little over a year ago our security firm had been hired by a prominent senator who'd received death threats from a fellow colleague. Turned out the death threats were real since both senators were killed. I worked the case and unraveled the conspiracy and brought those responsible to justice.

"Okay," I said, "so what do you mean by 'yes and no' then?"

"Well," the president replied, "I needed a reason to deviate from the motorcade and come here to see you this morning. I couldn't tell my staff that I was coming here to hire you to dispose of a well-connected foreigner, could I? The story I'm telling staff and secret service agents"—she waved to her entourage—"is for show."

"And what exactly are you telling them?"

"That you refused to come to the White House to receive this honor." She pointed to the Medal of Freedom in my hand. "That you've been stubborn and didn't want to be in the limelight and wouldn't accept the award. Which isn't much of a stretch, right?"

Probably not, I thought. But I didn't respond or nod in acknowledgment.

"But my staff knows me; they know I rarely accept no for an answer. Since I was in the area, and your place wasn't far off my original route south down the 101, I thought it was prudent to hand deliver you the award. That way you wouldn't dare refuse me." She smiled.

She's smart. I'll give her that.

"Let's get this show on the road," she said, picking up her phone and dialing. She exchanged brief words with her chief of staff. While waiting for Willy Blanco, she handed me the padded envelope. "There's some important items in there. A dossier on Juan Manuel Delgado. A full workup on the SEAL Team Six mission. There's also a thumb drive with two videos on it, a burner cell phone, a Canadian passport, and a credit card and driver's license in the same fake name."

I shot her a look.

"Just in case, Garrison. If things go sideways, and you need out of the country fast, don't hesitate to do so. But use the alias, and don't fly directly back here, not right away at least. Take a convoluted route back home. Got it?"

I did. "This is a lot to take in, Henrietta."

"Agreed," she said. "I don't need your answer right away, but pretty soon. It's Saturday now and Delgado visits his training facility every Wednesday, like clockwork. You'll need a day or so to get down there and get situated, so an answer by Monday would be appropriate. We can't wait another week. The longer Crossroads stays suspended, the greater chance we spook Delgado. And trust me, this isn't a man we want to spook. Not when the lives of two hundred innocent women are at stake."

Just then the president's chief of staff swept in front of my porch. After congratulating me, Willy organized a mini photo shoot. I put on a fake smile and tried my best to appear genuinely enthused as Henrietta draped the medal around my neck and Willy snapped some pics.

When Willy headed back to his SUV, the president stepped in close. "Once you've made your decision, text me from the burner phone. There's one number stored on the phone and it's to my burner cell. If you agree to the mission, text once more when the job is complete, then destroy the SIM and the phone. Regardless of your decision, everything in that envelope, including the cell, must be destroyed. I know you know that, but I have to emphasize how important that is."

I nodded. *Mission Impossible* instantly came to mind. "You mean, Madam President, all this stuff doesn't self-destruct?"

She ignored the comment. "Also, Garrison, the training facility sits slightly north of a surf spot in Northern Baja. I know you've frequently traveled down there to surf over the last decade, so you'll be very familiar with the terrain. I'm not trying to further sell you on this mission, I'm just saying you have the perfect cover story with family and friends for traveling there."

"Understood, though I'm not as concerned about my cover story as I am about this Delgado character. Is everything that I need to know about the man in here?" I patted the envelope. "I need to know everything about a person before I make a decision of this magnitude."

"Yes," she quickly replied, then backtracked. "Well, maybe n . . ." Her voice trailed off as she wrestled with something.

"What's not in the dossier that I should know, Henrietta?"

She cleared her throat. "I included only known facts about Delgado. I debated including conjecture because I'm simply not one hundred percent sure about one part of Delgado's life. What you need to know is Delgado's father recently passed. He was in his early eighties and spent his life in Mexican politics. He was the previous secretary of the interior."

She waited to see if I had a response to that, which I didn't.

"Right," she continued, "most people are unaware that in Mexico the second in line to the presidency is the secretary of the interior."

My eyes went wide hearing that comment.

"That's what I mean by how well-connected Delgado is within the Mexican government. Known as the wild, corrupt son, Juan Manuel Delgado pedaled his father's influence to achieve a near untouchable state. However, in the last decade or so, as his father reached the top political ranks, Delgado faded into the background and took on a new persona."

"What do you mean by that?"

"I mean, he claimed to be a reformed man; swore off any criminal activity. He even took on a new name, Jimmy D, after his own initials."

"J-M-D. Jimmy D. Okay, that's interesting."

"A name like Jimmy D immediately makes him affable and nonthreatening, which is exactly what he's trying to sell. And he's a hell of a salesman, Garrison. He weaseled his way into Crossroads by selling Ortiz on his personal reformation."

"You obviously don't buy his reformation then?"

She shook her head. "Not after Alejandro Ortiz's report and the video I saw. Jimmy D is all a front. All to hide his past and who he truly is."

"And who's that exactly?"

"Here's the conjecture." She pointed to the envelope and wiggled her fingers.

After I handed her the envelope, she extracted what looked to be a blown-up picture on a letter-sized piece of paper, but didn't show it to me. She kept it turned over as she said, "Juan Manuel Delgado aka Jimmy D is in his early sixties, Garrison. He's from Northern Baja. He's a criminal of ill repute with known government ties. Plus, he's a contemporary of El Chapo and rumored to have worked with the notorious narco, along with various other cartels. Probably the height of his criminal activity came in and around Tijuana during the early nineties."

I held out my hand to stop her since I knew where she was going. Suddenly I understood why this guy spooked her so much.

The president put her hand on my shoulder. "I figured those facts might prompt something in you."

I narrowed my eyes. "Based on that intel, you think he's the Butcher of Baja? Don't you?"

She turned over the picture in her hand so I could see it.

I'd seen the infamous photo many times, but it still made me silently gasp.

"I do think that," she replied. "In fact, we're pretty certain of it. Just not one hundred percent sure, though Ortiz said he can help with that, that he can provide the necessary proof."

My mind raced as I studied the gruesome photo of five butchered men. Eventually, I said, "If Delgado is the Butcher of Baja and responsible for that . . ." As I paused to swallow and point at the picture, the president finished my sentence.

"He won't hesitate to murder those women, Garrison. Not for one single, solitary second. The Butcher of Baja will do anything to cover his tracks. Anything."

CHAPTER FOUR

JAVI KNELT at the entrance of the tunnel and waited with bated breath, checking his watch every twenty seconds.

All he wanted to see was the soles of his granddaughter's tennis shoes as she backed out of the hole. He checked his watch again.

Forty-five seconds late, he thought. *Where is she?*

The tunnel in front of him was about seventy centimeters in diameter, approximately the size of an MRI tube. A red laser shot its vibrant beam directly through the center of the tunnel's hole. The laser level was mounted behind him on the scaffolding used to prevent a cave-in at the tunnel's entrance. The scaffolding also doubled as the exit point. After their twenty-minute shift, workers would climb the scaffolding to reach the surface. And the welcome relief of clean, fresh air.

Turning on the light mounted to his yellow helmet, Javi moved into the hole on his belly to get a better look. The light, however, only penetrated thirty or forty meters before fading into blackness again. During the first weeks of digging, he could shine his powerful headlamp into the hole and see the end. But the tunnel was now over two hundred meters long, so not a chance he could see the end.

Javi shouted, "Sylvia! Sylvia!"

No response, so he tugged on the extension cord lying on the dirt to his left, a vain attempt to send a signal to Sylvia to stop working, to put down her electric spade. Considering the length of the cord, and all the slack in the line, his scientific mind knew the tug would never be felt at the other end.

"Sylvia!" he yelled in desperation.

Suddenly he started scraping backward on his belly. He'd been so preoccupied with Sylvia's return he hadn't heard anyone climb down the scaffolding. Two hands yanked on his ankles, pulling his wiry body from the hole.

"Mr. White," the voice said, tsking. "What are you doing? You know better."

Javi knew by the voice it was the lead guard, a man known as El Patron. Patron ran the tunnel operation. He was a squat, powerful fellow. The rumor in camp was that Patron was former Fuerzas Especiales—a special forces unit in the Mexican Navy. Patron and the other guards referred to Javi as Mr. White, and they never told him why.

Still on his knees, with his back to Patron, Javi didn't respond. And he didn't dare turn around.

Patron's gun pressed into his back, though, demanding he do so.

Slowly, Javi turned to face him.

"Again," Patron said, pointing to Javi's face. "Remember what I said if it happened again? You know the rules." He shook his head. "The mask and oxygen are yours, not the workers'. Yours." Patron poked his finger against his chest. "You need that air."

It was true. Javi desperately needed the oxygen. Not just because he was underground all day, or that he was an elderly man, but he needed air to maintain mental sharpness and stay on top of his game. He oversaw the safety and straightness of the tunnel; that sole responsibility fell on his shoulders. But every time Sylvia came down for a shift, he couldn't help but force her to take the mask and oxygen with her.

Javi had no idea why she was involved. As a government engineer who'd previously worked in destroying drug tunnels made by prominent cartels, it came as no shock to him why he'd been kidnapped and conscripted into this position. What baffled him, however, was why they'd also taken his thirteen-year-old great-granddaughter.

Why is she being forced into this torturous labor? As payback for my involvement in destroying cartel tunnels?

"Rest of the shift," Patron said, "no more air. Maybe you'll learn then, Mr.

White." He checked his watch. "Your last check of the day is coming up. You'll have to crawl in there without oxygen."

Javi nodded. Twice a day he'd crawl to the end and check the hole, making sure it was centered and at a slight angle upward. Today, it would be laborious for his old body to crawl to the end, then inch backward, especially without oxygen. But, in the end, he felt it was worth it for Sylvia.

Where is she, anyway?

Sensing the same problem, Patron got down on his knees and peered into the tunnel. Twenty, maybe thirty years ago, Javi may have seized the opportunity and taken off his heavy-duty helmet and smashed Patron across the skull. Maybe even tied the man up and taken his weapon. During the evening shift, there was only one other guard topside watching the workers, so the odds of an escape weren't bad.

At seventy-two years old, though, Javi wouldn't stand a chance against the powerful guard.

"Here she comes," Patron said, backing up and standing.

Relieved, Javi crouched down. He immediately saw Sylvia's headlamp twenty meters from the tunnel's entrance, bobbing up and down as it pointed straight ahead. The beam from the red laser broke often as it bounced off her moving body.

When Sylvia reached the entrance, Javi helped her to her feet.

With the mask on, Sylvia's eyes bulged at the site of Patron. She ripped off the mask and began taking the oxygen bottle from her back to give to her papa.

"Save it," Patron said. "Keep it on, take everything up." He jacked his big thumb toward the surface. "Grandpa screwed up. He was warned."

"No!" Sylvia begged. "Please no."

"Up," Patron repeated. He used his gun to wave her up.

Sylvia clutched her papa. "I knew I shouldn't have taken it, Papa, I knew it. Never again."

"It's fine, dear," Javi said. "I'll be fine. Don't worry about me."

Patron pried them apart, then sent a distraught Sylvia topside.

"Go check it, old man." Patron waved his gun into the dark, cramped hole.

Javi got down on his knees and elbows and began inching into the tunnel.

He'd never done the trip without oxygen, so he wondered if this would be his last visit into the dark abyss.

CHAPTER FIVE

THE PRESIDENT LEFT me standing on the porch in a daze.

After blinking a few times, I refocused and watched the final SUV in the motorcade turn left onto Highway One and roar away. All that remained from the visit was some lingering dust in the air and the name "Butcher of Baja" swimming around in my head.

The Butcher was a man, a myth, a legend. Nobody knew for sure if he really existed. People conjectured that Joaquin "El Chapo" Guzman had an inside man—either with the Federales or a connected politician—that did all his dirty work in Northern Baja during the early nineties when Chapo warred with the Tijuana cartel. When murder and mayhem routinely filled the streets. When thousands were murdered, and even more were tortured into silence. The rumor was that a man named the Butcher of Baja orchestrated the bloodshed and protected El Chapo at all costs, but his identity had never been confirmed.

The Butcher's most notorious job, however, pertained to the slaughter of five prominent American businessmen from San Diego. It was also where the nickname Butcher of Baja originated.

By the late nineties, cocaine was pouring into America by the truckloads, and the cartels used American companies situated along the border to store their contraband. They even dug underground tunnels from Mexico that connected with these warehouses on the American side. A group of five prominent businessmen, who had big stakes in the area, brought national attention to the problem. The wealthy men flexed their muscles and demanded American law enforcement step up their game to curb the smuggling. They insisted the US government put an end to the pressure on American businesses from these drug cartels. Ultimately, law enforcement listened and ramped up their involvement, making several significant arrests.

But the fallout from the arrests were the murders of these five American businessmen. All five bodies were lined up and placed directly on the border between Mexico and the US. The gruesome part: the five bodies were sawed in half. The men's upper bodies were placed on the US side and their lower bodies were situated in Mexico. The crazy thing was that the lower body of each corpse was exactly sixty percent of the man's total weight. Coroners on both sides of the borders confirmed that fact, down to the ounce. The men were murdered with absolute gruesome precision and then strategically placed to send a clear message: Don't mess with us.

Naturally, this led to a deep fear by American businessmen working along the border. Nobody dared to stand up to the cartels anymore. It also led to a pissing match between the countries as to who was ultimately responsible for handling the murder cases. The case went to court and Mexico won because more than half of each victim's body was technically in Mexico. Despite losing the court case, though, America still committed considerable resources to establishing their own task force to bring the responsible party to justice.

Nothing came of it, however. Neither country solved the murders. And what still lingers to this day, all over the internet, was the picture in my hand. The one of the men's bodies sawed in half and lined up along the border.

In the end, the Butcher of Baja became a household name. Labeled a terrorist, he's currently topped America's Most Wanted List for several decades now.

I tucked the picture back into the padded envelope, then took everything to the kitchen table where my laptop was located. After fishing out the thumb drive, I stuck it in the computer's USB slot. There were two video files on there. I clicked the first one.

It was some silent drone footage. The footage was of a nondescript building sitting on a point overlooking the ocean. Clearly this was the training facility in Northern Baja that the president had mentioned.

The building sat a few hundred feet back from the cliff's edge. The beach below was rocky and getting pounded by incoming surf. The building itself was one-story and V-shaped, with the point of the V angled toward the ocean. It was a low-lying building of a muted brown color. The forest green window frames were the only other color on the building. The structure easily blended in with the surrounding desert landscape of dirt, rocks, and sparse cacti.

The drone flew a 360-degree pattern around the building. My eyes took in all the details from the elevated angle. Once the drone completed the full circle, the footage cut out.

I clicked the second video. When the recording kicked on, the point of view came from chest level of some unknown person walking toward a building. Either the person had a tiny camera hidden somewhere under their clothes on their left side, or perhaps there was a cell in their jacket pocket that poked over the top of the pocket and recorded everything.

Aside from the man with the recording device, based on the voices I heard, there appeared to be two other men walking beside him and speaking in Spanish. I had a limited vocabulary in Spanish—limited to ordering a cold beer and asking where the nearest waves were—so as the entourage approached the building, and the conversation picked up, I focused on the details in the video and not on what they were saying.

Since the footage started far enough back from the building, I could tell they were headed into the same training facility from the drone video. That was confirmed when I noticed a sign on the building that read Punta De Las Olas, which I knew roughly translated as Wave Point. Underneath that sign were the words Campo De Entrenamiento. Which I believed said Training Camp or something similar.

The men hustled past the main entrance to the facility. As they approached a side door, they got into single file position. The man recording the video took the middle position. You could see the left shoulder of the lead man, but you couldn't see his face. He led the men to a windowless side door that was solid metal and painted brown to match the building's exterior.

After punching in a code on a pad beside the door, the lead man pushed the door in, and the other two men followed. Immediately the video plunged into near darkness. But a cell phone light flicked on moments later and illuminated concrete steps in front of the men.

The narrow descent lasted about twenty steps of near silence. All I heard on the video was shuffling feet and the men's rhythmic breathing. A near identical metal door was at the base of the stairs. The lead man spoke into a walkie-talkie. I deciphered that he was announcing their arrival and saying something about the lights.

After punching in another code, the front man led the other two inside. In front of them was a narrow corridor. Though the lights had been dimmed, there was just enough light to make out the surrounding area.

As the men walked, I could see the floor underneath their feet was clean and made of polished tile. The walls were unadorned and appeared to be a vibrant white color. There were two closed doors on either side of the hallway. In front of the men, just barely visible about thirty or forty feet away, was a wall with double metal doors in the middle. Immediately the area reminded me of a small hospital ward, which it very well could be or could've been at some point in the building's life.

The lead man began talking. He appeared to be describing things to the other men. It became clear that these two men were visitors getting a rundown of the facility's operation. Unfortunately, the man spoke so rapidly in Spanish that I couldn't make out a word he was saying.

But that didn't matter. Because when he opened one of the doors, words became unimportant. The scene inside spoke volumes.

Eight women were inside the room. All eight were on hospital beds, which were chained to the floor. Worse, the women were restrained to the beds by cuffs on their right ankles.

They barely moved or looked up at the men as they entered the room. As the video moved closer to one of the beds, you could see the stone-cold, vacant looks on the women's faces, which indicated they were being heavily drugged.

The lead man grabbed the arm of the nearest victim. He spoke rapidly and pointed to the woman's forearm. I had no idea what he was saying, though I did recognize the words heroin and fentanyl. After that, he showed the men the woman's ankle cuff. Underneath the cuff, there was some thick padding held in place by some white medical tape. The man explained the situation, but again I couldn't decipher what he was saying.

The three men left that room, then peeked into the three other rooms. There were eight women in the same situation in each room. After that, the men proceeded through the double doors into a near identical ward.

The lights were dimmed in the hallway. Again, there were four rooms in total. About thirty or forty feet in front of the men was a big double door in the middle of a wall. Inside the room that the men visited were another eight women chained to beds. These women, however, were more awake and slightly more put together. One of them even listened to music on some headphones.

In the next ward—the third one—the women in the four rooms were no longer chained. Though they were all still physically in bed, many were sitting up and alert. Almost every woman turned to acknowledge the men entering the room.

The fourth ward the men visited was completely different. The lights were on in the hallway and the women were moving about. Some even talked to each other and smiled at the men when they entered the room. I noticed books on a shelf, a television with a DVD player, and some board games on a table. With the lights on, I could tell these women were attractive, aged anywhere between twelve and thirty, and all Hispanic. They appeared to be in good health, not to mention in decent spirits.

What the hell?

As the men ascended a concrete staircase at the end of the fourth ward, I was in shock at what I'd just seen. Had I'd just witnessed an intense, experimental drug therapy of some sort?

Unfortunately, I didn't have time to theorize. At the top of the stairs, the lead man punched in a code and opened the door. The men entered the ground floor of the training facility. And it couldn't have been in starker contrast to the underground hospital wards.

Everything was bright and airy, and the women moved freely about. The floors were hardwood, and the walls were a combination of shiplap and stainless steel, providing a very modern and clean look to the facility.

The end of the facility where the men entered was the living quarters for the women on the ground floor. To the left were four large rooms filled with bunkbeds. There was also a big kitchen between two of the bedrooms.

Several women were in the kitchen preparing a meal. To the right was a vast, open room. It appeared to be the main dining and living room for the women. One side of the room had floor-to-ceiling windows. The shades on all the windows had been drawn.

Women easily moved in and out of the rooms. Some were scantily clad and carefree. Others wore white bathrobes and looked like they'd just finished taking a shower. The palpable mood in the video was positive. I would say joyous even.

I mean, the women looked downright happy.

As the men moved from one end of the ground floor to the other, the lead man kept up his explanation. Down from the living quarters were all sorts of training rooms. One room they went into showed women getting all dolled up for what looked like an evening on the town. They were putting makeup on themselves or each other and trying on some tastefully tight outfits.

Another room the men peeked in showcased women getting and giving massages. An instructor was in the room providing some tips. It appeared these women were practicing their skills to be high-end call girls.

The president was wrong. This video didn't make my skin crawl. It made me sick to my stomach, not to mention mad as hell. And the anger only grew worse when the men entered the last room. There was a nurse in there doling out pills to several women. What commanded my attention, though, was a large whiteboard on the wall that contained a schedule, along with a ton of names, well over one hundred, I guessed.

Though the recording didn't dwell on the board too long, I got the distinct impression that this was the women's pill schedule. It tracked who got their drugs and when and how much.

The man recording the video excused himself to go to the bathroom. As soon as he entered a stall, he fumbled with the recording device and moments later the footage cut out.

I collapsed back into the kitchen chair and took a few deep breaths as I closed my eyes. But the image of the women in the first ward—chained to their beds while in a near drug-induced coma—was seared into the back of my eyelids.

I sat up and dumped the contents of the president's envelope onto the kitchen table. To clear my mind, I grabbed the files that were in there and quickly organized them. There were three stapled pages that looked like a screenplay in one of the files. As I glanced at the pages, I realized it was an English transcript for the video I'd just seen.

Immediately I replayed the video and followed along with the transcript as best as I could. The men's names were never mentioned at the beginning of the recording, but I did confirm that the visitors were getting a detailed explanation of the facility.

I fast-forwarded the video until I reached the part where the men entered the first room. The man explaining things was unabashed in the fact that these women were being heavily drugged against their will. He had no shame revealing that it began this way to get the women hooked on a very specific prescription painkiller. The man didn't name the drug because it was still experimental, though he likened the drug to being as euphoric as heroin and as addictive as fentanyl.

I wanted to reach into the video and throttle the guy.

He explained how important it was for these women to use pills and not snort or shoot up. He wanted them to have flawless skin and show no signs of being a drug user. No needle marks at all in the forearm, he insisted. The man seemed so proud of that as he showed off the flawless forearm to the two men.

Next, he alluded to the ankle cuff, explaining that they also didn't want the women to get marks or bruises on their ankles from the cuffs. Which was the reason they took great care, he said, to wrap the ankle and protect it from any injury or mark.

I needed a deep breath at this point. *So caring, aren't you?*

As the video moved from ward to ward, it proved that the people running this facility were scientific monsters. They'd perfected getting the women hooked on this incredibly addictive, euphoric drug. Following that, they slowly lowered the drug dosage until they were highly functioning addicts who showed close to no signs of dependency. However, the women were now dependent on an expensive and addictive drug that they couldn't live without, and definitely couldn't afford.

The man explained that after a prescribed time underground the women transitioned to the ground floor where they prepared for their new life and new profession. Of course, he never said exactly what that was. He spent most of the next part of the video pointing out just how happy these women were.

But the truth of the situation became apparent in the last room they visited. Each woman had a highly regimented drug routine they followed. To keep the women in such high spirits, the drug amounts in their system could be kept low because it was so powerful. It just needed to be consistent and never fluctuate.

All this, the man said gleefully, without exhibiting any harmful effects to their body. None at all, he claimed.

I was raging and deep inside my own head. So much so that I didn't hear the car approach outside. When my son rushed into the kitchen, I immediately snapped the laptop shut.

"Hey, pal," I said nervously, hoping he didn't see any of the video and ask questions.

"Hey, pops, whatcha doing?"

I wiped some donut crumbs from the corner of his mouth. "Just working."

"Dad, it's Saturday." He put his hands on his hips.

"You're right," I said, using that as an excuse to quickly stuff everything back into the envelope. Which was just in time since Mom suddenly appeared in the kitchen doorframe. Usually, Mom was nosy about things I was working on and had no problem looking inside any file I kept out.

But she paid no attention to the envelope. She said, "You'll never guess what we saw. Tell him, Simon. Tell your dad."

My son's eyes went big. "Five big black cars with dark tinted windows. Driving fast down the highway. So cool, Dad. Gramma says it was probably some dig—" He shot at look at Mom. "What was that word you used, Grams?"

"Dignitary, Simon. It was probably a dignitary." Mom looked at me. "I mean, who else could it be? Who else drives around with a posse like that?"

It wasn't the time to tell Mom about the president's visit. So, I deflected instead. "Posse and dignitary, Mom. You're teaching Simon some great old-school words. I like it."

She glared at me. "You don't see that too often in Morro Bay or Cayucos. Who else would it be, Gar?"

I shrugged. "A drug dealer. Maybe a famous rapper."

"You think?" Simon said excitedly.

Mom waved me off. "Listen, you left your cell in the car, dear. It kept buzzing over and over so I finally picked it up. It was Hans. You need to call him right back. That's what he said."

While she handed me my cell, I said, "Did he say what it was about?"

"No, just that he was here and needed to meet with you."

"Here?" I questioned. "What do you mean 'here'? Like here in Cayucos?"

"Not sure. Just call him, dear." She motioned to Simon. "Come on, let's give your dad some privacy and go find that so-called dog of yours."

What do you mean "here"? Slim lives and works on the East Coast. How could he be here without letting me know?

I immediately called my buddy back.

CHAPTER SIX

A LIFETIME AGO, Hans Schlimmergaard, aka Slim, was my trainer and commanding officer during my black-ops days. Slim taught me everything I knew about being an operative, including killing. We'd been through a lot, so our relationship was not one of beating around the bush.

He picked up the call and I blurted, "My mom said you're here. What does that mean? In town? In Cayucos?"

"No, pal. I meant here in California. Down south in LA."

"Why? What are you doing on the West Coast? Why wouldn't you tell me you're coming?"

He laughed. "You're not feeling threatened or getting territorial? Are you, buddy?"

"No, sorry, that came out wrong. I'm a little off my game since I had a weird morning. I mean, the weirdest. I believe surreal is the right word."

"Surreal, huh? Why don't you tell me all about it in person?"

"In person? Drive to LA today. Not on your life, my friend."

He blew a heavy breath into the phone. "Some boyfriend you are. Won't even take a short drive to chat with your buddy and visit your squeeze. Come on, Chase."

The woman I'd been seeing, Karla Dickerson, lived in the LA area. "Stay out of my personal life, boss. Isn't that a human resources violation I can report you for?"

"Listen," he said, "I figured you'd get all pissy and moany about driving to LA. Let's meet halfway then, in Santa Barbara. I've got some important things to tell you, and you can fill me in on this surreal morning of yours."

"Important things like what?"

"Not over the phone, Chase."

"Really?"

"Yes, really."

"Fine, I have an important thing to tell you as well. And I definitely can't talk about it over the phone."

"Oooh, the suspense," he said mockingly. "I can hardly wait."

After some more banter, we agreed on a time and place in Santa Barbara, then I hung up and proceeded to apologize to Simon and Mom about taking a work trip on Saturday.

Santa Barbara was an easy hour-and-forty-five-minute drive south on the 101. I jumped into my Chevy Caprice and was on the road earlier than I needed to be to meet Slim. But I wanted all the alone time I could get if I was to seriously consider taking another man's life, even if it was the notorious Butcher of Baja.

While driving, I weighed the pros and cons of the president's directive. Since it was such a heavy topic, I found myself in Santa Barbara before I knew it, about forty-five minutes before the meeting with Slim. After parking in a beach lot far from other cars, I pulled out the contents of the president's envelope and started reading. I wanted Slim's input and potentially his help if I decided to follow through on the assignment, so I wanted to know as much as possible about the job before speaking with my buddy.

I read the full workup on Juan Manuel Delgado, aka Jimmy D. The dossier provided a thorough understanding of his personal and professional life. It was a solid thirty minutes of reading. Based on that read, I felt confident that Delgado was indeed the Butcher of Baja. And without a doubt he was the man responsible for the operation at the Baja training facility.

Thinking about the video of enslaved women and the contents of the dossier, and the Butcher's history of torturing and maiming people, I now had a deep, urgent need to stop this man. But I didn't want to go it alone. I needed Slim.

Before leaving to meet him, I looked at the fake travel docs, which included a credit card, a Canadian passport, and a British Columbia driver's license. My mug was pictured on the two photo ID's.

The name on all three documents: Gary Pounds.

I looked in the rearview mirror and practiced a Canadian accent. *"Gary Pounds, nice to meet ya."*

The name brought a smile to my face. As I walked to meet Slim, I kept practicing a subtle Canadian accent, making sure not to overemphasize the double "oo" sound of out and about.

We'd agreed to meet at the Funk Zone. It was a trendy area of downtown Santa Barbara, a perfect hipster hangout. The place was filled with craft breweries, wineries, amazing food venues, and lots of shopping. Since it was still morning, we met at the Helena Avenue Bakery.

Slim was already there, sitting at one end of an outdoor picnic table. The man was so big that the opposite end of the table looked to be hovering off the ground an inch or so. He didn't see me coming, so I swooped in and surprised him.

"Geez, pal," I said, leaning on one end of the table. "I better sit here before the table flips up."

"A fat joke right out of the gate, huh? So surprising of you."

We both laughed.

"Listen," Slim said. "I'd get up to shake your hand, but I'm literally wedged in here."

"Right, picnic tables weren't exactly built with you in mind."

"Another one, really?"

"It's a girth joke, buddy, not a fat one."

And I meant that. Slim was far from fat. He was thick and meaty and a few inches taller than me, topping out at six foot six. The man was built like one of those World's Strongest Men competitors. I imagined he could enter a competition and do well, with little to no practice.

Aside from his size, Slim's other commanding feature was his short-cropped red hair. I motioned at his face. "How long you been in California? Looks like you finally got some sun. Your freckles are really popping. And your hair is turning a beautiful strawberry blond."

"And you're still follicley challenged, I see."

I slid down the bench and whacked him on the shoulder. It felt like I'd punched a rock. "So, what's up? What's going on? You on a job or vacationing or what?"

He glanced at his watch and didn't answer right away.

"What?" I said, eyeing him. "You have somewhere else to be? Someone else to meet?"

Slim looked up and hesitated. After a silent moment, he said, "Tell me about this surreal morning of yours."

"What's going on? Tell me what you're doing here. Let's start there."

"Listen, we both have important things to share. You start. Just trying to be polite here."

"Polite?" I waved him off. "Now that's a joke if I ever heard one. Fine, I'll go first, but it's too crowded here for my liking, and for my story. Let's get some coffee and baked goods and move over to Figueroa Brewing next door."

The brewery beside the bakery was closed, but they had tables outside that were not being used.

Slim nodded his approval.

"I'll get the coffee and food," I said. "By the time I'm back, maybe you'll have extracted yourself from the picnic table." I left to grab the food before he could respond.

About eight minutes later, I met Slim next door. He sat at a bar-height table. Since there wasn't a soul in the area, I felt confident about sharing everything above a whisper. I sat across from him, slid a coffee his direction, placed some chocolate croissants in the middle of the sticky table, then got right to it.

I said, "The president stopped by my house this morning."

He looked quizzically at me. "What president?"

"*The* president."

Still with a furrowed brow, he said, "Like the president of the Cayucos Lion's Club?"

"No. Like the president of the United States, jackass."

He coughed out some coffee while laughing.

I maintained a stone face.

"Wait," he said, leaning forward. "You're being serious."

I leaned toward him until our faces were two feet apart. "I am, and that's not the most shocking part." I paused, and not for dramatic effect, but because it was difficult saying it out loud. "POTUS wants me to eliminate a target."

"A target?" he snapped. "You can't be serious."

I nodded, then reached into the small backpack I'd brought and pulled out the president's envelope. After looking around to confirm we were still alone, I pushed the envelope across the table. "See for yourself."

Slim slowly pulled everything out of the envelope. He was such a meticulous man that even the way he laid the documents on the table was organized. After checking things over, he looked up. In his right hand he held the picture of the murdered San Diego businessmen.

"Okay," he said, flapping the picture. "Obviously this isn't an April Fool's joke. Tell me everything."

So I did.

I started with the presidential visit, moved on to the video, then discussed the SEAL Team Six mission outline, and ended with the dossier on Delgado and his alleged alias as the Butcher of Baja. As I spoke, I pointed to the relevant documents for Slim to follow along with. Though his head was buried in the documents while I talked, I knew he tracked with my every word.

Not surprising, after finishing the story, his first words were, "This is nuts, Chase. That's my first thought. Absolutely nuts. I mean, taking out the Butcher of Baja, or the supposed Butcher of Baja? By your own admission, we don't have irrefutable proof Delgado is the Butcher. You're actually considering this?"

I shrugged.

"My second thought," Slim continued, "relates to what I don't see here."

"And what's that?"

"An authorization letter, either from the president's office or from one of the intelligence agencies."

"Right, a letter authorizing the hit on a supposed reformed foreign national who may or may not be one of America's most wanted terrorists. POTUS would really want that in writing."

"Well, you'd be as nuts as her for taking a job like this without covering your back. You know how this works. You need at least some proof of the operation's existence and your authorized involvement in it."

I sighed. "Slim, you know as well as I do that this is way off the books, and it has to be that way. There's no way she'd admit to anything, especially not in writing."

"Exactly," he replied, pointing at me. "Exactly right. No way she'd admit to anything, or back you up. A suicide mission for you, pal. The slightest thing goes wrong, and you're hosed. There's no way you should entertain this. Plus, she's out of office soon. If you follow through with this, I imagine you'll do a good enough job to cover your tracks for a while. But what if they eventually trace the hit back to you? What if Delgado turns out not to be the Butcher? Now Henrietta Valenzuela is a private citizen and in no position to help. You'll be living in freezing cold Canada as Gary Pounds for the rest of your life. Alone, I might add." He flicked the passport my way. "Besides, Chase, it's clear she's using you."

"Using me? How so?"

"Her legacy is tarnished from the Nogales situation. She's in terrible political shape. Even worse if her immigration legacy falls through. Think about it. If her beloved Operation Crossroads becomes known as the operation that secretly drugged and trafficked Mexican women into our country to be call girls to the highest bidder, she'll be reviled. She's using your strong sense of justice to cover her ass, to make sure her political legacy and reputation doesn't go totally in the toilet. Maybe she's even lying about Delgado being the Butcher just to get you fired up on this job, to push you into accepting. Because she certainly doesn't want to risk using one of her many black-ops team to do the dirty work. Have you thought about that?"

I let his comments and questions sink in. Eventually, I said, "You may be right. I'll give you that. But at the same time, there's a clear sense of right and wrong here. If I wake up one day to a news story about the facility burned to the ground and hundreds of charred bodies found inside, I won't be able to live with myself. And you know I'm not being dramatic since we're possibly talking about the Butcher of Baja."

"Sure," he said, "but we're also talking about assassination. Think about the known Executive Orders that deliberately prohibit assassination. You got Ford's 11905, Carter's 12036, and, of course, Reagan expanded everything in EO 12333."

Slim was a fountain of information in realms like executive orders. I held up my hand to make sure he didn't carry on. "Got it, I know. You also know as well as I do that no one uses the word assassination anymore. It's all a semantic game now. Targeted killing is the new phrase. And targeting a known terrorist is certainly not unusual. Look at what you and I have done, what we've been ordered to do in the past. All under the guise of a targeted kill."

"True," Slim responded. "The difference there, though, was we were either in the middle of war or operating against a known enemy of the state. There must be an imminent threat of attack against national security interests to justify a targeted kill. And I don't think Delgado, or his situation, rises to that level, even if he is the Butcher of Baja and these women's lives are at stake."

Slim had a valid point, which ticked me off. I used the moment to deflect. "You're here now, pal. Why not come down with me to Northern Baja and check it out? See what we see, then go from there. I need you."

"Wait, so you *are* going down there? You've already made up your mind?"

"I need to check it out. Do some recon. For my conscience's sake, for these women's sakes."

He sighed. "I'd like to help, but my conscience is telling me no. It's too risky." He shook his head and looked away, muttering, "Way too risky."

I decided not to push him. But I did have one final thought. As I crammed all the documents back into the envelope, I left the thumb drive in front of him. "Take it back with you to your hotel. Watch it on your laptop, destroy it, then make your final decision about visiting Baja. At least do that for me."

Slim thought for a moment. He brought his hand out to pick up the thumb drive, but his cell buzzed and distracted him.

"Saved by the cell." He glanced at the screen.

"Who is it?" I asked.

Slim ignored my question and picked up the call. "No, no, we're here. Yup, we are. Just right around the corner at the brewery, sitting at an outside table."

Before I could ask again what was going on, the woman in my life, Karla Dickerson, bounded around the corner and headed toward us.

CHAPTER SEVEN

Since I was so articulate and poetic on my feet, I looked and Karla and said, "What the. . ."

Slim slugged me on the shoulder. "Geez, pal, hug your girl, will ya."

I snapped out of it and hugged her.

Typically, Karla would've poked fun at my dumbfounded look or said something sarcastic about it. But she stayed silent and squeezed me tight.

When I pulled back from the embrace, I noticed she looked nervous. I glanced at Slim, then back to Karla. As I held the stare, I noticed Karla's flushed cheeks. Though she maintained a vibrant look in her stunning blue eyes, she was definitely nervous. That was confirmed when she ran her hands through her short-cropped blond hair, fluffing it up. I'd never before witnessed a hair adjustment like that from her.

"What's going on?" I asked. "You here to break up with me?" I gave a nervous chuckle and pointed at Slim. "And you want him to be the mediator?"

"So negative," Slim said. "Only good things are going down here, brother. Trust me."

Karla took a breath and finally showed her cheerful smile. "If that were the case, think I'd choose this clown to mediate?" She motioned at Slim.

"Wait, is that a joke about my hair?" Slim said.

Karla slid in beside him. "Actually, it's a joke about that red nose of yours. Sunscreen's your friend, you know."

I laughed and took a seat across from them. "Okay, so seriously, what's up? What are you two planning? Conspiring, I guess, would be the more appropriate word."

Karla elbowed Slim. "This is your show. Tell him."

"We're a team, Karla. This is a package deal, just to be clear."

She sighed. "Sure, it's a package deal, I'll give you that. But I want to officially go on record that this was all your idea."

Slim waved her off. "You worry too much. Chase is going to love this idea."

Karla immediately looked down and away.

"Enough, you two," I said. "Spit it out, Slim. What's going on?"

He had a file with him and pulled it onto the table. While opening it, he said, "Business has been good, hasn't it?"

Now I was the one sighing. "I guess, but what do I know? It's your business."

"But you choose whatever job you want. You never want for an assignment. You turn down more than I offer, right?"

"What's your point?" I responded.

"My point is that I need help. Business is booming and we're leaving money on the table."

"Not *we*. *You* are, Slim."

"Exactly my point."

"Wait, what's your point?"

"It should be *we*. I want you to be my partner, Chase, not one of my independent contractors. I want to open a West Coast branch, and I want you to run it."

"You've got to be kidding?"

Slim motioned toward Karla, then pulled out some pieces of paper and spread them across the table. "We've been looking at some commercial property in LA over the past couple of days. Trying to find the perfect office location and building. We've narrowed it down—"

I held out my hand. "We? You're in on this?" I glared at Karla. "You two have been conspiring behind my back about my future? Looking to buy or rent an office building for me to run? Except I don't want to head an office or a branch. I don't want to run anything, for that matter. When have I ever—"

"I know you don't," Slim said excitedly, cutting me off. "But we have a plan, Chase, don't you worry."

"I don't care if you have a plan," I snapped back. "I don't need you two planning my life behind my back, that's for sure."

"At least hear me out, pal. Hear why I brought Karla in on this."

I shook my head like my five-year-old son would. If I was being honest, I felt like a five-year-old, too.

"*This*," Karla said, "was clearly a mistake. I knew it." She glanced at Slim. "It's going exactly as I told you it would. He's reacting just like I thought."

That irked me. How she so easily predicted my reaction. To prove I wasn't a child, I took a breath and changed course. "Okay, what are you in on, Karla? What's this so-called package deal you two have going?"

Slim leaned forward and put his monstrous forearms on the table. "I know you have no desire to run a branch. It's a lot of paperwork, hiring, budgeting, accounting, planning, organizing. Not your specialty at all. But it is Karla's. She's great at that stuff. You're a field man, Chase, I know that. Probably the best operative I know, besides myself, of course." He grinned. "You focus on running the investigative assignments, and Karla runs everything else. All the day-to-day operations will be under her purview. Perfect match. Plus, you two are finally living in the same city. Win-win. Am I right?"

I immediately looked at Karla to gauge her reaction. She stared wide-eyed for a moment, then glanced away. "Is this what you want, Karla? To leave your position with the Bureau and run an organization that spies on politicians? To do the budgeting and accounting and hiring and the like? Because we've certainly not talked about—"

"Exactly," she interrupted. "Exactly right. We haven't talked, Chase. Have we?"

"What does that mean?"

"You know what," she said, getting up, "forget it. Forget all about this. Like I said, it's a mistake. It was a bad idea." She shot a look at Slim. "How you talked me into this, I'll never know. If you ever lose your business, you should go into sales. Because you definitely sold me on the idea that he'd be interested and willing to listen."

She walked away.

I got up. "Come on, Karla, stay. Where are you going?"

When she didn't respond or stop walking, I hustled after her. She made it across the street and into her car before I could catch her. I came alongside the passenger door and motioned for her to open it.

She rolled down the window instead.

"Sorry, Chase. Like I said, I knew this was a bad idea." She shook her head. "I just got talked into it by Mr. Slick Rick over there. Can't believe I was that naïve."

I leaned onto the windowsill. "He can be a persistent one. Annoying, too. I totally get it. What I don't get is what you meant back there. About us not talking about it. Of course we've never talked about working together."

"You're such a dummy," she said. "I meant that in a more generic sense. I mean, we don't talk about our relationship or our future, do we? We don't even talk about living closer to each other."

She had that right, so I nodded.

Karla continued. "We see each other every couple of weeks, but only for a day or two. We both want to have fun and keep it light. I get it. We don't want to waste our limited time having a potentially awkward conversation about our future. But at some point, we do have to have that conversation, Chase."

"Agreed," I said. "But we need to communicate with each other about future plans." I motioned over my shoulder toward Slim. "Not via our red-headed intermediary over there."

"Agreed," she replied. "Don't know what I was thinking."

She didn't say anything more than that. I said, "Are you unhappy with our relationship? With what we have going on?"

"I wouldn't say unhappy."

"What would you say then?"

"I just want . . ."

I prodded. "Want what?"

"I want more, Chase."

More? More like marriage, more like living in the same town, more like running an investigative branch together?

She read my mind. "I know that's vague, but I can't tell you specifically what I want because I don't know. But I do know that we need to work through it together and talk about it as a couple."

"You're right. Maybe we should do it now. Get it over with."

She glared. *"Get it over with?* Geez, sorry it's so burdensome for you to talk about it, to converse about our future."

"That came out wrong," I pleaded, holding my palms out. "I'm sorry. I didn't mean it that way, Karla."

"It's fine, whatever." She turned on the car and motioned at a shoebox on the passenger seat. "I've gotta go, anyway. Have to get back home for a family thing this afternoon. It's Dad's birthday today. I got him a pair of those SeaVees shoes he loves. Their main store is just around the corner from here. That's why I was a little late to our meeting."

I nodded. "Surely you have a little time now to talk, don't you?"

"Later, Chase. When cooler heads prevail. Maybe next weekend when we see each other again."

Before I could plead my case, she backed out of the parking spot and took off.

I stood there for a moment and tried to gather myself. But anger at Slim took over. I knew that he just wanted to advance my career, and that he ultimately wanted the best for Karla and me. But I also knew he saw this business expansion as an opportunity for him to get a bigger piece of the pie. Plus, the man was trying to manipulate me into his plan by bringing Karla into the equation.

That didn't sit well with me.

No doubt I had a fuming look on my face, because as I approached the table, Slim immediately held out his hands. "Sorry, pal. Thought you'd be a little more open to this. I really did."

I started to unload on him, then stopped. I didn't want to start a huge argument and accuse him of manipulation and being money-hungry, though I knew that fueled his ultimate plan. Instead, I got straight to the point so we could bury the issue.

"Forget it all." I motioned at the commercial property listings on the table. "Not going to happen. Not with me involved. I'm perfectly fine doing what I do now."

Slim huffed. "Well, it *is* going to happen. With or without you, buddy."

"Really?"

"Really. And maybe even Karla still runs the day-to-day." He shrugged. "Who knows? That's up to her."

Slim was doubling down, which irritated me more. But I didn't take the bait. Instead, I pushed back from the table. "Good luck with that then." I stood and turned to walk away. "Good luck with everything."

"Don't forget this," he said. When I turned back, he pushed the thumb drive toward me.

"Listen," I said, pointing at the drive. "What's on that is far bigger than this squabble of ours. You owe me to at least look at it."

"I don't owe you anything, pal."

I stepped forward. "Is that so?"

"It is. You're not going to entertain the idea of running my new branch. I'm not going to entertain helping you."

"Tit for tat?" I said.

"Guess so," he replied, picking up the drive and thrusting it toward me.

But I backed off and left him holding the drive. I knew he wouldn't throw it at me or leave it behind. Slim knew covert information like that had to be protected and ultimately destroyed. I also knew that he couldn't help but watch the video the moment he sat in front of a computer. I know I would.

He cursed after me, but I hustled straight to the Caprice without looking back.

On the drive home, instead of wallowing in anger, I focused on the Baja mission. Specifically, how I could carry out the directive as a lone operative—without my good buddy Slim at my side. By the time I made it home and parked, I had a solid plan in my mind.

Before heading inside to hang out with my son for the rest of the afternoon, I took the burner cell out of the envelope and pecked out the words: *I'm in.*

Then I sent that text to the president of the United States.

CHAPTER EIGHT

JAVI USED his remaining energy to climb the final few meters of the scaffolding.

Once he emerged from the hole in the ground, and his feet touched the airplane hangar's concrete floor, he collapsed onto his chest.

"Papa!" Sylvia yelled, rushing to his side. "Papa, are you okay?" She helped roll him onto his back.

Javi began a coughing fit.

"Water," Sylvia said to the group of workers off to her right. "Bring water."

A man rushed over and handed Sylvia a plastic water bottle, which she unscrewed and fed to Javi.

"Papa, can you talk? Are you okay? Why are you all wet? Is that sweat?"

He took another few swigs of water and cleared his throat. By that point, Patron was by his side.

"Not sweat," Javi said, catching the eye of Patron. "It's water. We've hit the water table." He choked on the bottled water. "It's dangerous down there, very dangerous."

Patron remained silent and stared. Assessing his claim, Javi figured.

Eventually, Patron turned and gave Sylvia a once-over.

He gestured at her while looking back at Javi. "She was the last to dig, Mr. White, and she came back dry."

Javi nodded. "We haven't broken through the water table just yet, but we're close. When I reached the end, the wall and floor around the digging site was wet. It was likely dry when she finished her shift."

Sylvia nodded, then helped her papa to his feet.

"Water is seeping, not flowing," Javi explained. "Not yet at least." As he spoke, he noticed the other workers had moved closer to hear what he had to say. The eight men huddled together and shuffled forward as a group. Patron was deep in thought, thinking about the predicament, so he hadn't noticed the movement behind him.

He addressed Javi. "What are you saying, Mr. White? What does this mean?"

"We need to halt production."

"No way." Patron forcefully shook his head. "Not an option. Especially when we're so close."

That was the first that Javi had heard about their progress. Hearing they were near the end came as a mixed bag of emotions. The grueling shifts would soon end for Sylvia, but the danger of a flood was at an all-time high.

Plus, what will they do with us, Javi thought, *once the tunnel is complete?*

Patron jabbed a finger his direction. "You're the engineer. What's the solution here?"

"Dig again," he said. "Start deeper this time. It's a death sentence to keep going on our current path."

Again, Patron shook his head. Frustrated, he stepped out of earshot and made a call. A moment later, he returned. Patron held out a GoPro camera and thrust it toward Javi.

"Video," he said. "Crawl back and take some footage. We need to see this so-called seeping water."

"No!" Sylvia said, jumping in front of Patron. "He can't go down again."

Patron swept Sylvia out of the way.

To Javi's surprise, the thirteen-year-old lunged back and snatched the camera away. "I'll go," she said.

"Not a chance," he responded, eyeing Sylvia. Though he admired her immense courage, there was no way he'd let that happen. Sylvia was the youngest member of their family. She was their future. He'd protect her at all costs.

As the two wrestled with the camera, Patron said, "Doesn't matter to me who goes. Just get that video footage."

Suddenly one of the eight workers approached Sylvia and Javi. The middle-aged man stepped between the two, grabbing the camera in the process.

"I'll go," he said.

Momentary silence filled the hangar. Nobody knew what to say at such a grand gesture.

Javi stepped close to the man. He wished he knew the man's name, so he could thank him by name. He held the man gently by his shoulders. "It's very dangerous down there. Extremely."

The man solemnly nodded.

"You don't have to do this," Javi continued. "I'll go. I might as well. I'm the oldest here and have the least life expectancy."

"No," the man responded. "You're needed; you're of value. We need you to keep this operation safe, if it continues."

"But you may die. It's a distinct possibility."

The man stepped close. "I'm going to die anyway. We all are, aren't we?" He leaned in further. "They don't know our names, or even let us speak our names. Think about that, Mr. White. You're the only one of value. The only one they refer to by a name. We're dogs to them." He scoffed. "Worse than that actually."

After gesturing toward the hole, the man said, "This is all one big underground deathtrap." He swallowed. "I just may be the first to go."

Before Javi could respond, the man grabbed hold of the rungs and disappeared into the earth.

CHAPTER NINE

Exactly one month ago, President Henrietta Valenzuela sent a secure message to the upper echelon of the United States Navy.

With little to no explanation, the command called for a removal of all vessels in the Southern Pacific. The move was in preparation for the upcoming SEAL Team Six mission. What the president didn't want—I gathered from the mission documents she'd left for me to examine—was for any warship or submarine to be in the Baja vicinity. That way, when SEAL Team Six killed Juan Manuel Delgado and escaped via the water, the US had plausible deniability. The United States government could claim they had no vessels in the area that could've aided or abetted the hit on Delgado.

After reading and digesting the original mission outline, I had a better sense of the president's dilemma, and why she came to me. For her to assemble a small black-ops team still meant several people behind the scenes would be in the know. And if she had a leak or mole somewhere on her team, she couldn't use her resources without risking another potential Nogales situation.

For the original mission, two members of SEAL Team Six planned to infiltrate and exfiltrate Northern Baja via an undetectable submersible and some high-tech scuba equipment. Of course, I had access to neither, so I developed a much simpler plan. And sometimes, that was all you needed. My plan relied on a big surfboard and a CSR: a Concealable Sniper Rifle.

I considered it my Occam's razor plan.

It was eleven o'clock at night on Saturday. After Mom and Simon went to bed, I retreated to the back of my property where my run-down barn was located. I'd brought along one of my many sniper rifles from my operative days. The one in my hand was a Remington Defense CSR. I chose that rifle because it could be broken down into three parts, with no part longer than sixteen inches.

For about an hour, I cleaned and oiled the weapon. I also practiced assembling and dismantling it, which I hadn't done in a few years. The rifle was designed to be assembled and broken down in sixty seconds. Once I hit that target time, I moved on to the next phase of my plan, which involved a surfboard.

I had an old longboard that I'd bought at a garage sale for fifty bucks, probably close to a decade ago now. The surfboard was nine feet long, over two feet wide, and approximately three and a half inches thick at the widest point of the board. I nicknamed it *The Tank*. It was the perfect board for a beginner to learn on since it was so big and stable. And it was also the perfect board to conceal my Remington Defense rifle.

With an X-Acto knife in hand, I cut a large upside-down U shape through the board's fiberglass coating, directly in the middle where the board was the thickest and widest. Once completed, I peeled back the fiberglass, carefully folding it as far back as I could without creasing it. Then I duct-taped the cut edge to the board. Now the foam inner core was exposed and easily accessible.

I placed the rifle parts on the foam, then traced around them with a sharp pencil. Following that, I used the X-Acto to cut through the pencil marks. I dug the knife straight down as I traced, nearly piercing the board's underside. When I dug out the foam from inside the trace marks, it easily popped out and followed the shape I'd made.

After cleaning up the edges of the tracing with a flat-head screwdriver, I took the three rifle parts and placed them into their respective holes. Then I released the cut edge and smoothed the fiberglass over the holes.

Perfect, I thought, admiring my handiwork.

With the rifle hidden in the middle of the surfboard, I now had to seal around the

U-shaped cut to make it watertight. I placed strips of fiberglass cloth along the cut edge. Then I mixed up some resin and spread it over the cloth. Since the resin needed some hours to harden before I could sand it smooth, I turned in for the night.

Early Sunday morning, I woke and began sanding. Awkwardly, Simon visited me halfway through the sanding job and wanted to help. By the time I was finished, I had a perfectly concealed sniper rifle inside a surfboard. And my son had helped me do it.

Simon also helped me strap the surfboard to the top of my '86 Chevy Caprice. Naturally, he wanted to go along with me, but I told him I'd take him on plenty of surf trips in the future, just not this one. Mom was a little miffed about my impromptu four-day surf trip, but when I told her I'd take Ranger with me, she softened a little.

Mom had a love/hate relationship with my dog, so she cherished her moments away from him.

With Ranger in the passenger seat, and my car loaded with camping and surfing gear, I proceeded south to Mexico. It took me about five hours to reach the border. Before crossing, I stopped at a rental car place and paid a handsome fortune to rent a Jeep Wrangler.

I flashed my British Columbia driver's license and paid for the rental with my Gary Pounds credit card. Not only was it wise to have a four-wheel drive vehicle in Northern Baja, but it was also wise that Garrison Chase and his Chevy Caprice had no record of entering Mexico.

Once I'd transferred all the gear to the Jeep, Ranger and I were back on the road heading south on Highway One. This time, however, we were on the Mexican side of the highway.

As the president had mentioned, I'd done several trips to popular Mexican surf spots, breaks like Quatra Casas, San Miguel, K-38, and Salsipuedes, so I knew the lay of the land. And I also knew how to travel in Mexico.

It was no surprise, then, when I was pulled over by the Federales in Tijuana and Rosarito. Long ago, I discovered the key to success in these situations was threefold: stay calm, let the Federales search your vehicle without complaint, and keep just one fifty-dollar bill in your wallet at a time. Fifty bucks usually got the Federales off your back and on your way quickly. I tested that theory in both Tijuana and Rosarito, and it still worked flawlessly.

After leaving Ensenada, Highway One veered away from the coast. About a half an hour outside Ensenada, I pulled off the road and let Ranger out for a pee. I used that time to scan the topographical map and directions the president had left for me. Somewhere around my current position was a nondescript dirt road that angled west back to the Pacific. That road led directly to a small surf camp just around the corner from Punta De Las Olas, the training facility.

Eventually, I found the correct road after two failed tries. The road was long and bumpy, and I didn't reach the surf camp until late Sunday night. In fact, it was so late nobody was up, including whoever ran the place. So, I parked out front of what I believed to be the host's trailer and slept in the Jeep.

Ranger had a tiny bladder for a big dog, so he started whining just after sunrise. Since not many people were up, I pulled on my wetsuit and took *The Tank* down to the beach, leaving Ranger in the rental with the windows down.

My board was heavy enough without an embedded sniper rifle, so by the time I made it to the beach, I was winded from carrying it. Once I paddled to the lineup, however, I felt awake and alert. After some cordial head nods to the three other gentlemen in the lineup, I paddled toward the shoulder and waited my turn for a few wide set waves. After surfing like that for about an hour, I left the pack behind and paddled outside. I mean, way far out from anybody. Far from where the waves were currently peeling off the point.

My strategy was to establish myself as the lone surfer who paddled up the coast in search of his own wave. In reality, I simply wanted to go around the point to see the training camp on the next bluff and get a feel for the area.

Since the training facility was a low-lying structure, by the time I made it around the point, I could barely make out the top of the building. I decided then that I'd have to paddle to the nearest beach and climb the bluff to get an accurate lay of the land. But I wasn't going to do it now since it was high tide and the waves currently crashed against the bluff. My plan was to come back Tuesday evening and perform a dry run at low tide before the Wednesday evening show.

I paddled back to the surf camp and secured a spot with the host. The host was thrilled I had cash, so he didn't even ask my name. Since I wanted to be incognito and avoid conversation, I chose a small, weedy camp spot for my tent farthest from the main pack of campers. Ranger spent most of his time either inside the tent or sniffing around the small site. He was too scared to venture farther than that.

Without a doubt, I'd quickly established myself as a loner who was in no mood for company. That was evidenced by the fact that I had zero visitors and no conversations with other people during all of Monday. And most of Tuesday, too.

I spent those two days in and out of the ocean. Each time I went for a surf, I pulled the same move: I'd take a few waves with the other surfers, then paddle out of view for the remainder of the session. By the time Tuesday evening rolled around, not a soul paid any attention as I paddled around the point and disappeared from four to six o'clock.

According to the presidential package I'd studied, Delgado visited the facility every Wednesday evening, always arriving sometime between five and five thirty. On Tuesday afternoon at four thirty, I found myself on a small stretch of beach that only exposed itself at low tide. Punta De Las Olas was directly above me on the point overlooking the ocean.

I dragged *The Tank* as far up the beach as I could, then scouted the area for where to climb the bluff. At the north end of the beach, I discovered a jagged rock line that protruded from the cliffside. The rock jutted out a few inches and provided a decent ledge for my wetsuit booties to grip. It took me ten minutes to shimmy up the rock ledge to the base of the bluff.

Once at the top, I poked my head up slowly, like a gopher, to get a visual of the area. The first thing I saw was the training facility in all its brown and green glory. It looked identical to the video footage I'd seen. From that vantage, I had a solid view of the main entrance to the building.

After studying the structure and its surroundings, I refocused on why I was there: to visualize the shot and do reconnaissance for tomorrow's mission. So, I spent the next forty-five minutes studying the wind direction and waning light, calculating the distance to the main entrance, and examining the surroundings for any objects in my line of sight. I also envisioned my escape route back to the surf camp.

Once I had a solid plan, and felt comfortable with the shot, I focused on the part of the building where Delgado would enter. But the more I studied the entrance, the more I thought about the women inside. And the more I found myself getting emotional. Part of me wanted to abandon the Delgado hit and go rogue. Storm the building with my CSR ready to blaze. Pop any security guard who fired at me. Free all the women, get them to safety, burn the drugs and raze the building.

A real hero type move.

But I kept a level head. I needed to play the long game. I had to stop the Butcher of Baja and free the women. With the Butcher dead, he'd never torture or kill or dehumanize another person again.

Just as I was about to shimmy down the cliffside, the entrance doors burst open and a slew of children piled out, all wearing what looked to be the same white uniform. The scene stopped me in my tracks.

Who are these kids?

The children looked happy and carefree, breaking into a run as soon as they got outside. They played tagged and eventually disappeared around the corner of the building, no doubt headed toward the far parking lot on the other side.

For a moment, I was confused. Then I figured they must be the women's children coming for a visit. That had to be it.

And that revelation enraged me more.

I climbed down the cliffside, put my board back in the water, then paddled aggressively back to camp. The whole time I thought about those kids. At any given moment one of their moms may be sold into modern-day slavery to the highest bidder in the United States. The realization that some children may have just seen their mom for the very last time crushed my soul.

That night, the last thing on my mind before drifting off to sleep was placing the crosshairs on Juan Manuel Delgado's forehead.

And pulling the trigger.

CHAPTER TEN

TWENTY-TWO HOURS LATER, I was paddling toward the small stretch of exposed beach at Punta De Las Olas.

So far, everything was identical to yesterday's dry run. The only changes from Tuesday were that I had my Kershaw folding knife tucked into the top of my wetsuit booties, and I now wore a dark baseball hat. When I reached the beach, I dragged the board high onto the sand, then used my knife to reopen the U-shaped cut.

After quickly assembling the Remington Defense rifle, I went to the beach's north end and proceeded up the cliffside. I was in position with the rifle pointed at the building's entrance by approximately four thirty in the afternoon. Only the top part of my head and rifle protruded above ground. You'd never spot my minimal silhouette unless you were within a hundred feet. And currently there was nobody close to that distance. In fact, nobody was around at all.

And why wasn't anyone around? *Considering what's going on inside, shouldn't there be a few guards patrolling the perimeter?*

That thought concerned me. Did the lack of guards mean this could be the one Wednesday when Delgado didn't visit? To get my mind off that potentiality, I focused on my shooting position.

Though I was perched on a cliff, I'd achieved a stable position. My body was wedged into the cliffside, and I had a three-inch flat rock ledge for my wetsuit booties. I used the rifle's bipod on the ground to comfortably support the barrel. The stock was jammed into my shoulder. I had the scope dialed in after making the correct adjustments for bullet drop, wind, and distance. Which I'd pegged at 379 meters. Not a cakewalk shot, but not too difficult either. I felt confident I could get a clean hit and then disappear before Delgado's body hit the ground.

For the next forty minutes, I picked out targets on the building and practiced breathing and air-pulling the trigger. Just like my operative days, I was deep in mission mode. My mind and emotions were blank. Totally void. All I thought about was pulling the trigger smoothly, hitting the target, then exfiltrating cleanly.

Not once did I think of failure, of repercussions, of getting caught. Unlike yesterday, I didn't consider the women inside. Not at all. I was a robot operative on a mission from the president.

At precisely twelve minutes past five, I heard the roar of two car engines. After easing my eye from the scope, I glanced right. Two dark SUVs pulled in and parked twenty meters from the entrance.

Game on.

I put my eye back and patiently waited for the men to enter the scope's field of vision. Eventually, they did. There were five men in total. Delgado was one of them. In the president's package, she'd left no less than twenty different pictures of Juan Manuel Delgado. With his tall frame, square shoulders, and perfectly manicured ink-black mustache, he was an easy target to spot amongst the men.

The four men surrounding Delgado were clearly not guards. They didn't look like cartel men either. They carried no weapons, and each one was dressed in casual business attire. Since nobody wore a coat or suit jacket or bulky sweater, I could tell they weren't concealing any weapons on their hips or behind their backs.

Unsure of who these men were, I put them out of my mind and turned my attention to Delgado. Specifically, I put the crosshairs on his face, at the exact point where his left sideburn started. All five men had congregated out front of the entrance and were having a brief chat.

Now's the time.

I took a fraction of slack from the trigger. Held my breath. Just as I was about to ease my finger back, the men split up. Two men went to the main entrance while Delgado and the other two walked to the side door; the one that led to the underground hospital wards.

The sudden move didn't bother me. Instead, I realigned and thought it might be better to wait. The two men who entered the main entrance were now out of the picture. And the other two with Delgado were almost to the side door. Since they were in front of Delgado, I'd wait until they were inside the building before taking the shot. I'd drop Delgado just before his body crossed the door's threshold.

With no men outside to witness the shot, they'd have no idea what direction the shot came from.

Perfect.

But as the front man punched in the door's security code, I reconsidered because I currently had a good shot. Juan Manuel Delgado was perfectly framed in my scope as he stood and waited behind the other men.

Intuition told me to wait, though. *Stick to the plan, Chase.*

So, I did.

After the code released the locked door, the front man did something shocking. He pulled the handle toward him and stepped back as the door swung outward.

Wait, what?

The scene from the president's video was ingrained into my memory. In that footage the front man pushed the door inward, and the three men barreled in. Absolutely. I remembered it vividly. No way did the front man step back and pull the door outward.

What the hell? The door just swung the wrong way! Is this even the same building?

That detail distracted me, which ultimately ruined the hit. Because by the time I refocused, Juan Manuel Delgado had slipped inside.

And all I could do was watch the door slam shut behind him.

CHAPTER ELEVEN

My CHEST DEFLATED as I pushed out the breath I'd been holding.

Instinctively, I crouched down and dragged the rifle back with me, pushing my spine against the cliffside to maintain stability. A thousand thoughts spiraled through my mind.

Had I missed my opportunity? Did I blow it? *You didn't blow it, Chase. No way. Something's off here. Something isn't right. Is this the same building? It looks like it. I mean, it must be. There can't be two identical buildings like this. Right?*

My thoughts flipped.

It can't be the same building. It just can't. The hinges are on the outside; the door swings the bloody wrong way. The intel you got is bad, pal. Something is off here; something is definitely wrong.

In the end, I couldn't stop thinking about the door anomaly. It didn't make sense. Even if the building had a recent break-in or a problem with that side door, and the door had been changed since the footage I'd seen, it's not like they'd retool the door to swing outward. Plus, most exterior doors swung inward for security reasons and to protect the hinges from the elements.

They must be different buildings. But how? And why?

I decided I had to investigate. I absolutely had to find out if this was the building with the drug-induced women inside.

And I had to do it right away.

I got back into the shooting position and used the scope to scan the building. The first thing I focused on was the big glass doors at the main entrance. Inside, I could see the secretary who manned the front desk. She was currently packing up her stuff. No one else was in the lobby area.

I moved the scope toward the windows. Unfortunately, every window I focused on contained a dark tint, which prevented me from seeing in. Since I'd yet to spot any guards, and the men who'd accompanied Delgado appeared unarmed, I threw caution to the wind and decided to approach the building.

After the secretary left the lobby and headed to the parking lot, I climbed onto land and proceeded slowly toward the building with my rifle pointed straight ahead. Since the evening light was waning, and I was dressed in a full-body black wetsuit, I didn't stick out that badly. And during yesterday's recon I hadn't noted any security cameras on the building, so I wasn't concerned about being spotted on approach.

As I advanced toward the building, I steered clear of the main lobby. Instead, I shimmied along the open wall toward the point of the building's V. I knew that was my best bet to glance in and confirm the occupants inside. The tinted windows on my side of the building were about nine or ten feet above ground. I couldn't gain any visual confirmation from them, so I didn't waste my time trying.

I headed straight to the middle of the building. Even before I got there, though, I saw the problem: the floor-to-ceiling windows also had floor-to-ceiling blinds. And all of them had been drawn, just like they'd been in the video I'd seen. It made sense since the windows faced due west and the afternoon light blazed directly on them.

Undeterred, I kept moving. When I reached the other side of the building, though, I had the same problem: all the windows were high off the ground and provided no visual confirmation of who or what was inside the building.

So, I crept around the backside and slowly approached the main entrance. I didn't dare waltz up to the glass doors, knowing the mere sight of me would cause panic. Instead, I hung back and cautiously poked my head around the corner.

Nobody was in the immediate lobby area. I could, however, see a little way down the hallway and spotted some people. From what I could tell, they appeared to be young girls in lab coats. Like maybe middle-school-age girls.

What on earth?

I flattened my back against the wall and tilted my head upward. I wasn't sure exactly how long I stood in that position thinking about my next move. Maybe a minute or so. All I knew was that at the end of my thought process, I found myself heading straight at the side door with the Remington ready to fire.

Two thoughts were on my mind: shut this operation down, and take out Delgado.

I felt confident in the improvised mission since I had surprise on my side. Plus, I hadn't seen one guard this entire time.

Ten feet from the side door, I fired a round into the handle. The .308 caliber bullet made easy work of the doorknob and locking mechanism. Before I knew it, I was inside the building. While hustling down a dark staircase toward the basement, I rechambered a round. I hoped I wouldn't get into a firefight with anybody since the CSR was bolt action and fired one round at a time.

At the bottom of the stairs was a closed door. It didn't have a code pad beside the handle. In fact, it looked like a regular door without any lock at all.

I thought back to the video. *Isn't another code pad supposed to be here?*

After shaking off the thought, I brought the rifle up to my shoulder to hide most of my face. Then I charged in. Dead set on saving the women. Dead set on stopping this horrible operation.

Before making it two steps, though, I stopped in my tracks.

This was no underground hospital ward.

Not even close.

CHAPTER TWELVE

JAVI PEERED into the deep cavern below the tunnel's entrance.

He flicked his headlamp on, illuminating Raoul and Jaime at the bottom of the hole. For days the men had been digging a basin to help contain water in case of a flood. They'd been working without guards present, so they'd shared their names and grown closer while working together.

"Fine job, gentlemen," he shouted to them. "We're almost there, almost at twenty meters."

They gave him a thumbs-up, then returned to filling up the massive bucket beside them with dirt. Javi watched them until the bucket filled and they tugged on the rope attached to its handle. The workers on the surface would get the message, then do their part.

Moments later, the bucket passed Javi on its journey topside. At the same time, an empty bucket descended by him on its journey to the bottom. Javi helped thread the buckets through the large hole in the scaffolding's open floor.

Over the past few days, he'd utilized his engineering know-how. He'd designed the very pulley system he currently watched in action. With the help of Raoul, who was a welder by trade, Javi had designed a base for the scaffolding at the tunnel entrance. Using scrap pieces of rebar they found in the airplane hangar, they'd driven four long pieces of metal into the earth at the corners of the scaffolding structure. Then Raoul had welded a spiderweb flooring system for the scaffolding's base with various pieces of rebar.

With that in place, men took shifts digging a massive hole underneath the spiderweb floor. In pairs, they'd dig nonstop for an hour, then change shifts. It was all designed to anticipate a flood. Though Javi had begged and pleaded with Patron to start a new tunnel, the powers that be would not agree. They insisted the workers keep going since they were close to completion.

The best Javi could do was prepare for an emergency flood and level off the tunnel. If their continued digging broke through the water table, all the rushing water needed somewhere to go. Naturally, it would run toward the entrance because of the tunnel's slope, so it needed somewhere to reside.

When the next bucket of dirt passed through the spiderweb flooring, Javi knew that was it. The last bucket of the last shift. Patron and his superiors had granted them a few days of reprieve from digging, but no more than that.

Moments later, Raoul and Jaime climbed through one of the large holes in the rebar floor. Jaime carried two shovels while Raoul carried his welding torch and an extra piece of rebar.

Raoul nodded toward Javi. "Mission complete, Javi. We're done." Raoul put down the items in his hands at the tunnel entrance, then embraced Javi.

It amazed Javi how much everything had changed. A deep bond had developed over just a few days, not just between Raoul and himself, but amongst the entire crew. Since workers spent hours underground together, they had time to talk. And since it seemed inevitable that their time on earth was quickly dwindling, the workers shared their stories, who they were, their job or trade, their significant others, their life dreams, and their names.

It became an unspoken rule that crew members would refer to one another by first name while underground. But never topside. Never.

A triumph of the human spirit, Javi thought.

He pulled back from the embrace. Feeling himself getting too emotional, Javi got back to business. He motioned at the rebar beside him.

"Last one in place?" he asked Raoul.

"Yes," Raoul replied. "On our way up, we counted. Twenty in all."

Every time Raoul came down for a shift, he'd weld a pair of one-meter-long rebar to either side of the ladder that extended below the scaffolding floor, then he'd weld some crossbars for steps. That way, as the crew dug down, they built themselves a ladder to get out, but also so they could measure their overall depth.

Jaime motioned below his feet, concern in his eyes. "Javi, is it really big enough?"

Even though it looked like a deep, wide basin, it probably wasn't big enough. Javi could do the math in his head. Considering the diameter of the tunnel, and its massive length, a full flooding of the tunnel would eat up the basin's volume in record time. Hopefully they would survive a partial flood, though. But he wasn't about to tell the workers that. Javi bought as much time as he could, and the crew worked as fast and as diligently as they could. In Javi's mind, it was a tiny victory.

He placed his hand on Jaime's shoulder. "We'll be fine, just fine, Jaime."

"One more thing to do," Raoul said, grabbing his torch. "These holes in the floor are too big." He motioned to the spot where the ladder descended, and the other big hole where the buckets passed through. "I need to close them up now that we're finished digging below."

Javi nodded and watched Raoul work. The welder cut the final piece of rebar in half, then mounted the two pieces across the big holes and welded them in place.

When finished, Raoul eyed Javi with a big smile. "That way a small person like your granddaughter can't accidentally fall through."

Such a good man, Javi thought. Raoul was the one who risked his life to get video footage of the tunnel's leak for Patron. And here he was, still thinking of others.

"Great-granddaughter," Javi corrected. He hadn't mentioned that personal fact to any of the workers before.

Raoul quipped, "Not a chance. You can't be that old, Javi."

"I am." Javi nudged Raoul in the ribs and winked. "Started young, if you know what I mean."

Raoul gave a hearty laugh. "You mean you like young women. Just how young, Javi?"

The old man grinned and waved him off. "Never you mind."

As Raoul and Jaime started climbing the scaffolding toward the surface, Javi took a quick glance into the tunnel.

He spoke softly to himself, "Now the real danger begins."

CHAPTER THIRTEEN

THERE WERE no drugged women in the basement of Punta De Las Olas. Not a single person was in sight. There were no individual wards either. No rooms at all, in fact, or even a hallway, for that matter.

Directly in front of me was an open storage area filled with what looked to be scientific equipment. A faint smell of chemicals wafted in the air, which reminded me of my days in high school chemistry class.

It was so different from the video I'd seen, for a moment I thought I may be in a different part of the basement. But as I looked around, I couldn't see any doors to another area.

Suddenly, from the other end of the huge room, I heard shouts and the patter of footsteps. Following that, the lights flicked off and darkness took over. Then a door slammed shut.

No doubt Delgado and his two men fled the room via a staircase at the other end.

Move, Chase! Go after them before they get help. Don't give them time to mobilize.

I broke into a fast walk, dodging various large instruments in the darkness. When I reached the opposite stairwell, I smoothed my hand along the wall until I found a light switch. Though I wanted up the stairs quickly, I also wanted a quick glance backward.

So, I flicked on the light and stole a glance. Closest to the stairwell was what appeared to be a large centrifuge. It caught my attention because there were packaging materials haphazardly strewn around its circumference. Part of the centrifuge was still unboxed. I figured this new equipment piece was what Delgado and the men had been checking out.

Clearly, this was a storage area for some sort of scientific lab. And since I saw many different grow lights, I instantly thought of a hydroponic situation. I also looked around for any doors that led to a different part of the basement.

When I didn't find any, I moved into action and raced up the stairs.

Within seconds, I stood in front of another locked door with a keypad to its right. From behind the door, I heard movement and lots of shouting. After stepping back and taking a breath, I pulled my hat down tight, then propped the rifle on my shoulder and tilted my head until the right side of my face was covered by my shoulder. I squinted my left eye and looked down the barrel with my right and fired a round that blew apart the door handle. Immediately following that, I kicked in the door.

Shouts turned to screams. Upon seeing me, men and women in lab coats scattered and dropped to the ground. A few people yelled in English, "Shooter! There's a shooter!"

Since I didn't want to show my face, I kept my head tilted and my left eye squinted. I wanted to quickly look around, though, so I swung the rifle to increase my field of vision.

"*He's gonna shoot!*" someone screamed.

More chaos ensued.

Naturally, I had no intention of shooting anyone. But everyone else didn't know that. The way I was jerking the rifle around certainly didn't alleviate the anxiety in the room.

After a few quick glances around, I knew I'd been duped. There were no drugged women on this floor either. The vast, open space to my right was not the modern dining/living room for the women. This was a huge laboratory. In fact, with the floor-to-ceiling windows, this was essentially a greenhouse. Labs and workstations were set up everywhere in the open-concept room. Various plants were on countertops, obviously being tested and propagated for who knows what purposes.

As chaos in the room reached a crescendo, I knew I had to abort this improvised mission. All the intel I'd been provided appeared bogus.

No way would I follow through on a life-ending directive with bad intel.

Just before backing down the stairs, my eye focused straight ahead. I spotted Delgado frantically pushing digits on a numbered keypad in front of a set of double doors. Two men were on either side of him banging on the door.

Delgado turned, and for a second, he looked right at me. I could see the deep-set panic in his eyes. Just as quickly, though, he looked away when the doors opened. To put a scare in him, I fired a round high and to his right. The bullet lodged into a ceiling panel, and a *boom!* filled the room a fraction of a second later.

Upon hearing that, pandemonium in the greenhouse reached its apex. Which was what I wanted. I needed out of the building fast, and I didn't want anybody to have the gall to follow me.

As I crept slowly backward, I glanced toward the room where Delgado had fled. Right before the doors closed, I saw several children in lab coats backed up along the wall. They were sitting on the floor with their knees up and head between their legs. But I had no time to process that sight and what it meant.

Instead, I turned and charged down the steps, retracing my original route. With the lights on, I was up the opposite staircase in no time. I did, however, exit the side door cautiously, keeping the rifle pointed at the lobby area.

Since nobody was in there, I blasted one of the glass doors to jagged bits. I knew that move would put a further scare in people and hopefully keep everyone inside the building for a while. I didn't want anyone coming after me. And I certainly didn't want them to know which direction I'd fled.

I hustled to the cliff and dropped onto the ledge. After a quick look behind to make sure nobody had seen me, I sidestepped my way down to the beach. The sun had already set over the ocean, so it was close to dark. Enough to see for now, but I knew it wouldn't be long until nightfall. Which was good and bad. Good in the sense that nobody would see me paddling away. Bad in that I'd have to travel back in the dark.

Out on the water, I paddled swiftly. I'd smoothed the fiberglass sheet over the rifle holes. However, the rifle wasn't in its respective holes. It lay perpendicular at the front of the board since I had no intention of traveling any farther with it.

When I reached the furthest point out to sea before angling back to the surf camp, I sat on my board and dismantled the Remington Defense Rifle. Then I threw those three pieces into the sea, along with my baseball cap, and headed toward shore.

Fortunately, I'd completed this same trip numerous times, so navigating back in the dark wasn't too bad. Once on shore, I immediately stepped on my board and snapped it in half; directly in the spot where I'd dug the holes for the rifle. I broke off some pieces of foam around where the holes used to be. Now it looked like a trashed surfboard that had been broken in two by a large wave. The other good thing was that a broken board explained why I was out on the water through dusk.

If anyone asked, I'd tell them I had to paddle to shore to collect the broken board. Then I had to trek back to camp along the rocky shoreline.

With the two pieces of surfboard tucked under either arm, I trudged back to my camp spot. I made sure a few people saw me so nobody would think I'd vanished. Since everyone in camp was a surfer, they saw my broken board and deduced exactly what had happened to me. No mystery there.

Back at camp, Ranger was excited to see me. After feeding him and peeling off my wetsuit, I tucked into the tent for a few moments. I immediately wanted to call the president and give her a piece of my mind. Confront her about what the hell was going on. Directly ask her if she'd set me up. However, days ago when I first arrived at camp, I'd noticed there was zero cell reception. Calls in camp were impossible. You had to travel back to the main highway to get a signal.

That may have been a good thing. Because right now I needed to calm down and get a clear mind before taking further action. Plus, I needed to process everything I'd just seen and been through.

I never got that chance, however.

The throaty burble of multiple vehicles approaching the surf camp commanded my attention. I unzipped the tent's fly and looked out. Whirling lights and roaring engines were all I saw and heard. At least five vehicles screamed into the campground.

Doors flew open and a small band of armed Federales piled out of the SUVs.

CHAPTER FOURTEEN

Two FEDERALES quickly approached my tent.

I laid on top of my sleeping bag and pretended not to notice them approaching. Since the Federales immediately fanned out, I knew they were canvassing and didn't have a particular subject in mind.

That put my mind a little at ease. No doubt they'd heard from Punta De Las Olas that the shooter wore a wetsuit and baseball hat. Naturally, they'd come storming to the nearest surf camp to look for a suspect.

"Amigo, out," said one of the Federales. He pointed the tip of his Heckler & Koch MP5 into the tent, then motioned with his head for me to get out.

Since a rifle was mere inches from my face, I complied.

Ranger, however, didn't. He cowered in the far corner of the tent. His snout was buried under one end of my sleeping bag.

Once out of the tent, the same Federale looked at me and said, "Perro, out."

I coaxed Ranger from the tent. He immediately slithered under the dilapidated picnic table to my right.

Both Federales gave me the once-over, but they didn't say a word directly to me.

After the men had a brief, tense exchange in Spanish, which I couldn't translate, one of them prodded me forward. He led me toward the host's trailer.

The campground had zero outdoor lights. At night, the only light you could see came from the various campfires at different sites. Right now, though, a couple of SUVs had their bright headlights blazing on the silver camp-host trailer.

They lined five of us in front of that trailer. We all had our arms up to block the headlights from the blinding glare. Since we were all white and relatively the same height—that is, tall—I knew they were race- and height-profiling us.

There were lots of fast conversations in Spanish, which, unfortunately, I couldn't come close to understanding. One man in the line, two positions down from me, had a firm grasp of Spanish. He muttered a play-by-play of what they were saying.

Which basically amounted to: they're looking for a tall man who stormed a local building in a wetsuit while carrying a rifle and wearing a baseball hat.

Minutes later, they dumped our wetsuits in front of us. No surprise, though, since this was a surf camp after all. Plus, it was winter, and we were in Northern Baja, which meant you needed a 3/2 mm wetsuit to be comfortable in the sea for a couple-hour surf session.

All five of us had wetsuits, but there were only three baseball hats.

Thank goodness I threw mine out to sea.

One of the Federales asked in English, "Where were you tonight?"

He went down the line with the question. You couldn't see the cop's face because of the blinding headlights. All you heard was him asking the same question to each man, in relatively good English, and with only a hint of a Spanish accent.

When my turn came, I motioned toward the beach. "Out surfing. My board broke and I had to swim to shore to retrieve it, then walk along the beach in the dark."

After some conferring in Spanish, they hustled me back to my site. I showed them my broken board. In return, they showed me how to properly turn a campsite.

Six Federales tossed my site. No doubt looking for the rifle, or for anything else incriminating. They looked in, on, and under everything I'd brought to Mexico. Two of the men focused all their attention on the Jeep Wrangler.

They didn't find anything, of course.

The problem: they did take my wallet, fake passport, and burner phone. If I didn't get those back soon, I was screwed. The passport and phone were a huge hassle. Not only since I needed to text the president right away and demand to know what was going on, but also because I'd left my own cell phone and real passport in a hidden compartment in the Caprice. And that vehicle was currently across the border in a different country.

The Federales brought me back in line with the other four men, in front of the trailer with the blinding lights. I noticed that every man's passport and cell phone were on the ground in front of them, including mine.

Again, fast and loud conversations—bordering on arguments—occurred for the next few minutes. After that, some Federales emerged from the shadows and grabbed all the phones, wallets, and passports. They quickly retreated to their respective SUVs.

"Wait," I yelled after the elongating shadows. "Where are you going with my stuff? My ID. I need those things."

Since nobody responded, I walked in the direction of the blinding lights, straight toward the closest vehicle.

A few steps in, though, I heard some rifles engage, so I stopped. I held up my hands. "I just want my passport and wallet and phone back. Why are you taking them? What's going on here?"

Again, silence.

After some tense moments, I heard the man's voice who spoke earlier say, "You'll get your personal items back when we're done investigating. Now step back in line."

I didn't. "So, what, I just wait here? Till when? How long? What kind of treatment is this? I've done nothing wrong. I don't know who you're looking for, but it's certainly not me."

The speaker stepped out from the shadows. He must've been relatively my same height because his head blocked out the headlights.

I lowered my arm. But since the man was backlit, I still couldn't see much, only his silhouette. He was standing approximately fifteen feet away. I watched him open what I assumed was my passport.

"Listen, Gary Pounds," he said. "You're pushing it. Now back up."

I took a step forward instead. Not exactly to be obstinate, just to get a better look at him.

Not a good move. Two Federales stepped in front of me, seemingly out of nowhere. Their weapons were inches from my chest.

"Fine," I said, moving back. "Just tell me where and when I can come get my stuff, especially my passport. I need to get back home soon."

"Come by the station in a few days," the man said.

"A few days?" I shot back. "You're kidding, I hope."

"I don't kid around, Mr. Pounds."

Just as I was about to respond, a staccato of gunfire erupted. The man to my right dropped to the ground in fear.

I crouched.

"No more questions, Gary," the voice said. "Or the next rounds won't miss."

CHAPTER FIFTEEN

HENRIETTA VALENZUELA PULLED her chair tight to the desk and checked her watch.

There must be news, she thought.

The president glanced around. The Oval Office currently held several of her closest aides and advisors, all working late into the evening. She hoped to extract the burner cell from the 1920s walnut desk drawer to her right without anyone noticing.

As she eyed her staff members, waiting for the right moment, Henrietta tapped her fingers on the burled maple desktop and admired the desk she'd brought over from the West Wing study. It wasn't ornate and detailed like the Resolute desk; the desk most used by presidents. The C&O desk in front of her was straightforward, with zero frills. Only one other president had used the C&O desk in the Oval Office. And since she wasn't like most presidents, that suited Henrietta Valenzuela just fine.

With others in the room conversing, she sensed the moment was right. The president swiftly opened the middle of the three graduated drawers to her right. She slipped the burner cell out and placed it on her thigh. The expansive desktop easily hid the cell from view.

Looking up, she noted her staffers were still deep in conversation. Nobody paid her any attention. Off to her right, standing near the east door, were her chief of staff and deputy chief of staff. The two were in a lengthy discussion about an internal staffing issue. In front of her, on the left side couch by the fireplace, sat her personal secretary and the secretary to the president. And, yes, it was still confusing to her that those were distinct roles. The man and woman pored over tomorrow's schedule. Their eyes never once flickered toward their boss.

Still, Henrietta didn't want to draw attention to her movements, so she kept her head up while pushing the cell's power button with her right thumb. While waiting for the cell to power on—and hopefully buzz to indicate a new text—the president busied herself with the stack of paperwork on her desk.

As one of the rare left-handed presidents, Henrietta began signing the mundane documents with her left hand. Her right hand smothered the cell on her thigh, not just as an extra precaution to hide the phone, but to make sure she felt the buzz the moment the text came through. By the time she worked through the documents, however, the phone hadn't buzzed. She removed her hand and stole a glance.

Nothing. No new text. No call. No alert of any kind.

It wasn't like she had to rifle through a slew of missed calls or texts on this particular cell. Only Garrison Chase had the number to this phone. To double-check that she hadn't missed anything, Henrietta opened the text app. Nope. The only text in there was the one from Chase a few days back; the one that read: *I'm in.*

Just as her chief of staff was about to exit the east door into the Rose Garden, she said, "Willy, one second." She held up her finger.

Willy Blanco hustled over. "What can I do for you, ma'am?"

"While I go over tomorrow's schedule with Branch and Shelly, can you go next door and scan the networks? Give me a quick update."

He looked confused, which didn't surprise the president. Normally, it wasn't an odd request to ask for a news briefing, but it was when you had your final daily update just ninety minutes ago.

Willy recovered and said, "Sure, ma'am. Not a problem. Anything particular you're interested in? A domestic or foreign issue? Probably no news from Europe since it's the middle of the night there."

Henrietta paused for a moment. "Foreign, North American news is of particular interest."

He nodded. "I'll be back." Since there wasn't a television in the Oval Office, Willy walked across the office, through the west door, and into her private study.

For the next fifteen minutes, Henrietta walked through the intricacies of tomorrow's schedule with her two secretaries. At the conclusion, Willy entered the Oval Office. On his way to her desk, he gave a quick head shake.

"Nothing?" said Henrietta.

"Nothing new since the evening briefing, ma'am. I kept my ears open on all channels, as well as checked our standard news blog. Nothing popped up related to Canada or Mexico. And it seems there's no new developments related to the USMCA either, if that was what you're after."

The president didn't bite, she simply said, "Okay then, thanks."

Willy eyed her. "You sure everything's okay, Madam President?"

"Positive, Willy, thank you."

There was an awkward moment where Willy just stood there. The president's eyes glanced to the deputy chief of staff waiting by the east door. "You can join your deputy chief now."

"Yes, ma'am," Willy said, nodding and heading to the door.

"Madam President," Shelly said, motioning toward the Seymour grandfather clock. "You have a late meeting in the Cabinet Room."

Henrietta nodded. Typically, she never carried a cell with her into important meetings, especially when they were conducted in the Situation Room or the Cabinet Room. Tonight, however, she was prepared to make an exception since she needed confirmation of a job complete.

What if, she thought, *the mission fails? What do I do then?* As quickly as the thought came, she just as quickly shook it off.

The mission can't fail. It just can't.

Shelly cleared her throat, indicating the president needed to get moving.

Before standing, Henrietta discreetly slipped the cell into her right jacket pocket. It was a loose-fitting jacket, so she hoped she'd be able to feel the buzz of an incoming text.

74

CHAPTER SIXTEEN

THE ONLY ONE in the tent who got any semblance of sleep was Ranger. No doubt my dog was exhausted after shivering in terror under the picnic table while I was being grilled by the police. Sleep came easy for him.

Me, not so much.

I spent most of the night in and out of light sleep. When I was awake, my mind fixated on the president's directive and the evidence she'd provided. After hours of thinking, it became clear I was nearly duped into killing Juan Manuel Delgado.

Is he even the Butcher of Baja? Has the president lied about that?

My thoughts kept rolling: no way was I supposed to gain access to that building or see inside the place. My job was to take down Delgado from a distance and then run for the hills. And the president used the video to get me on board.

But she'd used doctored footage!

My bet was that at some point when the men approached the building's side door, an edit occurred in the video. Which meant the footage from the man's jacket pocket took place somewhere else; at the true spot where these women were being held, and not at the scientific lab I'd stormed.

The evidence was fabricated. A distortion of the truth. Hell, a total lie.

Who knows if Delgado was even involved with the human trafficking scheme?

Slim was right: the President of the United States used me. She handed me a basket of her dirty laundry and wanted me to do the cleaning. To clean up whatever jacked-up business she had going on here in Mexico. What exactly that business was? I didn't know.

But I was damn determined to find out.

By early morning, I was raring to go. I knew the Federales would take their sweet time returning my ID, wallet, and phone, so I planned to put some pressure on them.

After visiting with the camp host, an expat named Tobias Ranger, I got the address to the closest police station. Tobias gave me a bit of an education, too. He informed me that the officers last night weren't technically Federales, they were the local state police. He insisted that "Federales" was a Yankee slang term for Mexican police. That Mexico had a diverse law enforcement system like the US did. I informed him that I was aware of that fact, and that it was just easier to refer to them as Federales. Tobias told me to do better.

Touché.

Anyway, after my schooling, I packed up my tent, supplies, broken surfboard, and dog, then booked it out of the surf camp. Ensenada was the nearest city with a police station—three, in fact—so I headed there, which was a little over an hour away.

I visited the police command building in the north part of the city, and not the smaller substation or tiny portico that was by the side of Highway One as you entered Ensenada from the south.

I imagined a tall gringo like myself wasn't a frequent visitor to this state police station. That was evident when I entered the building. It wasn't like the place ground to a halt when I stepped through the front doors. The Mexican people were more subtle and polite than Americans, meaning nobody immediately shot me looks and stared me down like an American would. Instead, people slowly glanced over and glared for just a moment. A few people left their desks and congregated together to politely whisper about my presence. There was, however, no rude pointing in my direction.

At the front desk, a young officer with a smooth face greeted me. Honestly, he looked too young to be a cop.

"Hola, Senor," he said. "May I help you?"

"Hola," I replied, giving him a wide smile to be as disarming as I could. "I hope so. I'm looking for your commander."

I wasn't positive of the state police ranking in Mexico, so I wasn't sure if commander was the appropriate word, but I figured it was a generic enough term that this guy would know who I wanted.

"Our Comandante is not here," he quickly replied.

I sighed to express my displeasure. "That could be a problem," I said, tapping my fingers on the desk. "I'm pretty sure your Comandante has my passport, wallet, and phone. And I really need them back. Desperately, in fact."

No response from baby face.

"Your Comandante, is he about my height?" I asked. "Speaks good English."

The cop threw his head back in laughter. "No way. You very tall, mister. Not many Mexicans as tall as you."

I thought for a second. Since he used the term Comandante, it confirmed their ranking terminology. "What about your First Sergeant, or your Corporal? Are they here? Maybe they're around my height?"

That made him laugh more. He turned and shouted back. "Pepe! *Pepe!*"

A moment later, a man in plain clothes stepped out from behind a cubicle wall.

"Our Corporal," the young cop said with a grin. "What do you Americans say, 'At your service'?" He waved his hand toward Pepe and chuckled.

I nodded, and I immediately got the joke. Pepe would have a hard time touching my shoulders, even if he jumped off a stool to try. There was some more laughing, followed by some fast talking in Spanish by the two men.

To distract them from their sidebar, I said, "Were you gentlemen, or any other officers from this station, at the surf camp south of Punta De Las Olas last night? Some police rolled in looking for someone, and they ended up taking my personal effects."

"No, Senor, that was not us," Pepe replied. "Perhaps one of the other stations?"

After a cordial goodbye, I took Pepe's advice and tried the other stations. Though I didn't get quite the laughs I did at the first station, I didn't get any information or cooperation either. People were no doubt lying to me.

But there was a slight possibility that they were telling the truth, and that maybe the police came from the south. Tobias Ranger hadn't mentioned a station to the south, but it was worth exploring. I thought about the timeline. From the time I pulled the trigger inside the building, until the time I paddled back to camp, got undressed, and tucked myself into the tent, it was probably an hour and fifteen minutes at most.

Which put Ensenada in play, of course. But it also included some small cities south of Punta De Las Olas, too.

Climbing into the Jeep, I was greeted by Ranger licking my face.

I rubbed behind my shotgun partner's left ear. "Ready for a little road trip, pal?"

With the passenger window down and Ranger's long snout extending into the wind, we drove south down Highway One. My plan when I reached the turnoff to the surf camp was to start a timer. Since it was approximately thirty minutes from the camp to Highway One, I planned to drive and look for a police station no more than forty-five minutes south of the turnoff.

But as I approached the turnoff point, I had a sneaky suspicion that I may not get that far. I spied two old trucks idling on the side of the road with several men leaning against the tailgate. As soon as I turned onto Highway One, I glanced in the rearview mirror.

Damn.

The men immediately piled into the trucks. Before long, they were barreling toward me. Through the mirror, I watched the two trucks gain on the Jeep. They were old Toyota trucks, four cylinders, probably from the mideighties. Both were beaten up. One was faded yellow, and the other was originally red, but now it looked more orangey from years in the intense Mexican sun.

With a new Jeep, I'd have no trouble outrunning them. Which I started to do. That is, until I saw a man in the yellow truck bed lean against the top of the cab and point an automatic rifle at my tail. He fired a warning shot to the Jeep's right, causing Ranger to yelp, then slink inside and curl up in the passenger footwell.

Not wanting to be shot at, I pulled to the side of the road and prepared for a shakedown. The yellow truck pulled in tight behind me as I put the Jeep in Park. The red truck passed me, then backed up until its rear bumper nearly touched the Jeep's front grille.

This can't be good, I thought.

Our three vehicles stayed in that position, with nobody exiting or moving, for close to a minute.

By that point, the dust clouds from the vehicles pulling off the road had settled. The ticking of the hot engine and Ranger's rapid panting filled the Jeep's interior. In front of me, I had a nice view of the two men in the back of the red Toyota. Across their laps were two AR-15–style assault rifles. They were too far away for me to determine the exact make and model of AR-15.

Eventually, those two men hopped out of the truck and joined three others from the yellow pickup. The five men congregated to the right of the Jeep, facing me while standing in a semicircle. Though their rifles weren't pointed at me, their hands were on the weapons and in the ready position.

A tall man in the passenger seat of the red pickup eased out. He adjusted his slim-cut dark jeans and proceeded to roll up the sleeves of his black button-up shirt. The man kept the top three buttons undone, showcasing his hairless, tanned chest. He wore aviator sunglasses.

After looking my way, he pulled the shades down a fraction, then motioned me out.

I took my time.

Upon approaching him, I made the quick assessment that this was not the tall man from last evening. This man was close to my height, but he was too slim. No more than a hundred and eighty pounds at most. The silhouette I'd studied last night was much thicker and heavier set.

"Gringo," he said, pushing his glasses up. "What are you doing?"

The voice confirmed this was a different man. To my surprise, he had no discernible accent at all.

I came around to the Jeep's right side and leaned onto the quarter panel. It was a bit of an odd question to lead with, so I tried my hardest not to sound like a smartass. "Driving, it seems." I tapped the Jeep's hood with my left hand.

"Where to?" he shot back. "You missed your turnoff back there, amigo."

His comment threw me off, so I hesitated on my response. How would he know that was my turnoff? Suddenly I saw the situation through an entirely different filter. This was no shakedown for cash.

He repeated, "I wanna know what you're doing here, Gringo, and where you're exactly going."

I thought about it for a moment. "Trying to find the local police station.

Police made a visit to the surf camp last night. They took some personal belongings from me, which makes it hard for me to travel."

"The only place you're going," he said, "is back to the surf camp."

I straightened. "Is that so?"

He stepped forward. "It is."

I shook my head. "Don't think so."

"Tough guy, huh? Don't like taking orders, is that right?"

I didn't respond.

He motioned to the armed man closest to me. "Chuy, help me out here."

The man named Chuy stepped over. *"No problema,* Thiago." Chuy prodded me toward the other armed men, keeping his rifle, which I could now see was a Barrett REC7, leveled at my chest.

I kept my back to the leader, the man named Thiago, while eyeing Chuy's Barrett.

From behind, Thiago sighed. "Your avoidance of direct orders is causing quite the problems. Isn't it, amigo?"

I wanted to spin around and ask him what the hell he meant. Was he referring to me not jumping into the Jeep and heading back to the surf camp? Or was he talking about me not following my other orders?

I kept my cool, and my eyes on Chuy's trigger finger.

"Gringo, turn around when I'm talking to you."

I did, but not a complete one-eighty since I wanted Chuy in my field of vision.

"I said," Thiago continued, "you seem to have a problem with direct orders and following through, don't you?"

"I have somewhere to go," I replied. "And it's not back to the surf camp. So, I guess I do have a problem with your particular order."

He pulled his glasses down again. "I'm not talking about my order, amigo."

I did my best to show zero emotion. "Not sure what you're talking about then."

Again, Thiago sighed. "You're trying my patience, Gringo. I'm talking about your other order. About why you're here." He stepped toward me. "In Mexico." He said Mexico with a deliberate accent, accentuating the soft *h* sound that the *x* makes.

A million questions rifled through my mind, but my face and demeanor displayed nothing. I shrugged. "No clue, amigo. I really have no idea what you're talking about."

Since his aviator shades were still down, I saw his eyes quickly look at Chuy. Just as quickly, Thiago's eyes were back on me. But I'd seen enough. So, when Chuy turned his rifle around and grabbed it by the barrel and swung it toward me, I was prepared.

I crouched and blocked the Barrett from caning the back of my legs. My left hand grabbed the REC7 near the midway point, just above the magazine slot. Meanwhile, my right hand swung around and palmed the butt stock. Then I jammed the muzzle into Chuy's belly button. Hard.

Chuy groaned and collapsed backward, sucking in deep breaths on his way to the ground.

Since I had no intention of using the Barrett, I immediately dropped it and showed my hands.

That move probably stopped the other men from firing, but it didn't stop their anger. Four men tackled me to the dusty ground on the side of Highway One. I made a split-second decision to not fight back. Not only so I didn't receive a bullet in the head, but also so I didn't showcase my skills. I had no intention of coming clean to Thiago. I was still the quiet and reserved Gary Pounds, from the beautiful and peaceful nation of Canada.

Speaking of Thiago, after a few punches, he shouted, "Easy, gents, he still has a job to do. Mind his hands and eyes."

From that point on, I took a bunch of cowboy boots to the solar plexus, rib cage, and sternum. I'd taken far worse punishments in the past. In fact, after the kicking stopped, what hurt the most was coughing up some dirt balls.

Once the dust haze around me evaporated, Thiago approached. He knelt beside me as I laid on my back to catch my breath.

From his back pocket, he extracted what appeared to be my fake passport. "No sense," he said, "looking for your personal effects. The police won't have them."

I groaned inwardly.

He flipped open the passport. "Back to the surf camp for you, Gary." He craned my face so that our eyes met. "By the way, is Gary short for Garrison, amigo?"

I didn't respond.

"Wait for your new instructions," he continued, pocketing my passport. "Understood?"

I cleared my throat and kept up the ruse. "No idea what you're talking about. What new instructions? Instructions about what?"

Thiago grinned, showcasing a gold tooth on the right side of his mouth. "You really are a stubborn one, aren't you? Too stubborn for your own good."

Again, I didn't respond.

"Maybe you need something to jog your memory," he said.

The butt stock came out of nowhere. The oval shape approached my face too quickly to respond, so the stock of Chuy's rifle cracked against my forehead unimpeded.

I didn't pass out, but I certainly saw stars. Oddly, what I remember most was hearing Ranger barking, and that he had a deep growl between barks, which I hadn't heard from him before.

"Open the door," I heard Chuy say in Spanish. He rattled something else off, which I couldn't decipher entirely. But I knew it had something to do with using my dog as target practice.

"Leave him alone," I shouted.

Chuy didn't listen and opened the Jeep's passenger door.

No! Not Ranger.

I ran toward the Jeep. Ranger immediately scampered away when his paws hit the dirt. Chuy and the other men laughed too hard at my dog to fire a shot.

Once the men climbed into their vehicles and took off, Ranger trotted out from the short, scrubby bushes and licked my left palm.

"Good try, Ranger," I said, patting him on the head. "Good try, pal. Maybe next time."

CHAPTER SEVENTEEN

"THAT'S QUITE THE KNOT."

Tobias Ranger motioned at my forehead as he waved me into his compact Airstream trailer. "Have a seat." He pointed toward the table that also happened to be his bed.

"How'd you get a goose egg that size?"

I wasn't about to go into details about my recent altercation. "My board. Tried to do some fancy cross-stepping on a wave and wiped out. Smacked the old noggin on the front of the surfboard."

"Uh-huh," the camp host said, keeping his lips pursed.

Clearly, Mr. Ranger didn't buy my story.

"I'll get some ice for that, dude. And a few aspirin."

"Appreciate it. You know, my dog's named Ranger. Don't think I told you that."

"Far out," he replied, tucking his long hair behind his ears and nodding.

Tobias Ranger reminded me of Jeff Bridges in *The Big Lebowski*. Except Tobias was leaner and had longer hair than The Dude. In fact, Tobias's hair was so long and tangled that it hung in clumps that looked like dreadlocks. I didn't know if his hair had been deliberately weaved that way, or if it was simply a case of neglect.

Tobias opened a YETI cooler on the ground by his small kitchen sink.

Apparently, the cooler acted as his refrigerator. While he wrapped some ice in a partially soiled kitchen towel, I thought about my situation.

I hadn't come back to the surf camp because of Thiago's order, because I feared him and his men. I came back because I wanted to glean some important information from Tobias, who I assumed was somewhat knowledgeable about border crossing.

After taking the ice packet and pressing it on my forehead, I said, "So, Tobias, you saw the local police take my passport and ID last night, right?"

"Sure, man, totally bites."

"How does someone get back into America without proper ID? There must be some way?"

"There really isn't, bro."

"Even if I beg and plead my case at the border?"

He shook his head. "Nope, they'll just send you to the US consulate in Tijuana to sort it out."

I nodded. "So, no point at all in trying the border?"

"Don't waste your time. Why don't you just stay here and surf until the police come back? I mean, if you're not listed on the Mexican State watch list or with Interpol, the cops will be back with your stuff in a few days, a week max. A big, wintertime northwest swell rolls in tomorrow. Just chill here, man."

"I probably should."

"Let me get those aspirin and some water. I think that goose egg is getting larger by the minute."

While Tobias rummaged through his four cabinets, I thought about traveling home since I had no intention of chilling and surfing in Mexico. If I had shot Delgado, then I'd have to chill and wait to get my Canadian passport back since I'd want to travel back to the US as Gary Pounds. But since I did nothing wrong down here, I could plead my case as Garrison Chase to the Consulate, then hopefully they'd issue me a temporary identification to get across the border.

But what about these men who are after me?

My mind focused on the Toyota trucks. No doubt one or both were parked at the intersection of Highway One and the main surf camp road. "Tell me, Tobias, is there another way back to Ensenada from here, other than Highway One? Maybe a back road close by?"

He eyed me. "I take it you're not just going to chill then?"

I winced.

"Fine, fine," he said, holding up his hands. "I get it. You're certainly not the only one with a troubled past who's stayed here, and who has *muchos problemas* with the authorities. Ask me how many people have."

"Um…okay, how many?"

"Don't know, dude." He pointed at me. "'Cause I don't ask. Don't care to know. It's not my policy to pry."

"Got it," I said.

After Tobias gave me some aspirin and water, he wrote down some directions on a ripped envelope. I took the paper and stepped out of the Airstream. Tobias followed me to my vehicle.

He motioned at the Jeep. "Brother, you know this thing sticks out like a sore thumb around here, right?"

I nodded. When he didn't elaborate, I asked, "What are you getting at exactly?"

He motioned at the envelope in my hand. "You're taking back roads to be avoided, but at some point you'll have to get back on a main road, then head through some busy towns like Ensenada and Rosarito. No getting around that."

"Right," I said, eyeing him.

He held out his arms with his palms open. "Lookouts, dude! So many lookouts between here and TJ, man. So many."

"The police use lookouts?" I questioned.

"They definitely do."

"What about local militia or the cartel?"

"Man, everyone uses lookouts, bro. Cops, militia, cartel. They're one and the same in my mind. And lookouts have no allegiance really. They're the young kids on the side of the road playing soccer. Any kid aged five and up could be a lookout. They're given a couple hundred pesos to look out for a car, they look out for a car. It's simple. Doesn't matter to them who's dishing out the pesos."

I let that sink in, then eventually nodded.

"Just be careful, dude," Tobias said. "That's all I'm saying."

Before long, I was headed north along the bumpy dirt road that Tobias had sketched out. I knew he was right about the lookouts, so I planned to drive directly to the Consulate in Tijuana. Since I had more than enough gas, I wouldn't stop, not even for a pee break. I just had to avoid confrontation, make it inside the Consulate, and then plead my case.

The rough road didn't extend all the way back to Ensenada. It eventually connected with the One, but far north. Because the journey was so curving and uneven, Tobias told me it would be about an hour and a half drive.

Along the way, my mind couldn't let go of what Thiago had revealed. He knew I'd been sent to Mexico on a kill order. He knew where I was staying. He knew my real name was Garrison. And the only way he could've know those facts was from the president.

What incredibly shady business was POTUS into that she made connections and deals with banditos like Thiago and his crew?

My mind entertained various theories. Eventually, I found myself more confused than ever. So, I turned to my driving partner and used him as a sounding board to reason out loud.

"Ranger," I said, scratching behind his ear, "here's what I know so far about the president: she's desperate to protect her beloved Operation Crossroads, and she's equally desperate to get rid of Delgado. Somehow this Jimmy D character stands in her way or threatens her operation. She wants him out of the picture, so bad in fact, she fabricates a story to get me on board with his killing. When I don't follow through with her directive, the very next day she employs some shady characters to pressure me back on the job.

"Crazy, huh, buddy?"

Ranger stuck his snout out the window and didn't respond.

"You're thinking, I understand. Me too. The thing is, the evidence of this experimental drug therapy can't be fabricated. I mean, if that footage was staged, then we're talking about the most elaborate, over-the-top setup imaginable. I don't see it, pal. That doesn't make sense.

"What's more sensible is that there are two identical buildings like I saw in the drone footage. One is some sort of laboratory, and the other building houses this experimental drug therapy. That laboratory I saw with my own eyes is likely growing drugs. There are grow lights everywhere, plants are all over the place, and a brand-new centrifuge just arrived, which is probably being used to isolate chemicals. Maybe in the building I stormed they're growing the plant that's used in the drug that's given to the women, who are housed at a near identical building.

"Makes sense that these two operations are connected, right?"

Ranger's tongue whapped against the top of the window.

It felt good to get my thoughts in order, so I continued talking to my nonresponsive canine. "And maybe Delgado is running both these operations simultaneously. Maybe the drug-therapy building was way down the coast and the president just failed to tell me that. Maybe she thought it wouldn't matter.

"A good theory, wouldn't you say?" I stroked my dog's coat.

"If that's the case, though, then how do Thiago and his armed banditos play into the story? Would the president go to extreme lengths like hiring a cartel to force me to do the job? And if she *is* in bed with some cartel or militia, why not just order them to take out Delgado?"

As my thoughts continued, I bounced along in the Jeep for a while longer until connecting with Highway One. No banditos were anywhere to be seen, so I headed north toward Ensenada. Along the way, I stopped thinking about my situation since I knew my mind would keep going down endless rabbit holes. It was undeniable that I was a pawn in some international game. And when I returned home, I'd stop at nothing to figure out that game.

While driving, I focused on lookouts. As I weaved through Ensenada, I noticed how many kids were playing on the side of the road. I also realized—just like Tobias had said—that I stuck out badly in this Jeep. Most of the children looked my way as I drove past.

A few times I almost rear-ended other vehicles because I was watching kids in the rearview mirror, looking to see if they would pull out a cell phone and report me. Eventually, I kept my eyes straight ahead and only concerned myself with watching for the Toyota trucks.

For the next hour and a half, as I made my way to the Consulate in Tijuana, I saw no sign of the banditos. So, I was feeling good as I approached the US Consulate on Paseo de las Culturas street in Tijuana.

That feeling didn't last.

Surprisingly, the Consulate was not located in a busy metropolitan area. The building was of recent construction on a new street in an unpopulated area. On either side of the Consulate, and across the street, was nothing but bare, open land. There was nowhere for me to discreetly park and approach the building. The banditos knew that, of course, so they simply waited for me out front of the Consulate.

The orangey-red Toyota idled at one end of the street in front of the Consulate, and the yellow Toyota idled at the other end. Men were in the back of the trucks sitting up with their assault rifles on their laps. Clearly visible to any passersby.

Only in Mexico.

After pounding the bottom of the steering wheel, I parked on the side of the street, roughly halfway between the trucks. As my eyes flicked from the rearview mirror to the front windshield, I thought of my next move.

Should I run for it? Can I make it to the main entrance safely?

Naturally, I was concerned for my own health, but also for the safety of others. Though the vicinity wasn't crowded by any means, there were enough people milling about. That meant if these men decided to spray a barrage of bullets my direction as I sprinted to the main door, an innocent bystander could get hit.

"What do you think, Ranger? What's the best move?"

My dog panted and paid me no attention.

I sighed, then rolled down Ranger's window about halfway. After turning off the engine, I slowly unclicked my seatbelt while watching the men's movement in front and behind me. I tested them by opening my car door.

Immediately the four men in the back of the two pickups hopped out. They rushed toward the Jeep, not hiding their intentions or their weapons. When they were about halfway to the Jeep, I slammed the door shut, fired up the Jeep, and squealed off.

My thoughts were to try my luck at the border, but not at the Tijuana crossing. I figured Thiago's men would anticipate my next move to be a run for that particular border. And, for all I knew, they already had some other men waiting there. Or, at the very least, they would call ahead and get men there quickly.

So, I burned straight east along Mexico route 2-D. That highway ran directly to Tecate, about an hour away. And Tecate had a border crossing with US Customs that was much less busy than Tijuana. Hopefully, I could drive right into an open border lane and immediately talk with a US customs agent.

I had a third of a tank left in the Jeep, so plenty of gas to make it there without stopping. Within fifteen minutes of driving, I lost sight of the trucks.

As I made my way out of TJ, I pushed the Jeep. It was relatively barren along the 2-D. Nothing but desert, rocks, and rolling hills. With the sun setting behind me, I cruised for fifty-five minutes straight without incident.

The first sign of civilization as I approached Tecate city limits was a dirty, dilapidated garage on my side of the highway. A big sign above the garage said in faded blue letters—and minus the possessive apostrophe—Arturos Tires. The building was basically a two-bay mechanic's garage. Along the concrete wall facing my direction were hundreds of stacked up tires.

The next moments were a blur as I suddenly heard two loud gunshots. Almost simultaneously, I lost control of the Jeep as it skidded and swayed. Because the front and rear tires on the passenger side had been shot, the Jeep pulled heavy to the right. The vehicle ground to a halt perpendicular to its previous position, about thirty feet in front of the two garage doors.

A plume of dust drifted with the prevailing wind into the garage.

Ranger barked excessively at a dusty figure emerging from the left-hand bay holding a Barrett REC7 assault-style rifle.

The man with the hairless tanned chest stopped in front of the hood and pointed the rifle at the windshield.

Thiago pulled down his aviator shades and said, "Amigo, what are you doing?"

CHAPTER EIGHTEEN

THIAGO DIDN'T WAIT for my response. He held the Barrett in his right hand, with the strap over his right shoulder. With his left hand, he beckoned the Jeep forward and slowly walked backward.

"Nice and easy, amigo. You hit the gas and try to take me out, your dog will eat a mouthful of lead."

With the vehicle listing heavy to the right, I limped the Jeep toward him. Thiago guided me into the empty bay on the left. The bay to my right had a black and gold El Camino on its pneumatic lift, raised to about head-high level. It looked like the shop had just put brand new tires and rims on the vehicle.

Aside from the El Camino, the other thing I noticed was an office to my left. A large window extended its entire length, which ran about ten feet. Inside the office, a man was tied up in a swivel chair with his back toward the garage.

Since it was near dusk and no other workers were around, I assumed this was the garage owner, Arturo. Arturo had his head slumped to his left.

"Stop there," Thiago said, holding out his left palm. He maintained eye contact with me through the windshield and tsked. "You should've obeyed. You should've stayed put and waited for instructions, amigo. Now I'm going to have to step up the pressure."

I didn't respond or think about that statement. All I focused on was how to get out of this predicament.

"Keep it running," he said as he sidestepped toward the driver's door. Unfortunately, Thiago was smart enough to not step close enough to get hit by the door if I suddenly swung it open.

"Put your dog in the back," he ordered.

I didn't comply.

"Fine, I'll just put him down then." He aimed at Ranger, who surprisingly maintained a low, throaty growl. The second time I'd ever heard him make that noise.

I obliged and put Ranger in the back.

"Now move into the passenger seat," Thiago said.

After a momentary stare down, I shifted to my right and climbed over the middle console.

Once I was in the passenger seat, Thiago opened the driver's door with his left hand. The whole time he kept the Barrett in a steady, leveled position with his right hand.

With the driver's door wide open, he stepped beside the door and pushed the passenger side window button. My window rolled all the way down.

"Hook your right arm out the window," he ordered.

When I didn't budge, he pointed the rifle at Ranger.

Thrice he threatened Ranger's life, not mine. This proved he wanted me alive to finish the job on Delgado, which gave me some leverage. At least he wasn't going to kill me right away.

Thiago jabbed the gun at my dog. "I won't hesitate, amigo. Trust me."

I believed him, so I put my arm out the window.

"Wedge your armpit over the window."

I knew what he was doing. I'd do something similar if I needed to subdue someone and had no handcuffs. Though I'd probably put a person's fingers on the window.

As if reading my mind, Thiago said, "I could use your fingers, but you need your hands for later, so I don't want to mess them up." He laughed at his own comment. "I'm gonna roll this window up slowly until I pin your shoulder. I need you incapacitated so we can have a conversation without me worrying what you might do. Because I know who you are, Garrison Chase, and what you're capable of."

I didn't bite at that last comment. "A conversation about what, Thiago?"

"About why you're gonna finish your job. And how. Once and for all this time. You'll need to tell me when to stop so I don't crush your shoulder. It's up to you to tell me when."

He pushed the button and the window started up.

My right shoulder and side started lifting with the window. I had no time to panic or breathe. Instead, I put pressure on the balls of my feet and rose with the window.

Near the top, the window suddenly stopped. I looked to my left.

"Tell me when it's snug," he repeated. He grinned and flashed his gold tooth.

Arturo came into focus behind Thiago. The owner was still passed out, but Thiago didn't know that. It gave me a sudden idea.

"Shoot, Arturo!" I screamed. *"Shoot him now!"*

That outburst startled Thiago. He had to glance back. Most people would, right? When Thiago stole a glance, I capitalized on the error.

I retracted my arm and pressed my feet off the floorboards. Lunging across the seat with my left arm fully extended, I batted the Barrett's barrel to the left with my fingertips. The force caused the strap to slip off Thiago's shoulder, and the rifle clanked against the concrete.

As Thiago turned back, I brought my right arm around in a sweeping arc and drove my fist into his sternum. It cracked against his ribcage, but it didn't break anything since my arm was stretched out so far that I had no weight behind the punch.

Thiago was not a heavy man, however, so his slight frame stumbled backward on impact with my fist. As he dropped onto his butt, I grasped the edge of the driver's seat and used both hands to grind my body over the console and out of the vehicle. I collapsed on top of the rifle when I hit the ground.

Witnessing this, Thiago yelled, *"Cabrón!"*

He knew I had the upper hand, so he scrambled into the office on his knees while I grabbed the rifle.

By the time I stood and pointed the assault rifle at the large office window, Thiago had regained the advantage. He'd spun Arturo around in the chair and had a knife pressed to the man's throat.

Arturo was now awake. The garage owner's brown eyes were wide, and he was frozen in terror. There was a faded red bandana tied behind his head and across his mouth.

Thiago was kneeling behind the chair, so his body was covered by Arturo. All I could see of Thiago was his right arm and hand holding the curved knife, and the right side of his face.

"Like I said," Thiago yelled, "I know you. I know what type of man you are. You come after me, you kill an innocent man. You don't want that on your conscience."

I aimed at the small section of Thiago's head that I could see.

Thiago retreated even more behind Arturo. He kept yelling. "You really going to do this, *cabrón*? This man's life is in your hands. That's on you."

Thiago was beyond nervous. His shaky hand had caused the tip of the blade to dig deeper into Arturo's neck. Blood dripped from the puncture wound.

Being in a predicament like this after having the upper hand infuriated me, especially while holding an assault rifle. My body tremored. Only for a moment did I entertain the idea of taking out these two men, then fleeing for the border.

What stopped me, of course, was my conscience. Arturo was innocent. For all I knew, he was an upstanding man with a wife and children, a family who depended on him.

"Put the gun down," Thiago said.

"Put the knife down first," I replied.

He laughed. "No way, you first. Nonnegotiable."

I didn't put the rifle down, not right away at least. Instead, I thought about the situation. Thiago could've easily killed Arturo prior to me arriving. For some reason, he didn't want Arturo dead. Plus, if I dropped the rifle first, he'd gain nothing by slitting Arturo's throat.

"Putting it down," I said, dropping the rifle's barrel until it pointed at the ground. "Take your knife off his throat."

Slowly, Thiago complied. He said, "Drop the AR."

If I wasn't going to use the AR, I didn't want Thiago to use it either, so I released the magazine and cleared the chamber. After throwing the magazine over my shoulder, and kicking away the chambered round, I bent and lowered the rifle to the ground.

As I stood, I said, "Now put away the knife."

Thiago straightened, then resheathed his knife.

"Step away from Arturo," I said.

But Thiago didn't step away. Instead, he wheeled Arturo out in front of him. When they were outside the office door, Thiago stopped pushing the chair and stood still. He kept his hands on the back of the chair and eyed me, from about fifteen feet away.

"Now," he said, "you're going to take that El Camino back to the surf camp. You okay with him taking the Camino, Arturo?"

Arturo slowly nodded.

Thiago said, "And you'll wait there for further instructions. Like you were supposed to all along. As soon as we locate the target, you'll get your new instructions."

I scoffed. "And I thought you said you knew me."

"You received a comprehensive dossier on your target, didn't you, Garrison? Think we don't have a dossier on you then? Think we don't know your address in Central California and who you're bedding in Los Angeles? Come on now. You seem smarter than that."

He did his annoying tsk-tsk.

I wanted to slam my fist through his mouth, hopefully break off his gold tooth, and then feed it to him. How dare he bring my family and girlfriend into this? It shouldn't have surprised me, but it did, and it pissed me off.

"Let's just say, Garrison, if you don't comply with your orders, a special woman in your life is going to pay the price. In fact, maybe she already is."

I tensed at that comment, then fought the urge to panic. No way did I want to give him the satisfaction that he got to me.

While narrowing my eyes at him, I thought of Karla and what she might be going through. But that wasn't productive thinking, so I focused on my next move instead. Unfortunately, I didn't have any time to formulate a plan. The sounds of vehicles approaching the garage distracted me. No doubt Thiago's band of misfits had arrived.

Within seconds, you could hear the men trying to lift the garage doors.

"They're locked," Thiago shouted, "use the side door."

Five men barreled through the metal side door moments later.

Thiago went straight into boss mode. "Weapons away," he said. "We have it worked out in here, so I don't want anyone shooting and ruining our plan.

Got it?" He waited for his men to lower their weapons, then he said, "Leave the rifles outside, and two of you stay out there to keep watch."

The men seemed fine with those orders. Everyone except Chuy—the man I'd jabbed in the gut with his own rifle. He complied with the orders, but he clearly wasn't happy about it. And it wasn't just his red face that informed me of his displeasure. As the three banditos approached our side of the garage, Chuy had a heated conversation with Thiago in Spanish.

He wanted a piece of me. Clearly.

Thiago, however, held him off.

"Chuy," Thiago said, "Mr. Chase has been informed of an update in his life and is now more than willing to obey. Isn't that right?" Thiago shot me a look.

I wasn't going to acknowledge that with a yes, but I also didn't have a plan. "I'll be taking my dog and leaving in the El Camino, I suppose."

As I turned to open the back door for Ranger, Thiago said, "Not so fast. The dog stays with us." He flashed his gold tooth. "You can have him back after the job is complete."

"No way," I said, lifting the door handle and opening the door.

Thiago held up his hand. "Nonnegotiable, amigo."

Before I could respond, Thiago's cell rang. He pulled it out and glanced at the number, then addressed Chuy. "You're in charge for a few minutes. I have to step out and take this call."

On his way out, Thiago swept up the REC7 and its magazine. After he exited the garage, Chuy swept in behind me and slammed the Jeep's door shut with two hands. Then he two-handed me in the back to get me moving. Again, Ranger surprised me by standing on the back seat and giving Chuy a low, throaty growl.

Where is this aggression coming from?

Slowly, I proceeded around the Jeep's rear bumper. Chuy stayed close behind, itching to get a piece of me. As I angled toward the El Camino, one of the banditos was by the car lift pushing a large red button. The El Camino slowly lowered on the lift. When the vehicle reached eye-level, at least on me, I could see directly behind me in the reflection of the driver's side rear window. Being so short, Chuy couldn't see the window yet, so he thought he was being sneaky with the X-shaped lug wrench in his hand.

While he swiveled the lug wrench back, I spun and intercepted the wrench as it swung forward. Chuy's eyes bulged at the sudden move. As I tore the lug wrench from his grip with my left hand, I exploded my forehead down, cracking Chuy on the top of the head. He crumpled to the ground.

The move stung because of my previous goose egg. Instead of knocking me for a loop, however, the pain brought me alive. I turned toward the man who'd been working the pneumatic lift. He'd stopped the lift and was lunging toward me. With the lug wrench in my left hand, I threw it like a frisbee as hard as I could. One of the ends connected square with his chest.

He grunted on impact. Clutching his chest, he dropped to his knees.

Out of my periphery, I saw the third bandito scrambling around the Jeep's hood and rushing my direction. After the throw with my left hand, I pivoted fast to my right and brought my right elbow up and exploded it forward.

It collided with the approaching man's throat, sinking deep into some spongy cartilage. He gagged and turned red, then collapsed to the ground in a coughing fit.

Chuy had regrouped and charged toward me like a stampeding bull. With his body bent in half and his thick head leading the charge, he slammed into my gut. I stumbled backward. Fortunately, I'd grasped Chuy under the armpits and was able to bring the man with me.

We slammed into a tower of tires stacked against the wall. There was some give to the rubber tires, so it wasn't a hard impact, and I didn't lose my wind. Chuy drove his legs forward and tried to plough me through the tires and grind me into the wall.

But being so short and bent over like that, the man was a ripe target for my knee. So, I smashed him in the face with my left knee, splitting open his nose in the process.

Bloody and raging, he came at me with outstretched arms. Before reaching me, his chin met the sole of my boot. Chuy's head snapped back, and he dropped to the ground.

Looking around, I grabbed the first thing I saw: a tire. As Chuy struggled to his knees, I stacked a tire over his head. The tire dropped over his body and rested on the back of his calves. Then I quickly grabbed two more tires and thread them over Chuy's head. At this point, Chuy had managed to stand. Unfortunately, for him, his hands got tied up within the inside of the tires.

I took that opportunity to open his nose some more with a ferocious right hand to the face. With Chuy seeing stars, I stacked two more tires over his body. I grabbed a smaller tire for the final stack and had to jump up and use my body weight to wedge it over his shoulders.

The extra work was worth it, though, since Chuy was now incapacitated and looked like the Michelin man.

Glancing back, I saw that the other two banditos were recovering. The man I'd elbowed in the throat was on all fours breathing deeply and getting ready to stand. The other man who'd taken the lug wrench to the chest was already on his feet and approaching me. He was still unsteady on his feet, however, so I clotheslined him and flattened him on his back. Then I clubbed the man on all fours in the middle of the spine until he dropped onto his stomach.

The pneumatic lift gave me an idea. Working quickly, I dragged each man underneath the lift on the El Camino's driver side. I positioned one body at the front and the other at the back. Then I pushed the lift's down button and slowly lowered the El Camino.

With the men positioned under the front and back tires, I eased the lift down until the tires touched their bodies. As soon as the men felt the weight of the tires, they screamed.

One yelled, "*Cabrón!* You *cabrón!*"

Apparently, bastard was my new nickname.

I gingerly tapped the down button two more times, just enough to pin them against the concrete without squishing out their insides. Though I felt great about subduing the three men quickly, their screams brought Thiago back. He kicked open the side door and jabbed the REC7 my direction.

While walking around the lift to face me, Thiago spoke, but I couldn't hear what he was saying since the garage was a cacophony of sounds. The Jeep had never been turned off, so the burbling of its muffler filled the background. To my right, Chuy sputtered and wrestled with his encasement. Behind me, the two men pinned under the El Camino tires were no longer screaming. Instead, they groaned loudly. No doubt the weight of the vehicle was crushing their chest and making it hard for them to breathe.

The most surprising sound, however, came from Ranger. He barked excessively while standing on the rear passenger seat. He acted like he wanted to tear Thiago apart.

Thiago, now with his back to the Jeep, started to speak again. I motioned to my ear that I couldn't hear.

He shouted, "You're more than capable, amigo, just like I thought."

Behind him—through the Jeep's windows—I watched Arturo wrestling with the rope around his body. Since the cheap swivel chair had a low-back, Arturo had managed to get some of the loops free over the chair's top.

"Now," Thiago continued, "you need to lift that vehicle off my men."

At this point, Arturo had freed himself from the chair. However, his hands were behind his back and bound tightly around the wrists with another rope.

To keep Thiago distracted, I again motioned to my ear. "What'd you say?"

While Thiago repeated his command, I saw what Arturo had planned. He was at the Jeep's driver's side rear door. He'd turned backward and was struggling to open the door for Ranger, who still barked repeatedly. No doubt Arturo thought the German shepherd was an attack dog. I knew better. I knew Ranger barked because he wanted out of the vehicle so he could go cower somewhere.

"Will do," I said to Thiago, just as Arturo had managed to pull the door handle.

Ranger jumped out. Fortunately, there were so many noises Thiago had no clue what was happening behind him. To my surprise, instead of cowering and heading for cover, my dog scrambled around the rear bumper and charged toward us.

My eyes stayed on Thiago since I didn't want to draw attention to my stampeding dog. While slowly inching the lift off the men, out of the corner of my eye I watched Ranger leap in the air and plant his front paws square in Thiago's back.

As Thiago stumbled forward, I rushed in and focused on the Barrett. I collided chest-first with a stumbling Thiago. With my hands on the rifle's barrel, I jerked it up and away from my face as we collapsed backward and crashed to the ground in a heap.

The rifle fired some deafening rounds over my head. The bullets lodged into the El Camino's quarter panel. Ranger was on Thiago's back and had chomped on the back of his neck.

And my boy wouldn't let go.

Since the Barrett singed my palms from being fired, I quickly scooted it away.

Screaming in pain, Thiago rolled to his right to shake Ranger free. When the dog kept clutching on, Thiago unsheathed his curved knife and plunged it toward Ranger.

"*No!*" I yelled. But I was too late to intercept the stabbing motion.

Ranger yelped like I'd never heard a dog yelp before. He'd taken the stab to his hindquarters. In a rage I rolled toward Thiago. As Thiago extracted the knife from my dog, I grabbed his knife hand and quickly snapped his wrist. Picking up the dropped knife, I jammed it into Thiago's left hamstring, twisting it for good measure.

He yelped louder than Ranger had.

On my knees, I scrambled toward my dog. Ranger had collapsed on his side. When I reached him, I straddled his body and applied pressure to the wound with my left palm. I heard footsteps behind me but didn't pay them attention since my focus was on Ranger. Besides, I figured it was Arturo rushing over.

Suddenly, though, I took a blow to the back of my head and collapsed forward onto my forearms. Dazed, I had no idea what just happened.

As I fought to stay conscious, I heard a quick staccato of gunfire. Expecting to feel warm blood fleeing my body, I was surprised when I didn't. And I was downright shocked when a body dropped to my left.

With blurry vision, I fought to see who it was. Between blinks, I saw Chuy's lifeless eyes staring at me. Then I heard a voice I hadn't heard before.

It said, "Mister, you okay?"

The last thing I heard before passing out was that same voice:

"Mister, you saved my life."

CHAPTER NINETEEN

"MADAM PRESIDENT," the chairman of the joint chiefs of staff said, "perhaps you'd like to weigh in here?"

Since Henrietta hadn't been listening to the debate, she paused on her response. Long enough that Willy Blanco left his seat and whispered in her ear.

"What's going on, ma'am? You seem a million miles away. You understand the dilemma the generals are having here, right?"

When the president didn't acknowledge, Willy quickly brought Henrietta up to speed on the conversation that had been happening in the Situation Room. Basically, the top generals had a clash of opinions about how to proceed in light of a brewing crisis in the Mideast.

To save face, when Willy finished whispering his recap, she addressed the room. "I need to step out of the room for a few minutes, everyone, I apologize for that. My chief of staff just apprised me of a situation that needs my attention." She glanced at Willy.

Willy played along by nodding and heading to the door.

"My apologies," Henrietta said to the room. "Be right back."

Outside, the president rushed in the direction of the Oval Office. Willy hurried along beside her. "Let's walk and talk," she said to Willy.

He nodded.

"Obviously you know I wasn't paying attention in there, but I know you were. When I go back in, what's my position regarding the matter at hand?"

Willy started in with a lengthy explanation. Midway through, Henrietta cut him off. "Get to my position, I'll wing it from there."

"With all due respect, ma'am, you're not a winger."

She sighed. "With all due respect, Willy, keep your opinions to yourself."

Though Willy kept pace with her, he stayed silent, which was unusual for him. Made sense, though, since the president had never spoken to him like that before.

He recovered and quickly explained the position he thought she should take. After that, he said, "Ma'am, you're clearly distracted with something. Can I help with that matter?"

She stopped short of the Oval Office door. "You can, absolutely. I need you and a few members of the communications team to sit on the news cycle. I want updates by the hour, through the remainder of the day. Understood?"

"Sure. What are we looking for? North American again?"

She nodded and turned toward the door.

Willy stopped her before entering. "Henrietta," he said.

She spun. He'd never referred to her as Henrietta within the confines of the White House before. However, the president let it go. She glared at him. "Willy."

"It may help me and the team I put together to know specifics about what we're actually looking for."

The president mulled it over for a moment. "Mexico. I want to be apprised of any developments within moments of breaking news in that nation." She pointed at Willy. "But only you, Willy. Let the coms team scan for North America news; don't specifically mention Mexico to them. You can filter from there and bring me any news from Mexico."

He nodded.

Out of the corner of her eye, the president saw one of her secretaries approaching the Oval Office door.

"Branch," she said, holding out her hand. "I need a moment in my office." He kept coming, curious, no doubt, as to why she'd abruptly left the Situation Room.

"Alone, Branch. Alone."

He stopped and skulked.

Henrietta whisked open the door, then closed it and leaned against the backside.

After a few exhales, she extracted the burner cell from her pocket and approached her desk. She glanced once last time at the empty screen, then powered down the phone and shoved it in the middle drawer.

Then she headed back to the Situation Room to save face.

CHAPTER TWENTY

I woke up flat on my stomach with my forearms pressed against the cold concrete.

I guess I hadn't moved an inch since being smacked from behind.

Though I hadn't changed positions, several things in my vicinity looked different. For one, Chuy's lifeless body was nowhere to be seen. In fact, none of the banditos were nearby, including Thiago.

And where's Ranger?

I moved my head too fast, looking for my dog. Pain shot through my skull, so I grabbed my pounding noggin. That was when I realized I had some ice on the back of my head, held in place with something. After extracting the temporary bandage, I saw it was the red bandana that had been in Arturo's mouth.

Where is everybody?

Slowly getting to my feet, I performed a panoramic sweep of the garage with my eyes and confirmed there was no Ranger. No Arturo. No Thiago or his men.

However, there was a small woman in the office with her back to me. She was busy shifting a pan around on a hot plate. Suddenly, the aroma in the garage registered: she was frying some meat. My guess: carnitas.

I made my way toward her, feeling steady on my feet when I was about halfway there. The woman was demure, dressed in an olive-green, floor-length skirt and a colorful, tasseled blouse. Her long brown hair went midway down her back.

Since I didn't want to startle her, I tapped on the large office window.

Turning, she seemed surprised and came running out. "Senor!" She rattled off in Spanish and pointed at my head. *Su cabeza* is all I really understood, which meant your head.

I waved it off and then fired some questions back to her in English. Immediately I realized her English was worse than my Spanish.

I motioned to the spot where I'd last seen Ranger. "Donde esta mi perro?"

She struggled for a second, trying to find the words. She gave up and simply said in Spanish, "*El veterenario.*"

I nodded since that was easy enough to interpret. "Did Arturo take him?"

She thought for a moment. "*Si*, Arturo. Back soon." She pointed to the chair where Arturo had been tied up. "Sit." Then she motioned with her fingers and thumb toward her mouth. "*Comida,*" she said.

The woman waited for me to sit, then she rushed back into the office to attend to her sizzling pan.

Unbelievable. Who were these kind people? Taking care of my dog and feeding me like this. What hospitality, especially since I brought Thiago and his thugs here and upended their little world.

Keeping still helped alleviate the pounding in my head, but it didn't stop the myriad thoughts from rattling around in there. Knowing Ranger was at the vet provided some relief, but then my mind focused on Karla. So many questions:

Where is she? How's she doing? Is she hurt? Tied up? Incapacitated? I had to get back to the States. And fast.

But how?

The woman distracted me with a plate of food. She put three tacos in front of me, each piled high with crispy carnitas and some salsa verde.

As I ate, we tried our best to communicate. All I could gather, though, was that she was married to Arturo. She kept saying that her *esposo* would be back soon.

And she was right.

Just after downing the third taco, Arturo was back.

He looked happy to see me, informing me right away that Ranger was in surgery and that the prognosis was good. His English was decent.

I asked him where Thiago and the men were and what had happened after I took the blow to the head. He informed me that he'd freed his wrists with Thiago's knife, and that when Chuy had rushed toward me, he'd picked up the Barrett and shot Chuy in the back after Chuy had clobbered me.

"Where are the men now?" I asked. "And where's Chuy's body?"

Arturo didn't answer, and I sensed he wasn't going to. So, I tried a different approach. "Arturo, who were those men? Can you tell me that?"

He didn't hesitate on this question, immediately responding with, "No idea, Mister. Never seen them before. *Nunca.*"

"Really," I questioned. "You've never seen any of those men before?"

He nodded and performed the sign of the cross.

I kept at it, though. "They weren't local cartel men?"

"Oh, no, Mister," he said, shaking his head.

"Please, Arturo, call me Chase. That's my last name, you can call me that."

"Okay, Mister Chase, will do."

I grinned. "Arturo, were those men local militia then?"

"No, they're not from around here, Senor."

That shocked me. "Are you in trouble for taking one of them out?"

"No, not at all. They shouldn't have been here. They're not supposed to be here." He pointed downward when he said that last sentence. "Besides, Mister Chase, you saved my life."

His ear-to-ear grin was contagious.

I assumed Chuy or Thiago weren't going to kill me, so it wasn't exactly accurate, then, to say that Arturo saved my life. I nuanced my response. "You saved me, too, Arturo, and helped me greatly."

He patted me on the back and checked out my head, pointing to the goose egg on the front and large nodule on the back.

I laughed. "Now I'm balanced out."

"Funny, Mister Chase."

"Tell me, Arturo, were those men part of another cartel, a rival one perhaps?"

"Not sure," he said, shaking his head.

"But they aren't part of the local cartel then, right?"

Arturo backed up toward the office, clearly uncomfortable at my line of questioning. He said, "More tacos?"

"No thanks," I quickly replied. "Arturo, do you work for the local cartel?"

He immediately turned.

I stopped him before he could retreat into the office. "Please, Arturo, I have to know who those men are. They're making me do an unpleasant job, and they're threatening a loved one at home until I do it."

Arturo turned back. I watched his shoulders sag, then he lowered his head.

"I have no interest in you," I continued, "and whether you work for a local cartel or not. In fact, I need to get back to the States as fast as I can. That's my number one priority here. It will really help me if I know who those men are."

He opened his mouth but then just as quickly closed it.

"My girlfriend's life depends on it. Please, Arturo."

He shook his head emphatically. "I don't work for the local cartel, Mister Chase. I want you to know that."

I nodded.

"Jalisco cartel," he said, "has moved into the area recently. Tecate"—he pointed to the ground—"is their new base."

"Wait, I thought this was Sinaloa or perhaps Tijuana territory?"

"In the past, yes, not now. Jalisco has been very active here in Tecate, and here at the shop. They, they . . . I can't think of the right English, Mister Chase."

I took a guess. "They shake you down for money?"

"No, not money." He pointed to the El Camino. "Once, maybe twice a week they bring a vehicle to me."

Now I got it. "You hide drugs in vehicles destined for border crossings in Tecate?"

He sighed, looking disappointed with himself.

"I understand, Arturo, you have to do it for your family."

With his head down, he said, "*Si, mi familia.*"

"Arturo." I waited for him to look up. "These men today aren't with Jalisco, so are they Tijuana or Sinaloa men?"

Again, he shook his head emphatically. "Outsiders, Mister Chase. No idea who they are. Jalisco will take care of them; this is not their territory." Again, he pointed to the ground.

I assumed that meant they'd all be killed, if they hadn't been already, but I wasn't about to clarify that with Arturo. I moved on. "Can you get me across the border?"

He eyed me and pointed north. "Mister Chase, the border is right there. Sure, I can drive you."

I shook my head. "Those men took everything, Arturo. My wallet, passport, all my ID."

"*Cabróns,*" he muttered.

"I need to get across the border and check in with my girlfriend. As soon as possible. I don't have time to go to the consulate or embassy. I have a car and ID on the other side. I just need to get over the border. I'll be safe there. Can you help?"

After a long pause, he nodded. "It will cost you."

"How much?"

Arturo walked to the Jeep. "Are you willing to part with this?"

He didn't need to know it was a rental and that a fake credit card was on file for the security deposit. "Absolutely."

He nodded. "Then I have calls to make and work to do."

Just like that, Arturo whisked into his office. He sent his wife home and then shut the door. As promised, he made some calls. About thirty minutes later, he came out.

"Okay, Mister Chase, all set. You go early morning."

"Thanks, Arturo."

"You get everything straightened at home, then come back for your dog. I'll take care of him until you return."

There was something sincere about the way he said it, so I knew Ranger would be in good hands. "I really appreciate it."

"Now I have work to do, Senor," he motioned to the Jeep. "And you'll need to wait outside, I'm afraid."

"But I can help."

"No, the less you know, the better. I must insist. Besides, it's evening now and cool outside."

Arturo wheeled his office chair to the side metal door. Before I knew it, I was sitting outside on the chair amidst a stack of used tires. Arturo's understanding of a cool evening and mine were worlds apart.

Instead of focusing on the heat or what trouble Karla could be in, I thought about the border crossing. I wondered if I'd do a more traditional crossing like through the desert with others while being led by a coyote. Or would they smuggle me across in the Jeep somehow? Maybe that was what Arturo was working on right now.

When Arturo finally finished his work and joined me outside, I directly asked him. Again, he played coy. He distracted me with more food delivered by his wife, then with tequila and Jarritos grapefruit soda, which made for a pleasant cocktail and helped us pass the time.

About two-thirty in the morning, after our fourth tequila and soda, a filthy white-paneled van eased around the backside of the garage. Immediately Arturo hopped to attention. He rushed over and spoke with the driver, then went around back and opened the doors. After a brief conversation with someone inside, he motioned me over.

Before I could see inside the van, Arturo stopped me and handed over a water bottle. "Drink this now. Get lots of water in you. No matter what happens, Mister Chase, just know that you're going to be okay. And so is your dog."

He led me to the van, which was crammed full of people. Maybe fifteen. As I quickly scanned the crowd, the count eased up to around twenty. Several children were in there, all cowering behind their parents.

Guess I'm doing a traditional crossing.

"See you soon, Mister Chase." Arturo patted me on the back as I climbed inside.

The women, children, and three men inside the cramped quarters all stared at me. Not a soul said a word, though. Arturo struggled with the back doors, eventually leaning all his weight on them until they latched shut. The left side of my body squished against the doors. My right side pressed against the woman beside me. Though she didn't seem perturbed, I apologized profusely, nonetheless.

Within a minute of driving, the stifling air made my throat drier than the desert we would cross soon. I downed the sixteen-ounce water bottle, then wondered if that was a mistake.

I'll get more, right?

As we rumbled along for the next twenty minutes, my shirt soaked through with sweat. I tried to think about what I was going to experience being smuggled across the border, but my mind started going hazy. At first, I thought I'd probably had one too many tequilas and sodas. But as time passed, and my head grew increasingly thick with cobwebs, I wondered if my mind was shutting down from heat exhaustion.

It wasn't until I started having superlong blinks that I knew I had a problem.

A woman near me held out a folded piece of paper. I had a hard time grasping it. When I finally got hold of the paper, then opened it and read the contents, it took my mind a minute to process.

The note read: *Sorry, Mister Chase. They don't want you to know anything about their operation. Very sorry. Arturo.*

The last thing I remembered was glancing at the empty water bottle in my lap, then to the twenty other sets of eyes fixated on me.

Apparently, I was the last person in the van to know I'd been drugged.

CHAPTER TWENTY-ONE

When I woke, the first thing I felt was heat. Blazing heat. It blasted my face and chest and legs. I also felt wetness underneath my back.

Since my eyes felt welded shut—probably crusted over from salty sweat —I had to exert some energy to open them. As soon as I pried them open, they clamped shut. A full dosage of sunlight was too much to handle.

I turned onto my side and put my forearm across my face. Slowly, over the next few minutes, I released my arm and blinked rapidly until my eyes could handle the brightness.

All I saw was desert. Flat, dry land stretched out around me in all directions.

I saw no wall or chain-link fence. Nothing to tell me that I was close to the border, or even what side I was on.

Am I still in Mexico?

After some deep breaths, I sat up and checked myself over. Aside from a splitting headache, I was fine. Next to my left leg was a full water bottle, which gave me pause. It couldn't be spiked with anything, right? It made sense that Arturo and his contacts had drugged me. Like Arturo's note said, they didn't want me to know the ins and outs of their operation. And they certainly succeeded at that. No real reason to drug me again.

So, I downed about a quarter of the water, then studied the sun's position and got my bearings. Soon I was walking in what I believed to be a north-west direction. That seemed like the clear, smart strategy.

After just five minutes of walking, I crossed a dirt road that appeared to have fresh tracks. The road stretched east to west. My immediate thought was that this was a border patrol road. No doubt four-wheel-drive border vehicles cruised this road looking for trespassers.

That was my hope, anyway. Since I didn't have much water, I prayed they traveled the road frequently. As I walked west along the road, I first thought about Karla. What it potentially meant for her once it was discovered I wasn't in Mexico, and that I hadn't followed through with my orders.

Since that thought turned quickly dour, I focused my attention on border patrol. Hopefully I got picked up soon, then I'd have to feed them a story. My best bet was to tell them a tale as close as possible to the truth.

I'd tell them I was on a short surf trip in Mexico with my brand-new Jeep. While getting carjacked, I tried to fight the thieves but ultimately failed. They took my vehicle, money, ID, and dumped me in the desert. Then I wandered northwest until I came across this very road.

The alternative was convincing border agents to take me to the Caprice, where I'd stashed my passport. Then I could easily prove who I was, and that I was an American citizen. Of course, they'd ask me why my car was there, why I rented a vehicle to enter Mexico, and most importantly, why I'd entered Mexico without my passport. The first question asked by an astute border agent would be: *How'd you expect to get back into the US, sir?*

No, unfortunately, I couldn't go down that road. Instead, I'd play it safe and stick with the surfing/carjacking story and see how that fared.

Approximately thirty minutes later, I knew my chance to try out the story was fast approaching. Off in the distance, straight west of my current position, a dust cloud plumed in the air. Moments later, a vehicle materialized; a Chevy Tahoe, from what I could tell from this distance.

I stopped in the middle of the road. I didn't put my hands up or anything. Instead, I stood there with a pleasant look on my face. Oh, and I downed the rest of my water.

The Tahoe pulled up quickly, and the two agents, a man and woman, got out even quicker. They didn't storm toward me and draw weapons, nothing like that. They seemed more perplexed than anything.

Which made sense. I figured they didn't come across too many tall, bald white dudes walking alone on the Mexican-American border.

They moved in closer, scowling at me. Their name badges stood out, metallic and shimmering in the bright sun. I assumed the badges listed the agents' last names. Otherwise, the woman's first name was Henry. The male agent to her right was named Garcia.

I gave Garcia and Henry my best smile and said:

"I'm American. And, please, I need help."

CHAPTER TWENTY-TWO

"PLEASE, PATRON," Javi pleaded, "look at these men."

Javi pointed to Raoul, Jaime, and David standing against the eastern wall of the airplane hangar. "Look at their clothes; they're drenched. The water's increasing down there. Give it some time to drain and allow the catch basin to do its job. I beg you. A flood is imminent."

Patron sighed in exasperation. "Can't do it, Mr. White."

Javi jabbed at the men again. "They're working round the clock, risking their lives. Please!"

That part was true. These three men wouldn't allow the older men or Sylvia to take their regular digging shift.

True men. Real men, Javi thought. *Salt of the earth.*

The imminent-flood part, however, wasn't exactly true. Yes, the water increased a little, but not by much. Javi knew the tunnel was just about completed, so he was desperate to stall. He knew that completion most certainly meant death. For everyone.

Today, he hatched his plan with the three men during their shifts. He instructed them to get as wet and muddy as possible before returning, then Javi would do the rest.

He stepped in close to Patron, so he could see the man's eyes. "The smart thing here is to wait, let that water slowly filter into the tunnel and work its way into the basin. We may have hit an aquifer or a water pocket that needs slow draining. If we forge on, we may break it wide open and flood the tunnel permanently."

Patron shook his head.

Frustrated, Javi's voice rose. "What's the point of all this if the tunnel gets flooded? People won't be able to go down there and access the tunnel. And if you intend to smuggle humans, what are you going to do, give them scuba equipment? And—"

Patron held out his hand, saying, "You don't stop, do you, Mr. White? You *won't* stop, will you?"

Javi gestured to the people behind him. "I care about them, about all of them. So, no, I won't stop."

Patron lowered his head for a moment, then gestured for Javi to follow him.

The airplane hangar was split into separate wings. Javi and the workers had never been on the other side; they'd been confined to their respective wing for months. Only the guards and Patron accessed the other side through a locked door.

While Patron brought his keys out and unlocked the door, he cautioned Javi. "I probably shouldn't be doing this, but you should know what we're hoping to accomplish." He opened the door and waved Javi in. "That way you'll understand, and maybe, just maybe, stop bugging me. Stop with all your questions."

Javi stepped into the vast room on the other side. There was a ton of equipment and supplies in there, but what caught Javi's attention was a small office to his left. The door to the office was open and a white woman was inside.

Javi tried to get a better look, but Patron rushed over and closed the door. Since Patron was as wide as a locomotive, Javi couldn't see around him to get a good look at the woman.

After closing the office door, Patron spun to face Javi. "No questions about her, Mr. White. Not one. You'll meet her soon enough. She's a new worker."

Javi nodded.

Patron gestured to the supplies laid out on the hangar floor. "I imagine an engineer like yourself can piece together what we're doing below," he said. "What our ultimate goal is."

It didn't take Javi long to figure out the operation. A huge portion of the concrete floor was covered by rows and rows of large-diameter conduit piping. The conduits were made of hard, white plastic and looked to be about the same diameter as the tunnel. An immense engine, which could be confused with an oversized generator, was in the center of the floor.

Clearly, it was a vacuum system. The tunnel would be used to send packages—not human cargo—to the other end.

"Understand now?" Patron said.

"Yes and no," he replied. "This hangar must be by the border, so you'll be sending contraband to America via these pipes using a vacuum system. Right?"

"See, you are an intelligent man, Mr. White. What don't you understand then?"

"Why you're doing this? Why you're not more concerned about a flood or cave-in?"

"That's where you're wrong. We are deeply concerned about the tunnel collapsing or flooding before we get the pipe laid, which should start tomorrow. We just need to chance it and finish the last few meters today.

"We have a dedicated crew coming tomorrow. They'll insert and connect the piping, which shouldn't take long. Once everything is in place, we'll welcome a cave-in around the scaffolding. In fact, if it doesn't happen, we'll initiate one. Understand now?"

Javi nodded. "Then the tunnel will be harder to detect that way." As a former engineer with the government, Javi had seen his share of "supertunnels" that cartels had built in the past. "So you're moving away from bigger tunnels then?" Javi asked.

"Yes, ground-penetrating radar keeps getting more sophisticated, so it doesn't make sense to invest the time and capital into huge tunnels anymore, not ones that can be easily discovered. We've come full circle and are back to smaller, less costly alternatives. We'll just build more and more of them. I'd love to share more of our operation, especially what we're doing on the other side of the tunnel we're digging, but that's all you're getting from me, Mr. White. The quicker the men finish the last fifteen meters of the tunnel, the safer everyone will be."

"Is that so?" Javi said with a hint of skepticism. He feared that since Patron was sharing part of the plan with him, he was preparing to get rid of him.

Patron eyed him. "It is."

Eyeing him back, Javi said, "What exactly are your plans for us?"

The boss laughed. "You think we're going to get rid of you all, is that it?"

"Something like that."

Patron ushered him to the door. "Mr. White, as long as you and the workers prove useful, why would we get rid of you? We have plenty of tunnels to dig. Plenty. Now get out."

After the door closed on him, Javi stood and faced it for some time, wondering which was worse: Knowing your death was imminent, or being forced into grueling labor for the rest of your life?

CHAPTER TWENTY-THREE

As the Tahoe pulled into the rental car lot, Agent Henry turned toward the back seat. "You certainly have some friends in high places, Garrison Chase."

Instead of responding, I simply nodded.

Slim had pulled some strings. That was a perk of having him work closely with members of Congress. Apparently, he'd asked a senator to make a call vouching for me, which expedited my time at border patrol headquarters.

When I spoke with Slim on the phone, I wasn't sure if the call was being monitored by headquarters, so I hadn't debriefed him in detail. I spent most of the conversation asking what he knew about Karla. Unfortunately, after the Santa Barbara meeting, Slim and Karla hadn't reconnected, so Slim didn't know her whereabouts or if she was in any trouble.

"Here you go," Agent Garcia said, pulling in front of the customer service entrance.

"Appreciate it, you two," I said.

Before I got out, Agent Henry addressed me. "How exactly are you going to rent a car to drive home without ID or a credit card? Thought about that, Mr. Chase?"

She's the astute one.

"I'll figure it out." I winked. "Like you said, I have some friends in high places." Before she could respond, I was out of the vehicle and standing in the rental car office.

"Can I help you, sir?"

I waited until the border patrol vehicle exited the parking lot, then I turned toward the check-in employee. I wasn't about to tell him that I rented a Jeep last week and left my own car around back. That would certainly prompt him to inquire where the rental car was.

"Thanks for asking," I said. "On second thought, I'll take the bus instead of renting."

I hustled outside. I kept a spare set of keys in a magnetic box attached to the underside of the rear passenger tire well. Before long, I had my door unlocked and was sitting in the driver's seat.

The first thing I did was peel back the inside paneling on the driver's door, then fished out my passport and cell phone. Flipping it open, I was annoyed to discover a dead battery. That didn't surprise me, though. I still used a Motorola Razr from the nineties, so the battery barely lasted a day. I didn't want to upgrade to a fancy phone with multiple cameras and social media integration. All I needed was the ability to talk with people, and to send an occasional text or two.

I plugged in the phone and took off. When I was just north of San Diego, I figured the phone had enough juice for a call or two, so I pulled off the freeway and into a gas station. The first number I dialed was Karla.

I held my breath as the phone rang.

No answer. I sighed in exasperation, then immediately called Slim, who picked up on the second ring.

"Tell me some good news, buddy," I said.

Since he didn't immediately respond, I knew he had none.

"Didn't find her, huh?" I asked.

He blew a breath into the phone. "Still looking, pal. She's not answering her cell, as I'm sure you tried, and she's not at home either."

"Damn," I muttered under my breath.

"But I'm at her work right now," he continued. "It's just . . ."

"Just what, Slim?"

"Just not making any headway. I'm at her field office, and all they can tell me is that she's unavailable. They're tight-lipped people, Chase. What gives? You're from their world. What does 'unavailable' even mean?"

"They're not going to give you any details on one of their agents' whereabouts. No way. Not unless they know you or you flash a badge. And your private dick badge doesn't count, my friend."

"Maybe you'll have better luck since you're a former agent and may know some coworkers to ask."

"Didn't leave on great terms with everyone, but I'll definitely try." I looked at my watch. "I'm probably ninety minutes out from the field office, if traffic is okay. In the meantime, why don't you check out her dad's place. They're close. Then circle back to her FO and we'll meet there."

"Copy," he said.

"Hey, pal, thanks for doing this. I know we left Santa Barbara on bad terms."

"Like you said, my friend, there are far more important things to deal with than our little business squabble."

After giving Slim the address to Karla's dad's, I hung up and pushed the Caprice. Traffic was never okay in LA, especially in West Los Angeles where Karla's field office was located. I had to finish my drive on the 5, then travel far up the hellacious 405 freeway, all the way to Wilshire Boulevard to be exact.

Ninety minutes turned into over two and a half hours.

Since Slim hadn't called back, I knew he hadn't found Karla at her dad's house. But I found Slim easily since he'd told me his rental was a burnt orange Subaru Outback. He was parked in the open-air parking lot across from the Wilshire Federal Building. I'd parked a few rows over, so I walked up and surprised him by opening the front passenger door.

He gasped, then said, "Geez, pal, you almost gave me a heart attack." I motioned to his girth, but he stopped me before I could say anything. "No fat jokes, buddy. We don't have time."

"You're right," I said, nodding. "I'll go see what I can find out."

"You know anyone in there? Maybe someone who works the front desk?"

"Doubt it," I said. "I worked out of the Long Beach Resident Agency. I came up here a lot, but not enough to remember anyone except Karla and the assistant director. I'll see how responsive they are to my presence."

Though they were somewhat receptive, they still didn't provide any useful details concerning Karla's whereabouts. Before long I was sitting in the passenger seat of Slim's rental car. He didn't ask if I found out anything. I guess he could tell by my dejected look that the mission was unsuccessful.

Instead, he simply said, "I watched the video of the drugged women."

I let the comment hang for a moment.

Eventually, he gestured at me. "I get it now. I get why you felt so compelled to go down there. Sorry I was being so bullheaded about helping."

I nodded.

Slim shifted toward me. "So, tell me what the hell happened."

"A lot, Slim. A lot." After a deep breath, I told him the condensed version of events, outlining my past few days. My story stopped at the point where I called him from the border patrol office.

He pointed at me with an even redder face than usual. "I told you she was using you, pal. I told you. Dammit, Chase."

I diffused his anger by stating, "You did, you certainly did. I'll give you that."

While he took a moment to compose himself, I continued. "No real clue what's going on in Mexico. What our president is mixed up in. If she's in bed with some drug cartel, why not use them for the hit? Why recruit me? And then why reach out to these criminals to put the pressure on me to finish the job?"

"You sure it was the president who sent the cartel after you? Positive?"

"How else would they have gotten that intel? These guys knew my mission directive and my real name. Unless you told them—"

"Got it," he said, holding up his hand. "Let me get this straight: the president uses you to take out Delgado, who she badly wants killed. So much so, in fact, she fabricates or distorts or makes up evidence, whatever you want to call it, to get you down there."

"Yup."

"When the directive fails, she gives up your identity and sends these men after you to finish the job. I'm assuming you know what that means?"

"Been thinking about that a lot. It means after the job they were going to take me out. Unequivocal. Because the president knew I'd come straight to her and ask what the hell was going on. Demand to know why she sent these thugs after me, not to mention threatening Karla."

"This is so messed up."

"It's useless sitting here," I said. "We need to start building our case against the president. The burner cell from Henrietta was taken from me in Mexico, so I never followed up with her. Does it make sense to confront her at this point? I know I can't text or call her, and I certainly can't ring the White House and ask to speak with her, but you know some Washington elite that could get us in touch."

"I do, but don't think it's wise. The prez is clearly into something sinister here, and since she's the most powerful person in the world, it's best she doesn't know your whereabouts, or what you know. Keeping her in the dark is to your benefit until we get more evidence and figure out what exactly she's involved with."

"Agreed. We have to nail her, pal."

He nodded. "We will."

"Let's get moving."

"Shouldn't we wait to see if Karla checks in at work?"

"This place is a zoo." I pointed toward the building. "We'll never spot her entering."

Wilshire Federal Building didn't just house the FBI field office. It also housed Veteran Affairs and a passport agency. A day didn't go by without hundreds of people lined up outside.

"What do you have in mind?" Slim asked.

"Tell me you didn't destroy the video."

He whistled. "I was going to tonight since I have a flight back to the East Coast in the morning. You're in luck."

"Let's go watch that video and build our case against POTUS."

CHAPTER TWENTY-FOUR

"THERE IT IS," I exclaimed. "Did you catch that?"

"I think so." Slim backed up the video.

We were hunched around the tiny desk in Slim's hotel room. His laptop was open, and we were watching the president's video. Right at the point where the three men approached the side door of the Punta De Las Olas building.

"Here goes again," Slim said, pushing the play button.

We watched in silence. "There," I shouted. "You saw it this time, right?"

As the man recording the video stepped inside the building's side door, a nearly imperceptible flicker on the recording occurred.

"Yup," Slim said. "Not sure what technicians call that, maybe a jump cut or something like that, but it's there. The video changed after that point. Those men stepped into a dark room in some different building. I'm sure of it."

"Me too. You'd hardly notice if you weren't looking for it, but it's there."

We let the video play out in its entirety, just to see if we could spot more anomalies. Which we didn't.

After the video played, Slim turned to me and shook his head. "This whole case unraveled on that one tiny detail. You realize that, right?"

"I do. If I hadn't remembered the details in this video—that the door pushed in—I wouldn't have thought twice about it when I had Delgado in my scope. When I saw his front man pull the door outward, I wouldn't have paused like I did."

"You would've dropped Delgado right there, before he crossed the door's threshold, correct?"

I nodded. "I had a good shot, Slim. And I would've taken it."

Slim blew out a big breath. "If you weren't a details man, you'd have killed him, slinked back to the States undetected with your head held high."

"Right. And unbeknownst to me, I would've contributed to whatever conspiracy the president is involved with. And maybe, maybe not, killed an innocent man."

"Heavy stuff. I need a drink. Want one?"

I saw the bottle of Buffalo Trace bourbon on the bedside nightstand. "A double, please."

Slim opened his mini fridge and pulled out the round ice bucket. "Still have some cubes that haven't melted. On the rocks? Or have you manned up and will finally drink bourbon straight?"

"Two cubes," I said, smiling.

"Sorry I don't have any highball glasses. Plastic will have to do."

Slim glugged two healthy pours into the plastic cups. When he handed me the one with ice in it, we didn't bang cups and cheers. It wasn't a celebratory drink. Far from it. To have evidence the president used me to try to kill someone was a sobering moment. This was more of a cope-with-it type drink.

Slim settled his girth onto the bed while I turned the desk chair around to face him. We worked on our drinks for a moment. He broke the silence.

"Just to play devil's advocate here, what if the president was duped? Just like you were."

"Why would you think she was duped?"

"I don't know, maybe because of her management style. Because of her too-trusting nature. I mean, Nogales proved that about her, right?"

I shook my head. "I don't know the details about what went wrong with the Nogales operation, but I guess I should. It could be tied to my operation. What really happened there?"

Slim took a slug of bourbon. "It all goes back to Operation Fast and Furious. Remember that?"

"I do."

That famous operation occurred in the late 2000s when the government entered the business of gunwalking. The ATF was a major player in the controversial sting operation. Gunwalking basically allowed licensed firearms dealers to sell weapons to illegal straw buyers. The premise was to track those sold guns as they made their way across the border and up the Mexican cartel chain. With the ultimate purpose, then, to arrest high-level cartel members.

Long story short, it didn't work. No significant arrests were made. Worse, only around seven hundred of the two thousand guns that had walked across the border were recovered by the US government. It led to the total embarrassment of the ATF.

Slim continued, "So, solid intel came in a few months back which showed the location of a huge cache of these gunwalking weapons in Nogales, Mexico. Naturally, the ATF was champing at the bit to save face and go in there to get their weapons back. The ATF director lobbied the president, and POTUS gave the director carte blanche access and approval. She told him, 'Do whatever it takes, and do it fast.'"

Slim shook his head. "The ATF director took that to heart and rushed a mission together. He didn't thoroughly vet his small team. And as you know, it only takes one bad egg."

"A team member sold them out?"

"Yup," Slim replied. "Apparently, one greedy member sold the information to the cartel of what time the raid was going to take place, though there's some speculation that the team member didn't act alone. That hasn't been proven, however. Anyway, the traitor thought the team would show up for the raid and the warehouse would be empty. No harm, no foul. The blame would simply fall on bad intel."

I finished the story. "The warehouse was empty of weapons, but not of cartel members."

Slim sighed. "They walked into an ambush and lost half the team."

"Plus," I added, "Mexico was pissed that an American operation happened on their soil without their knowledge."

"And the buck stopped with POTUS since she authorized a fast mission at all costs. Everyone knows her greatest strength is not being a microman-ager. She appoints people, steps out of the way, and lets them do their job. Which is mostly a good thing. But *not* micromanaging can be her weakness, too. In the Nogales case, she gave a hothead director free rein on a controver-sial mission."

"And it couldn't have gone worse."

"Right."

"Your ultimate point, though?"

"Her weakness is her MO, Chase. She moves fast, gets thing done, but she doesn't do a lot of oversight or vetting. That's my main point. What happened with the Nogales operation, maybe that's what's happening with your case? Maybe she's being fed manipulated evidence and hasn't bothered to vet it, to really check it out."

"You're saying somebody else is behind this, then. Somebody's duping the both of us?"

"Could be. It's a possibility."

"It's a valid point, it's just that POTUS is way out on a limb here. I mean, giving a civilian like me a kill directive. She told me this operation was solely between me and her, and I believe that considering the serious nature of her ask. Why would she bring in another party to be privy to such a controver-sial directive?"

Slim frowned.

Before he could say it, I added, "I get it, Slim, she could be lying. I don't think so, though. I think she picked me for the job to be as discreet as possi-ble, and to ensure it gets done. But when I never texted her to confirm the kill, and she didn't see the story blasted all over the news, I think she panicked and used some shady Mexican ties to pressure me."

He finished his drink. "Damn, you're probably right."

I finished mine, too.

A moment later, Slim said, "What about the building from the video? We have a dire situation there. Do you agree that the president's footage about the drugged women is likely real, even though you were sent to the wrong or different place?"

"I do."

Before we could go on, my cell buzzed. On the front folded part of the phone, I could see the phone number scrolling across the screen.

My eyes must've been popping because Slim asked, "Who is it, Chase?"

"It's Karla's number."

For a moment, I froze and didn't take the call, wondering if this was indeed Karla or maybe her kidnappers.

"Answer it!" Slim said.

I took a breath and flipped open the phone. "Who's this?"

CHAPTER TWENTY-FIVE

KARLA'S VOICE was on the other end.

Relief flooded my body. I instantly felt my blood pressure drop. She was already midway through her first sentence when I finally tuned in to what she was saying.

"I mean, geez, Chase, I know you missed me, but why so many calls today?"

"Where were you?" I blurted.

"On assignment all day. I left my cell in the car. Even if I had it with me, I doubt I'd respond. You know that, Chase."

"Are you still on assignment? You're safe, though, right?"

She sighed. "All right, what gives?"

Slim nudged me, to ask what was going on. I mouthed that Karla was fine, then responded to her. "A lot is going on, Karla. Just glad you're safe, thought you could be in trouble."

"Which means you're in trouble," she shot back. "Tell me what's going on."

"Not over the phone."

"Really?"

"Really."

I gave Karla the address to Slim's hotel. She told me she'd be there when she could. I signed off with a "Be careful." She replied with: "Shut up."

Karla Dickerson did not like being kept in the dark.

As soon as my Razr flipped shut, Slim said, "She's totally fine, right?"

I nodded. "A valid scare tactic by Thiago and his band of thugs."

"It worked," Slim said. "But total hogwash in the end. They don't have an American crew."

"Seems to be the case."

"Now we can cheers." Slim filled our plastic cups with more Buffalo Trace, and we toasted to Karla's safety.

I blew the fire from my lungs, then said, "Back to the buildings."

"Tell me about the one you stormed, the Punta De Las Olas building. When did you figure out it didn't house the women?"

"As soon as I opened the basement door."

"What was down there?"

"A giant storage room with a ton of scientific equipment. I followed Delgado and his crew down to that area. My guess is they were checking out a new centrifuge that had recently been unboxed. They heard me coming and split via the far staircase."

"So the entire basement was one big, open storage room?"

"Yup. I didn't stay down there long because I had my focus on Delgado. But it seemed clear the equipment was all related to plant growth."

Slim nodded. "You go topside and what happens?"

"Chaos," I said. "I fired into the door at the top of the staircase, then kicked it in. To my surprise, hundreds of people, scientists I suppose, were in this open-concept lab. Tons of workstations and grow tables. It appeared to be some sort of hydroponic growing lab on the main floor."

"What stuck out the most to you?"

I thought for a moment. "Naturally, pandemonium happened when all these people saw me standing in the door frame pointing a rifle their direction. What I remember was that people shouted out in English. 'There's a shooter,' 'get down,' that sort of thing. And that stood out to me because those cries were spoken in English."

"That is odd. What do you make of it?"

"My guess is that it was an international gathering of scientists, a collaboration, if you will. As I scanned the room with my scope, I noticed a lot of faces weren't Hispanic. There were several people of color in the lab. Quite a few were Germanic and/or Scandinavian-looking scientists, and some Asian people, too."

"Interesting," Slim responded. "Anything else stand out?"

Again, I took a moment. "Obviously, I knew right away my intel was bad. I fired a warning shot at Delgado. The oddest part was when Delgado absconded to the other side of the lab, he opened a door to get away, and I caught a view on the other side of the door. I witnessed several young children in lab coats lined up along the wall. They were being told to put their head between their knees."

"Why were kids in this lab?"

"Not sure. The day before, during my reconnaissance run, I'd also seen kids leaving the facility. At that point, I thought they were children of the women inside. Now, I have no clue what they were doing there."

We took some time to think while we worked on our drinks.

Eventually, Slim broke the silence. "What do you think they were growing? The drug used on the women in the other building?"

"That was my first guess since these two buildings are definitely related. But now I'm not that confident they're growing the drug there, if I'm being honest."

"How come?"

"Kids being involved like that. It seems crazy if we're talking about an illicit and highly addictive drug. But more importantly, if that place was growing a fentanyl/heroine superdrug, why wouldn't there be security and patrol guards, and a perimeter set up? There should be all those types of security precautions."

"You're right, you're totally right." Slim polished off his second drink.

My cell buzzed again.

"Karla?" Slim asked.

I shook my head, not recognizing the number. A moment later, it came to me. "It's my neighbor."

Slim frowned. "You're not going to take it?"

"I'll call her back. I'm sure one or more of our chickens got loose and wandered over to her property. Mom's probably out somewhere with Simon."

"So where do we go from here, buddy?"

"That's the question, definitely *the* question."

Slim and I strategized for a few minutes. The more we talked, the more something nagged at the back of my mind. Speaking Mom's name brought her to my mind's forefront. For some reason, I kept revisiting the interaction with Thiago in Arturo's garage.

I visualized what I remembered from that confrontation: Thiago said if I didn't comply with my orders, a special woman in my life would pay the price.

A special woman. Those were his exact words.

"Dude," Slim said, waving his hand in front of my face. "You're off in never-never land. What on earth are you thinking about?"

I swallowed. My cell beeped, alerting me to a voice mail from my neighbor. My heart started pounding as I had an ominous thought that the voice mail had nothing to do with chickens.

"Seriously, Chase," Slim said. "What's wrong?"

I held up a finger to Slim, then listened to the voice mail.

After it played, the cell dropped from my hand.

"Okay, pal, start talking. You're worrying me."

I gathered myself, then looked at my buddy. "I had it all wrong, Slim, totally wrong."

Again, I thought of the phrase, *a special woman.* Karla wasn't the only special woman in my life.

I blinked, and held my eyes shut. "They grabbed Mom, Slim, not Karla. They have my mother."

CHAPTER TWENTY-SIX

JAVI and the workers sat at some plastic tables inside the airplane hangar eating lunch.

All eyes were riveted toward the corner of the hangar. The new woman—who'd just served them lunch—was in a rather heated debate with Patron. She spoke in rapid English, which appeared to confuse Patron. Javi figured Patron spoke some English, but certainly not enough to follow the conversation with the woman.

One of the workers, a man named Jaime, shuffled toward Javi on his butt.

"What's going on? What are they arguing about? Is the new woman with the guards?"

"No," Javi replied, shaking his head. "She isn't. I saw her on the other side; she's one of us."

Jaime nodded. "What are they arguing about then?"

"Food," Javi responded. "She needs help preparing food." He leaned in. "Especially since that new crew I told you about is coming soon."

Frustrated with the woman, Patron grabbed her by the arm and dragged her toward the workers. They stopped in front of Javi.

"What's she saying?" Patron asked.

Javi quickly studied the woman, who he guessed was probably ten years younger than him. He figured she was early to midsixties. She had vibrant blue eyes and curly, dark hair with tinges of gray around the edges.

"I couldn't hear the full conversation," Javi answered in Spanish, "but basically she needs help in the kitchen, Patron."

The woman pointed at Sylvia. "I need her. She shouldn't be working down there." The woman jabbed toward the open hole in the middle of the hangar. "She needs to help me prepare food."

Patron glanced at Javi and spoke in Spanish. He asked Javi if he was okay with having Sylvia out of his sight. Javi thought it would be much better for Sylvia to work with this woman than be stuck underground.

"What's he saying?" The new woman glared at Javi.

"It's fine," Javi replied to the woman, "go ahead and take her."

The woman smiled and gestured toward Sylvia. "Come dear. Come with me."

As Sylvia approached, the woman knelt beside Javi. "She has your eyes. You two must be related."

He nodded as Patron barked orders at them to stop talking.

The woman placed her hand gently on his arm and gave a comforting squeeze.

She whispered, "I'll take good care of her. Don't you worry."

CHAPTER TWENTY-SEVEN

I LEFT my neighbor Sandy's place after getting a rundown of what had happened.

Earlier, I'd burned out of the hotel room and raced to the Caprice and shaved forty-five minutes off my record driving time between LA and Central California. Slim had stayed back and waited for Karla. The two were about an hour behind me in Slim's rental.

Apparently, Simon had woken at Gram's place this morning. All alone. My mother was nowhere to be found. Simon had heard strange men's voices in the house the previous night, but he thought it was a dream. When he couldn't find his grandma in the morning, he knew he hadn't dreamt about the men and feared they would come back for him. So, he cowered under the bed for most of the day, eventually gathering enough courage to head to Sandy's house.

I looked at my son in the rearview mirror as I drove down my gravel driveway. He was wrapped up in a blanket, fast asleep. Naturally, I was a mixture of emotions. His safety gave me a huge sense of relief, but that feeling was quickly sapped by not knowing where Mom was or what condition she was in.

After parking, I scooped Simon up and took him to his bed, laying him gently on top of his covers. Since I didn't want to wake him, I kept all the lights off in the house. I eased into bed beside my son and lay in the darkness.

Stillness surrounded me. There was no wind tonight. All I heard outside were crickets chirping and insects buzzing. I lived in a one-story, well-built ranch-style home, so there were no creaks or groans from the house. Aside from the sounds of nature, silence filled my home.

My thoughts, however, were vivid inside my head, buzzing around and making their own noise. I knew if I had any chance of finding Mom, I'd have to figure out what was going on. That meant I'd have to get on the move. Maybe head back to Mexico, hopefully with Slim this time. Of course, Simon couldn't come with me, which would devastate him. I knew he'd be in a fragile state for a while. Most of my thoughts revolved around that.

How do you balance being there for your son with an important mission that takes you away from him? How do you push your kids to be brave while also potentially terrifying them if you do? The more I thought about the answers, the more questions came. My mind kept coming back to the same question: How do you build courage without permanently scarring your child? The last thing I wanted was one of Simon's earliest memories of me to be abandoning him after this terrifying ordeal.

Those thoughts meandered through my mind until the sound of an approaching car pulled me back to the present. Looking at my watch, I knew it was Karla and Slim. For the next five minutes, I listened to the crunching gravel, car doors opening and closing, discussion between Slim and Karla as to why the place was so dark, then the opening of my front door, followed by the flicking on of lights.

Since light from the living room flooded into his bedroom, Karla could see me snuggling with Simon. I held up a finger and whispered I'd be there soon.

Unfortunately, all the noise stirred Simon. He wiggled in my arms, then his eyes fluttered open.

"Dad!" He clamped onto me and hugged me like he never had before.

I enjoyed the moment. Eventually, he pulled back. Before he could speak, I said, "I'm here, buddy. I'm sorry I wasn't earlier. So sorry."

"Where's Grams? Is she okay?"

"She's okay. We'll all be back together soon."

Silence for a few moments.

"Dad, I was scared. Nobody was here. It was—"

"I know it was scary, son, but you were brave. I'm proud of you."

He hugged me again. I stroked his hair, pulling it away from his eyes. "Do you wanna talk about it, pal?"

He immediately shook his head.

"Maybe tomorrow?"

"Maybe," he replied.

I clutched my son tighter and held him for some time. When he fell back asleep, I gingerly retracted my arm from under him. Just as I pivoted on the bed, he woke.

"Don't leave, Dad. Please don't!" He tugged at my clothes.

"Of course, buddy," I said, easing back into bed. "I won't leave."

I kept my word and spent the night with him. I knew my guests would understand that Simon took priority. Karla was familiar with the ins and outs of my house, so she could easily make up the couch for Slim.

For a long while that night, I couldn't sleep. I passed the time by thinking about my next moves, and all the necessary details that surrounded them. I thought about going it alone, with just Karla and Slim at my side. Would they want to do that? Was that the right thing to do?

Then my thoughts flipped, and I considered contacting the feds. Was that what Karla would think was best? If so, what would I say to the FBI? How would I convince them to investigate, especially when it involved the commander-in-chief? Plus, where would I tell them to look for my mother? Who would I tell them kidnapped her? Sure, I could tell them some Mexican thugs, but not much more than that. I didn't even know the specific cartel these men worked for, or even if they were part of a cartel at all.

Before drifting off to sleep that night, I knew—without a doubt—I needed to gather more intel and data before bringing in the authorities.

I just hoped Slim and Karla would agree.

CHAPTER TWENTY-EIGHT

"He's good with kids, isn't he?"

I looked at Karla. "He is, he's had quite a bit of practice, raising three boys and all."

She stepped beside me and wrapped her left arm around my waist. "I think that extra night of snuggling with you really helped Simon get over his fears."

"I think so. He's finally focused on something else."

Slim stood about thirty feet away. He worked with Simon on his shooting stance. Slim had set up an array of tin cans on top of some old wine barrels I had kicking around my property.

Simon held an Airsoft pistol I'd bought for him a while ago, though I only gave it to him yesterday. Originally, I wanted him to be older before we practiced shooting. However, Slim insisted Simon was the perfect age to learn. I acquiesced since I needed Simon distracted so the adults could talk.

"Nice work!" Slim shouted after Simon knocked a can over with a plastic pellet.

My son turned to look at me. He had a huge grin on his face.

I gave him a thumbs-up. "Good job, pal."

It was the morning of the second day since I'd been home. Yesterday, Slim, Karla, and I strategized about the next steps in our plan. Fortunately, everyone agreed we needed more intel and evidence before taking this further. It was a rough day for me since I needed to stay positive for my son while my countenance was down, and my mind was elsewhere. All I thought about was Mom: whether she was safe or not; where she was; how to find her. The biggest thing on my mind was if I was wasting time staying at home. Taking time to strategize was essential, but we also needed to be out looking for her. Since I had no idea where to start, Karla thought it would be best to stay home at least one full day in case the men who took Mom delivered a message. That made good sense, so I expected some contact. Maybe a ransom note. A threat. Something like that.

But nothing came. All was not a loss, though, since an extra day with Simon really helped calm my son down.

Today was a different story. We'd be on the move. No more sitting around and waiting.

Slim gingerly stepped back from Simon, leaving the boy engrossed in his shooting.

When he reached us, he said, "I'm shoving off. I'll get down there and get the details arranged, then text you later tonight."

"Are you sure he'll come through?" I asked Slim.

"He will. You were wrong about him before, weren't you?"

"I guess."

Slim slapped me on the back, said farewell to Simon and Karla, then hopped into his rental and roared off. He was headed to northern San Diego to visit the congressman from California's 49th district. The 49th covered from Dana Point to just above La Jolla. It was an incredibly rich area, so they were represented by a disgustingly wealthy businessman. A man named Valen Jackson.

My second job for Slim was working for Valen. A couple of years back, Valen Jackson was in a heated campaign battle with an opponent and needed whatever edge he could find to win. Unfortunately, I provided him that advantage.

As if reading my mind, Karla pulled back from our embrace. "What's up with Valen Jackson, anyway? You've never told me much about him. And I thought it was a cut-and-dried case. But yesterday, hearing you speak with Slim about him, I couldn't help but notice the disdain you had for him. What's that about?"

I motioned to Simon. "Shouldn't we get on the road? We're off schedule."

She needled me in the ribs. "Such a deflector. No way, I'm not letting you do that. I want to hear what happened." She motioned toward Simon. "Let him have some more fun shooting before we get in the car. I'll grab you another cup of coffee, hear your story, then we can leave."

Before I could object, she said, "Meet you on the porch."

Reluctantly, I made my way there.

Minutes later, Karla handed me a steaming cup of black coffee. She didn't waste any time. "Why the dislike for this guy?"

I took a sip. "What do you remember about that case? We were dating then. Remember, I stopped by your place before and after?"

"I definitely remember the case, and you stopping by. What was Valen's opponent's name? I can't seem to remember that."

"Theodore Brody."

"That's right. Teddy B. The man who liked to portray the image he was a soft ol' teddy bear."

"The one and only."

"I remember there were some unsubstantiated rumors that Teddy was cheating on his wife with someone on his campaign team. Somebody high up."

"Yup. Valen hired me to find out if that was true. And, if so, to get him some evidence."

"I also recall you telling me it wasn't that hard of a case."

I nodded. "It wasn't. Took me about three days. Three days to get video proof of Teddy hooking up with his head campaign manager."

Karla snickered. "Not good. What happened from there?"

After a deep sigh, I said, "I remember thinking I had this sucker. But then I thought about his situation. I mean, Teddy B was no saint, that's clear. None of us are. Here I had evidence that would embarrass the heck out of him, ruin his marriage, and possibly also his career. And that got me thinking about Valen. Because that man seemed equally sleazy, if not more so, than Mr. Teddy Bear. Potentially then, I'd be responsible for Valen's victory in the election. Maybe I'd be responsible for putting a far worse person in office than Teddy B."

"That's a lot of assumptions, Chase."

I nodded. "Agreed. And that's why I started investigating Valen Jackson, off the books, of course. Slim had no idea, and still doesn't. In fact, Slim doesn't know that I still do this with most clients he sends my way."

Karla's eyebrows raised. "You do?"

"I feel I have to, Karla. And that's why I don't want to run a West Coast branch for Slim. I'm like the worst, most inefficient security contractor out there."

"What do you mean 'inefficient'?"

"I don't log the hours when I'm vetting my own clients, of course, so most jobs I accept take me twice as long as the hours I bill. But the main point is, I'm not supposed to be investigating my own clients. That's not how our business works. Slim would kill me if he found out. In his world, you take the job, do the job, and then move on. But I don't operate that way, and I don't think I ever will. I'm the last person who should be in charge."

There was silence on the porch for a moment. Then Karla broke it. "This is good," she said.

"Good?" I narrowed my eyes. "Really?"

"Really. You're opening up. I know you hate that word, Chase, but it's true. I didn't know this about you, about your relationship with your job. It helps me understand why you didn't spend a second entertaining the idea of running a branch for Slim, not to mention working with me. Like not even a millisecond."

"Okay, it's good." I smiled. "Everything's good here then."

She smirked. "Back to Valen. You go off the books and start investigating him. What'd you find out? And why did Slim say you were wrong about him?"

I finished my coffee. "Valen Jackson put on a front. He was the quintessential politician: smiles and handshakes and baby-holding and lofty promises. Everything I hate, and Slim knew that was how I felt about him. The odd thing, though, the more I watched Valen, the more I realized at home he was a different guy."

"How so?"

"Subdued, calm, caring even. I tailed him for days and learned the most about him at night. One evening he took his wife on a date, paid attention to her, opened the car door, even pulled out her chair at dinner. Never once looked at his phone while in her presence. He had no idea, of course, I was watching him, so it was a genuine look into the type of person he was. He was also the same around his teenage children. Even during the day, with his campaign employees, he was kind and thoughtful. It didn't really look like a front. I mean, it could've been, but I just didn't get the sense from studying him."

Karla nodded. "But when that camera turned on . . ."

"Right, Valen Jackson turned on. Or more accurately, he turned *into* somebody else."

"What'd you do with the evidence on Teddy?"

"Showed it to Valen."

"And his response?"

"Ecstatic. He wanted to blast the video footage everywhere. I probably overstepped my bounds, but I took a firm stance and said I would handle what to do with the evidence."

"Why's that?"

"Teddy B had three kids, two high schoolers and one middle schooler. I didn't want Valen to go splashing the video on the web or leaking it to a news outlet and totally shaming Teddy and exposing the affair. Then the kids become victims. I envisioned them being endlessly harassed, having to change schools, going to therapists, that sort of thing. With the video leverage, I thought Valen could get Teddy B to bow out gracefully. Without making a big media splash."

"And did Valen agree?"

I nodded. "He did. Totally promised to keep the video evidence under wraps. Understandably, though, he wanted to keep the footage as backup. At that point, I trusted Valen. Or at least I thought I did. I thought he'd be a man of his word."

"He went back on his word then? I'm confused. Because I don't remember anything about Teddy B sex tapes being released."

"I left Valen's house that night feeling good about the situation. I went back to the hotel and packed up, but then noticed my sunglasses weren't in the room or in the rental car. I figured I'd left them at Valen's. So, on my way home, I swung by his house. There were several cars there, but I didn't think twice about it. Valen's wife let me in and said her husband's team was in the den strategizing, which of course piqued my interest. I listened outside the den door and became enraged. His team was in there planning the release of the videos for the morning news. In fact, they'd already contacted the local media outlet."

Karla was at the edge of her seat at this point. "What'd you do?"

"Stormed in there and grabbed the footage and gave Valen a piece of my mind. I reminded him of his promise. That he gave me his word. I reminded him that I wasn't one of his constituents or media darlings who would go soft on him and let him get away with anything."

"Basically, you lectured your own client."

"Oh, yeah," I said, smiling. "I totally let him have it. Then I left with the evidence."

"And what'd you do with it?"

"Went to Teddy B's house and gave it to him. Lectured him, too. Told him to smarten up."

"What about Valen? Wasn't he pissed you left with the evidence?"

"You know, I don't think so. I told him to forget the final payment he owed us. I even returned his retainer check."

"And Slim didn't find out?"

"Nope. Days later, Valen squeaked out a victory without using the evidence. He never contacted me or Slim. To keep Slim satisfied, I sent him the money that Valen owed us out of my own pocket. Told Slim that Valen paid me directly for everything, and that I was cutting Slim a check for his share. For all Slim knew, Valen was a satisfied client."

"Okay, so your lie has been buried for a while and now it may rear its head?"

"Right, that's why I'm concerned about Slim approaching Valen for help. Don't want Valen double-crossing us because he's holding a grudge. I don't think that's the case, but you never know."

"You should get out in front of it. Tell Slim everything. And I don't just mean the true Valen Jackson story. You should tell him why you don't want to run a branch, and your concerns about the nature of your job."

"You're right, I should."

She sighed. "That means you won't, Chase. I know you."

"I'll come clean to Slim, let me work on the timing of when."

Karla stood and put her hands on her hips.

"I promise, Karla."

"You better."

She snatched the coffee mug from my hand just as a distant buzz caught our attention. We both looked straight out from the porch toward the source of the sound.

Karla saw the drone first. She leapt off her chair and ran out to meet the descending multi-pronged drone. I watched in surprise as it hovered about twenty feet above her and sent a fluttering white envelope to the ground.

Snapping into action, I raced to Karla's side. As she picked up the envelope and opened it, I focused on the drone, which was now buzzing away in the direction of the Pacific. Soon I lost sight of it as it blended in to the horizon.

When I looked back at Karla, she had the envelope open. Inside was a lone Polaroid picture. It only took a quick glance at the picture to realize what this was all about.

Immediately I backed up and started looking around.

"They can't be far, Karla. Whomever is controlling that thing must be close."

She tucked the picture away and joined me in scanning the area. "Yes and no," she said.

While looking up at the surrounding hills, I said, "What do you mean?"

"Our FO is working with different drones these days, so I recognized that particular model. It's one of the best commercial drones out there. It has an incredible range. The person operating it could be quite far."

"Like how far?" I asked.

"Six or seven miles."

I looked at her. "Really?"

"Really. It needs to be line of sight, though, so the controller is somewhere out there." She pointed to the myriad hills surrounding my place. "Has to be high up on one of the hills."

I scanned east to west for about a minute in silence. Karla did the same.

Eventually, I sighed. "It's useless. Six or seven miles is far away, especially for my eyes."

"And we have no clue which direction either. There's a lot of ground to cover behind your property. This is futile."

"Can I see the envelope and picture again?"

"Sure," she said, handing it over facedown. "Check out the message scrawled on the back of the Polaroid."

I read the hastily scrawled words: "GO BACK TO THE SURF CAMP."

I flipped the picture over. Mom was front and center, holding a Mexican newspaper against her chest. She was in some sort of building that I couldn't quite make out because the background was a little fuzzy. The flash from the camera made her sweaty face glisten from the bright, concentrated light. Mom had a red bandana in her mouth. Her eyes were wide, and her pupils clearly dilated.

Trying to stay positive, I looked at Karla. "She's alive. At least she was yesterday." I motioned at the date on the newspaper.

Karla rubbed my back. "You were headed back to Mexico anyway."

I nodded. "Let's get on the road. Like now. And double-time it."

CHAPTER TWENTY-NINE

FOR THE SECOND time in one week, I headed south to Mexico.

First, I'd driven with Karla and Simon to LA and spent the night at Karla's. In the morning, Karla left with Simon to Disneyland. To distract my son from his missing dog and grandma, we thought a day at Disneyland and another at California Adventure Park would do the trick. Since Karla had a couple days off, she was excited to spend some alone time with my son.

I'd just left my buddy Mick Cranston's place in San Clemente and was headed to La Jolla to pick up Slim. Slim and I were determined to figure out what was going on. In our minds, the most logical place to start was the Punta De Las Olas building. Figuring out what was going on inside there was key—the key to potentially unlocking other mysteries, too.

We needed answers, and we knew Alejandro Ortiz would be the one to provide some. He was the main man working with the US on Operation Crossroads, and he was the one who turned on his partner, Juan Manuel Delgado. Of course, everything we learned about Crossroads and Ortiz came from the president, who we couldn't really believe.

Our intel was questionable at best. But since we had to start somewhere, we chose Ortiz.

Valen Jackson was our ticket to a meeting with Ortiz. Valen had been working across the border for decades now. He had thriving farms up and down the Baja California coast. Prior to working with the US government, Ortiz had also made his mark in agriculture. Slim surmised that the two would know each other.

And that guess turned out to be correct.

Slim had called last night to inform me he had the details worked out for the meeting. Since he didn't want to get into those details on a call, he simply told me to pick him up promptly at 10:00 a.m. in La Jolla, at a chain hotel just off the 5 freeway.

I arrived ten minutes early.

Slim squeezed into the passenger seat of my Caprice. "Simon doing okay?"

"I think so. At the very least, he'll be pretty distracted the next couple of days."

"Good to hear. How's Mick doing? Did you get him on board without much hassle?"

"I did. He has teenage girls, so it didn't take much convincing to get him out of the house for a couple days."

"He'll meet us later this evening at the surf camp then?"

"Not exactly."

Slim furrowed his brow.

I explained. "He's already left for Mex. He's headed to the surf camp first. That will give him the afternoon to scout out the camp, identify any threats. Then he's going to pick us up later this evening in Tecate."

"Why Tecate?"

"To pick up my dog."

"Really?"

I nodded. "Really. Then he'll drive us back to the surf camp."

Slim thought about it for a moment. "All right, at least Mick is doing reconnaissance; it can't get better than that. But you do know we may be walking into a trap here. The drone note you received may not be about you completing the Delgado job. It may be about getting you into Mexico so they can off you in the remote desert because you know too much."

"Very much aware, pal. That's why it'll be nice to have my two closest and most-skilled buddies protecting my six."

"With what?" Slim said, shaking his head. "My hands? I'd feel much better if we were armed, but I know we can't bring any weapons across the border."

"I wish we could, believe me. So, fill me in. Where are we headed?"

"CBX in Otay Mesa."

"We're flying out of Tijuana?"

"You got it. We sure are."

CBX stood for the Cross Border Express in Otay Mesa, California. The interesting thing about the Tijuana International Airport was its location. It was positioned directly by the border. Americans could park in the US, at the CBX parking lot, then walk across the border and straight into the airport terminal.

I asked Slim, "Where are we flying to, and in what?"

"We lucked out. Valen's company flies out of Tijuana twice a week, and there's a flight today. Various company execs are brought along to check on the Mexican operations. Valen owns a few dozen farms stretching from Tijuana to Cabo. Since there are a lot of stops, they use a helicopter—one of those rescue copters, a Sikorsky S-76."

"Great," I said, shaking my head. "That's the Kobe helicopter."

Slim looked confused.

"The model of helicopter that Kobe Bryant went down in."

"That's right, forgot about that. Hopefully we have better luck. So, listen, we're hitching a ride with some of these execs. I think the chopper has like eight executive seats, but only three execs are on board today. We're going to Punta San Carlos, about a third of the way down the peninsula."

"Why there?"

"That's where Alejandro Ortiz currently is. He has a vacation place there. Punta San Carlos is a renowned windsurfing spot. Though Ortiz was an avid windsurfer, and is now too old to enjoy the sport, it's still his number one vacation spot."

"Vacation? After all that's going on, Alejandro Ortiz decides to go or stay on vacation?"

Slim shrugged. "I guess, don't know more than that. Valen called him yesterday and Ortiz agreed to meet us in Punta San Carlos."

"And what story did you sell Valen? Did you tell him the truth? That we needed this meeting with Ortiz to talk about the government operation and Punta De Las Olas?"

"Heck no, pal."

"Good. What'd you say then?"

"Real Estate. I told Valen that you and I were interested in some vacation property in Baja. We're looking to buy a particular property and did some research and found out that Ortiz owns the land. We wanted to meet to see if he'd be interested in selling."

"And Valen was fine with all this? Not upset at the sudden request for help?"

Slim waved me off. "Buddy, he was more than happy to help out. The Sikorsky wasn't full, and Punta San Carlos is right by their last stop today. Plus, Ortiz is an old buddy of Valen. No problem at all."

I guess I had a concerned look on my face because Slim followed that up with, "Why so skeptical?"

"No reason."

Slim sighed. "You've always been weird around Valen. You know that, right?"

I wasn't about to launch into what happened with the Valen job, so I changed subjects. "Let's talk about our play with Ortiz. Do we come clean about our intentions from the get-go? Or keep up with the real estate ruse? We could mention we love surfing and fishing and are interested in the Punta De Las Olas property, or in any surrounding property that he could part with."

Slim stroked his short, red hair. "Not sure. Been thinking about that. What do you think?"

I reflected for a minute before responding. "I imagine we have to do both. Eventually we'll have to come clean with him and apologize for the ruse. Initially, though, I want this guy totally unprepared so we can gauge his reaction when we mention Punta De Las Olas. Does he speak freely about that property or immediately shut down when we mention it? That will tell us which direction to proceed."

"Okay," Slim said, nodding. "I'm with you."

"Why don't you do the talking first, about the property and our interest in it. I can sit back and study his reactions. Then I can assess and come clean, if need be, and do damage control about our ruse. Remember, Ortiz knew a hit on Delgado was imminent. He was the one who informed the president, or so she claims. For all I know, he may be aware the president approached me with the kill directive."

"You think?"

"Before everything went down, I would've said categorically no. The president wouldn't have divulged important mission details like that. But now, who knows? Anything and everything are on the table. We can't trust anyone."

We let that comment hang for some time. In fact, we didn't talk much the rest of the way into southern San Diego. Eventually, we pulled into the CBX lot, checked in at the CBX terminal, then walked across the 390-foot pedestrian bridge into Mexico.

Before stepping into another country, Slim turned to me. "We could potentially be walking straight into a lion's den here."

"You're absolutely right. Sometimes you have to, though, right? We need answers, Slim, and we need to find Mom."

He nodded and stepped into Mexico. "We're in the fire."

I stepped beside him and slapped his broad, sweaty back. "Directly into the furnace, buddy. No turning back now."

CHAPTER THIRTY

"MADAM PRESIDENT," Kendra Winfield said, "this is going to turn a lot of heads. We're going to get a lot of questions."

Henrietta had been getting pushback from her team for the better part of the last hour; from the very moment she proposed an impromptu campaign return trip to California.

The president let out an exasperated sigh.

Winfield, her head campaign manager, kept at it. "It's challenging to explain, ma'am, especially since you were just in California and there's nothing on our schedule to suggest you were going back soon. And you want to go to San Diego, but you're polling so well there."

"Fine then," the president said. "Here's my compromise: a campaign trip to Arizona. Get me there, somewhere right by the border. Spin it however you will. Maybe there's a hot-button issue in Arizona I'm interested in."

Winfield turned to the others in the Private Study and held out her hands. "Well, gentlemen, anything?"

Willy Blanco said, "No issue that I'm currently aware of."

Branch, the secretary to the president, said, "The border, of course. It's always the hot-button issue there, ma'am, always."

Henrietta was sitting at the Roosevelt desk. She'd pulled up a map of Arizona on Google on the computer in front of her. "Yuma," she said, pointing to the computer screen. "That's our next campaign stop. That's where we'll go. Make it happen, team."

"And our rationale for a sudden trip to Yuma?" Winfield asked.

Without looking up from the computer, Henrietta said, "That's why you get the big bucks, Kendra. I trust you'll come up with something good." Her eyes flicked to Branch and Willy. "Gentlemen, clear my schedule for the next day or so and inform the staff. You have some details to work out."

Willy, Branch, and Winfield stood awkwardly still.

"Come on, team," the president urged, "get a move on. And, please, leave me for at least half an hour. No disturbances. I need some time."

When the three filed out of the room, Henrietta turned her attention back to the computer. She clicked on another tab and studied a different map. This map was of Northern Baja. She'd been tracking Garrison Chase's burner cell location, which, from what she could tell, was in Tecate, and it had been there for some time.

She studied the map for a while, eventually nodding and tapping the screen.

"Here I come, Garrison Chase, here I come."

CHAPTER THIRTY-ONE

"SURELY YOU AREN'T HERE to talk real estate," Alejandro Ortiz said, shooting looks between Slim and me. "Can we skip the ruse now, gentlemen?"

And here I thought Slim had been doing a reasonable job selling our vacation property dreams.

My buddy glanced at me and sighed. I nodded.

He looked back at Ortiz. "When'd you get suspicious?"

Ortiz laughed. He was a portly man, so his midsection jiggled long after his laugh stopped. "My dear boys," he said, condescendingly, "from the beginning. The very beginning."

I'd had strong reservations from the beginning, too, from the moment we stepped off the helicopter after a three-hour flight time. An armored vehicle had picked us up from the tiny Punta San Carlos airport. Professional security men patted us down and drove us to Ortiz's property. Ortiz's vacation home was a modern beachfront estate that could've easily been mistaken for a Malibu beach home. Three security men surrounded the property. It didn't take me long to realize Ortiz wasn't here on vacation.

He was in hiding.

Slim prodded for more information. "Like beginning when you first met us, or even further back than that?"

Ortiz dabbed at his sweaty forehead and smiled. It was the first smile I'd seen from him. "From the moment Valen mentioned you two." He dabbed his forehead yet again.

Even though the air conditioner was pumping in the opulent den, Alejandro Ortiz seemed to have a perpetual bead of brow sweat. The man reminded me of Marlon Brandon in *The Godfather*, but from *Part III* of the series, when Brando was much older. The two men shared a near identical mustache. A big difference, though, was that Ortiz didn't have the crooked, drooping mouth of Brando.

I spoke for the first time. "Why agree to see us then, sir? Especially if you knew it was all a cover."

"He speaks!" Ortiz exclaimed. "Was beginning to think, my dear boy, you were mute."

"Just cautious," I fired back.

"Got it," Ortiz responded. He motioned to Slim. "He's the brawn"—then looked back at me—"and you're the brains, I assume?"

Slim was about to interject, but I interrupted. "Why agree to see us? Let's start there."

Ortiz nodded. "I'm sure you're both very much aware that I've been working with your government on an important operation. Things took a turn for the worse, shall we say, in recent days. So, when I heard two Americans suddenly wanted to meet with me, I couldn't help but think it was no mere coincidence. I'm intrigued at your presence, to say the least."

"Intrigued?" I questioned.

"More than intrigued," Ortiz admitted. "I'm in a bind, gentlemen. I'm not here for long beach walks and the lovely weather. As you can tell from security, I'm quite concerned about my safety, borderline paranoid I'd admit. But considering who I'm dealing with, I think it's prudent and wise. Anyway, I know you two are former G-men turned investigators, so you're somehow involved in this fiasco or investigating the situation or perhaps doing a bit of both."

He paused for a moment to touch his lips, then proceeded. "Course, you could also be here to kill me. And if you were here to take me out, well, you wouldn't have gotten very far with my security detail. Right? Not much risk for me there. And if you're thinking of something a little more personal, perhaps a little more close-up, well . . . "

Ortiz must've pushed a button under his desk. Wooden panels on either side of the bookshelf behind his office chair suddenly hinged open. Two of his security men stepped into the room. Their pistols were not in a threatening position, but they certainly weren't being hidden either.

As quickly as they stepped into the room, they just as quickly stepped out.

Ortiz eyed us. "What do you Americans say, 'Just trying to keep it real'?"

Though I appreciated his honesty, something didn't sit right with me. "Tell me, Mr. Ortiz, why would you think Americans would be sent to kill you?"

"Potentially sent to kill me," Ortiz corrected. "And that stems from the fact that your president is incommunicado."

Slim and I exchanged curious looks.

"Suddenly she's stopped returning my calls," he continued. "I haven't heard from her in days, and considering we've been working closely on Crossroads, well, it makes a gentleman pause and think. Especially a paranoid one like myself."

Before I could process that comment, Ortiz said, "Shall we move on, gentlemen? Since clearly you aren't here on a sinister mission. It seems my paranoia has indeed gotten the best of me." He focused his attention on me. "I'm a businessman at heart, so always looking for a deal. I thought perhaps we could work together because I'm quite sure we have a common enemy. When you mentioned Punta De Las Olas, I immediately realized you gentlemen were in the know. How much? Well, I'm not sure. How about we all put our cards on the table then? What do you say?"

Neither Slim nor I responded.

Sensing our hesitation, Ortiz directed us to the back of his office.

"Like I said," he continued, "I'm a businessman, so I know you two may want to discuss first before agreeing to anything. How about you fix yourselves a drink? Maybe have a quick chat in the process? Totally understandable."

Before I could ponder that move, Slim headed to the drink cart. I reluctantly followed.

With our backs to Ortiz, Slim scanned the cart, no doubt looking for bourbon. He spoke softly to me. "What do you think?"

"I think Ortiz is scared to death of Delgado. He gave the man up to our government and set everything in motion. When the hit didn't go as planned, Ortiz probably thinks Delgado believes he's the double-crosser."

"Sure," Slim said. "I could see that."

"I'd be on edge and prone to hiding if the Butcher of Baja was after me, too."

Slim nodded. "Hey, sorry, but the only brown liquor here is some tequila reposada."

I cringed but agreed to a shot.

After we both blew fire, I said, "The problem here is the men forcing me to go back and finish the job, not to mention snatching Mom. I mean, Delgado's obviously not behind that. He's not responsible for enforcing his own hit."

"Right, the president and Mr. Ortiz are the ones who need Delgado dead. And desperately from what we understand. Plus, it sounds like those two may be on the outs for some reason. We obviously can't trust Ortiz then, or the president."

"Agreed, but the problem is we need answers. And this guy"—I thumbed discreetly behind me—"has answers."

"I'll let you take the lead, then," Slim said. "You do the talking this time."

I leaned in. "I'll reveal a lot but stop short of the whole truth. I'll tell him everything except for Mom's kidnapping and the pressure to complete the job. Since he could be behind that."

"Not positive, but I think that's the best move." Slim took another tequila shot.

I waved off his offer for a second drink and headed back to my chair, thinking about my strategy. I felt getting in step with Ortiz was the best play. Playing up a mutual interest in disposing of Delgado, even if that wasn't my ultimate intention, at least not at this point.

As I took a seat, I came out swinging. "Juan Manuel Delgado aka Jimmy D aka the Butcher of Baja. Our common enemy. Correct?"

Ortiz straightened in his chair but didn't say a word.

"We can say his name," I continued. "Can't we? It's not like the guy is he-who-shall-not-be-named. He's not Voldemort from *Harry Potter.*"

Slim laughed, but Ortiz didn't seem to get the reference.

I shook it off. "You and Delgado have been running Operation Cross-roads with the president, but it turns out your partner hasn't exactly turned his back on his old ways. Has he? And that didn't sit well with you, Mr. Ortiz, so you approached our president for help."

I paused and stared at him, waiting to see if he'd acknowledge.

He did. After his subtle head nod, I said, "The president had a plan in play, but that all went south when the Nogales operation went public. She was desperate to work with you to get rid of Delgado so that Crossroads could continue—and ultimately fulfill her legacy, of course—so she reached out to me with the burn notice on Delgado."

Ortiz blew out a big breath. He was at a momentary loss for words, which seemed rare for him. He recovered nicely, though. "I knew she had a backup plan, just wasn't sure exactly what she had in motion. I certainly wasn't privy to any details. What happened then, since Juan is very much alive, Mr. Chase? From my understanding, he knows that I'm the one who gave him up. Hence the security. How did the hit get botched? Did you miss the shot?"

I shook my head. "Intel was questionable, which gave me pause before pulling the trigger. Correction: intel was misleading. Totally fabricated, in fact."

"How so?" Ortiz asked.

"The video the president left with me didn't line up with reality. Didn't line up with what was truly going on inside Punta De Las Olas. Do you know what video I'm talking about?"

"Goodness," Ortiz said, standing and pacing. After some back-and-forth striding, he stopped. "That was me, the video was all my doing."

Slim snapped, "What do you mean that was you?"

"I mean, I put that video together for the president. Wasn't sure if anyone else would see it."

I shot to my feet. "And you doctored it? Or at least knew it was doctored?"

He reluctantly nodded, then resumed pacing.

"Mr. Ortiz," Slim said, "you better sit and elaborate."

Ortiz complied. He began rambling before fully seated. "Yes, I edited the video but didn't think that mattered, not much, anyway. I agree it's misleading, but the video isn't fabricated, and my intentions weren't bad. It's just—"

"Stop," Slim said, holding up his hand. "Start at the beginning, the very beginning."

I nodded my approval.

Ortiz gathered his breath. "I had suspicions about Juan, right from the start, considering what I knew about his past and all. Then when rumors started happening with our Crossroads operation—"

"Can you go further back?" I interrupted. "To the absolute beginning. How did you and Delgado become partners in Crossroads, anyway?"

"Right," Ortiz said, tapping his fingers on his desk. "I'd transitioned out of agriculture and into human resources about five or so years back. I'd built the employment agency from the ground up and eventually got into business with your government. It was lucrative, to be blunt. I needed an infusion of capital to keep up with your government's demands. And I also needed help with Sinaloa."

"How so?" Slim asked. "What was going on with them?"

"As I'm sure you know, cartels run Mexico. Anything lucrative and they want their piece, they want their dirty hands in the pie, so to speak. Juan and I had known each other for decades. I knew about his past, but I also knew he was a changed man. Juan was a natural fit to partner with since the Sinaloa cartel was making some lofty demands. He had the capital, and he had experience dealing with cartels. He promised me he'd handle that side of things, keep Sinaloa at bay. Considering his past, and who his father was, I thought it was a smart deal. I had no reservations bringing him in because I believed in his reformation. Boy, I had that wrong. Way wrong. He really sold me on his past being in the past. Anyway, I didn't know what Juan meant by 'handling' the cartel and keeping them at bay until much later."

I wanted to hear Ortiz admit to the drugged women scheme, even if he wasn't involved. I said, "And how did he appease the cartel then?"

"You saw the video," he shot back. "Didn't you? Juan started that operation to keep Sinaloa appeased."

I played somewhat dumb. "I saw the video, but the men spoke in Spanish, so I got the gist just not the details. Tell me more."

Ortiz nodded. "Listen, I had no idea Juan and the cartel were skimming these women for their operation. I promise. They went over the top in the scheme, in both scope and money."

"How so?" Slim asked.

"I mean, heavens, they built a nearly identical building to house the women."

I leaned forward. "What do you mean by that?"

"Let me back up," Ortiz responded. "Juan, I refuse to call him Jimmy by the way, has this little pet project. Basically, he's trying to develop drought-tolerant plants that can grow and thrive in desert-like conditions. With little to no water. His goal is to make the dry, arid land of Northern Baja a thriving agricultural area. He wants to make the land prosperous for the people. So, he started this scientific foundation of his, which comes with substantial support from the Mexican government. Courtesy of his late father, I suppose. It's also a learning center, so he allows local school children weekly visits. He shows off the lab to get the kids excited about science and plants and farming. And the future, as Juan likes to say."

I nodded to myself. "So that's what's going on at Punta De Las Olas."

"Yes and no," Ortiz said.

He addressed my confusion. "That's what the converted saint named Jimmy D would have you believe. But what Juan Manuel Delgado is really doing is using the place as a front. He has a select group of scientists in that facility who've developed and now manufacture their own superdrug."

When he paused, I clenched my fists. "To experiment on these women, who are then sold into modern-day slavery."

Slim kept me from going down anger road by keeping the conversation on point. "Why an identical building? Explain that."

"Confusion," Ortiz said. "That's what I gathered from Juan at least."

"Confusion?" I repeated.

"The women are flown to that location blindfolded, so they have no clue where that Punta De Las Olas building is actually situated. Though the women are confined inside the building, Juan wanted it to be a beautiful building and a pleasurable place for them to live—the main floor, that is, since we know the basement is far from that. Anyway, the problem with creating a beautiful place like Punta De Las Olas is that it's memorable. What if one of these women leave the program and start making wild accusations against Juan? Saying they've been drugged and kept at a facility against their will. All they can remember and describe is Punta De Las Olas."

I saw where this was going. "Delgado says they're delusional and describing his foundation building, right? The one in Northern Baja perched on the cliff overlooking the ocean. Where people clearly aren't being held against their will."

"Correct," Ortiz said. "It's right there in the open. Public can even visit it, and often do. It looks identical on the outside, and the inside main floor has the same basic rooms and setup. Instead of the main dining room, though, the Baja facility is a large scientific lab."

"It would," Slim said, "create confusion for the women, that they're mistaking a place they've been with somewhere they haven't."

"Ultimately, their story would be hard to believe," I added, "since they were opiate addicts and surely must have flawed memories."

"When I discovered all this," Ortiz said, "it blew me away. I mean, the time and money involved to build a replica building like that, just as a precaution, is mind-blowing. But that's the power of Mexican cartels, which terrifies me. And always has."

I asked, "How did you discover the scheme?"

"Family," Ortiz responded. "A few family members I was distantly acquainted with mentioned that they hadn't heard from their daughters in a while. I did some digging to help the families out, but I couldn't find the women. When it kept happening, I approached Juan to see if he knew what was going on. He said he didn't, but I didn't buy it. I kept pushing the issue until he acquiesced."

Ortiz stood and made his way to the back of the den. "Need to pour myself a drink for this next part."

Slim and I waved off his offer for another drink.

After pouring himself a shot of some silver tequila, Ortiz walked back to his desk and said, "Juan agreed to show me the operation, saying it was necessary to keep Sinaloa satisfied. Said he'd fly me to the location but that I had to be blindfolded, and I wasn't allowed to bring my phone either. He said the operation wasn't that bad, that the women were ultimately happy in the end. And that I would see all this firsthand."

He paused to take a shot. After a disgusted head shake, he continued. "They toured me around the building, bottom to top. Since I didn't trust Juan, I'd worn one of those Western shirts with black snap buttons. I replaced one of the buttons on my left front pocket with a tiny camera so I could record whatever I found."

"You took the footage," I said.

"Yes, not sure if you could tell, but by the end of the tour I was enraged and shaky and ran into the bathroom. Following the visit, I put together the video for the president, to show what was going on."

Slim leaned forward. "And you personally doctored the footage?"

"I did. A mistake in retrospect. At the time, though, I felt it didn't matter much. Didn't see the point in going into all the details about identical buildings. I knew Jimmy checked in on his foundation every Wednesday, and I knew what was going on with the women at the other building. But I didn't know when Juan visited that building. The video ultimately conveyed what was really going on. Why delve into the weeds, isn't that what you Americans say?"

Neither Slim nor I responded.

"Juan needed to be stopped," Ortiz said flatly. "That was my focus. I understand now why you'd be confused when entering the building." He eyed me. "What exactly happened to make you go inside? That wasn't supposed to happen. What gave you pause?"

"Door hinges," I replied.

Ortiz furrowed his brow.

I explained. "When you went through the side door in the secret video you shot, everyone barreled inward. But when Delgado and his men approached the side door, when I was watching them through my scope, they pulled the door outward before entering. And I was pretty sure I remembered it swinging in from the video."

Ortiz shook his head. "That's something: door hinges. I'll be. I guess Juan didn't make an exact replica."

"Any idea where this replica building is?" I asked. "I know you said you were blindfolded."

Ortiz grinned. "I do, gentlemen, I do."

Slim and I glanced at each other.

Ortiz's grin ballooned to a full-blown smile. "In fact, I know its precise location."

CHAPTER THIRTY-TWO

"WHERE," I said, scowling at Ortiz. "Where are these drugged women being held against their will?"

Ortiz didn't answer my question. "Mr. Chase, my assumption is that prior to coming here you had grave concerns about your president's directive; that perhaps you'd been fooled into the assassination of Juan Manuel Delgado. And that would've been a result of my doing because of the doctored video footage. Let me assure you, this man needs to be taken out. He needs to be stopped, once and for all. And I'd like to implore you to finish the job."

My scowl deepened.

Ortiz held up his hands. "Before getting into details about the women's location, I just wanted to make sure we're on the same page about Juan Manuel Delgado."

I nodded to appease him. "Like I said earlier, he's our common enemy."

"Speaking of assumptions, Mr. Ortiz," Slim interjected, "my assumption is that you have the means"—Slim gestured to the opulent den—"to more than adequately protect yourself. As is evidenced by this property and the men you clearly have at your beck and call. Why not go after Delgado yourself? Why implore us to finish the job?"

"Point taken," he acknowledged. "I'm certainly a man of means, not wanting for much as you can see. My men tried right away to locate and dispose of Juan, but they failed. Which isn't surprising considering Juan's deep connections. No doubt Juan is in hiding and has commissioned my death. Now I have the Sinaloa cartel after me, and potentially the leader of the free world, so I need all the help I can get."

He paused. When Slim and I didn't respond, he continued. "As I said, I'm a businessman and always looking for a deal. The fact that you gentlemen are here suggests you still want to be involved, and perhaps finish the job you started. Which is what I ultimately want, too. In exchange for Juan's death, I can offer three things: One, proof to your government that Juan Manuel Delgado is the infamous Butcher of Baja and responsible for the— let's just say—dismantling of those American businessmen. Two, I can provide the location of Punta De Las Olas where you'll find the women. You'll most assuredly find the Butcher of Baja hiding there as well. And three, I'll provide the necessary weaponry and transport to get there, to get the job done right. Sound good?"

I said, "Can you give us another moment?"

"By all means," Ortiz replied.

I pulled Slim back to the mini bar. Before I could say anything, Slim asked, "What do you think?"

"I think we may be getting off priority here. We need to figure out who else wants this job done, what the president's exact involvement is, and where the hell my mother is."

Slim took a moment. "I understand, and I agree. Your mother, though, may very well be at the building with these women. And this may be our best bet for some answers."

I didn't respond. After some moments of silence, Slim said, "What do you want to do?"

"Ask more questions," I replied. While walking back to the desk, I asked Ortiz, "How'd you get the precise location of the building? After all, you told us you were blindfolded with no phone on you."

"Prior to departure, Juan informed me we'd be walking over some pretty rugged terrain from the helicopter landing site. I prepared by wearing my trainers, those particular trainers used for running that have a small GPS unit in the sole so you can map your runs."

Not bad, I thought.

Ortiz hinged open the laptop on his desk. He beckoned us over. Pointing to a map on the screen, he said, "The building is in the northeastern Sierra Madre mountain range, technically called the Sierra Madre Oriental." He zoomed out on the screen. "You can see its location is at the base between these two mountains, but you can't see the actual building from the air because of the dense forest."

I nodded and glanced at Slim. He didn't say a word or move a muscle. His eyes were fixated on the screen. I turned back to Ortiz.

"What were your intentions with this intel? You obviously knew what was going on there, inside that building." I motioned to the screen. "And I assume you wanted it stopped."

"Very much so," he said. "For my safety, I wanted Juan out of the picture first, especially since I knew he was the infamous Butcher of Baja, and what he was currently up to." Ortiz motioned to the laptop screen. "Upon Juan's death, I was prepared to give your government concrete proof of his identity since the major threat on my life would've been taken care of. And that also would've put a stop to Juan's operation."

I glanced at Slim to see if he had any input or questions. He was still transfixed on the screen, and I noticed his lips were slightly moving. What was his deal?

"You all right, buddy?" I asked.

He snapped out of it. "Maybe tequila isn't my thing." He glanced at Ortiz. "You have a bathroom nearby?"

Ortiz motioned behind us. "Door at the back on the left."

Slim, still murmuring, excused himself.

I turned my attention back to Ortiz. "What happened between you and Henrietta? If she won't return your calls, obviously something happened. What? Aside from the hit not going down, of course."

He snapped the laptop shut and eased back in the chair. "I can only conjecture."

"Then conjecture away."

"She's cleaning up her failed operation. That's what I think is going on here."

I'd thought about that, too. A lot. It was a valid theory. "Go on," I said, motioning with my hand so he would cough up more details.

"Her operation was built on stealth and surprise. It was all about hitting

Juan when he least expected it. When you didn't pull the trigger, everything changed. The moment Juan Manuel Delgado left the Northern Baja building alive, the president pivoted because she knew she was screwed. She'd missed her one chance at getting the Butcher. She knew he'd go into hiding and have the support of a massive drug cartel behind him. And she would never get another chance to take him down. But what she feared the most, and I'm conjecturing here, was Juan claiming that Americans were behind his attempted assassination. Think about that. She'd never survive that story. Never. Not another unauthorized, failed operation on Mexican soil. Operation Crossroads then, and her legacy, forever tarnished."

Slim returned and eased into the chair beside me. I glanced over. He looked perfectly fine.

Ortiz continued. "The fact that she won't return my calls, gentlemen, leads me to believe that she may be out to silence me. Which would mean you, Mr. Chase, and now your associate here, might be on her list, too. If that's what's going on with your president, then we"—Ortiz motioned at us —"are loose ends. No telling what your president may have set in motion to get rid of us since we're the only ones who knew about the Punta De Las Olas hit."

I couldn't help but think of Thiago and his men pressuring me to finish the president's directive. *Did she really reach out to them and set that in motion?*

I didn't have time to think since Slim suddenly—and quite assertively— brought himself into the conversation. He put his arm on my shoulder and gave it a friendly squeeze, then a pat. "Mr. Ortiz," he said, "we're with you. Chase and I are on board. Absolutely. Let's work together to rid the world of the Butcher of Baja."

As he pulled his hand off my shoulder, he dropped it out of sight and gave me a quick pinch on the scapula. My pal was slick. Obviously, he was up to something. Though I had no clue what, I got the signal and stayed quiet.

"You had it all wrong, Mr. Ortiz," he continued, "he's the brawn"—Slim thumbed at me—"and I'm the brains. Don't let size fool you. Now, let's talk details."

Incredulously, I listened for the next ten minutes as Slim hammered out a deal with Alejandro Ortiz. Ortiz wanted us to stay the night, work out a plan in Punta San Carlos, then leave the following evening on our mission. Slim convinced him that we needed to get back to Tijuana, for my dog, and to leave the following evening from Tijuana. The whole conversation was hasty since Slim kept mentioning Valen's helicopter was leaving soon, and we needed to catch that flight back to Tijuana. However, I knew we had another ninety minutes before takeoff.

The best part of the plan was Slim convincing Ortiz that we needed to take the weapons with us; that way we had a day to familiarize ourselves with their operation. In the end, Slim loaded a canvas duffel bag of weapons, then Ortiz's men dropped us off at the small airport outside of town.

Surprisingly, the helicopter's pilot, a man named Clayton, was already in the cockpit. It looked like he was going over his preflight instrument check. Only when the car had dropped us off, and was well out of view, did Slim let me ask a question.

"What the hell was that all about?" I asked. "You don't trust Ortiz, do you?"

"Hell no," he said, smiling. "Which is why we're going to get those women and Delgado long before our planned mission with Ortiz tomorrow evening, and hopefully save your mother, too."

I furrowed my brow. "And how, my dear friend, are we going to do that?"

Still smiling, Slim pulled out his cell and opened the notes app on his phone. "Coordinates," he said, holding out the cell so I could read the screen. "Coordinates to the building in the Sierra Madres."

"Wait, what? How'd you get coordinates?"

"When Ortiz showed us the laptop screen, the cursor was hovered over the Punta De Las Olas building in the Sierra Madres. The software or app or whatever program he was using showed the latitude and longitude in the top right-hand corner of the screen. The numbers were tiny, so it was easy to miss."

I slugged him on the shoulder. "You genius. I wondered what the hell you were doing."

"I was repeating the coordinates in my head over and over, committing them to memory. Then I excused myself and went to the shitter to put them into my phone before I forgot." He laughed. "I also texted Clayton and told him we could leave early."

"You were always good with numbers, buddy. That's for sure."

As we walked toward the helicopter, Slim motioned toward the pilot. "You saw me talking to him on our way down here, right?"

I nodded.

"Clayton did two tours in Afghanistan. He's perfect to drop us off somewhere close to these coordinates"—Slim held up his cell—"and exfiltrate us if things get hairy. I'm sure Valen will be okay with us commandeering the bird for a quick mission. Don't you think?"

I shrugged.

"I'll call Valen when we land in TJ. When should we head out?"

"As soon as possible," I replied. "We'll hook up with Mick, bring him up to speed, get a quick plan together, then the three amigos will hit the building before dawn. Agreed?"

"Agreed."

We climbed into the helicopter and took our seats. Slim and I were alone in the executive passenger area of the Sikorsky S-76. I unzipped the duffel bag at my feet.

"Now," I said, "let's check out what type of weapons you secured."

Slim said, "My pleasure."

CHAPTER THIRTY-THREE

Javi liked the new woman. She was a real firecracker who rarely followed the guards' orders. In fact, the new woman insisted on learning and calling the others by name, even in front of the guards.

Her name was Isabelle, but she preferred Izzy for short. Izzy was born and raised in California and spoke some Spanish, but not nearly enough to carry on a proper conversation.

Javi and Izzy were currently in the middle of a conversation in English, which was great practice for Javi. They stood beside the sink in the makeshift kitchen of the guards' quarters. Izzy had insisted Javi help her with the dinner dishes. The night guard wanted nothing to do with an upset Izzy, so he acquiesced and let Javi help. Izzy had been probing Javi for details about what was happening underground.

"We'll finish the tunnel during tomorrow's morning shift," Javi was saying, "unless . . ."

Izzy stopped washing the dish in her hand and placed her hands on her hips. "Unless what, Javi? What?"

He looked around.

"For heaven's sake," she said, "nobody's around. The guard is clear on the other side of the hangar."

Javi cleared his throat. "Unless the men sabotage the tunnel."

"Sabotage? What do you mean? Why, why would the guys do that?"

"It's not my idea; it's Raoul and Jaime's. They want to do something drastic."

"And why's that?"

"When we're finished with this tunnel, Patron suggests we'll all be forced into digging another tunnel, then another, and another. Raoul and Jaime don't necessarily believe that. They believe it will be the end of the line for everyone, so they want to take action now."

Izzy eyed him. "What do you think will happen?"

"Honestly?" he asked.

"No, Javi, lie to me." She smiled. "Of course, I insist on your honest answer."

"Fifty-fifty for me. Could go either way."

"How exactly would these men sabotage the tunnel?"

"Dig up, toward the surface, for the last few meters. Break through the water table or into the aquifer and flood the tunnel, which may cause it to collapse."

"Wouldn't that . . ." Izzy didn't finish her question.

Javi nodded. "Most likely, it may kill the man who breaks through. Their survival would depend on how much and how fast the water flows in."

Izzy shook her head. "No, no, no, no," she repeated. "We can't let that happen. We can't have one of them sacrifice their life. We need to buy time; we need to prolong this. We need to be patient and do nothing rash. Help will come."

"You honestly believe that?" he asked.

"Absolutely, Javi, absolutely."

"Seems like wishful thinking."

"No," she snapped back. "It's not. I just know help will arrive. I'm here because of my son, and whatever he's involved with. He traveled to Mexico last week, said it was an impromptu surf trip. Now I know it wasn't."

"What was he doing in Mexico then?"

"No clue, but it wasn't some harmless surf trip. Once I was across the border, they took a Polaroid picture of me with a Mexican newspaper held under my chin. That must've been sent to him. I'm being used as leverage for something, but I have no idea for what."

Javi took a moment to process that news.

Izzy said, "What are you here for? No offense, Javi, but considering your age, it can't be for your brawn and exceptional digging power."

He thought about his family. Could he be here because of his family, too? As quickly as that thought came, he dismissed it. He pointed to his head. "I'm assuming my mind. I'm an engineer who used to work for the Mexican government."

"Okay," she said slowly, eyeing him. "How does Sylvia being here make sense then?"

Again, he pointed to his head. "I know, that's been nagging at the back of my mind this whole time. Maybe to make sure I follow through with their orders? As payback maybe. Honestly, I don't know."

Izzy thought for a moment. "Neither do I. What I do know, though, is my son. By now, he knows I'm being held, and he'll stop at nothing to find me. He's relentless like that. It's one of those traits he inherited from his father—God bless his soul."

Javi wanted to ask more about that, but the timing wasn't right.

She continued. "I just hope Simon is safe in all this. He . . ."

"Who's Simon?" he asked.

"My grandson. I was looking after him when they abducted me. They left him alone in the house. He's whip-smart, so I'm sure he went to the neighbors when I didn't come back. He must've been awfully scared, though."

Izzy braced herself against the sink's edge and stared straight ahead.

Javi placed his hand on her left forearm and gave a comforting squeeze. "I'm sure he's just fine, Izzy, totally safe."

After a moment, Izzy looked over at Javi. Her countenance was serious, and her eyes locked on to his.

"Promise me, Javi, promise you'll convince Raoul and Jaime to abandon their plan."

He hesitated to respond.

She grabbed him by the shoulders. "Promise me. Please, Javi."

He nodded.

She turned back to the dishes and said, "Nobody dies. We're all going to survive this; we're going to be fine."

He wasn't so sure.

Izzy must've sensed his doubt, because without looking at him, she said, "Have faith, Javi. Just have a little faith."

CHAPTER THIRTY-FOUR

"Only in Mexico," I said to Slim as the giant Sikorsky S-76 made an impromptu landing off Federal Highway 2D.

We were on the outskirts of Tecate, just a few hundred yards from Arturo's tire shop. Not even close to being a proper landing site for a helicopter, but that didn't matter in Mexico.

Slim patted me on the back as I exited. He said, "Clayton and I will take the chopper back to TJ. You can go back with him." Slim gestured in the direction of Mick Cranston, who stood by his beloved Toyota Land Cruiser, which was parked in front of Arturo's place.

After the helicopter cleared the area and I wiped myself clean of dust and dirt, I proceeded toward my buddy. Mick and I had become close friends ever since working together as partners in The Activity.

Mick leaned against his prized Land Cruiser, a two-toned blue 1977 FJ55. He fiddled with a strand of hair that had poked free of its gelled casing. Though Mick tried his best to tame his hair each morning by using a tub of hair gel, his dark hair was so thick and wavy he constantly had to fight with it to keep it in place.

I patted the Land Cruiser's hood. "You barely drive this thing in America, and you bring it out here to the Mexican desert?"

"It was built for off-roading, my friend, not cruising six-lane California freeways. This baby's in her element."

We embraced for a moment. Since Mick was a combination of muscle and sinew, his back and sides felt like they'd been wrapped in ropes. When he wasn't training Marines at Camp Pendleton South, or parenting his teenage daughters, the man hit the gym to stay in shape.

I got straight to business. "Anything suspicious at the surf camp?"

"You know I'm in the dark here, so nothing really struck me as odd. A bunch of surfers surfing and an expat running the place. Nothing seemed out of place."

Mick didn't know much about what I'd been through in the past few days. I'd kept things extremely vague during our phone call.

"Good," I said, "and I guess it doesn't matter since plans have changed and I don't think we're going back there."

Before Mick could respond, Arturo emerged from the garage.

"Lo siento, lo siento," he repeated while approaching me. "So sorry, Mister Chase, so sorry about the water." He winced. "I'm just glad you're okay. So glad. Again, so sorry."

I held up my hand. "I understand, Arturo. I know it wasn't your idea."

Relieved, his eyes lit up and he motioned me into the garage. "Come see, I have your dog. He's doing fine."

"Your dog?" Mick questioned. "What the hell is going on here? You have lots to tell me, pal."

"I certainly do."

As we walked toward the garage, I put my hand on Mick's shoulder. "We have about an hour drive back to TJ, I'll fill you in on everything then."

"Sure that's long enough?" he asked.

"Over here," Arturo said, waving toward the office.

To the left of his office door was a pile of colorful Mexican blankets. Ranger was plopped on top of them. His tail thumped as he tried to get up.

"Easy, boy," I said, sweeping in beside him. "Stay right there." I sat on the cold concrete floor beside my dog and gave his ears a good scratching. He groaned in compliance and eventually laid his head on my lap and licked my forearm.

"He's a good dog," Arturo said. "And the doctor said he'll fully recover.

He can walk a little but should stay off his hind legs for at least another two weeks."

I nodded.

Mick wasn't paying attention to Ranger. He surveyed the garage, no doubt wondering why the heck he was here and what exactly went down in this place.

"I have something else for you, Mister Chase." Arturo grinned ear to ear. "I think you'll be pleased."

He whisked into his office, opened a desk drawer, then returned to the garage absolutely beaming. In his right hand was my fake passport, burner cell, and wallet.

I was at a loss for words.

Arturo handed everything over. "What I don't understand, Mister Chase, is the passport. It's your picture but the name is different: Gary Pounds. What's your real name?"

Now Mick was finally paying attention to us. He grabbed the Canadian passport, glanced at it, then held up his hands. "Yeah, what gives, Mr. Pounds?"

I didn't address his question since I was too dumbfounded as to how Arturo had secured my possessions. "How'd you get these? I thought that thug Thiago had these items. And I thought Thiago was dead."

Arturo nodded. "A lot has happened in the last few days."

"Fill me in," I said.

"Turf war, Mister Chase. The men who were here"—he pointed to the ground—"are part of a new cartel trying to move in to the area."

"Which cartel? Jalisco? You told me before that Jalisco had already moved into Tecate, and pretty recently, too."

"*Si,*" he said as he nodded, "they have. But this cartel is different, even newer." He held up three fingers. "There are three cartels warring for control of the border area."

"And what is the newest cartel called?"

He shook his head and shrugged.

I kept up with the questions. "There's Sinaloa, Jalisco, and some new cartel warring. Is that what you're saying?"

"*Si.*"

I held up my passport, phone, and wallet. "Okay, then, how did you come into possession of these?"

"When you were passed out over there"—Arturo pointed beside the car lift—"I called my contact in Jalisco to help clean up the mess. They came and took the man I shot as well as the others, then . . ."

I waited to see if Arturo would continue, but he clearly struggled with carrying on. "It's okay, Arturo," I said, "I gather Jalisco disposed of the other men?"

After a deep breath, he nodded. "But not all the men. They wanted to send a message to the new cartel, so they kept the leader alive, the man you call Thiago. They beat him pretty good, stripped him down to his underwear, then sent him on his way." Arturo motioned to the items in my hand. "Those were on him, and I insisted on taking them. I knew you would be back because of your dog."

My mind spun as I considered this new piece of intel. It was big news. Thiago and his band of misfits were part of an up-and-coming cartel that wanted to move into the area. No doubt they also wanted to take over Sinaloa's operation with the women at Punta De Las Olas. Pieces started to fall into place.

"You okay?" Mick waved his hand in front of my face. "You're deep in thought, buddy. What's going on?" He sat down on the other side of Ranger.

I looked at Arturo. "You happen to have some tequila left?"

"Absolutely, Mister Chase. I'll get some."

When Arturo left, I turned to Mick. "A third cartel makes sense, totally. They wanted me to take out Delgado and kept pressuring me to do that. They probably preferred that in order to stay clean of any involvement in the hit. That way Sinaloa would blame Jalisco for Jimmy D's death. Jalisco would then get pissed at the accusation since they had nothing to do with it. Those two cartels would do serious damage to their numbers in battle, then the new cartel sweeps in after the carnage ends and takes over the area, including the Puntas operation. That's my best guess, anyway. And it seems our president may be taking her chances with this new cartel. Maybe she sees this as her only winning scenario. She gets rid of a notorious cartel like Sinaloa, and still keeps her beloved operation alive." I shook my head. "I don't know. Putting her in bed with any cartel just seems like a stretch, but it's plausible. I don't really know."

"No," Mick said. "I don't know. I don't know a thing, Chase. What hit? And who's this Jimmy D character, anyway?"

My thoughts stopped as I remembered that Mick had no clue about Delgado's alter persona. "Sorry, buddy. Jimmy D is who I was commissioned to take out. His real name is Juan Manuel Delgado, who you may or may not have heard of. The name I definitely know you've heard of, though, is the Butcher of Baja."

Mick's jaw dropped. A second later he recovered and said, "The president ordered a secret hit on the Butcher of Baja, a man wanted by our government for decades, and she chose you for the job? That's what's going on here?"

"That's right."

"I can't wait then," he replied, "until our car ride back to hear the full story. No way."

I nodded.

"Start talking, pal."

Before I could, Arturo walked over and handed Mick and me glasses of tequila and Jarritos soda. "Appreciate it, Arturo. Would you happen to have any food? Would love some if it isn't too much of a bother."

"No problem at all. My pleasure, Mister Chase."

Once Arturo was busy making food in his office, I brought Mick up to speed. Though he didn't say much, about halfway through the full story, Mick stood and began pacing. Over the years, I'd put Mick in some dangerous positions, so I sort of expected him to berate me when he learned everything. Surprisingly, he didn't mention a word about the danger of the mission, or about being pulled into an international conspiracy involving the president. He was, however, focused on the women in the Sierra Madre mountains.

"So we leave tonight then? To get these women, but you're not positive the Butcher will be there or your mother."

"No, not positive about either."

"How many women are we talking about, approximately?"

I sighed. "Hundreds."

Mick paced again, looking up after twenty seconds. "This is more reconnaissance then, right? 'Cause we can't get hundreds of women out of there tonight."

"Definitely reconnaissance. Hopefully we can shut down the operation when we're there. Slim's working on securing our ride for tonight, and seeing what options exist in that part of Mexico to help with extracting the women."

Just then, Arturo entered the garage holding two plates. They were piled high with rice and beans and some carne asada. The sight and smell of good food brought an end to our conversation. Arturo joined us on the garage floor as we ate.

About midway through our meal, Arturo started apologizing again. Seemingly out of nowhere.

"Lo siento, lo siento," he said, motioning toward the office. "The door was open, guys. I, I . . ."

"It's fine, Arturo. I take it you heard our conversation. Is that what you're apologizing for?"

He pinched his fingers. "Little bit, just here and there. When you mentioned the women in that operation, I couldn't help but listen in. You see, it's my niece, Mariana." He paused to take a breath.

I said, "What about your niece, Arturo?"

"Mariana joined that employment agency months ago, but my sister hasn't heard from her at all."

Mick and I exchanged glances.

Arturo swallowed. "She's sixteen, and very beautiful."

For a moment, I didn't know what to say. Eventually, I patted him on the shoulder. "If she's there, Arturo"—I motioned to Mick—"we'll bring her home. Mariana will be safe."

"You have our word," Mick added.

"Okay, thanks," Arturo said. But then he quickly shook his head. "You don't understand, though. You don't understand."

"Understand what?" I questioned.

"I want to come with you. That's why I'm telling you. Not for you to feel sorry about my situation. I want to help. I can help."

I shook both hands at him. "No, Arturo, it's far too dangerous."

"How will you communicate with these women?" he said. "My niece speaks little English, as do all the women, I imagine. Bring me along as an interpreter. Please. I'll be of use."

The look on his face was killing me. I glanced at Mick to see if he would help me out, but Mick didn't say anything. He appeared deep in thought.

"Arturo," I said, "you would indeed be helpful as an interpreter. I get that. It's just you have a family, a wife, a business. It's too dangerous. Too much risk."

He placed his hand on my shoulder. "If we don't stop this new cartel, if they succeed and push Jalisco from this area, Mister Chase, they will come for me. For killing one of their men. Right away. I won't have a family left. Not a wife, not a business. Nothing. So, please, let me help you. I want to control my own fate. *Por favor.*"

I held up a finger. "Give us a minute, Arturo." I pulled Mick outside and said, "Is it crazy to bring him? I know interpreters who have helped us out of some jams before. They've been invaluable in past missions. Between the three of us, including Slim, we don't speak much more than a few sentences of Spanish. We won't be able to explain very much to these women. What do you think?"

"Listen," he said, "you don't trust the president or Alejandro Ortiz, right?" He didn't wait for me to respond. "And we don't really know what's going on. So, the important question is: do you trust Arturo?"

I didn't think long. "I do. He's innocent, brought into this based on the location of this shop. And he has some skills, beyond speaking Spanish, that is."

"Like what?"

"Like using a Barrett REC7, and not hesitating to shoot someone."

"Fine then," Mick said. "I'm okay with it."

We walked back into the garage.

"Arturo," I said. "You're in. Are you sure you want to do this?"

He nodded, then hustled over to some storage cabinets mounted on the wall. He pulled out the Barrett. "And I kept this. Can I bring it?"

"Absolutely," Mick and I replied in unison.

CHAPTER THIRTY-FIVE

THERE WERE five of us in the spacious Sikorsky S-76, which sat idle on the Tijuana airport tarmac. Arturo, Mick, Slim, Clayton, and myself. The Sikorsky had two rows of comfy seats that faced each other. Arturo was across and to the left of me. Mick, Slim, and Clayton were near the cockpit examining aerial photographs of the Sierra Madre Oriental range.

I was in my seat with the burner cell on my right knee. I'd been eyeing the phone for quite some time, wondering what my best move was.

Eventually, Slim broke away from his group and walked over.

"What gives, buddy? We need your input."

"I should text her. Shouldn't I? I mean, why not? What do we have to lose?"

Slim looked confused, so I motioned to the burner cell. "The cell the president left for me. I was supposed to text her when the job was complete, then destroy it."

"Oh," he said, "I see. Okay, let's think about this. What do you hope to gain from texting her?"

"That's the problem. I don't know. Naïvely, I'd like her to respond and explain that she had nothing to do with all this, but . . ."

"But you don't think there's any chance she's innocent of recent events."

"We're dealing with warring cartels, Slim, a notorious terrorist, and a questionable Mexican business. I just don't see how she could be innocent of any involvement, or how she could even explain those things away. On the other hand, I have a hard time believing she's involved in any operation that would overlook the plight of these women."

"I get it, pal," he said, "totally. Remember, though, what we've learned about the politicians we've been working with, and all the things we've uncovered while investigating them. You know what I always say?"

I nodded. Slim had a few maxims he often repeated. One of his favorites spoke to me as well. "Humans have infinite capacity for self-rationalization," I said.

"What people convince themselves is okay to do is mindboggling. You and I have seen it hundreds of times, and politicians are by far the people who rationalize their actions the most."

"For the greater good, for the people," I added.

"The president could have some twisted justification for overlooking the Punta De Las Olas operation and working with a new cartel."

"You're right," I said, "she could." I thought about a few different things the president may be thinking to justify her actions. After a moment, I looked at Slim. "I'm texting her. Why not?"

Slim stared at me, mulling it over.

While he thought about the wisdom of texting the president, I said, "In my mind, one of four things will happen."

"And what are those four things?"

"One, and this is highly unlikely but at least plausible, she responds with an explanation that makes total sense, something we hadn't thought about, and it vindicates her involvement in everything."

"I'm with you," Slim replied, "that's highly unlikely to happen. What else you got?"

"She replies with some BS explanation that we immediately see through. If that happens, we know she's definitely involved."

"More likely to happen," Slim said. "What else?"

"She replies and states she has no idea what I'm talking about, feigns ignorance in the whole matter. Maybe even says we need to meet and talk about it."

"Which could be a trap," Slim pointed out.

"Absolutely."

"What's the last possibility?" he asked.

"She doesn't respond."

"Right," Slim said, nodding. "And if that happens, she's involved."

I conferred. "That's right. That's absolutely right."

We sat silent for a few moments.

Eventually, Slim broke that silence. "Don't think you have anything to lose then, buddy. In fact, I think we can only benefit from contacting her."

"Agreed."

"So." Slim motioned at the cell on my knee. "Go for it."

I typed out: *I won't do your dirty work, Henrietta. What the hell are you up to?*

Then I sent that text to the president of the United States.

Following that, I sat and stared at the phone for minutes, patiently waiting for a return text. I looked forward to seeing those three little moving dots indicating a return text was in motion.

Nothing came, however.

After staring at the phone for ten minutes, Slim pulled me away. Before long, we were in a deep planning mission that lasted hours. We constructively argued over our helicopter landing site, who would approach the building, and who would stay back and provide cover. We were three bullheaded gentlemen, so the planning phase took us into the dead of night. In the end, though, all three of us felt we had a solid plan to infiltrate the Punta De Las Olas building.

While Clayton prepared for an imminent departure, Mick did a weapons inventory check. He pulled out everything we had and used the empty seats to lay out the guns.

He motioned us over. "We have a problem, boys. A pretty big one."

Slim and I went over. "What is it?" I asked.

"Ammunition," Mick stated.

Slim sighed. "I know. It was a stretch to request the weapons before the mission, so I held back on pushing for more bullets; thought it might've raised suspicions."

"I think you did the right thing." I motioned to the weapons. There were two pistols on the seat to my left and three rifles on the seat to my right. "You secured some solid gear, Slim, that's for sure."

Mick nodded in agreement.

The two pistols were Belgium-made, a pair of FN Five-seveN semiautomatic pistols. Solid, reliable pieces. I knew they included either a ten- or twenty-round magazine. Looking at Mick, I said, "Tell me they both have the twenty-round mag."

He shook his head. "Wish I could. Both ten-round."

My shoulders sagged, but I quickly recovered and motioned to the rifles. The two Slim secured were less familiar to me, though they looked like AK-47s. "What about them?" I asked Mick.

"WASR-10s," he said. "Romanian-made semiautomatic rifles. They're a modernized variant of the AK-47. Each contains a standard thirty-round magazine."

"Older or newer models?" Slim asked.

"Worried about trigger slap?" Mick said.

Slim nodded.

Trigger slap was caused by the bolt slamming backward into the trigger assembly, which could result in incredible pain to the shooter's trigger finger.

"Fortunately, new ones," Mick responded. "The old WASR-10s, prior to 2007, were known for significant trigger slap. These ones were manufactured in 2010, so we're good to go."

I motioned to Arturo's Barrett. The standard magazine in the REC7 held thirty rounds. "What's left?"

"Twenty-four rounds."

Mick had already done the math in his head. "A total of 104 rounds, gentlemen. Not great, especially when we have no idea what's ahead for us. No clue how many security men are inside and outside the building."

I nudged Slim, who had a notoriously happy trigger finger. "Judicious use of bullets, my friend. Judicious."

He nudged me back. Considering his massive elbow, I stumbled back upon impact and collapsed into the seat behind me. "Judicious?" he said, shaking his head at me. "What were you, an English major in college?"

Before I could respond, the helicopter's blades started up and Clayton shouted back, "Take your seats, gentlemen. We're off."

Slim and Mick took their seats, and we all clipped in.

Slim sat across from me. He motioned at the burner cell. "Anything from the prez?"

Henrietta Valenzuela had most of the evening, and all night, to text me back. So far, I hadn't been alerted to a text. I checked one last time, however, just in case.

With a blank screen on the burner cell, I looked up at my buddy.

"Nothing, pal. Not a word."

We both knew what that meant. I didn't verbalize it, but Slim did.

He shook his head. "She's involved, the president of the United States is definitely involved."

CHAPTER THIRTY-SIX

WE ARRIVED at the Sierra Madre Oriental range slightly before 3:00 a.m. Clayton dropped the four of us off on the backside of the two mountains that faced the replica Punta De Las Olas building.

Mick, Slim, and I felt it necessary to land the helicopter on the backside of the mountains to avoid detection. It meant a longer trip to the building than we'd first anticipated. Which was just fine with us. With limited ammunition, the reconnaissance mission relied on stealth. Our mission was simple: confirm the occupants of the building. If we could confirm that women from the Crossroads operation were inside, Mick believed he'd have leverage with his superiors to send in a rescue squad.

Since we had the cover of night, the four of us took a high elevation route around the eastern mountain. The eastern and western sides of the Sierra Madres contained a combination of subtropical pine and oak forests. The higher elevation meant less trees, so we were able to travel much quicker and make up some time. Once the building neared, about a half hour before dawn, we dropped into the thick forest, then split up.

I was currently flanking the east side of the building while Mick flanked the west side. Mick and I carried the Five-seveN pistols. He also had one of the WASR-10s strapped to his back.

Since the building was V-shaped, it had the footprint of a giant triangle. The point of the V faced straight north, and I imagined the big room with all the windows, when the blinds were open, had a great view of the two mountains in the daytime. Or perhaps the forest at this elevation was too dense, and all that the windows revealed was a tangle of fat, mossy trees.

Slim and Arturo had the other two rifles, and their job was to provide cover. They hunkered down on either side of the V while Mick and I snuck around to the south side where the building's entry was located.

From the V's point to the glass entryway at the rear of the building took me about fifteen minutes of creeping. I could barely see ten feet in front of me, so most of my strained looking was directed toward the ground, being careful not to step on something and alert to my position. Along the way I spotted no security men. All was eerily quiet. So quiet, in fact, I could hear my heart thumping over top of my shallow breathing.

With the glass doors just barely visible to my eye, I tiptoed in to get a better look. As I approached, I scanned the top of the building, searching for a flood light or motion sensor or video camera mounted somewhere. But I found nothing. As far as I knew, the eastern side of the building was secure, deserted and void of people, lights, or any cameras.

You'd think I would've been relieved at that fact.

I wasn't.

To me, that meant one of two things. Either this was a trap and men were waiting inside, or the building was deserted. Which meant the women had been taken from this location, and the Butcher and Mom weren't here. And that meant our trip was in vain.

I crept back and stowed myself about fifty feet from the entrance, crouched down in a thicket of dense bushes. Approximately five minutes later, I heard Mick's subtle approach. We'd agreed to meet on this side and compare notes.

Once I confirmed it was Mick, and not an animal or security man on patrol, I stood and waved him over.

He crouched into the bush beside me. "Well?"

"Nothing," I whispered. "Whole side is deserted, not a person in sight. Definitely no security patrolling the perimeter, and I couldn't spot any security features on the building."

He looked down and shook his head. "Me neither. The other bad news"—he held up his cell—"is no signal. The last reception I had was on the other side of the mountain. I don't like this, buddy, not one bit."

"Me neither."

"What now?"

"We go in. You know we have to, right?"

"I know." Mick sighed. "We definitely have to, in case those women are inside. I just don't want to."

My buddy pulled out one of four Motorola SABER handheld radios he'd brought along on the mission. I had one in my back pocket. Slim and Clayton had the other two.

"We're going in," Mick quietly said into the radio. "Need you to shift. One of you needs to cover the glass entry."

A moment later, Slim's voice said, "Copy. Moving now."

As Mick and I proceeded to the glass doors, I said, "Looked like a pretty standard pin-and-tumbler lock on the glass door. You bring your tools?"

Mick patted one of his pants pockets. "Always."

At the door, Mick pulled out a tension wrench and a couple different-sized picks. I turned and faced the forest while he worked on the lock.

It took him just under a minute to open the door.

Once inside, Mick and I crept slowly through the lobby. I took the lead since I knew the layout of the building from the video I'd studied. Mick stopped me before I got too far in front.

"Remember," he whispered, motioning at my outstretched gun, "conserve."

I nodded. "I'm only firing if my life depends on it. Or yours."

I kept moving, working in reverse order of the video. The first room I checked was the pill room. The room where I'd seen the large whiteboard outlining all the women's dosages.

Nothing there. No people, and by all looks, no pills either.

The next few rooms I checked I swear I held my breath. We didn't dare turn on any lights, so every door I opened I expected to be ambushed. Either shot at or charged at. At any second, I expected to hear the staccato of gunfire, which would, unfortunately, be directed at me.

But I didn't find, or even hear, a soul on the ground floor. Mick checked all the rooms on the left side, and I checked all the ones on the right. We reconvened in the large V-shaped room with all the windows, which was currently being used as the women's dining room. The tables were bare and empty, so no signs of a recent meal.

"Where to now?" he asked.

I pointed to the door behind him. "That leads down below to where they keep the women they're pumping full of drugs."

He hustled over, then quickly turned back before I reached the door. "It's open," he said. "I don't trust open doors."

"Me neither," I whispered.

Mick opened the door and beckoned me down. "You first."

I nodded and headed down the dark stairs, the pistol leading me forward. At the bottom of the stairs, the heavy steel door into the hospital ward area was locked, but Mick had it opened in forty-five seconds.

The fourth ward—the one I'd seen on the video where the women were unchained and freely moving about the four rooms—was empty. After we cleared the rooms, we turned on the lights. Though we found no women, we found signs of recent life. The rooms were a mess. Trash was strewn all over the place. The garbage cans were overflowing with various food wrappers and tissues and toilet paper and water bottles. The amount of trash in the ward suggested there were many more women than the thirty or so I'd seen in this area on the video.

Mick had the next door open in under thirty seconds.

The third ward was empty, too. That was our sense as soon as we stepped into the area. The place was dark and eerily quiet, and it was also full of trash. Once we cleared the four rooms, Mick and I walked back toward the door we'd come through and flipped on the hallway light.

Within seconds of the shining light, we heard a sound. We immediately looked at each other.

"What was that?" Mick said.

I held up my finger and strained to listen. The sound grew louder with each passing second.

"Murmuring," I said to Mick. "Sounds like people murmuring."

He nodded but didn't say a word.

The hallway in front of us was about fifty or sixty feet long, so we slowly paced our way toward the next steel door. Instinctively, when I stepped forward, Mick didn't. Then vice-versa. We cautiously approached the next door alternating our steps. Though it felt like it took five minutes, it was probably more like thirty seconds. All I focused on was listening.

"Lots of murmuring," I said.

At five feet from the door, I turned to Mick. "Like hundreds murmuring together."

He nodded in agreement.

We sidestepped and shuffled the last few feet toward the door. We both leaned forward and turned our heads. My left ear led me forward. Mick's right ear led him forward.

A foot from the door, our eyes met as we deciphered the voices.

Women, I mouthed to Mick.

He blinked and held it for a second, then opened his eyes and nodded in agreement.

My countenance dropped when I deciphered a few Spanish words: water and food. Plus, I also heard the words, *please, please, please*. Over and over. *Por favor, por favor, por favor.*

Following that, I heard some light pounding on the door, I turned to Mick and motioned to the pocket where he kept his lock-picking tools.

"We have to open the door, buddy, but . . ."

Suddenly fear took hold, and I couldn't finish my sentence. I sensed that Mick understood my fears, too. Perhaps this was a trap. Perhaps some men were present with the women. And as soon as we opened the door, we'd get mowed down. Or perhaps we'd cause chaos when the women on the other side saw two white men armed to the teeth.

I needed a second to think.

"Stand back," Mick said, pulling me back from the door. "We could take direct fire any second. It could be a trap."

The light pounding on the door turned fierce. Then the murmuring turned to hysteria. Our eyes were drawn to the floor. Multiple sets of fingers protruded under the steel door. In the light, each bony finger stretched and wiggled in desperation.

I swallowed and tried to clear the massive lump in my throat.

Mick turned to me with wide eyes. "What's our plan here?"

I grabbed my handheld radio. Considering the noise coming from the other side of the door, I didn't need to be discreet and whisper.

I shouted into the receiver, "Slim, get Arturo down here."

"Copy that, buddy."

"Now, pal. I mean, like right this second."

CHAPTER THIRTY-SEVEN

MICK BACKTRACKED to the receptionist area to intercept Arturo and lead him to the basement.

I waited in the hallway of the third ward, far back from the steel door. Though the pounding and screaming reached new heights, I spent the five minutes it took for Arturo to arrive blocking the noises out. I focused on what I wanted Arturo to communicate to these women before opening the door.

But Arturo didn't wait for me. He didn't even listen to me when I yelled at him to stop.

He brushed by me and proceeded to the steel door without so much as a pause. More than likely, Mick had brought him up to speed and coached him on what to say.

So, I let it go, then moved forward to listen to what he was saying.

Once Arturo began shouting at the door, it only took a few moments for the hysteria to subside. Though I was not well-versed in Spanish, I could immediately tell that Arturo was calling out for his niece. He kept repeating the name Mariana. Each time he said her name I assumed he was describing her features. He also kept mentioning his own name.

Eventually, I interrupted and asked Arturo to inquire about my mom, then I described her to Arturo. He spent some time inquiring about Izzy, to no avail, then transitioned back to asking for Mariana.

After a few minutes, I grew impatient and approached him.

"Arturo, Mariana may or may not be in there. We must move on. You need to—"

"No, Mister Chase," he interrupted. "She's inside, she's coming to the door." He nodded excitedly. "She obviously trusts me, and I trust her, so we'll know what's going on soon."

Since that made sense, I stepped back and let him do his thing.

He turned back and said, "I'm sorry, Mister Chase, but your mother isn't in there, it seems. There are no white women, unfortunately."

I nodded.

Mick and I listened and tried to decipher the quick conversation Arturo was having with his niece from behind the door. When Arturo finally turned back to address us, Mick and I leaned forward.

"There is a man in there," he said, "one man." Arturo held up a finger.

"I knew it," Mick said. "I knew it."

"No," Arturo said, shaking his head. "Not what you think. He's..." Arturo struggled with the English word. I noticed he'd grabbed his wrist and kept his hand clamped there while looking up at us and stammering.

"He's cuffed," I said. I thought of the women on the video. "Or chained? Or both."

"*Si, si.*" Arturo nodded quickly.

Mick and I exchanged a glance.

Mick spoke first. "We're going to open the doors, Arturo. Let them know we're armed but not a threat."

"No problem," Arturo replied. "They know we're here to help."

Mick worked on the lock.

I stood back and dropped the Five-seveN to my side. I didn't tuck it away since I wanted to confirm with my own eyes that there was only one man inside, and that he was chained or cuffed and not a threat.

When Mick had disengaged the lock, he stepped back and joined me.

Arturo told the women to be calm. "Tranquillo, tranquillo," he repeated, then opened the door.

Several women immediately burst into the hallway. Arturo and his niece embraced amidst the chaos. Dozens of women rushed over to Mick and me, totally unfazed by our weapons. They touched us and gushed and murmured their praise. The other hundred women behind the first wave held back. They didn't rush us, though they stood together en masse in the hallway, staring at us with wide eyes.

The women looked sick. Pale and sweaty and shaky, a far cry from how they looked on the ground floor during the footage Ortiz had shot. It didn't take much guesswork to realize these women were abandoned and now in the first stages of withdrawal after months of forced, drug-induced "therapy."

Mariana waved us over. Arturo didn't get a chance to introduce us since Mariana immediately headed down the hallway and beckoned us to follow. The throngs of women parted until we came to the second room on the right.

I motioned for Arturo to hold back while Mick and I flanked the door. Though I took the far side of the door, I didn't see inside while passing the threshold since several women were still vacating the room.

Mariana shook her head and told us to enter. "*No problema.*" She repeated that twice and waved at us to put our guns down.

After a quick glance inside, Mick and I stuffed our weapons away and entered.

Indeed, there was only one man in the room. And, like the women I'd seen in Ortiz's video, the man was handcuffed to the bed, and the bed was chained to the floor. He was passed out or unconscious, but not dead. I could see his chest slightly rising with each breath. He had an IV in his right arm. The pole beside his bed held two IV bags, one full, the other half-empty. Though it was clear-looking fluid in the IV bags, I guessed it was not a simple saline solution.

The man's face was beaten and swollen, so I didn't recognize him. That is, until I approached the bedside and got a solid look.

The lump in my throat was back.

Mick, of course, stood there with a blank look on his face. He looked over at me. "Take it you know this guy, pal? 'Cause you look like you've seen a ghost. You're as pale as these women."

I nodded.

"Who is he?" Mick prodded.

After swallowing and pushing out the breath I'd been holding, I said, "That, my friend, is Juan Manuel Delgado. You're looking at the infamous Butcher of Baja, Mick."

CHAPTER THIRTY-EIGHT

NOT SURE HOW long I stood there staring at the Butcher's face.

Though his face had taken a beating, I'd seen enough pictures of him to know without a doubt the Butcher was the man chained to this bed. Plus, I'd caught a momentary look at Delgado's face through my variable, high-powered scope not long ago, so his mug was fresh in my mind.

But I didn't have long to dwell on what the Butcher of Baja beaten and unconscious and cuffed to this bed meant. Because Slim's voice crackled on the radio in my back pocket.

"We've got a problem," he said.

That snapped me out of it. Mick was on attention, too. He stared at the radio in my left hand.

"Arturo," I said, "can you clear the room?"

Arturo complied. It didn't take him long since there were only a few stray women inside. He shut the door, keeping himself and Mariana inside with me and Mick. I was about to tell him to let his niece out but thought better of it. He didn't look like he'd ever part from her side.

"Go ahead," I said into the radio.

"Sounds approaching," Slim replied. "Men are out there. Coming in fast on foot. Not even being careful. Stepping on branches and scuffing rocks. Multiple footsteps."

"How many exactly?" I asked.

"Can't tell yet. Will know soon, though. Sun is just coming up."

"Where's the approach coming from?"

"Directly south," he replied.

I looked at Mick.

He said, "I knew it. This was a trap." He pointed at Delgado. "All of it, a trap to lure us down here. We gotta move. We're in terrible position. The worst."

And that was an understatement, though I didn't dare say it since I didn't want to freak out Arturo and Mariana even more. I gathered, however, that Mariana couldn't understand the conversation. She repeatedly asked Arturo for an explanation, and Arturo reluctantly replied.

After his explanation, Arturo asked, "What do we do with the women?"

My mind was already tracing out an emergency plan. I stepped over and conferred with Mick for a minute, then addressed Arturo. "We'll go topside and assess the threat. Can you and Mariana stay back and keep the women down here? We need them calm and quiet."

He nodded.

"Let's move them to the next ward," I said. "There are stairs that lead to an outer door. If we can neutralize the outside threat, we can let them out. Then Mick can call in help when we're on the other side of the mountain."

I turned to my buddy. "Can you open the next two doors, then join me upstairs?"

He was off before giving a response.

I hustled back through the wards we'd come through, stopping when I reached the main-floor dining room. That was when I pulled out the radio and asked for an update.

"Not going to like it," Slim replied.

"Go ahead," I said. "Give it to me straight."

"So far I've counted six men."

Six?

"And more are coming," he added. "The tally keeps going up every few seconds."

More? "What are they doing?" I asked.

"Spreading out near the entrance, spacing out about thirty yards from one another."

I winced but asked anyway. "And they're carrying?"

"Oh, yeah," he replied. "Can't tell the makes or models, but definitely AR-style rifles."

I squeezed the handheld as my mind calculated the layout of the building. There were only two exits from the replica Punta De Las Olas building. The main glass doors at the entrance, and the side door that led down to the first ward. And both were on the building's south side.

"We're screwed," I said to Slim. "They're spreading out and covering the only exits. They'll mow us down when we attempt to vacate."

"Copy that. We'll have to lay down massive cover fire to get you guys out. I can blaze and keep them from popping you on exit, but you three will have to fire everything you have at them to make it to cover, to stand a chance."

"Copy. Then we're out of rounds and will have to run for it. Use the forest as coverage."

There were a few silent moments between us.

I shook off my spiraling thoughts and crept toward the reception area. Since that space was floor-to-ceiling glass, I stayed low on approach. As I neared the entrance, I pressed my body against the outside-facing wall and got down on my belly.

From the floor, I peered outside and strained my eyes toward the trees. Unfortunately, I was too far away and at a bad angle, so I couldn't get a good view into the foliage to spot any men. I shuffled back on my elbows and asked Slim for another update.

"Eleven," he said in a whisper. "I've identified eleven men spread out thirty yards apart."

My head dropped between my shoulders.

"And they're engaged," Slim added. "I repeat, weapons engaged."

My mind raced for a new plan. "Stay in position, pal. We're regrouping inside."

"Copy."

I retraced my steps, meeting up with Mick as he climbed the steps to the main floor.

He held up his radio. "I heard. Eleven? Beyond bad. Beyond, pal."

"Agreed. We can't go out either exit. It's a death sentence. A half dozen men, maybe we survive, but not eleven. No way."

"How do we get out then?"

I started descending the stairs. "I've got an idea."

He shouted after me, but I kept going, not stopping until I returned to the room that held Delgado. When Mick was inside, I again asked Arturo to shut the door. He complied and kept Mariana with us.

Arturo spoke first since I was catching my breath. "Bad, Mister Chase?"

I nodded. "Too many men, Arturo, far too many."

Mariana's face grew concerned as she could tell I was delivering bad news.

"What do we do then?" Arturo asked. His eyes were huge and wide, and his creased brow was as deep as a trench.

"Our best chance," I replied, "is to get help. Bring help back for the women." I looked at Mick.

Mick reluctantly nodded. He'd already done the risk analysis in his head, just like I had. Leaving with the women was a surefire way to get them killed. And us, too. Leaving them inside until we could bring help was the slightly better option of two terrible ones.

"Who gets help?" Arturo asked. "Who goes?"

"We all can," I replied, circling my hand to include the four of us. "Though it's best if someone stays behind with the women."

"You sure we all can't leave?" Arturo inquired.

"Eleven men," Mick replied. "Eleven are out there, Arturo."

"And they're heavily armed," I added. "Perhaps with enough ammunition to kill us all."

There was a moment of pause as Arturo processed the gravity of the situation. He turned and quickly filled Mariana in. Eventually, he turned back and said, "I'll stay with the women. I'm not abandoning them. No way."

Another brief pause.

I broke the silence and tried to stay positive. "They didn't kill the women prior to our arrival, Arturo, and they could have. They certainly could have. They probably just want Mick and me. Hopefully we'll draw the eleven away. Hopefully they won't care enough about the women to come back."

He didn't seem encouraged by that. And I wasn't buying it much either.

"You hunker down with them," I added, "lock yourselves in the next ward. We'll get out and bring help back as quick as we can."

"I saw there was some food and water in the next ward," Mick said. "Enough to tide you over until my team comes."

Courageously, Arturo nodded.

Mick held up his cell phone. "I took brief video of the women, and I'll send it to my commanding officer as soon as I can get a cell signal. That's proof enough to get an American team here from the Camp Pendleton base where I'm stationed, especially since these women are part of Crossroads. You keep these women calm and safe until they arrive. Got it?"

"*Si,*" he replied.

"Both doors, on either end of the ward, stay locked." I stared at Arturo, then motioned toward the REC7 still in his possession. "You keep that and protect the women with it."

Mick came up behind me and touched me on the shoulder. I knew he was concerned about leaving a weapon behind since we needed as much firepower as we could get to survive our exfiltration. I turned and held his gaze but didn't say anything. After a moment, he nodded.

I walked over and placed my hand on Arturo's shoulder.

He spoke before I could. "Go. Go get help, Mister Chase. I'll protect them. Or die trying."

"You're a good man," I said. "A very good man, Arturo."

Mick nudged me. "We gotta move. What's your plan for getting out?"

I motioned at Delgado. "We need to take him with us."

"You can't be serious," Mick stated.

"I am. We need to take him; we need him alive. And he can help us get out of here. Just trust me, no time to explain."

Mick hesitated.

"Help me with his cuff," I said, walking over to Delgado's bedside.

"You sure?" Mick asked.

"Positive."

"Fine," he replied, "but I'm not wasting a bullet shooting the cuff off."

"Agreed." I walked over and pried off a metal drawer handle from one of the dressers in the room. Then I used that as leverage against the end of the cuff that was linked to the bed frame.

Meanwhile, Mariana rushed to the Butcher's side and extracted the IV from his right arm.

Mick and I took turns cranking on the bed frame until it broke. Then we were able to slide the cuff free. He was about to grab the unconscious body and sling it over his shoulder.

I stopped him. "I'll take him. Can you lock the door by the stairwell?"

While Mick rushed off to do that, Arturo helped me get Delgado into a fireman carry across my shoulders.

As I hustled down the hallway with the unconscious body, I tried not to make eye contact with the women. By the time I approached the door into the second ward, the murmuring in the hallway had reached its peak. It seemed the women were rapidly catching on to what was happening.

I pivoted back, just for a moment, and saw Mick fighting his way through the throngs of stressed-out faces. Arturo was behind me and tried his best to keep the women back. I believe he was telling them that we would be back soon, and to stay calm.

Mick caught up with me just a few feet from the door, but the crowd was advancing fast on us. Arturo was now screaming for everyone to be *tranquillo*. For everyone to stay back.

But no one was listening.

We sprinted the final two feet and cleared the door's threshold, moments before the crowd did. I pitched Delgado's body into the open hallway as Mick wheeled the door shut. Or at least tried to. Women slammed against the other side before it fully closed.

By that point, I'd spun and exploded both hands against the door to help Mick. We gained a few inches of closure, but then started to lose ground.

The whole time this was happening I could feel the handheld in my back pocket crackling to life. But there was too much commotion and noise for me to make out Slim's muffled voice.

Women's arms now extended into the door's opening. Mick and I leaned all our weight into the door. These desperate, emaciated hands and sinewy forearms reached out to us.

The sight was devastating. A knot in my stomach tightened by the second. I had to peel my gaze away. I closed my eyes and pushed with everything in me.

More women must've piled against the door because we started losing more ground. Second by second, the door inched open further and further. More arms reached out to us in desperation. I envisioned these women succeeding, stampeding down the open hallway, clamoring up the stairs, then heading to the exit they were familiar with.

Only to be slaughtered by gunfire.

I turned and rammed my back into the door, dug my boots into the polished floor as hard as I could. Mick followed suit. We gripped our thighs with both hands and fought to stay stationery.

Meanwhile, the radios in our back pockets kept squawking.

Since we hadn't answered the previous calls, Slim's voice suddenly shouted. Even though the radios were mashed against the door, Slim's voice was so loud there was no mistaking his words. Not now.

"RPG!" he screamed. "RPG! *Incoming!*"

And then a topside explosion rocked our world.

CHAPTER THIRTY-NINE

THE EXPLOSION WAS DEAFENING, and the whole building shook for a moment.

Naturally, the blast startled us, but not enough that we cowered and dropped to the ground in fear. After impact, Mick and I instantly felt the pressure on the door give way. No doubt most of the women had dropped and taken cover.

With our backs still pressed against the door, it slammed shut within seconds of the blast. Wasting no time, I heaved Delgado across my shoulders and hustled through the next ward. Mick closed and locked that final door behind me.

We paused at the bottom of the stairs and listened to an update from Slim.

"One of the men stepped out from the trees with a launcher on his shoulder. The RPG took out the entire glass entrance."

"They in the building yet?" Mick asked.

"Negative. They're regrouping. Won't be long, though."

With that, we got moving. At the top of the stairs, I needed a moment to gather my breath since I'd just climbed the steps in record time with a body draped across my shoulders.

"What now?" Mick asked.

I motioned at the dining room, toward the array of floor-to-ceiling windows. "There's our exit." After another deep exhale, I said, "Slim rotates back, covers us as we smash through the window and hustle to the tree line. Then we run for our lives."

I maneuvered Delgado until his back and rear end faced in front of me, then I tapped his backside. "He's gonna take the impact through the glass. I think we keep the fabric blinds closed to minimize any cuts."

Mick nodded. "As long as you leave this monster on the other side of the broken glass."

I shook my head. "We can't, Mick."

"Really?"

"We need him. We need his intel to piece everything together. And my guess is he knows something about Mom's whereabouts. Plus, for all we know, these men could be here for him, and not us. I mean, we saw zero cameras and arrived here unplanned and unannounced. The arrival of these men could be coincidental. Maybe they were already on their way to kill him or rescue him on a predawn mission. Who knows?"

"Neither of us believe in coincidence," Mick stated.

"True, but that doesn't mean these men are only here for us. And if they need Delgado, dead or alive, taking him away from this place protects the women."

Mick sighed, knowing I could be right.

"Taking him to the helicopter might draw these men away from the building. It may save hundreds of lives, Mick."

Slim interrupted us with, "Men approaching! Permission to engage."

"Negative," I said. "Pull back and cover the V. We're going through the windows."

"Wilco," Slim replied.

"Time to move." Mick pointed his gun at one of the lowest windows. "Take the lower-left window. I'll double-tap the glass right before you crash through. Depending on the glass type, that should smash it or at least weaken it where the rounds penetrate."

I nodded. "It's worth two bullets."

I moved into position, about forty feet from the window, enough for me to gain maximum speed before the crash.

"I'll take your six after impact," Mick said. "Unless you're winded and need me to carry the body, then you cover my six."

"I'll be fine. I'll give it my everything to the tree line, then we'll switch, and I'll cover you. Let's rotate the body between the three of us, maybe five-minute shifts each, until we reach the helicopter."

"I like it."

"We should refrain from firing a single shot once we're in the forest. Use trees for coverage and conserve every bullet. Then use everything left to protect us while boarding the helicopter. Taking out the man with the rocket-propelled grenade is top priority."

Just as Mick nodded, Slim was back on the radio telling us he was in position.

Mick and I tapped fists, then I was off, pumping my legs as hard as I could while my two hands gripped the sides of Delgado's belt. Mick waited until I was approximately ten feet from the window to fire.

The glass didn't shatter. But I did hear it crack.

At two feet away, I heaved Delgado directly at the spot where Mick's bullets had torn through the blinds. Then I followed the body, crouching and protecting my head from behind Delgado's pancaking body.

We crashed through a tangle of blinds and shattered glass, which rained down on my head and sprinkled across my back. Since Delgado's body was dead weight, he flopped straight down on the either side of the shattered window. I stumbled over his midsection and collapsed onto the dirt ground.

Mick kicked through a jagged piece of remaining glass, then stepped out and pointed both his weapons toward the tree line. I scrambled backward and lifted Delgado over my shoulder while Mick popped a few cover shots.

Following Mick's shots, bullets zipped by us.

"*Move! Move!*" Mick encouraged me.

Suddenly Slim joined in the fracas by blitzing the tree line to my left. I angled toward the spot I saw his muzzle flash. When Slim paused on the trigger, Mick took over with a few shots of his own.

But when he finished, a volley of bullets sprayed back, kicking up the dirt around our feet. I felt at least one bullet had connected on my left side. Fortunately, that bullet tore into Delgado, and not me. Of course, I was running for my life and had no time to inspect where it had penetrated his lower body.

Mick ran to my left side. By this point, my chest heaved, and I fought for every breath. The lactic acid in my legs burned; it felt like an elephant was on my shoulders, driving my feet into the ground.

Mick's eyes met mine, just for a fraction of a second. "Go! Go!" he shouted, waving frantically toward Slim's position. "We're so close."

Slim was only twenty yards away. He'd moved out from behind a large pine tree to show me his exact position. Adrenaline spiked and I screamed atop my lungs, willing my legs to move faster. Maybe it worked. Maybe it didn't. There was a lot of fatigue in my body, so I had no idea if I gained any speed with the guttural shout.

To protect my final lunge into the forest, Mick stopped running and pivoted. He unloaded a few rounds into the trees where the shots were coming from. Not exactly what we had planned—conserving our ammunition—but firing those final few bullets may have saved my life.

Seeing Mick covering me, Slim dropped his rifle and beckoned me behind the tree. I staggered the last few steps toward him. He came along my left side and immediately grabbed Delgado's bloody, dangling legs and threw them over his head. Then I slid the rest of his body onto Slim's massive shoulders.

"Who's this?" Slim asked.

"The Butcher," I said.

His eyes bulged, then he pointed to the WASR on the ground. "Grab the rifle."

As I picked it up, Mick sprinted into the forest and blew past us, all the while circulating his arms to get us going. "Move! Move!" he yelled.

Slim was already trudging forward with Delgado on his shoulders. I followed suit, sneaking a quick glance behind me. Though I saw no one, I heard and saw rounds coming at us. Bullets either zipped by or sunk into tree trunks with a near silent plunk. The forest was our only hope. Dodging tree-to-tree was our one chance at making it to the helicopter alive.

"Conserve," I yelled to my buddies in front of me.

Mick and Slim had spread out some distance. They'd decided not to follow each other in anything close to a straight line. Which was smart since it would divide the shots from the men behind us. If we grouped together, it would be easier for them to pick us off.

So, I spread the pack out farther, choosing different trees to dodge between. We moved forward like that for a solid ten minutes. Incredulously, Slim didn't slow down, turn back once, or ask to be relieved. But after ten minutes of running and dodging and nearly being shot, I was the one who broke the conservation rule.

I had to.

The men chasing us quickly learned we weren't counter attacking. Since we didn't fire a single shot behind us in those ten minutes, our pursuers gained ground. I knew they'd made progress because I could hear their voices behind me, along with their fast footsteps.

Being the farthest back, I stopped and took stock of the situation while peeking out from behind a huge oak tree.

Damn!

My eyes ballooned when I spotted two men only forty yards away. The eleven men had sent their two fastest runners ahead to catch us. Fortunately, the fact that we hadn't fired back meant that these two weren't being as cautious as they should be.

I spun and pressed my back against the big tree, took three slow and steady breaths, lulling the two men closer. My past missions—not to mention all the years of training—prepared me for the moment. Though I hadn't been in a situation like this for some time, or practiced at an action pistol range in years, the muscle memory was there.

I felt it. Though I was being hunted, I was calm and controlled.

Completely hidden from view, I teetered the WASR-10 against the tree and eased the pistol from behind my back. Then I suddenly spun fast to my right, simultaneously drawing the Five-seveN to shoulder level.

The two men were maybe fifteen yards apart. Both had just stepped out from behind their respective tree. Neither had been advancing with their weapons outstretched. Both AR-style rifles were down at their side.

Their mistake.

I tagged the man to my left first, a direct forehead shot. Then I swung right and tapped the other man in the chest. Before the second body had dropped to the forest floor, I'd turned and grabbed the rifle.

With the lead chasers out of the way, I beelined it in the direction of Mick and Slim, no longer darting between the trees as cover. Just sprinting like a madman.

Unfortunately, I'd lost sight of Slim and Mick, but only for about thirty seconds. They'd paused their advance behind a large bush, waiting for me.

No doubt they'd heard the double-pop of the Five-seveN pistol. When I approached them, I saw they'd transferred Delgado onto Mick's shoulders.

I waved them ahead, yelling, "Two down! Keep moving! Move!"

Mick spun and was off. Slim gave me the thumbs-up but waited for me. Without stopping, I handed him the WASR-10 and proceeded forward. As I did, I could hear Slim behind me contacting Clayton on his radio.

Then, about a minute later, after gaining good ground, I heard a sound I wish I hadn't: the distinctive whoosh of an RPG. Turning toward Slim, I witnessed him tumble onto the ground as two large trees growing together, about twenty feet to his right, took the brunt of a rocket-propelled grenade.

A deafening explosion filled the quiet forest. Following that, the two trees toppled to the ground into a tangled mess. Then the burning and crackling of fire roared to life.

"You okay?" I yelled toward Slim while circling back to his position. "*You okay?* Talk to me, buddy."

Mick had circled back, too.

I helped Slim to his feet and repeated my question.

"I'm fine," he said, "totally fine. No injuries. None that I'm aware of."

Fortunately, there was lots of dirt, smoke, and fire in the air from the explosion at the tree base, so we quickly moved behind the blast site to take cover. After a quick once-over to make sure Slim wasn't bleeding, I stepped away from the blast area and looked back. Immediately I saw three men advancing quickly, approximately seventy-five yards away.

"We gotta move," I said.

"Change of plans," Slim said, catching his breath.

"What change of plans?" Mick shot back.

"We'll never make it to the backside of the mountain, not at this rate, not with nine men chasing us while carrying that body. Not without serious fire-power covering our ass."

"What then?" I asked.

"Been in contact with Clayton. He's been circling the area, looking for a closer spot to land. He's found a relatively clear area a few hundred yards that way." Slim pointed behind himself. "You two divert the men that direction." He pointed to our right. "I'll use this diversion to sneak off to the clearing undetected. When you've drawn the men far enough away, I'll call in the bird."

When he paused, Mick said, "Then what?"

"I'll take the Butcher with me, Clayton will pick the both of us up, then we'll head your direction. There's a rescue long line in the helicopter you guys can use. Clayton spotted a thick canopy in the direction you'll be headed, about half a click from here. He'll stay above the canopy and drop the line down. Then we'll pull you both up and out and get you to a safe landing spot. Unfortunately, it's not a rescue helicopter, so there's no winch to pull up the rope."

"That's okay," I said, "at least a thick canopy will make it hard for the RPG to take out the helicopter."

"Exactly," Slim said.

"Cover us from the air," Mick said, handing Slim his WASR-10. "With both rifles. Use every single round. I won't be able to effectively use the WASR with one hand on the long line. Chase and I will be able to use the pistols, though."

I nodded.

As Slim slung the two rifles in front of him, he also nodded.

I helped transfer Delgado from Mick's shoulders to Slim's. Then my big buddy charged off toward the direction of the clearing.

"Just hang on, gents," he yelled after us. *"Hang on!"*

With the men approaching, Mick and I had no time to talk, so we took off to our right. As soon as we emerged from the blast site, we no longer had cover from the smoke and fire. That was when the onslaught began.

The rat-a-tat of semiauto rifles roared over the sound of two trees burning.

Mick and I literally ran for our lives, crouching and dodging and using every trick we could think of to stay alive. We'd spread out, approximately fifty yards apart. We made sure we were on a staggered plane and not in line with one another. We also moved from tree to tree at the same time, that way our chasers would have to choose which person to fire at, effectively dividing the bullets that were sent our way.

Everything in me wanted to turn and fire shots to cover Mick when he was on the move. I knew Mick felt the same way because every minute he'd turn back to check up on me, making sure I hadn't been hit or fallen behind.

Unfortunately, we didn't have the firepower to cover each other, so we simply pressed on and managed to survive the half-kilometer trek. The only positive of not firing back was that we gained some ground on the men behind us.

Because of the lighting, I knew we'd arrived at the area Clayton had spotted. There was a denser canopy above us, so the morning sun didn't penetrate as much. Mick sensed it as well. I watched him pause behind a tree and pull out his radio. We were on the same channel, of course, so I could hear their conversation. I could also hear the helicopter's rotor blades between pauses of gunfire.

Slim and the pilot were close.

I knew Mick had a tactical watch with GLONASS, a Russian satellite-based navigation system that worked alongside GPS. Using the additional satellites that GLONASS offered, it was faster to get your position than GPS alone. I listened to Mick feed the coordinates to Clayton, then I watched my buddy wave me over.

After a cautious approach, Mick and I strategized.

He said, "I'll go up the rope first, about halfway, so we can spread out on the line. You take the bottom of the rope and tie a foothold. We'll do this as soon as Slim starts firing."

"I can climb, too, pal, and give you the foothold."

"No offense, my friend," he said, "but when was the last time you climbed a rope?"

I paused on my response.

"Right," he continued, "so I'm climbing. Once we're solid on the line, we fire every round on our way up and through the canopy."

Just then, about seventy-five yards south of our position, I saw the long line drop to the forest floor. I pointed. "Let's move, get as much distance as possible."

Mick nodded and was off. We threw caution to the wind and raced directly to the dangling rope. Above us was a slight break in the canopy, so I could see the hovering helicopter. Slim was kneeling at the open doors with both rifles at his side. At the ready.

The break in canopy would allow us to be pulled straight up without getting raked by branches. But the break was also dangerous if our pursuers got close to this position. All they'd have to do was aim straight up and take out the helicopter.

The sounds of incoming bullets got us moving. The rounds sprayed the surrounding trees. Immediately Slim started firing the WASR-10s.

Upon hearing that, Mick tucked the pistol in the back of his pants and hopped on to the rope, slinking his way upward. While he did that, I bent down, grabbed the rope's tail end and tied a quick loop for my foot. While grasping above me, I motioned to Slim, who'd paused on the trigger, to started lifting us up.

Seconds later, we lifted off the ground.

At that moment, Mick and I unleashed some rounds toward the approaching men, who we could now see about a hundred yards away.

The ascent was terrifyingly slow. I knew the helicopter had to rise cautiously, otherwise the long line would sway and potentially knock us into the surrounding trees and branches.

Dangling like that, with a slight sway, was far from the ideal shooting position. And our pursuers knew it. They suddenly broke free from their cautious approach and started sprinting toward our position.

I let them have it. Each time I pulled the trigger, I counted down my remaining bullets. Mick and I both focused on the lead man to our right: the man holding the RPG. I saw our rounds missing him to the left and to the right. We were off by twenty feet in each direction. The man paused after our bullets stopped and took a second to gather himself before pulling the trigger.

I said a quick prayer as the hissing RPG snaked its way through the air toward us.

It missed left by fifty feet and roared off into the distance.

When I heard Mick stop shooting, I glanced up. He was currently passing through the canopy top. Either he was out of bullets, or he had no visual on the men.

With eight bullets left, I took aim as best I could and pulled and pulled and pulled. When I emptied the magazine, return fire started immediately. I dropped the empty pistol and clutched the rope with both hands.

Suddenly I felt blood on the side of my neck.

Am I hit?

This time I felt the blood spatter on my bald head. Instinctively, I looked up.

And saw Mick bleeding profusely from a bullet hole in his leg.

CHAPTER FORTY

THE AIRPLANE HANGAR'S door screeched open, waking Javi from a dead sleep. Following that, the hangar's large overhead lights flicked on. Immediately panic set in. Javi's eyes bulged, and his heart pounded.

He wasn't supposed to be here.

Javi crawled toward the window and slowly eased up until he could see out the window's bottom right-hand corner. His fists clenched upon seeing Patron, who was on a cell phone in what appeared to be a serious conversation.

Since extra men had arrived the other day to help with the pipeline installation, Javi had been helping Izzy and Sylvia at night with the dishes, as well as in the morning with breakfast prep. This night—of all nights—he'd decided to sleep on the floor of the break room with his granddaughter and Izzy. Patron hadn't been around much in the past two days, and the current night guard didn't care much for the goings-on inside the hangar, so Javi thought he was in the clear.

Not so.

Izzy and Sylvia were awake, staring at him with wide eyes.

He met their gaze. "I'm going to sneak out while I can, while he's still on the phone and distracted."

"Hurry!" Izzy said.

"Be careful, Papa," Sylvia added.

He kept his old body hunched over as far as it could go, which wasn't very far. Though the tunnel had connected with the other end, and the vacuum pipeline system had been completed, there were lots of extra pipes and machinery still inside the hangar. So, Javi was able to hide his movement toward the door to the other side.

Javi stopped his retreat, though, when Patron angled toward his side of the hangar. Though Patron's back was to Javi, Patron was close enough to hear Javi's footsteps if he kept moving. Javi stayed crouched behind a large pipe. Being so close, he could hear every word of the one-sided conversation now.

"Are you sure this is necessary?" Patron was saying. "You sure this is what you want to do?"

A pause in the conversation.

Patron added, "It's finished, boss. It's ready to go. The tunnel's complete. This will destroy it, obviously."

Javi's ears were on fire now.

"Yes, yes," Patron continued, "sacrifice, I get it. It's just a huge sacrifice. I mean, it's—" Patron stopped himself.

Javi couldn't decipher the voice on the other end, of course, but he could hear the voice's muffled speech. And that voiced appeared to be rising in volume.

Patron finished his sentence. "It's a lot of people, a ton of bodies, boss."

The voice shouted back at Patron.

"Understood," Patron replied, trying to calm the person on the other end. "Shouldn't be a problem. I have an idea of what we can do. It's gruesome, but it's a solution."

As the conversation de-escalated, and Patron paced to the other side of the warehouse, Javi quietly made his way to the inner door, which he'd kept unlocked. After turning the doorknob and easing onto his side of the hangar, he shot a look toward the break room before closing the door.

Izzy and Sylvia were beaming, happy he'd slipped back to the other side undetected. He gave them a thumbs-up and closed the door. Placing his back against the door, Javi reflected on the devastating conversation he'd just overheard.

He was anything but happy.

CHAPTER FORTY-ONE

MICK CRANSTON WAS A WARRIOR.

Though he'd been shot in his upper-left thigh, he held on to the swaying rope. A lesser man would've fainted from blood loss and fallen to his death.

Clayton, noticing Mick's condition, slowed the helicopter's ascent even more. That helped. But it also meant we took more bullets than we wanted.

Fortunately, the slightly swaying rope made us hard targets for the men below, so we escaped the line of fire without another bullet hole. As soon as the rope's bottom passed the top of the canopy, Clayton swung the helicopter north.

"Hang on, buddy!" I yelled up to Mick, wiping blood from my forehead. I'd noticed Mick sliding down the rope as the helicopter gained momentum. *"Hang on! You got this!"*

But he really didn't.

With one useless leg, Mick couldn't grip the rope with his lower body. All that was keeping him alive was his upper-body strength, which I noticed was waning with every passing second.

I looked past Mick and saw Slim frantically yelling at Clayton. Now that we were out of firing range, Slim was telling him to slow down. Focusing back on Mick, I started to panic as I envisioned him losing strength, then tumbling through the canopy to his death. Mick had two daughters, and I couldn't imagine explaining his death to his wife, Julie.

As I refocused on what to do, an idea suddenly popped into my mind.

"Slide down to me, Mick, slide down. Slowly!"

Mick was so weary, he followed orders without a word.

When he was ten feet above me, I shouted, "Ease down onto my shoulders. I have a solid foothold in the rope. I can support your weight. You're gonna make it, buddy."

On the final five feet of Mick's descent, I noticed his forearms shaking. They were as taut as the rope itself. Blood from his leg wound started dripping onto my head again.

I shook it off and said, "Hold on, just a little bit more, almost there."

But Mick couldn't hold tight the last few feet.

His arms lost strength and he started sliding fast down the rope. Fortunately, I was ready for him. I threaded my head through his rapidly approaching legs, and my shoulders caught his bony butt from descending farther. Mick was wiry and strong, but he weighed only one hundred and ninety pounds, so my shoulders easily took his weight.

"Keep holding on, pal," I encouraged him. "Don't want you tipping forward or back."

He grunted something, and I took that as a good sign. At least he hadn't passed out.

I threaded my right arm over Mick's right leg and latched my hand onto the rope in front of Mick's belly. That secured him some more.

Slim must've seen we had a solid position because I felt the helicopter gather speed. Looking ahead, I saw that Clayton was cutting between the two mountains and angling around the backside of the mountain to the original drop-off site. Which was probably best. Below I could only see treetops and no sign of a clear landing site anywhere.

The wind blew hard on my face, which not only dried the blood on my head, but also revived my body. Which was exactly what I needed. Every muscle was tense as I supported Mick's full weight on my shoulders.

Mick and I held on to the bitter end. The descent to the landing site was excruciatingly slow. Just when we were a few feet from landing, and my free foot was dangling and stretching for the ground, Mick's arms finally gave out.

He toppled about six feet to the ground, landing on his right side, which protected his bad leg. I ran to him after stepping off and freeing my foot. Using my Kershaw folding pocketknife, I sliced at the bullet hole in his pants, then used both hands to rip open a wide tear in his pants near the wound.

The fall seemed to have woken Mick from his daze. He asked, "Is it bad?"

I didn't respond right away. Instead, I dabbed at the wound with the torn flap of pants. When I finally stemmed the blood flow long enough to get a visual, I let out a huge breath.

A small win.

"Not bad, pal," I said to Mick. "Not bad at all. You'll be fine."

The bullet wasn't lodged inside his thigh; it had grazed the outside. Before the blood flowed back to the wound, I saw the track it had carved. The bullet's path had left a four-inch-long groove on the side of his thigh. I guessed the track was about an inch deep.

Relieved, I put pressure on the wound and took stock of my surroundings.

Clayton had landed the helicopter fifty feet from our position. Surprisingly, Slim hadn't rushed over. Upon further examination, I realized he was busy attending to Delgado. He looked to be doing what I was doing: stemming blood flow from a wound on Delgado's leg. The man's lower left pant leg and shoe were covered in blood.

Soon Clayton was out of his seat and rushing toward me. As I watched him hustle over, I suddenly had a thought. A somewhat paranoid thought, maybe, but a plausible one, nonetheless.

Without a word to Clayton, I grabbed hold of Mick's legs while Clayton hooked his arms under Mick's shoulders. We carried Mick into the helicopter, placing his body a few feet from Delgado's. Clayton attended to Mick right away. I saw that he had a first aid kit by his side, and he was busy tying a tourniquet. Following that, he applied a pressure bandage to the wound.

"How's he doing?" I asked Slim, motioning at Delgado.

"At one point better. While waiting for the bird, he was coming to. But before fully waking, he conked out again. Not from whatever he was drugged with, though." Slim pointed to Jimmy's left calf. "Two bullets are lodged in there. He's lost a bunch of blood."

I nodded, remembering when we took fire hustling to the tree line. Those two bullets likely saved my life. If it weren't for the Butcher's dangling legs, I probably would've taken those rounds to my left side.

"I need a quick word, Slim." I met his gaze and immediately nodded my head to the side. Slim picked up on the hint that it needed to be out of Clayton's earshot.

"Now, though?" he asked. "Why not in the air?"

I glanced at Clayton, whose back was to me, then glared at Slim.

"Be right back," Slim said to Clayton.

Clayton responded with, "Off the ground in five. Mick here is stable, I'll get this other man stable, then we're off."

I pulled Slim to about the spot where Mick had fallen.

Before I could speak, he said, "What's this about?"

"Nobody knew we were coming this morning. There were no security cameras anywhere inside or outside the building. And look at where we are right now. Nobody saw us landing here. We could've landed a supersonic jet here and nobody would've been the wiser."

"Okay," he said. "So what?"

"That building was a clear trap. Nobody knew we were coming, but eleven men were waiting for us to descend on it. How would they have known we were coming? We didn't even know that until a few hours before takeoff. Our plans were only known by us and Clayton."

Slim motioned toward the pilot. "You think Clayton called it in? He just saved our lives, pal."

"Listen, I think Ortiz obviously set us up. And Ortiz and Valen Jackson were in the same business together, and we also know they're friends. You called Valen to get permission to use the helicopter. Valen could've easily let Ortiz know we were coming early."

Slim's shoulders sagged. "Back to Valen Jackson. Always back to him. Unbelievable. You totally have it out for him, Chase."

"I don't have it out for him," I shot back. "I simply don't trust him. And I have reason to, reasons I don't have time to go into right now. Just trust me."

Slim sighed. "And I have reasons to doubt your conspiracy theory, buddy."

"Like what?" I asked.

"Like why Clayton would save us and Delgado if he was in on this?"

I immediately thumbed at Delgado. "Maybe to get him. That man was drugged and held in the building's basement. And we're dealing with warring cartels here. Maybe one wants him dead, the other alive, maybe the third is holding him for ransom. Who knows? But perhaps we were used by one of these cartels to get Delgado back to safety. For whatever reason. It's plausible, right?"

Slim reluctantly nodded his head. "It is. But you're dead wrong about the security camera thing."

"How so?"

"I spotted at least three cameras in the trees, pointed toward the building. Yes, you're right, no cameras are in or on the building, but that's because they're in the forest."

I straightened. "Really?"

"Absolutely. You wouldn't have seen them in the dark. I didn't see them until the morning sun broke through. And I only picked them up because I was closely studying the approaching men. When you came smashing out of the building, you were a little too preoccupied to see them, let alone having me tell you about them."

I was at a loss for words.

"Let's put your theory to bed, okay?" Slim said.

"Back burner," I replied. "That's the best I can do. We both know we can't trust anyone. We need to keep our eye on Clayton for the time being. And, please, no more using Valen Jackson."

He nodded. "Let's go."

I looked at Clayton, who was waving us over.

After piling in, I noticed Mick was awake and sitting up. He was a little pale but doing okay. He had his phone in his hand. He told me he just sent the video to his superiors.

Delgado was flat on his back between the seats. His eyes were flickering open.

"Both stable," Clayton shouted back as the rotor came to full speed. "But we need to get that man to a hospital." He motioned toward Delgado. "Get those rounds out of his leg."

Once we were at flight altitude and underway, I left my seat and checked in with Mick first, then Delgado. Kneeling beside Delgado, I said, "What happened? How did you get to that building? Talk to me."

Nothing. He stared at me without blinking.

"Who took you there?" I asked. "Who brought you to that building?"

Still, nothing. No eye movement or response.

I kept at it. "Come on, Delgado, talk. Tell me what's going on. Tell me something."

Juan Manuel Delgado, however, continued to stare straight up at the helicopter's ceiling.

I took a moment to restrategize. I wasn't sure if he was still under the effects of whatever drug had been administered through the IV, or if he was in shock from his wound. Or perhaps he could hear me just fine and was simply ignoring me.

I bent over and repeated myself. "Delgado, you need to talk. Or should I say Jimmy D? Or perhaps I should say Butcher."

He blinked. Three, maybe four times. The blinks were so fast I couldn't count accurately.

"That's right," I continued. "I know you're the infamous Butcher of Baja. And soon the whole world will know."

Delgado subtly shook his head and tried to speak, but no words came out.

I scowled at him. "Of course, you deny it. Why wouldn't you?"

Between labored breaths, he mustered, "No . . . not me."

"Uh-huh," I said.

Delgado swallowed and licked his lips. His eyes fluttered open and closed. He repeated, "Not me." After another deep swallow, he added, "Know who is."

That got my attention. I leaned closer until our faces were only a foot apart.

He whispered something, which I couldn't decipher.

I turned my head and brought my ear to his lips, our heads now inches apart. I waited in that position for a solid ten seconds, for Delgado to say something. Anything. When he didn't, I looked back and sighed.

The man was unconscious once again.

CHAPTER FORTY-TWO

JUAN MANUEL DELGADO didn't regain consciousness, not once during the flight to Tijuana.

Slim and I took turns attending to him. We applied all the emergency field training knowledge we had. That kept the man alive for the time being. After realizing he wouldn't come to and give us the intel we desperately wanted, we turned our attention to Mick.

He was stable and doing well. Of course, he now had only one useable leg. Currently, he was in the copilot seat talking on a headset with his Commanding Officer at Camp Pendleton.

Mick Cranston and I had worked together in black-ops years ago. Prior to that, he was part of an elite group of Marines at Camp Pendleton called Detachment One or Det One, for short. That group was disbanded in 2006. Following his stint in black-ops, Mick returned home to Southern California and settled down as a trainer for elite Marines at Pendleton. Since he was cagey about the exact unit he currently trained, my guess was he trained another elite group of Marines like Det One, some type of new unit that wasn't public knowledge.

That hunch was confirmed when Mick signed off with his CO and brought Slim and me up to speed on the plan.

"All right, here's the deal," he said. "We have a subset of specialized

Marines at Pendleton that I work with. I'm talking small, a team of just eight. They exist for this exact type of mission, and, in fact, are already en route as I speak. Fortunately, it doesn't raise flags for them to simply up and go like this. As of now, only we and my CO know about this mission. I was able to convince him to release the team based on the cell video I took of the women. Once we get boots on the ground in Mexico and confirm the situation, my CO will go up the chain and arrange transport. Primary focus right now, though, is getting there and securing the women. There's only eight on my team, but that's enough to take out the men on the ground and protect the women. Trust me."

He waited for our reaction.

Slim and I nodded.

"Needless to say," Mick continued, "we're going in low to avoid radar. We're rendezvousing with the incoming team a couple hundred miles east of Tijuana, smack in the middle of the desert. I'll join up with them there." He motioned to his leg. "Obviously not going on ground but overseeing the mission from the air and bringing them up to speed."

I figured the answer but asked the question anyway. "Can I join? I know the layout of the building better than anyone, Mick."

"You know you can't, pal."

I reluctantly nodded. "We need to get him medical attention." I motioned toward Delgado. "We need him alive, but we also need to take him to the US, Mick. If he is the Butcher of Baja, he needs to stand trial in the States. This is our chance."

Mick thought about it, eventually nodding and saying, "You two get him medical attention in Tijuana, but obviously keep it on the down low. You'll need to protect the hell out of him. Once my CO is fully on board, I think we'll have the leverage to do whatever it takes. Once Delgado is on the mend, maybe we take this helicopter to rendezvous with my team in the desert, and we'll transfer Delgado to Pendleton."

"Good plan," Slim said. "I like it."

I wasn't as enthusiastic as Slim. Since the tentative plan relied on using Valen Jackson's helicopter once again, I had some hesitation. And Mick sensed it.

"You good with that, buddy?" he asked.

"Maybe," I replied. I wasn't about to get into it with Mick and Slim since the pilot was two feet away.

Mick sighed. "Well, if you come up with something better, let me know."

I slapped him on the back to ease the tension. "Will do."

Mick checked the coordinates on his watch. "We're twenty out from our rendezvous."

Slim and I went back to our seats and argued softly for the remainder of the flight to the rendezvous site. Our argument revolved around my distrust of Valen Jackson and the pilot.

"We have no vehicle on this side of the border," Slim pointed out. "Remember, we walked across. And since we must keep a low profile with Delgado, it's not like we can call an ambulance or taxi. The pilot's an expat and lives in Tijuana, so he'll have a vehicle at the airport, and he'll know the closest, best hospital."

I held up the keys Mick had given me. "You're wrong. We have Mick's FJ55. Remember, he drove it there from Arturo's."

"That's right. Still, I think we should ask Clayton about what clinic to go to or if he knows of a discreet one."

"I don't know, buddy."

"What I know is that we may still need Clayton and this helicopter, so let's not cut him out of the loop prematurely."

I thought about it for a moment. "If we're going to use him, then I want him by our side the whole time, so we can keep an eye on him."

"Agreed," Slim said. "Listen, if this transfer in the desert goes off without a hitch—no one intercepts the Marines team, that is—will you feel confident then that Valen and Clayton have no part in this?"

"It will help."

"You're something else, pal." He shook his head. "Serious trust issues."

"Slim, if all this is about using us to get Delgado out from the grips of whichever cartel took him, then we could still be in the middle of a setup here, right? I mean, think about it: we use Clayton and his knowledge to get Delgado to some specific hospital or medical clinic, and if Valen is somehow or in some way a part of this, then Clayton feeds his boss that intel and suddenly we're intercepted en route or at the hospital."

"Sure, I'll give you that. It's possible, but unlikely. We have no reason to believe Clayton is compromised or Valen is dirty." He held up his hand to stop me from interjecting. "We'll be cautious, okay? Any weird sign from Clayton and we abort. He sneaks off and makes a call, we're out. You have my word."

There really wasn't another option at this point, so I reluctantly agreed.

Minutes later, we landed. As promised, it was a remote site in the middle of the desert. There were some sand dunes around, so my assumption was that Mick's men and their helicopter were behind one of the nearby dunes.

Mick had coordinated the site and exchange flawlessly, so everything happened quickly. Before we knew it, two Marines were hustling toward our Sikorsky. With a quick goodbye, Mick was picked up and carried off. As we left, I turned in my seat to get a visual of the area to see if I could spot the Marines' location. But the moving rotor kicked up a huge sandstorm and blocked my vision.

About an hour later, we landed at Tijuana International Airport. During the last leg of our flight, Slim brought Clayton up to speed on our next steps. Since I wanted to keep an eye on Clayton, I'd taken the copilot seat to watch him.

Slim stood behind Clayton, feeding him the plan details.

"Sure, I got just the place," Clayton said. "Mr. Jackson takes good care of all his employees, so I've picked up some injured and sick workers before and brought them to TJ, to a doctor we trust. Shouldn't be a problem."

Slim slapped him on the shoulder. "I knew you'd come through."

Clayton looked back at Slim. "No worries, this is quite exciting. Not my typical workday. It's like I'm back on tour, you know. May I ask: who's this guy you've brought along?" He thumbed over his shoulder.

I took the question before Slim could. "Probably best to keep that quiet. The less you know, the better." I studied Clayton's response. The pilot shrugged it off like my comment didn't bother him, so that provided some measure of confidence.

At the airport, things moved quickly. Before long, we were carrying Delgado into an emergency room at a local clinic just fifteen minutes from the airport. I insisted quite strongly with the clinic staff that I needed to be in the room when Delgado was being worked on. Clayton, being fluent in Spanish, helped me articulate to the staff that my presence was nonnegotiable. It also helped that I gave them a few hundred dollars.

While I waited and watched the doctor work, Slim stayed in the waiting area with Clayton to keep an eye on the pilot. We'd been there about an hour when my personal cell buzzed and alerted me to Mick's call, which I'd been anticipating since Mick's team must've landed in the Sierras within the last half hour.

I stepped into the hall and answered it. "Talk to me," I said.

Mick's voice cut in and out. There was a ton of static in the background. Plus, I could hear the helicopter gearing up to leave.

"You're in and out," I said to Mick. "Can't hear well. Repeat."

A brief pause, then Mick's voice came in loud and clear. "Nobody's here."

"What?" I fired back.

"Everyone's gone. The militia, the women, nobody's here. No bodies either."

I was stunned, so I gave no response.

A moment later, "You there, buddy? You copy? The place is deserted."

I reluctantly replied, "Copy. Heard you, Mick, loud and clear."

CHAPTER FORTY-THREE

"IT'S TIME, MADAM PRESIDENT," Kendra Winfield said, looking at her watch. "Motorcade is ready, and the town hall starts in thirty."

Henrietta nodded. Though her entourage was prepared to leave, she wasn't. And she knew Kendra would be upset about that.

"I need to speak with Willy first," she said to Kendra. Before Kendra could object, the president held up her hand. "It'll be quick, don't you worry."

As Kendra reluctantly left the hotel room, Henrietta opened her laptop, then double-clicked on the tracking software program. While it reloaded, she stepped in front of a mirror and surveyed her outfit, then touched up her makeup.

Moments later, a knock came to her door and Willy announced his presence.

She signaled to the secret service agent to let him in.

"What can I do for you, Madam President?" he said.

She waved him in as she took a seat behind the small desk and glanced at her laptop. "I need you to pick somebody up."

He stopped midstride. "Somebody? Who?"

"Garrison Chase. I need you to pick him up in Tijuana and bring him to me."

"Across the border?" he said, approaching the desk. "Right now? Surely you can send someone else, or I can find someone else for the task."

"No," she quickly replied. "Just you. I trust you'll be discreet about his retrieval."

"May I ask—"

She held up her hand. "No, you may not ask why. I'm sorry. Just get this done for me, Willy, okay?"

He nodded.

Henrietta glanced at her computer screen. Garrison Chase appeared to be on the move, no longer at the airport. "I'll text you a precise location when you're closer to TJ."

Willy looked at his watch. "We're in Yuma, ma'am, so Tijuana is a few hours away from here."

She pointed to the hotel door. "Then I suggest you get going."

CHAPTER FORTY-FOUR

I'D SPENT the afternoon in Delgado's recovery room. The doctor said the surgery to remove the two bullets went off without a hitch, and that he'd be able to talk by early evening.

I hoped it would be earlier, so I waited bedside for Delgado to wake and be lucid enough to speak. Not sure, though, what kind of intel I would get from him. Or if I could even trust what he had to say. But I was running out of options.

The cell connection with Mick had been spotty at best, so I didn't get too much information from him. I knew Mick's CO was pissed, and I also knew they had a working theory about the women. The team had found some fresh, wide tire tracks directly beside the building. Based on the size and pattern of those tracks, they were certain a convoy of military vehicles had swept in and picked up the women and headed west. However, Mick's CO wasn't about to scour the Mexican countryside for the women. And it wasn't even in question to rendezvous in the desert and have Mick's team transport Delgado back to Camp Pendleton. I assumed the team was already headed straight back to their base.

So, for hours, I sat in that recovery room with only my spiraling thoughts as company. I had no idea where my mother was being held, or if she was even alive. And the women? Well, they were an utter mystery. Exactly where two hundred women and Arturo and his niece were being taken was beyond my scope of understanding. I couldn't even venture a guess.

On a positive note, that fact that Mick's team found no bodies meant at least the women and Arturo weren't slaughtered in the building's basement. But the more I thought about that, the less positive I became. I mean, the cartel obviously knew that we knew the location of the Punta De Las Olas replica building. And whichever cartel was responsible for locking the women in the basement wouldn't want Americans to return and find hundreds of dead bodies there. In my mind, that meant the women and Arturo were being taken elsewhere to be killed. Somewhere we'd likely never find them. Ever.

To keep my mind from going too dark, I thought about my next steps. If I didn't get any trustworthy intel from Delgado, the only thing I could think to do was go back to Punta San Carlos. I could get Clayton to fly us back down there, then Slim and I could stake out Alejandro Ortiz's compound. See what we see, and if we felt it necessary, pay Ortiz a personal visit. Of course, we'd want to confront him and really lean on him for information. And that meant we'd have to take out his team of five.

I spent some time thinking about that possibility. We still had some weapons in the Sikorsky but no ammunition. Which I didn't think was too big of a problem for being in Mexico. Since Clayton was turning out to be a potential asset, I figured he would know where to go for military equipment and ammunition.

Early evening, I took a break from the recovery room and reconvened with Slim. I brought him up to speed on everything I'd been thinking, and I also asked him about the plan to revisit Ortiz. Just after we agreed on heading south to Punta San Carlos, the doctor who'd been working on Delgado came out to the waiting area and waved me over.

"He's awake," the doc said as I approached, "and he's doing fine. Give us five minutes to get him sitting up and stable, then he's all yours."

"Sure, doctor, thanks."

I went back and spoke with Slim. I wanted him in the room to help with questioning Delgado, but I still didn't trust Clayton 100 percent, and since Clayton couldn't be in the room with Delgado when I questioned him, we agreed that Slim would stay with the pilot.

A few minutes later, I walked into Delgado's recovery room.

As promised, the man was sitting up. Delgado had thick, dark hair and an equally thick and dark mustache. He looked all right for being shot up and losing a ton of blood.

"I take it you're the man I owe my life to?" he said.

To hear that from his mouth was weird, even though what he said was partly true. But what he didn't know was that I almost killed him, too. I paused momentarily on my response and walked the few remaining feet to his bedside.

"What's your name?" he said. "I need to know the name of the man who saved my life."

"Chase. Garrison Chase. But you need to know right away there was a team of us responsible for your extraction." Since I didn't exactly know which name to refer to him by, I avoided calling him anything.

He held out his hand and I shook it.

"Juan Manuel Delgado is the name," he said.

Looks like he doesn't remember the conversation in the helicopter.

"That name's a mouthful," he continued. "You can call me Jimmy D, for short."

Not likely, I thought.

"I trust, then, Mr. Chase, that you'll give my thanks to your entire team for getting me out of there safely."

"Wasn't exactly safely." I motioned at his leg. "You took fire on extraction. Obviously, you don't remember since you were out cold."

"True, I don't remember much."

I wanted to know what he remembered about the extraction and how he got to the Sierra Madres. But I also wanted to remind him about our brief conversation in the helicopter when he denied he was the Butcher but said he knew who was. I figured I'd work up to the latter.

I began with, "What do you recall? How'd you get to that building in the first place?"

"Wish I could tell you. Until now, I didn't even know I was in a building. What building?"

"The Punta De Las Olas building," I replied. "The one in the Sierra Madre Oriental range."

Immediately he furrowed his thick brow. "Not following, Mr. Chase. My building is on the coast in Northern Baja."

"I'm talking about the replica building."

His scowl deepened. "Perhaps it's the drugs they had me on, maybe they haven't fully worn off, but I have no clue what you're talking about. What do you mean *replica building*?"

Okay, interesting. The man seemed genuinely perplexed. I stared and studied him for a few silent seconds, then knew I had to get to the point.

"Do you remember our conversation in the helicopter, Mr. Delgado? When you came to, I was leaning over you, and I asked you a question. Do you remember?"

He sunk back into the pillows. "So that *was* real, was it? I thought it was a dream. I was in and out most of that ride, and mostly out, for the record."

"It was real all right."

"You asked me if I was the . . ." He paused and swallowed. "The Butcher of Baja."

"Correct. And you denied it but said you knew who was."

He subtly nodded but didn't elaborate.

"Who is?" I prodded him. "If you're not the Butcher, then who is?"

He deflected. "Mr. Chase, you and your team rescued me, and I owe your team my life. You're obviously American, as I can tell from your accent, but I need to know why the US is involved and what your role is before I divulge what I know. I hope you can understand."

I could. It was a fair question; one I would ask if the tables were reversed. I decided to give him the truth since I had nothing to lose. Naturally, I'd hold back some key details.

"The US is involved because Operation Crossroads is a shit show, sir, it's a front. It's a—"

"A front?" Delgado interrupted. "How so? I don't follow."

Again, he seemed genuinely perplexed. Maybe he was just a good actor, though. "Mr. Delgado, it may be best if you get out in front of this and come clean. I don't appreciate being played."

He held up his hands. "How can I get out in front of something if I don't know what you're talking about, Mr. Chase?"

I sighed and decided to play his game. "Crossroads is skimming beautiful women—two hundred, to be precise—from the employment program and training them to be high-end call girls in the US. All done in a building built identical to your foundation building. The Butcher of Baja is behind this, working with a local cartel, Sinaloa is our guess, to accomplish all this. And you, Mr. Delgado, are being pinpointed as the mastermind behind this, as the infamous Butcher of Baja. From your very partner, no less. If you aren't the Butcher, then it goes without saying, you better get out in front of this."

Delgado closed his eyes and shook his head, clearly exasperated. "That rat bastard," he said.

"Who?" I asked. "Who are you talking about?"

"It all makes sense now," Delgado replied.

Before I could ask who again, Delgado blurted, "Ortiz. It's Ortiz."

It didn't surprise me to hear Ortiz's name, but I still blew out a deep breath.

"Alejandro Ortiz," Delgado continued. "He's the man you're after. He's the Butcher of Baja."

CHAPTER FORTY-FIVE

"WHAT ON EARTH IS GOING ON?" Izzy said. "What do you mean they're taking you somewhere? Where?"

"I don't know, Izzy," Javi responded. "I don't know what's going on. Really. No clue."

Moments ago, one of the guards had entered the makeshift kitchen and demanded Javi and Sylvia come with him. Javi had broken free of the guard's grasp and ran back to Izzy.

"You must know something, Javi. Please tell me. You've been acting strange ever since you snuck back to the other side."

Javi placed both hands on Izzy's shoulders. He thought of the conversation he'd overheard Patron having. He wasn't about to burden her with that information, but he also wasn't about to gloss over it either.

"Promise me," he said. "Promise me something, Isabelle."

"You're scaring me here, Javi. What's going on? What do you know?"

"Whatever you do, please, please, don't go down into the tunnel. Do whatever it takes, but don't go down there."

Suddenly the guard grabbed Javi and yanked him back, pulling Izzy with him.

"Leave him!" Izzy shouted.

The guard rudely pushed Izzy back. He dragged Javi and Sylvia out of the room and slammed the door behind him, then locked Izzy inside.

She pounded on the door, repeating, "Leave him! Leave him alone!"

Before the guard spun him around, Javi mouthed: "Don't go down there, please, I beg you."

CHAPTER FORTY-SIX

"You're positive?" I said to Delgado. "Positive Alejandro Ortiz is the Butcher of Baja. Unequivocal?"

He nodded. "That's what this is all about. He knows that I know. Speaking of getting out in front of it, that's what he's doing. All along he's been trying to frame me. It's clear now."

I needed a moment to process, so I grabbed the plastic chair I'd been sitting in and scraped it to his bedside. Crossroads was an operation between our president and Ortiz and Delgado, so it wasn't surprising that these two men had turned on each other, that each were pointing to the other as the evil mastermind. I thought about my meeting with Ortiz in Punta San Carlos. Ortiz had made a solid case against Delgado being the Butcher and responsible for everything. Naturally, questions rifled through my mind about who was telling the truth and who was lying.

In the end, I wanted to hear Delgado's version of what was going on. I asked, "How long have you known this about your partner, about Alejandro Ortiz being the Butcher? A long time?"

"Heavens no," Delgado responded. "Just recently, in fact."

"And how'd you find out?"

Delgado motioned toward the open door. I got up and closed it.

When I sat back in my chair, he avoided eye contact and said, "My father. That's how I found out."

It appeared painful for him to admit that, so I let his words hang for a moment.

Soon, he turned and made eye contact. "May I ask: What do you know about me and my father?"

"Some, I'll admit."

"How much?" he pushed.

"Assume not much, Mr. Delgado, and tell me everything. Start at the beginning."

For a second, he looked like he was going to fight me on that, but then he settled back. "I wasn't a good kid. Or an adult, for that matter. At least not my first forty years on this planet. I really wasn't. I was loosely connected with the Northern Baja cartels, as I'm sure you know. But I promise, I didn't do ninety percent of what people thought I did. I'll admit, I pedaled my father's influence and did things I wasn't proud of. Certainly, I did. But I wasn't involved in killing and mass bloodshed, and I didn't protect or work to protect El Chapo. No way."

"Did you try to squelch the rumors then? Maybe work to protect your reputation?"

"I didn't, and I regret it. I was young and stupid and, admittedly, loved the attention and the rumor that I was this bad boy with unscrupulous power. I didn't find wisdom until a decade ago, and that's when I decided to turn my reputation around."

"Starting with your name. That's why you started going by Jimmy D, I assume?"

He nodded. "Absolutely. That was just a beginning point, though. Subsequently, I've poured my time and finances into my foundation for the past decade. Because I truly want to make up for my past indiscretions. I want to give back to my people. Do you know what my foundation is about?"

"I do. Is Ortiz part of the foundation? Do you work with him on that? After all, he has some history with successful agriculture businesses, doesn't he?"

He shook his head. "He does, but not with my foundation, that's all my doing, my life's work. Ortiz isn't involved in that."

"So how did you and Ortiz begin working together?"

230

"Many years ago, he and my father were in business together. But when my father became too busy with his political career, he sold his share of that business. That's how I first became acquainted with Ortiz." Delgado paused, and I noticed he was gripping the sheets on his bed in frustration.

To nudge him back on track, I said, "What about you and Ortiz working together? Ortiz told me he approached you for financial help with Operation Crossroads. Is that true?"

Delgado relaxed his grip. "He did, and, yes, that's true. I saw the good work he was doing with that program—at least that's what I thought at the time. When he approached me, I was happy to be part of it. I joined as mainly a financial partner, a silent partner. I had my work with the foundation, so I didn't have time for his work, but I believed in what he was doing, and I didn't think twice about infusing capital into the Crossroads program."

"When did things start going bad?"

"To this day, Mr. Chase, I wouldn't say—from my perspective, anyway—that things were ever going bad."

"Really?"

"Yes, really."

"Red flags then?"

He sighed. "Certainly. With hindsight, I see them. It makes sense why my father was so against my involvement with Ortiz from the very beginning."

"Why? What happened with your father?"

"Seven weeks ago, he had a massive heart attack. He didn't die right away, but his condition was bad, you know. The family rushed to his side to say our final goodbyes. At one point, he cleared the room and wanted to only speak with me. That was when he unloaded, said he'd done terrible things and apologized. I apologized, too. It was a beautiful moment for us, but then he started babbling on about me being careful, about me not trusting Alejandro, about me severing ties with the man. I didn't know if it was the meds speaking because he rambled somewhat incoherently about Ortiz."

"And what did he say exactly?"

"He was vague at first, so I pushed him on what he meant. That was when he made the claim that Ortiz was the Butcher of Baja."

I leaned back in my chair. Naturally, each man pointed the finger at the other. They both had different versions of what was going on. But who was telling the truth?

"The story goes, Mr. Delgado, that the Butcher of Baja helped protect El Chapo, and that there was a rumor he did that by having a government man on the inside. Did your father admit to being that man?"

"Basically, yes, he did. That was his secret, the guilt he couldn't live with. He had to come clean on his deathbed for his conscience's sake. And to protect me."

"What else did you gather from your father's relationship with Ortiz?"

"That he was given no choice in the matter."

I furrowed my brow. "What do you mean?"

"I mean, it wasn't like my father was a terrible man that was working with Ortiz for profit. My father didn't elaborate, but he did repeatedly say that Ortiz made him do things. I assume he meant that Ortiz blackmailed him, likely by threatening our family."

I nodded. Could be the truth or could not be. His father may have been trying to make himself look better to his son.

"Listen," Delgado continued, "I understand you may be skeptical of the story. I mean, I was a little skeptical, too, and that was probably my downfall."

I leaned forward. "How so?"

"After my father died six weeks ago, I started to investigate. It wasn't that I didn't believe him, I was skeptical of his story because of his condition and the meds he was on. I wanted to perform due diligence. If Ortiz was indeed the Butcher of Baja, I had to be beyond careful. I started speaking with Ortiz more, asking questions of him and his business. In hindsight, that must've been a red flag for him, the way I suddenly poked and prodded into his affairs."

I nodded. Sure, that could've set things in motion. "From your perspective," I said, "were there any other red flags prior to this? In terms of working with Ortiz and Crossroads."

"The only thing we argued about were the cartels. Looking back, that's a red flag."

"How so?"

"Not surprisingly, Ortiz mentioned early on that he was being pressured from Sinaloa. I was adamant that he ignore any pressure or request from cartels. Told him not to give an inch, lest they take a mile. He scolded me on how naïve that approach was, and, honestly, he was right. But I was stubborn. I'd turned over a new leaf and didn't want to go down that road again. Refused to, in fact."

Delgado looked peeved at himself, so I gave him a second, then said, "What did you do then? Turn a blind eye?"

He sighed. "Sort of. I wouldn't listen to his concerns. I stuck my head in the sand any time he mentioned what was going on. I simply didn't want to know. I told him to stand firm and hire a security force to deal with any threats. I told him that's what I was going to do if they started coming after my foundation."

I thought about his foundation building, and the fact that there weren't any security men there. "You never felt threatened by the cartels? Because it's pretty clear you don't have any security measures at your foundation."

He scrunched up his face. "You've been there?"

I realized I tipped my hand, so now it was my turn to deflect. "I've been investigating this whole affair and have tried not to let any detail escape scrutiny."

"And why's that?" he replied. "Who put you up to this task, anyway?"

I steered the conversation toward the women. "The women are why I'm involved with this."

"Women?"

"The two hundred women who were skimmed from Crossroads, Mr. Delgado."

"Right," he said, sighing. "Forced to be high-end call girls."

I nodded. "They're missing."

He cocked his head. "Missing? I had no idea. Tell me more."

I brought him up to speed as fast as I could, covering details like the replica building in the Sierras and how we'd found him there with the women, drugged and chained to the bed. By the end of my story, I'll admit, he did look somewhat pale.

"This is terrible," he said. "Horrible, in fact. I can't believe the lengths Ortiz has gone." He looked away from me and toward the wall. "He tried to kill me outright, didn't he? That man who stormed the foundation building was hired by him."

I didn't want to languish here, so I kept the conversation moving. "After the attempt on your life, what happened? Where did you go and how did you end up in the Sierra Madres?"

"In to hiding," he replied. "I didn't want to draw a ton of attention to my whereabouts, so I took a small team of men and hid out east of Tijuana at a family property most don't know we own. But they found me anyway."

"Who found you?"

He shook his head. "No clue, but I'm assuming cartel men. They stormed the property in the middle of the night, took out my men, and blindfolded me right away. As soon as they put me inside a vehicle, all I remember is a prick to my arm, then I was out. And I didn't wake up until your team rescued me."

I stood and began pacing. I had to. My mind needed to work out the big picture and aimlessly walking back and forth helped.

"You all right, Mr. Chase?"

"Fine, just need to work through some things in my mind."

"Understood," he said, holding up his hands.

Moments later, I stopped pacing and said, "Earlier you said you began poking and prodding and looking into Ortiz's affairs. What exactly did you learn?"

"A little," he replied. "I used some of my former cartel associates to try to figure out some things. I learned the general gist of what was going on, but I didn't find out any specific details."

"What was the general gist then?"

"Ortiz was deeply indebted to Sinaloa. They were pressuring him more and more from what I gathered, to Ortiz's breaking point, in fact. They wanted more money from him. And if you know Alejandro Ortiz, you know he doesn't give up money easily. Anyway, the rumor was he wanted to part ways with Sinaloa, but it's never easy to break ties with a huge cartel like Sinaloa. At the same time, Jalisco had been moving in to the area. They'd already taken over the Tecate area."

Delgado took a sip of water and continued. "Ortiz apparently has ties in the northeast, in the Coahuila state. He wanted to bring in a relatively unknown cartel from that region. Not sure their name. Anyway, my understanding was that he wanted to get into business with them and push out Sinaloa. The idea was to start a war between Sinaloa and Jalisco."

I nodded. "Hopefully to clear a path or opportunity for this northeastern cartel to move in."

"That's what I gathered," Delgado said. "And like I said, I didn't know the details. I didn't know he was working with Sinaloa to skim these women, and that the operation was in the Sierra Madre Oriental range. But if you think about it, it makes some sense now, right? That range, and the replica building, is in the northeast where this new cartel is from. They could easily take over that operation from Sinaloa since it's in their backyard."

Just then, a nurse came in to check his vitals, so I resumed pacing and thinking.

The cartel part made sense to me, and it aligned with what I'd learned from Arturo. No doubt this northeastern cartel was headed by Thiago, or Thiago was relatively high up, at least, within that criminal organization. No doubt it was Thiago's cartel that had tried to kill us at the replica Punta De Las Olas building.

But which man was working with Thiago and his cartel? And how did this new cartel know about me and my directive? Plus, who the hell had Mom?

After some more pacing, I knew I had two conflicting stories without any solid evidence or proof. Honestly, I was fifty-fifty in my mind as to who was the Butcher of Baja and responsible for everything. Since I couldn't figure out the Butcher angle, I turned my attention to our president.

How exactly was she involved? Was Henrietta in cahoots with one of these men, along with this new cartel? For her, could this be not only about killing an infamous terrorist but also about payback for her failed Nogales operation? Sinaloa or Jalisco was likely responsible for Nogales, so maybe she needed to befriend this new third cartel to exact revenge on the cartel responsible for the dead American soldiers. Was she vindictive like that? Was that her motivation?

I kept thinking about her, and that her main connection, the person she worked most closely with on this side of the border, was Ortiz. If Ortiz was the one lying, had she simply been duped by him? Maybe the president did share details about hiring me for the job and that's how Thiago and his thugs knew my name and my directive, because those men ultimately reported to Ortiz? Could the president be innocent?

A knock on the door interrupted my thoughts.

Slim pushed in before Delgado or I could respond.

He pointed at me. "You have a visitor, and you'll never guess who."

CHAPTER FORTY-SEVEN

"WILLY BLANCO?" I said, cautiously shaking his hand. "What are you doing here?"

"Obviously you haven't been checking your cell, Mr. Chase. The president needs you."

It took me a second to realize he meant my burner cell. Since the president never texted back on the flight to the mountains, I'd turned it off and hadn't thought twice about it.

I pulled the cell from my back pocket and powered it on. Within seconds, the cell beeped and showed three short texts in my queue, all three sent not long ago.

Willy grabbed my arm. "Let's find somewhere private to chat."

While he steered me around looking for a quiet place, I read the texts.

The first one said, *Sorry I've been out of touch, will explain everything.* The follow-up text read: *Before Willy brings you to me, I have a job for you.* And the final one: *Ask Willy about FTU Logistics. He'll explain everything.*

Willy had found a small catholic chapel down the hall. There were a few rows of semicomfortable chairs in the room, incense burning in the air, and a ton of Mary statues. One woman was also present, but Willy used his Spanish and politely shooed her out.

We turned chairs to face each other.

He gestured at the cell in my hand. "What did she text you?"

"You don't know?" I asked.

"No. Originally, she wanted me to come get you. She's in Yuma doing some campaign work and wanted to speak with you. But then she called while I was en route and said plans had changed, that I was to bring you to the FTU Logistics warehouse we've been monitoring. She said she'd follow up with you via text."

"I take it she's tracking my cell, and that's how you knew I was here?"

He nodded.

Naturally, I wanted to know about the FTU warehouse, but I also wanted to know what Willy knew. I asked, "Do you know why she wanted to speak with me? Do you know what our connection is?"

"I know a little about your past and why the president wanted to give you that medal, of course, but nothing beyond that. To be honest, the president has been acting pretty strange ever since you two met."

"How so?"

"She's been deeply preoccupied. Not paying attention in important meetings, short with people, that sort of thing."

"Preoccupied with what?"

He didn't respond right away. I sensed his problem and guessed at it. "I know you can't divulge classified information, Willy, and I'm not asking you to. Can you vaguely allude to her preoccupation?"

He nodded. "It's okay, there's nothing really classified. She's simply not acting like herself lately. She's been obsessed about whatever is happening on this side of the border. I've been closely monitoring the news cycle here in Mexico for her."

"And you don't know why?"

"Not until now," he responded. "Or until I spoke with her on the way here. Obviously, she's had me watching the news, so I suspect she's also had the CIA closely monitoring their Mexican intelligence channels for any chatter. And it looks like they picked up something, that's what she relayed to me."

"Picked up what?"

"There's chatter about an American hostage being held in Mexico, right along the border, in a building just across from the FTU warehouse in Otay Mesa. There's also chatter that a tunnel has been dug linking the two."

I tensed. American hostage? Mom maybe? "What do you know about this hostage?"

"Me?" He pointed to himself. "Nothing. I have no information other than what I just told you. That's all the president said."

"Okay, one of the texts said you'd explain everything about FTU Logistics. Explain away."

He settled back in his chair. "What, if anything, do you know about the company?"

"Not much," I replied. "I know they're an up-and-coming shipping company. I think FTU stands for 'Fast-to-you.' Right?"

He nodded.

"I also know they're competing in the ultracompetitive package delivery business with FedEx and UPS and the like."

"Yes and no," Willy said. "They're competing, for sure, but they're nowhere near the size of those two. They're directly competing with smaller delivery companies like DHL."

"Got it. So why is FTU on the president's radar?"

"Because they hire a ton of Mexican immigrants."

When he paused, I said, "Isn't that a good thing?"

"Sure, sure it is. The president loves that fact. However, our administration eventually discovered that more than half of these immigrants have fake social security numbers, so that put them on our radar about a year ago because of the sheer volume of immigrants FTU has on the books. When we see that many fake work documents from immigrants, we assume corporate malfeasance. When a company like FTU is into malfeasance, one situated so close to the border, we also think cartel involvement is a high probability. The president put a small team together to investigate if that was the case. They were stationed around here but had to pull out because of the hot water from the Nogales operation."

"Before they pulled out, what did they discover?"

"FTU was a major player in the drug smuggling trade, and that this particular warehouse in Otay Mesa was the central hub of distribution."

"Pretty good idea," I said, thinking. "FTU is all about the package delivery business, so they have vehicles and routes already in place. Hide their contraband in plain sight, so to speak. And the drugs come into the States via this tunnel, that's the new development, I guess. Is that the gist?"

"It is. We can't prove it, of course, but we're confident FTU is run by the cartels or perhaps the company execs are being paid handsomely from the cartels to use their network. At any rate, the cartels sponsor these immigrants. They get them fake identification and a good job in the States. Pretty much a win-win for the immigrants."

"Except they're heavily indebted to some bad players."

"Exactly. Once Stateside, these immigrant drivers pick up and transport the contraband, carry the drug packages alongside their legit packages. The whole operation is coordinated from the Otay Mesa facility."

He pulled out an iPad from his valise and started fiddling with it. "The president wanted me to show you the latest satellite images, less than an hour old, of the FTU warehouse and its proximity to an airplane hangar just over the border, where we assume this supposed tunnel originates. I just need to get a decent cell signal here to download the image."

While Willy stood and searched the room for a signal, I immediately thought about his words: airplane hangar. The picture of my mother holding the newspaper popped into mind. The background was fuzzy, and earlier I couldn't place it, about what I thought it looked like, but now I did: an airplane hangar! The Polaroid could've been taken inside a hangar, for sure.

Suddenly my thoughts flipped. *Or am I simply seeing something I want to see?*

"Here it is," Willy said, rushing over and showing me the iPad screen.

I studied the image while Willy pointed out a few things. "This is the main FTU warehouse. At the far eastern end is their production and recycling facility for boxes."

I glanced at him.

"They manufacture and produce all their own boxes in house, and that's where all the illegal action happens. What's interesting is this." His finger pointed directly south of the recycling facility. "It's an abandoned airplane hangar at the far eastern end of the TJ airport, only about 250 meters between the recycling facility and the hangar. Recently, I'd say within the past month or so, there's been a clear increase in activity there. . ."

Willy continued speaking, but I didn't pay attention to what he was saying. My eyes and attention were laser focused on the four military convoy trucks parked alongside the eastern wall of the airplane hangar. I thought about the timeline and the approximate distance from the Punta De Las Olas building to Tijuana. It was a three-hour flight time for a helicopter, probably eight or so hours by car. For these big military vehicles, more like nine or ten hours. It was enough time, though, since the convoy had all day and early evening to travel.

The women! The missing women must be in the hangar. And likely Mom. The American hostage.

"Mr. Chase," Willy said, "are you listening?"

"Give me one second," I said. "Hold tight." I didn't wait for his response. Instead, I raced out of the room and found Slim and quickly brought him up to speed. We discussed what to do, eventually deciding on Slim staying with Delgado and Mick helping me at the warehouse.

After the call to Mick, I went back to the chapel. "Take me there," I said, pointing at the iPad screen, which was on Willy's lap. "Take me to the warehouse now. You can explain the rest on the way."

He hesitated.

I headed to the door. "*Vámonos*, Willy, *vámonos*."

CHAPTER FORTY-EIGHT

Darkness hid my approach as I hustled west toward the FTU recycling facility. I hadn't seen another human since Willy dropped me off five minutes ago. As a result, it didn't feel necessary to move slowly and cautiously, and I wasn't worried about anyone overhearing my cell conversation with Slim. I'd called him to fill him in on some details.

"At some point," Slim was saying, "you're going to have to trust one of them, pal. At the very least, you need to trust your instinct on who you think is telling the truth. And you need to start doing that now."

He was right, of course, but I hesitated to admit that.

"People change, Chase," he continued. "That's something you have a hard time accepting."

Damn, he knew me. He was right again, but I still deflected. "I take it from that statement you buy Delgado's story then. That's he's truly a changed man and innocent of all this. Which means you think Ortiz is really the Butcher and is the one lying about everything."

"I think Delgado has the story that makes the most sense. And since, yes, I do believe people can change, I think he's telling the truth. I think Ortiz has been manipulating everything and everybody, especially us and the president."

"You think she's clean in this?"

"I do. She may have her faults, but she's not involved in a plot with these missing women. No way."

I trudged on while thinking about that, eventually agreeing. "I'm with you. What bugs you the most about Ortiz and his story?"

"Nothing," he was quick to reply. "It's a distinct possibility he's telling the truth about Delgado. But if Delgado is the one lying, then our mission in the mountains doesn't make much sense. That situation bothers me."

I'd been thinking the same thing but wanted to hear Slim articulate his concerns. "How so?"

"If Delgado is lying, then he's really the Butcher and responsible for the replica building and drugged women. Why then would he be drugged and chained to the bed with the women in his own facility? The only explanation would be to convince us he's not the Butcher, and to try to sell us that he was the real victim here."

"Right, which is quite a stretch and an elaborate setup. It would mean those were his men chasing us and shooting at us."

"And ultimately wounding him badly."

I thought about that last point by Slim. Perhaps it was all a ruse by Delgado, and it *was* his men chasing us. Maybe they simply made a mistake by shooting him in the leg. "Man, Slim, I wish we'd spoken with the women when we were there. Asked them how Delgado got to the basement. The women could've provided some information and confirmation to help us figure out who's telling the truth."

"True," Slim said. "But the whole situation was rushed and pretty dire. Is Mick on his way?"

"An hour out," I replied. "It would've been nice to have set up a communication system with Arturo, too. Don't you think?"

"Buddy, nothing we can do about those things now. Let's forget the past and look forward. You have a job to do."

I thought about Arturo and his niece and their fate. Those thoughts turned quickly dour, so I pushed everything aside and said to Slim, "I do have a job to do, so I'm gonna sign off now. I'm close to the recycling facility."

After saying our goodbyes, I settled into some low bushes and surveyed the area. Nobody was around at ten at night. The far eastern side of the recycling facility was a construction zone, and all the workers had been off for hours. Since I didn't know if they had a security patrol or not, I needed to lay low and wait at least a half an hour before making another move.

While waiting and watching, I thought about what had transpired since rushing out of the clinic. Originally, I'd wanted Willy to drive me directly to the airplane hangar, but he convinced me otherwise. The mission Henrietta had for me was to confirm the tunnel's existence from the US side, then follow up with her. The president would take it from there. Though I didn't particularly like that plan, I agreed that approaching from the US side made most sense.

Before taking on another presidential mission, though, I needed to first speak with Henrietta. Unfortunately, Willy couldn't get a hold of her because she was in an evening campaign town hall in Yuma, so I couldn't question the president's motivation or involvement. I was still somewhat skeptical as to her role in all this. So, I devised my own plan, which was to confirm the tunnel's existence, then wait for Mick and his team.

Willy and I had entered the States via the crossing in Otay Mesa. It was not a busy crossing and having government plates on our vehicle helped us breeze through. After dropping me off about a half-mile from the FTU compound, Willy drove to an industrial business park across the street from the main FTU warehouse and waited for me there. Prior to crossing the border, we'd swung by the airport and picked up the one pistol we'd left in the Sikorsky. I'd dropped my empty Five-seveN pistol into the jungle canopy, but Mick had kept his. We still had the WASR-10s but no ammunition for them. I'd assumed Mick had emptied his clip, so I was happily surprised when I discovered two bullets were left. The pistol was currently tucked into my belt, behind my back.

After about a half hour in the dark, my eyes had adjusted. I could see the area where the tunnel exit was proposed to be. There was a collection of large, wheeled recycling bins just outside the far eastern corner of the construction site. Underneath one of those bins was the tunnel's access point.

Apparently.

Feeling confident there were no security men patrolling the perimeter, I made my move. This time, however, I did move slowly and cautiously until I reached the four big, blue bins. The bins were lined up on a slab of concrete. A curb was behind the bins, and behind the curb was nothing but dry, open land. I couldn't see details of the airplane hangar across the border, but I could tell how close the building was, and that this far corner lined up directly with the middle of the hangar.

I looked inside the first recycling bin. Nothing but empty boxes stacked up two-thirds to the top, so I rolled the bin to my left until I could see the full area underneath. The concrete continued. I pulled the next bin into the position the first one had been.

Again, nothing but solid concrete underneath.

The third one was different, however. This bin had one of the two lids opened, and as I pulled it toward me, into the open position where bin number two had been, I noticed how much heavier it was. Immediately I figured it had been weighed down, that way it didn't accidentally wheel away and reveal what was underneath. I wasn't surprised when I saw a square metal grate in the concrete.

Jackpot.

Rushing over, I noted it looked like a standard storm run-off grate. I bent over and peered through the grates, but I couldn't see much from lack of light. After lifting off the grate and setting it aside, I pulled out my personal cell and flashed the light down the hole.

Since I couldn't see down that far, I grabbed the burner cell from the president and used its light as well. With both lights, I could see more, but I still couldn't see the bottom. To me, it looked exactly like a sewer and/or ground water run-off hole. The sides of the hole were smooth concrete, and a metal ladder was embedded into the concrete.

I sat by the hole for a moment. A moment turned into several minutes. My mind raced with theories about this hole. Part of me thought this was perfect cover for a tunnel exit, totally ingenious to build a fake run-off system to hide a tunnel's true intentions. The other part of me thought I'd simply discovered an actual run-off grate, that the intel I was given was wrong or misleading. I knew I needed to descend the hole and confirm whether this was a tunnel exit from the other side. But should I do it now? Or should I wait another half hour for help to arrive?

After mulling that over for a minute, I made my decision. My mother's life, along with hundreds of innocent women, were at stake here, so no time to waste.

Just as I prepared to climb down the ladder, I heard some noise to my left.

Very subtle, but a noise, nonetheless. It came from inside the third recycling bin.

The heavy one!

Suddenly I understood. Scrambling to my feet, I knew the heaviness wasn't to weigh down the bin. The heaviness was a person inside.

Sure enough, as I got to my feet and charged toward the bin, a man popped up. Boxes above his head peeled away, revealing a disfigured face.

But I wasn't paying attention to who the man was.

My focus was on his rising gun arm.

CHAPTER FORTY-NINE

HIS GUN LEVELED at my rapidly approaching chest.

I had no time to extract my pistol. Instead, I zeroed in on his trigger finger. As soon as I saw him pull, I spun ninety degrees to my right, exposing my left shoulder. At that exact moment, I angled my upper body backward.

Boom!

Instantly I felt the round pierce my left arm. I didn't drop to the ground, so I knew my chest was spared. I slammed into the bin hard, leading with my wounded shoulder since I had no time to pivot to my other shoulder. The second shot rang out above my head, which drowned out my scream from the searing shoulder pain.

Directly behind the bin was the curb, so the wheels banged into it and the bin teetered backward. Since it was a heavy bin, it didn't topple over. While it was teetering, though, I plowed ahead like an NFL lineman and flipped it on its side.

The man inside toppled backward and ended up flat on his back amidst a tangle of boxes. Meanwhile, I scrambled over the bin and fought my way through the slippery, flattened carboard. I grabbed his ankle with my good hand—my right—and yanked him toward me. Simultaneously, I was reaching around with my injured, bloody left arm to extract the Five-seveN.

Fortunately, the man had lost his gun in the melee. But he sprang forward, pivoting at the waist. He immediately latched on to my left arm with both hands. My pistol had been coming forward, but I instantly drop it when he squeezed my wound.

He had a wild look in his eyes, and I quickly recognized the man as Thiago.

"You're a dead man, Gary," he seethed, squeezing harder.

Instead of yelling in pain, I reacted by dropping my hold on his ankle and feeding Thiago the punch of my life. I connected flush with his left cheek and left side of his nose. He flopped backward so fast I couldn't tell how much damage I'd added to his already disfigured face.

With Thiago dazed, I used the moment to glance left to locate my pistol. As I spotted it and reached across with my right to grab it, I noticed Thiago's legs flailing in my periphery.

Suddenly the chunky heel of a cowboy boot connected with my jaw. I spun backward from the impact. My right hand failed to grab the pistol, but it did grip the edge of a flattened box. As Thiago recovered and sat up, I used that box and swung it sideways in a slicing motion. The box cut through Thiago's neck.

"You're the dead man, Thiago." My eyes focused on his bloody neck. He would've felt the wound, of course, but he wouldn't know how bad it was. He had no idea it was only a centimeter deep slash.

Naturally, his hands went to his jugular.

Capitalizing on that, I grabbed the Five-seveN and pistol-whipped Thiago.

While he cursed in pain, I used my considerable weight to pin him to the ground. I fed him two more solid right-hand punches until he went limp. Then I tucked the pistol away, stood and grabbed his ankle again.

I dragged Thiago backward; his head bumping off the curb and smacking against the concrete. With his body in front of recycling bin number two, I dropped my grip on his ankle and opened the bin's heavy, black plastic lid. Next, I grabbed the man's skinny frame and flopped him over the edge of the bin. Since he was positioned front forward, he was bent at the waist. His upper body was inside the bin, and his lower body was outside it.

I slammed the lid against his lower back, then hopped up and sat on it and attended to my arm. It was bleeding decently, but not out of control. Taking off my outer shirt, I examined the wound. The bullet had passed through the outside edge of my left bicep. Fortunately, it was only about a half-inch-deep wound. I ripped my shirt in a few pieces and tied one of the pieces in tourniquet fashion above the wound.

Then I waited for my dear friend Thiago to come to. Naturally, I had questions for him. It seemed pretty clear he was waiting for me. So, how did he know I was coming? Who fed him that intel? The president or Ortiz? Or could there be another explanation for his presence?

Unfortunately, I didn't get a moment to think since a shot rang out and buzzed over my shoulder. Atop the recycling bin, I was totally exposed, so I reached around and grabbed the pistol with my right and pointed it toward the direction of the shots.

Two armed men were fifty yards away, approaching fast with rifles extended. Immediately I assumed they were Thiago's backup men.

Pulling twice, I dropped the man on my left, then swung the pistol right and pulled.

Nothing. I pulled again. Nothing but an empty sound. That was when I remembered I only had two bullets to work with.

The man on the right fired a short blast. Those rounds hissed by me, missing by a mile. I realized with Thiago so close the man wasn't about to risk killing his boss. The problem for me: as soon as I jumped off the bin and moved left or right, or tried to roll backward, this dude wouldn't miss again.

All I could do was hold my hands in the air and pray he didn't shoot.

I held my breath as he advanced on me. By this point, Thiago had come to, and he was pissed. The weight of my body kept him subdued, however.

The man swept in fast with an aggressive look on his face. The assault rifle was still extended, bouncing up and down as he covered the final twenty yards. His right index finger was taut on the trigger. I saw he held another Barrett REC7 assault rifle. When he slowed and stopped and aimed the Barrett, I closed my eyes.

My mind pictured Simon. A happy image of him smiling. That was how I wanted to go.

Instead of shooting, though, I heard, "Off."

I opened my eyes to the man waving the rifle, demanding I get off the bin.

Letting out a huge breath, I complied. Immediately Thiago straightened.

In frustration, he pressed the lid off his head and slammed it open. He nodded a thanks to his man, then turned to me.

No addressing me as amigo this time. "*Cabrón*," he said, "you are indeed the dead man now."

The man holding the REC7 spouted off in Spanish. Thiago glanced at him and replied in English. "Not yet. And I want the pleasure of doing it, not you."

Thiago turned to me. My punches had opened a few prior facial wounds. Those wounds wept blood, streaking down his cheeks and leaving a crimson trail.

"Cell phone," he said. "Take it out and kick it away."

I didn't. "So, your cartel and Ortiz are working together. And my president is feeding information to your cartel. Is that it? What are you all hoping to gain, anyway?"

Thiago wasn't in the mood to converse. Instead, he turned to his man and motioned him toward me.

"My guess is moving in on Sinaloa territory," I continued, "is that right? Your main competitor. Is that ultimately what's in it for you and your men? My president wins, at least in the eyes of the public, because the notorious Sinaloa cartel is taken out of power. I bet they're responsible for the dead American soldiers in Nogales."

"Cell phones," Thiago said, this time using the plural. That confirmed he knew everything, that I even had two cells on me. And he could have only known that from the president.

Thiago rushed over. "You move, you're dead." He shot a look at his man, who had the Barrett pointed at my face, then looked back at me. He spun me around and patted me down.

After fishing out my two cells, I heard him say to his man in English, "Take them to the coast, right now. Make sure they're on and throw them off one of the cliffs in Pacific Beach. Before you go, I'll take the rifle."

I listened to the exchange, then moments later I felt the barrel poke me in the back.

"Move," Thiago said, prodding me toward the sewer grate.

When I reached the hole's edge, I said, "So this is the plan, is it? Shoot me in the back, I fall into the hole, then what?"

Surprisingly, he responded. "Then you join the same fate as the others."

I glanced over my shoulder.

He motioned toward the hangar. "Everyone on that side, including your mother. It will be a quick burial, at least for you, maybe not so for the others."

Just then, a radio squawked. Still looking over my shoulder, I watched Thiago take out a handheld radio and respond, "Not yet. Wait for my signal."

I tried to control my breathing, tried not to let the gravity of the situation get to me.

Think, Chase, think!

"The others," I said. "You mean two hundred innocent women? That's who you're referring to. You're going to murder two hundred innocent women, Thiago. Just like that, with no conscience or remorse."

"Turn around," he commanded. "Look at me straight on."

I did.

"If you had done your job," he said through clenched teeth, "if you had taken out Delgado as instructed, like we implored you to do, those women" —he jabbed the rifle toward the hangar—"wouldn't be in this situation."

I blew up at that statement. "Oh, so it's *my* fault. I just needed to kill an innocent man, set him up to go down as a notorious terrorist, then the operation to drug these women and sell them to Americans could continue. You take that noble cause away from Sinaloa, and then carry on their tradition, is that right? I bet you've convinced yourself that these women are better off as sex slaves in America, haven't you?"

Thiago didn't respond.

"Oh," I said, "so you *have* bought that line."

He pointed the rifle at me, took up some trigger slack. "You're a smart man, Senor Chase, too smart for your own good. But we're done talking now, amigo. *Finito.*"

Suddenly something Ortiz had said in Punta San Carlos came to mind.

"You need me far away from here, don't you? That's why your man is taking my cell to the coast in San Diego. You know people are tracking my cell, right?"

He sighed. "What's your point?"

"I have a GPS tracker in the insole of my boot. Like the ones runners use."

His finger eased a little.

I kept going. "They're standalone, these small GPS devices. In the past, they had to be tied to an app on your cell. They're more sophisticated now, so you don't need your phone with you. It's too bulky to be running with, anyway, so these new trackers have their own storage and signal built in."

His finger eased some more. I was getting to him. Which was good since I was making this stuff up. It rang true to me, but I wasn't sure if it really was true or not.

"You shoot me," I said, "and I fall down this hole. My body will be traceable. Hans, Mick, and my girlfriend know about the tracker. They'll know exactly where my body is. And you don't want a soul to know about this tunnel, not when you're planning to bury hundreds of women alive and two Americans."

He thought for a moment. Suddenly he jabbed the rifle my direction. "Step forward. Now. Or you're a dead man."

"Not a chance," I said.

I watched his brow furrow.

"I'm a dead man," I replied, "no matter which way you look at it. If I step forward, you shoot me, but my body doesn't fall down the hole. You simply take my boot off, push me down the hole, then take the tracker to the coast. Nope, not doing it. Why would I?"

To emphasize my point, I stepped back and dangled one foot behind me, hovering it above the hole.

"Fine, I'll shoot you," Thiago said. "Then I'll climb down and take your boot off, then drive to the coast. Correction: I'll climb down and check your boot, 'cause I think you're lying."

Damn, he made a good point. I countered with, "But my boys are already on their way. That will take you some time to climb down and back up, and they'll be here by then."

"We know exactly where Hans and Delgado are, and that pilot of yours."

"Yeah, but you don't know where my military buddy Mick is."

"I've had enough of this." He took aim. I saw him put pressure on the trigger.

Fearing he was about to pull the trigger, I blurted, "Don't shoot!" I held up both arms. "Fine, I'll prove it to you." I immediately bent over and started untying my boot.

"Easy," he said. "Easy!"

But I didn't slow down or take it easy. As I unlaced my boot, I pretended to be really pissed. The moment the laces were untied, and I pulled the boot apart to create some room to free my foot, I straightened. At the same time, I whipped my foot forward.

The boot flung like a missile at Thiago. I dodged to my left as it sailed through the air and connected with Thiago's upper chest. He fired a shot, but it went high.

As the rifle tracked up, I barreled into him with my head, connecting hard with his lower abdomen. The REC7 flew backward, and so did Thiago. We both landed on the concrete in a heap.

Since I had the upper position, I picked him up under the arms. In a fury, I spun Thiago around and took a few steps and heaved him backward. He stumbled a few steps, tripping over his feet. He collapsed onto his butt and kept sliding.

Then Thiago slipped down the hole and clear out of sight.

CHAPTER FIFTY

By Thiago's three- to four-second-long scream, I estimated the depth of the hole to be about fifty or sixty feet.

I grabbed the REC7, put my boot back on, then rushed to the toppled recycling bin. After a moment of searching, I found the gun Thiago had used to shoot me. It was an Obregón, a Mexican designed .45 caliber semiautomatic pistol.

Taking both weapons, I scrambled down the ladder. Nearing the bottom, where it was pitch-dark, I stopped on the ladder and listened. I wasn't sure of Thiago's condition. No doubt he was dead, but I had to check to be sure.

When I heard no movement or moaning, I proceeded to the bottom and immediately stumbled over Thiago's dead body. I rummaged through his pockets and took out his cell and radio.

The first thing I checked was his phone. No bars. *Damn.*

Since I desperately needed to call Slim—to warn him that they knew his location—I raced up the ladder, about two-thirds to the top, until a bar of reception registered on the cell.

Hanging on that ladder, I called Slim and told him everything.

"Just wait for Mick," he said.

"I can't. My mom, Slim, these women, they're going to die. Pretty sure the plan is to bury everyone in this tunnel at any given moment. They're tying up every loose end possible, which is why you have to be careful."

"I will, don't worry about me." The handheld squawked to life and interrupted me. "Gotta go, pal."

The radio voice had spoken rapidly in Spanish, but I deciphered the word *listo* and knew that meant *ready* in English. I hesitated to respond and pretend to be Thiago. The fortunate thing was that Thiago didn't have much of an accent, and earlier he'd replied in English.

I pushed the button, thinking about how Thiago had responded. "Not yet. Just wait for my signal."

With no time to waste, I rushed to the bottom, using the light on Thiago's cell to see. His body had landed at the ladder's base in an open area, which was sopping wet from a few inches of water. The entire space was maybe twelve feet by twelve feet. If it wasn't wet, it would've made a good spot to store extra contraband.

I needed to move. The walls, however, gave me pause. At first, my eyes were drawn to them because they were slick and seeping water. But as I scanned the cavern, the explosives embedded in the dirt walls made me freeze in place.

They are definitely prepared to bury this tunnel. Move, Chase!

I refocused on my surroundings. A few feet behind the ladder's landing area was the main tunnel. That tunnel ended abruptly after only thirty feet. There was one offshoot, however.

I raced to the offshoot, which was about two and a half or three feet in diameter. Lining the inside of the tunnel was a hard plastic sleeve. I fit inside the pipe, just barely. Unfortunately, the Barrett REC7, which was slung around my back, wouldn't fit. I could've carried it out front with me, but that would've significantly slowed me down.

And time was my enemy.

I left the Barrett behind and took the Mexican pistol and radio into the tunnel with me. The tube's plastic floor was angled down slightly. Not steep enough, though, for me to use gravity and slide to the other end. Normally, I'd have quite a problem with a tight fit like this, due to my slight fear of enclosed spaces, but all I could think about was rushing to the other end and saving Mom and the other women.

As I slinked down the pipe, my left arm throbbed in pain. I distracted my mind by thinking about the time it would take to travel 250 meters. Since I was a tall man, I knew I could easily stretch my arms forward a whole meter. By quickly pulling my knees in after stretching out, I figured I could cover a meter distance in about two or three seconds. That put my time at 500-750 seconds to cover the total distance. Somewhere between nine and thirteen minutes to get to the other end.

But could I keep up that pace, especially with an injured arm?

I surprised myself and made it approximately 200 meters in ten minutes. At the 200-meter mark, I was exhausted, but at least I could see the tunnel's origin. There was a dim light coming from that end. Seeing the end wasn't what got me moving quicker, though, it was what I heard that did.

Screams and panicked voices traveled down the pipe and filled my ears. They were clearly women's voices.

With all the noise, I didn't have to slow my approach or worry about being heard. When I reached within ten meters of the tunnel's opening, I could see one man standing just outside the entrance. He was hunched over with his back to me. The other thing I could see was a welding arc. It looked like he was welding something onto the tunnel floor.

What? I couldn't tell at this distance.

I slinked forward and stopped a meter and a half from the end. That was where the light stopped its penetration into the pipe.

When I saw what was going on, I immediately pulled out the Obregón.

The man stood on a floor made of welded pieces of rebar. The whole thing looked like a giant, metallic spider web. He was bent over welding a final bar across the biggest opening in the web.

Below him were women's voices. Screams, to be precise.

I almost pulled the trigger right then. But I didn't. The sound of gunfire would travel to the surface. And that would draw attention to the situation, which would send more men down.

Nope, wasn't going to do it.

Instead, I tucked the pistol away and pulled out my Kershaw knife, gripping it with my good hand. I slinked to the end as fast as I could, got to my feet and immediately lunged forward.

Knowing what this man was doing—sealing the women alive in an earthly grave—I didn't hesitate for a second. I jammed the knife in the back of his right thigh.

His scream added to the cacophony of sounds.

As he collapsed forward, I fell with him, pulling out the knife in the process. After flattening him on the metal rebar floor, I finished him off with a stab to his right side.

Next, I pushed his body toward the wall and grabbed the construction light that hung on a scaffolding system above my head. I brought the light down to the floor. My heart sank.

All the women were there, and some men, too.

Hundreds of eyes looked up at me. Hands stretched out above their heads. A chorus of "helps" ascended to my ears. I moved the light around to see faces. It was hard, though, to make out particular faces since two hundred bodies were cramped in the basin below, but I eventually did, spotting Arturo first, then Mom. She said something to me but I, obviously, couldn't hear.

"One second!" I yelled down.

Turning, I grabbed the welding equipment, but then realized I'd never welded before and didn't know where to begin. So, I looked back at where the man I'd stabbed had been working. He hadn't quite finished welding the last piece of rebar in place.

I stomped on the joint he'd been working on. Over and over. Ten kicks later, the rebar broke downward. During my frantic stomping, I hadn't noticed a man climbing the ladder underneath the floor. As soon as that last rebar piece broke free from the joint, the man on the ladder cranked it back and out of the way.

Without a word, he climbed through the small opening, then grabbed the welding equipment and began making the hole in the floor bigger. At the same time, women started rushing up the ladder.

What should I do with them?

All I knew was that I couldn't send them topside. Surely, there were more men inside the hangar, and those men wouldn't hesitate to kick the women back down the hole or shoot them on sight.

"Arturo! Mom!" I shouted while bringing the construction light toward the floor. "Send Arturo and Izzy up quickly."

By the time they made it up, the tunnel floor was packed with twenty or so women.

"I knew you'd come," Mom said, embracing me. "I knew it, son, just knew it."

I wiped some misty tears from her eyes.

"Are you okay?" she asked. "What happened to your arm, dear?"

Pulling back, I said, "Never mind me, Mom. I'm fine. Are you hurt or injured?"

She shook her head.

"You're doing okay then?"

"I am now."

I turned to Arturo. Before I could speak, he said, "So glad to see you, Mister Chase. So glad."

I nodded. "We need to move, get these women to safety. Is it clear topside?" I thumbed toward the surface.

He vigorously shook his head. "No way, a number of armed men are up there."

"That way it is." I pointed down the tunnel.

He paused for a moment, then nodded and said, "Our only way."

I grabbed his shoulder. "Take them to the States, my friend. Lead the way. There's a REC7 at the other end. Protect the women, Arturo. Mick and his team should be there to help."

I didn't wait for him to respond. I also didn't want to cause a panic and mention the explosives at the other end. "Now go," I commanded. "Be safe. And be fast."

Before rushing into the tunnel, Arturo grabbed Mariana and brought her to the front of the line. She hugged me without saying a word, then Mariana was the first into the tunnel.

Mom surprised me by not following Arturo into the tunnel. Instead, she encouraged the women hesitating in front of it. "Quickly, quickly." She began taking charge and directing traffic.

I helped her by repeating, "*Rapido, rapido.*"

Before long, though, I knew I had to go to the surface. My fear was the explosives at the other end. I'd bought some time by using the radio, but soon they'd get suspicious as to why Thiago hadn't given the go-ahead.

"Mom, I have to go up there." I motioned to the surface.

She turned. "No, you don't, son. It will take some time, but we can get everyone out safely this way."

When I hesitated on my response, she stepped toward me. "What's wrong, Gary? What aren't you telling me?"

"We don't have much time, that's all I'll say. If you hear a loud explosion, Mom, climb this scaffolding and get to safety. I'm going up there to hopefully clear the area."

She grasped my wrist. "You sure?"

"It's our only way, Mom, maybe our only chance at surviving this."

"Be careful, hon, I'll stay back and help the women."

"Are you sure?"

She nodded and said, "Hon, if you do clear the area, look for two people. They aren't down here, they were taken earlier, so I thought they were among the first to be forced into the basin. But I can't find them anywhere, and they're dear to me."

"Who, Mom?"

She quickly described an older man and his great-granddaughter. A man name Javi or Mr. White and a young girl named Sylvia. I asked a few quick questions, then knew I had to go.

As I started ascending the scaffolding, Mom said, "Take Raoul with you." She motioned to the man who'd been using the welding equipment. "He's proved invaluable and speaks good English."

"It's too dangerous," I said, shaking my head.

"Mister," Raoul responded, "danger is everywhere. There's no escaping it. You may need help, so let's go."

Raoul followed me up.

The scaffolding was well built, so it was a relatively easy climb to the top. I hung back a few feet below the surface and listened, for longer than I would've liked. There were some arguing voices, but there was also a distant sound of gunfire. Since I couldn't decipher any parts of the conversations I heard, I waved Raoul up.

He climbed to my position and immediately began listening. Soon, he acted as my interpreter, whispering to me, "They're arguing about what to do. Apparently, there are men outside and the building is surrounded."

While Raoul paused to listen some more, I thought about what was going on outside. Perhaps Sinaloa or Jalisco had caught wind of the operation and was fighting back? Or was it Mick's team? Had they crossed the border and surrounded the building?

Raoul interrupted my thoughts. "There's also talk about explosives and a man named Thiago. They haven't heard from him. They're about to call him again."

Immediately I grabbed the radio from my back pocket and frantically tried to turn it off. Just as it crackled on, I shut off the radio.

Did they hear the static?

I held my breath, listening for footsteps, waiting for a head to peer over the tunnel's opening. I stretched out the Obregón toward the surface, figuring I'd take out the first head I saw. Then I'd rush from the hole with the gun blazing.

Raoul and I hung there for a few tense seconds.

Fortunately, nobody came. I imagined that was due to all the chaos around. It was clear the men inside the hangar were preoccupied with the surrounding forces and what to do about Thiago's silence.

I used the distraction to climb the remaining few feet, then eased my head above the surface to see. Alejandro Ortiz was the first man in my field of vision, directly in front of my position. His presence solidified his identity as the Butcher of Baja.

The Butcher was approximately thirty feet away, standing by a line of heavy-duty, gray plastic tables that were clearly used as dining tables for the workers. Two men surrounded Ortiz. They were the arguing voices that Raoul and I had heard.

The Butcher's men held REC7 rifles, but they weren't drawn. The men surrounding Ortiz weren't the same men from his compound in Punta San Carlos. The fact that they held REC7 rifles meant they were part of Thiago's cartel. In the middle of the closest table was a handheld radio and another smaller device. I guessed it was a detonator.

Turning a full rotation, I noted three more cartel men in the hangar. Those men stood by the main hangar door and were paying attention to the noises going on outside. Their weapons were at the ready. I noted they were also REC7 rifles.

Slinking down, I brought Raoul up to speed on what I'd seen. The whole time I whispered to him I cursed myself for not bringing the REC7 with me.

After speaking with Raoul, he popped his head up and surveyed the hangar for a few moments. "You need a diversion," he whispered to me after surveilling the area.

"Right," I replied, "I definitely do."

"I'll be the diversion," Raoul said. "I'll draw attention from the men at the hangar door. You take out the men by the table."

"It's a death sentence, Raoul."

He shrugged and motioned below him. "So is down there. This is our best chance. It's a large hangar and I could make it to safety on the right side by one of those old planes."

I was about to argue, but Raoul held out his hand.

"No time to argue, Mister Chase."

With that, Raoul climbed the remaining few feet and pulled himself from the hole. The last thing I saw was him heading in the direction away from the plastic tables.

Immediately there were shouts, then a brief pause before gunfire.

I raced to the top with the Obregón drawn. Exploding from the hole, I fired toward the Butcher and his two men, angling to my left since the men at the table had turned right and were aimed at a retreating Raoul.

I took out one of Ortiz's men. The other one swung his rifle toward me and pulled the trigger. I stayed ahead of the blast by a few feet, eventually sliding and pulling down the last table in the line. I turned the table on its side and took refuge as another blast came.

It shredded the right side of the plastic table like it was swiss cheese.

I immediately returned fire to put the man on defense. When a brief pause between gunfire happened, I quickly glanced up.

Ortiz and his man had also turned over their closest table. The other three cartel men by the hangar door were now firing their weapons and advancing toward one of the planes on the hangar's other side. I couldn't see Raoul, so hopefully he'd made it to a plane unharmed.

Banging could suddenly be heard on the hangar door. Following that, bullets pored through the sheet metal. From behind the closed door, tons of muffled shouting could be heard.

A spray of gunfire erupted from behind Ortiz's table. I flattened on the floor as bullets sailed just over my head. Since the hangar was about to be breached, and things would get even uglier, I angled toward the end of my table—still flat on my stomach—and moved away from the table's protection for a moment. As soon as I could see Ortiz's table, I pulled the trigger rapidly five times.

One—maybe two—bullets penetrated the table and hit Ortiz's man. His weapon dropped, then he clutched his stomach as his eyes rolled back.

Ortiz started shouting, adding to the chaos. "*Don't shoot!*" he screamed. "I have the detonator. *I have it!* I'll push it, I swear."

He stood, dragging the plastic table backward and using it as a shield. Ortiz's free hand waved the detonator. He frantically scrambled back toward the hole, screaming at me over and over.

I advanced toward him, cautiously. My mind calculated the various options. "Stop moving," I shouted. "Stop Ortiz, and I won't fire."

But Ortiz didn't stop. He was inching back toward the hole, still shouting at me not to shoot.

The tension only grew worse when the hangar doors were ripped off their hinges as one of the military convoy vehicles crashed through. Following that, a flash grenade lobbed into the building, which stunned everyone and brought me to my knees. After the initial shock and impact, I looked up and surveyed the scene, stretching out the Obregón to protect myself.

The three cartel men who were by the planes and shooting at Raoul had stopped. They spun and turned their gunfire toward the military vehicle. A team of commandos were piling out of the back and fanning out in various directions. Within seconds, I watched the three men by the planes get shot and killed by sniper-like accuracy.

Then I heard, "Aug, don't shoot. Repeat, don't shoot."

Immediately I lowered the Obregón. Aug was short for my former operative codename: Augustine. Mick was here, yelling at me. These commandos were his elite unit.

Dropping the gun, I advanced toward Ortiz with my arms up. "Drop it," I yelled at him.

Ortiz dropped the table but not the detonator.

In my periphery, I could see Mick's men assembling and about to act. "Don't shoot him," I said. "Please."

"Hold fire," Mick commanded his men.

Twenty feet from Ortiz, I stopped. "It's over, Alejandro. Your reign is over. You're finished, Butcher."

Ortiz glanced at me, then shot a look at his dead men. His eyes flicked toward Mick's commandos, who were to his left and ready to take him down. Finally, he looked back at me.

"Agreed," he said. "It's over for me, indeed. You're a formidable foe, Garrison Chase. Didn't think you'd get to the Sierra Madres early like you did, you caught us off guard there. You and your team and Juan were all supposed to die in that building's basement. I must've made a mistake somewhere, just not sure where."

I didn't engage. Instead, I said, "Just ease your thumb off the detonator, Ortiz."

He replied, "One mistake in my business is a death sentence. I've always said that, guess I'm now living proof it's true."

"No need to make it a death sentence for all. Please, put the detonator down."

Once again, Alejandro Ortiz looked around at his surrounded position. "You will not, though, be taking me back to the States alive. Not a chance."

Suddenly Ortiz jammed his thumb down on the detonator.

"*No!*" I yelled in vain.

There was a short pause after Ortiz pushed the detonator, and in that brief moment, I thought maybe, just maybe, the explosives had malfunctioned.

Then we all heard it: a deep thundering *boom!* It sounded far off, so it was clearly from the other side of the border.

As the ground trembled beneath me, I looked at Ortiz. The Butcher had a sinister smile on his face.

"You're not bringing me anywhere," he said calmly. "Not over my very dead body. And you certainly won't bring that back to the States either. No way."

In seemingly slow motion, Alejandro Ortiz, aka the Butcher of Baja, laid back into midair.

Then I watched his large body plunge silently into the cavernous hole beneath him.

CHAPTER FIFTY-ONE

As I RUSHED toward the giant hole in the hangar's floor, my mind raced with worry. I thought of Mom and the women below. Had Ortiz's body flattened and maybe killed someone?

I also thought about the explosion at the other end, knowing that the plan was to bury that end of the tunnel, which would no doubt send a tidal wave of water down the pipe and flood this end.

Peering down the hole, I held my breath.

The makeshift floor was only sixty feet down and the construction light was still on, so I could see. I exhaled when I saw a man pushing the Butcher's fat body through the large opening in the floor. Ortiz's body plunged into the basin below. It appeared Mom and a few women were still down there with the man.

"Mom! Hurry!" I shouted. "Up the scaffolding. Get out of—"

Right then, the man who'd just pushed Ortiz took a pair of feet to his chest as a woman shot from the pipe. About five more women shot out of the tube, crashing into each other, one by one. Following that, a man who I immediately recognized as Arturo, smashed into the women's bodies. Everyone was piled up in a tangle of arms and legs. Then a cannon-sized blast of water burst from the pipe's end like a broken fire hydrant.

In horror, I watched as two or three women got swept into the basin below.

Turning to climb down, I heard Mick say, "What the hell are you doing?"

I looked up to see my buddy limping over.

"Get your men, Mick, hurry. Get 'em down this hole. It's filling with water and there's maybe ten people that need help."

He peered down, but just for a second before turning and wheeling his arm toward his team members. I was already gone, racing down one side of the scaffolding. Fortunately, Mom and a few others were on the other side of the scaffolding climbing up.

I raced down to Mom's level and noticed that she was struggling.

As I moved to her side, I said, "Get on my back, Mom. Link your hands around my neck. I'll take you to the top."

"No," she immediately replied. "Get down there, a few women need your help. Jaime stayed back to help, too."

"Mom, you might fall."

She thumbed up. "I'll get one of these young men to take me."

I looked up. Five of Mick's men were descending the scaffolding.

"Go!" she commanded.

After climbing down a few more levels, I stopped. Arturo had his niece clinging to his shoulders. He said, "I think everyone is safe on the other side, but they need help below."

I kept descending until I reached the floor. The cannon of water was relentless. It slammed into the opposite wall and drained straight down into the basin. The man who'd pushed Ortiz into the basin, who Mom had referred to as Jaime, was helping a woman up through the opening in the floor. The woman was panicked and sputtering water and obviously terrified.

Jaime looked at me and held out a finger. *"Una mas."* He pointed below.

"I'll get her." I motioned at the girl beside him. "Take her to the surface."

As I grabbed the construction light, I looked up to see Mick's men helping Mom and the other women on the scaffolding. I brought the light to the floor. The basin was half full of dark, filthy water and was rapidly rising. My hope was to see the woman in the water.

I didn't.

I tried to locate her hair floating somewhere on the water's surface, but I saw nothing. So, I dropped through the floor's opening and tin-soldiered into the water, my body slicing through and traveling straight to the basin's floor. It was pitch-dark in the muddy water, so I didn't open my eyes. Instead, I brought my arms out to the side and started moving them all around, hoping to touch the woman's body. I kept doing that while slowly ascending. By the time my body surfaced, I hadn't found her.

Above me, one of Mick's commandos was bent over and shouting, asking me what I was doing. Now that the wider part of the basin was submerged in water, I noticed the water level rose even faster in the narrower opening.

With no time to explain things to the man, I dove straight down to the bottom again. As I searched the basin's floor, I pushed out all the air in my lungs to keep me at the bottom. Within ten seconds, I stumbled over something.

Grabbing the first body part I could, which turned out to be an arm, I heaved.

All I felt was dead weight. The body didn't budge.

I pulled on the arm, which brought me close to the body. With my free hand, I touched the person. Almost immediately I knew it was Ortiz because of the bulbous midsection. Letting go, I kicked toward the nearest wall, then pushed off that wall toward the other side. As I zig-zagged wall-to-wall, up the basin and toward the surface, I swiveled my arms in all directions in hopes of touching something.

Anything.

As my breath waned, I fought to keep the course. All I wanted to do was kick straight to the surface and gulp some air. But I held on, and about two-thirds of the way to the surface, my right hand brushed something.

Both hands reached out to that area. After some frantic searching, I latched onto a body part: a thigh, I think. I righted the woman's body, grabbed her by the midsection, and kicked straight up with everything in me.

Like a breeching whale, we crashed above the water's surface. When we settled, I saw that the woman was unconscious. I treaded water and delivered a few breaths into her mouth.

To my joy, she came to a few moments later. Her eyes fluttered open.

"I got her!" a man's voice shouted. "I got her."

Looking up, I saw that we were near the spiderweb flooring, and that the commando had been waiting for me to surface. Kneeling by the basin's opening, he reached down with his two long, powerful arms and scooped her out of the water.

"You okay on your own?" he asked.

I waved him up. "Go, go. Take her, I'm fine."

He threw the woman over his shoulder and started up the scaffolding.

After climbing out, I took a moment and caught my breath and stared at the rapidly rising water. Looking down, I hoped there wasn't another woman who'd been swept into the basin.

Hopefully Ortiz is the only body down there.

As the water reached thigh-high, I left all thoughts behind and climbed to the surface. Halfway to the top, I could hear Mick's voice yelling down for me, asking me if I was okay.

I paused to give him a thumbs-up, and to rest my aching left arm. As I hung there for a moment, I noticed a bunch of explosives embedded into the wall, at about the thirty-foot mark. I'd been in such a rush before I hadn't noticed the explosives.

Obviously, the plan was to bury the tunnel's exit *and* entrance. Earlier, when I'd popped my head up to survey the area, I saw an industrial-sized cement mixer. I knew once the entrance had collapsed, they planned to fill in and smooth out the hole in the hangar floor.

Minutes later, Mick helped me out.

"So glad you're okay, buddy. You sure you're the last one?"

"I think. I hope. Pretty sure only Ortiz was left down there."

As Mick helped me to a nearby plastic chair, I looked around. Mick's men had made a makeshift triage area by the military convoy vehicle. My Mom was busy helping them out. Currently, she was by Raoul's side. Raoul looked to have a leg injury, but he was sitting up and alert and appeared to be okay.

I turned to my buddy. "What about the other side?"

"What about it?" he replied.

"Did you confirm the women's safety?"

He shook his head. "Not sure. We left Slim in charge over there."

"Slim?"

"Yup, he didn't stay put at the clinic."

"What about Delgado?"

"Clayton stayed with him."

Before I could respond, Mick said, "We knew you needed help here, buddy, so the team came over to this side."

I nodded. "I'm surprised you crossed the border."

"Me too."

I furrowed my brow, not sure what he meant by that comment.

He clarified. "Surprised that we were given authorization, I mean."

"Wow, I'm shocked that you even asked. What exactly happened?"

He pulled a plastic chair close. "As soon as we got to the recycling facility, I saw the convoy vehicles and confirmed that with my CO. He wouldn't authorize our crossing, not on his own, so he went up the chain. I mean, high up, Chase. It all happened fast, too."

I leaned forward on the chair. "How high up?"

"As high as it goes, buddy. All the way to the top."

"You mean, the chairman of the joint chiefs of staff?"

"No, I mean your pal, the president, gave us approval to act."

I stood, pushing the chair back. No doubt I had a confused look on my face because Mick asked, "What gives, Chase?"

"But she's involved in this," I said. "Why would she give you authorization to act, especially on this side of the border, in a cover-up she must've known about? She set me up on the other side, Mick."

"I don't think so, pal. I don't think she's involved in burying this tunnel and potentially murdering hundreds of innocent lives. She helped stop all this."

Confused, I stood there without responding.

Mick interrupted my thoughts. "Listen, I'm supposed to call her and update her on mission status. In fact, I have her direct number."

"Really? You're kidding."

He pushed a button on his cell, then handed it to me. "I'm not. You speak with her."

I reluctantly took it, not believing him. Needless to say, I was shocked when POTUS picked up and said, "Mick, what's the status?"

"Not Mick," I said. "It's Garrison Chase, Henrietta."

"Garrison, finally. My goodness. Finally, finally I get to speak with you."

Finally? What does *finally* mean?

"Garrison, are you there?"

"What do you mean you finally get to speak with me, ma'am? What's that supposed to mean? You're the one who's been unresponsive."

"What do you mean?" she snapped back. "I haven't heard a peep from you. I monitored the burner cell I gave you for days. In fact, this whole time I've been monitoring it. Nothing from your end. Nothing."

Before I could respond, I felt someone hugging me. Pulling away from the conversation, I saw that it was Mom. She squeezed me tightly from behind.

"So glad you made it, hon. I think everyone got out safely, at least on this end."

I gave her a quick squeeze back and said, "Hold on, Mom. I need to finish this call."

Mick came over and quickly explained to Mom that I was on with the president. As I turned back to the conversation with Henrietta, Mom was loud in my other ear as she questioned Mick.

She repeatedly asked him about Javi and Sylvia. When she referred to Javi as Mr. White, I tensed. That name triggered something in me.

And suddenly, all the pieces fell into place.

"Garrison, are you still there?" the president asked. "Did I just hear you refer to your mother? Your mom? Exactly what the hell is going on there?"

"Sorry, Madam President, I'm still here." I cleared my throat. "And, ma'am, I'll tell you exactly what I think is going on here."

CHAPTER FIFTY-TWO

BY THE TIME my lengthy conversation with the president had ended, and I'd had some emergency medical attention on my arm, I stepped outside the hangar for the first time.

People swarmed the area, buzzing around like insects. The area was filled with Mick's men, local Mexican authorities, border patrol agents—both from Mexico and the US—and what I believed to be Fuerzas Especiales, the Mexican Special Forces.

Special Forces had secured a fifty-yard perimeter around the airplane hangar. Outside the perimeter were airline workers, press, and numerous onlookers. The only person I recognized out there was Willy Blanco. He waved me over. I held out a finger to tell him I'd be there in a minute.

I tracked down Mick just outside the west side of the hangar. "What'd you find out? Any sign of the missing Javi and Sylvia?"

"No sign," he said, shaking his head.

"What about on the other side? Did we confirm everyone's safety?"

"We did. Slim has it under control."

As I breathed a sigh of relief, I looked around. My eyes focused on the military convoy vehicles parked at the side of the hangar. I pointed toward them. "Wait, did you guys use just one vehicle? Or two?"

He looked over, at where I was pointing. "Just one," Mick said. "It's still inside. The other two are right there."

"No, there were four total."

"Four?"

"When I arrived at the warehouse, there were four convoy military vehicles lined up on that very wall."

"Really?"

I nodded.

"Okay," Mick said. "We obviously have one missing military vehicle to account for."

"You should let Special Forces know. I would, but I have plans."

"Will do," Mick replied. "What plans?"

I motioned toward Willy Blanco, who was frantically waving me over. While I walked in his direction, a large helicopter landed some distance behind him. It was dark and far enough away for most people not to notice or pay attention. But I could tell by the shape it was Marine One, the president's helicopter.

When I reached the president's chief of staff, he said, "Glad to see you're alive." He motioned to my left arm, which was in a sling. "You okay?"

I nodded.

He patted my back. "President called. We got you a ride out of here. Ready to go? She'd love to officially get things in writing from you, especially when everything is fresh."

"Sure thing."

As we walked, Willy asked a ton of questions about what had happened. Along the way, we detoured and stopped by his government vehicle so he could grab a small duffel bag from the trunk. Willy motioned at the car as we left toward the helicopter. "Guess I'll send an aide back for that."

A few minutes later, right after we boarded Marine One, I said, "You know what, Willy? I forgot to tell Mom what I'm doing, and she doesn't have a cell on her. I really need to tell her where I'm going and make sure she goes back with Mick's team. Sorry, I'll hurry."

"No problem," he said.

I hustled back and found Mom and brought her up to speed. I also took the time to speak with Raoul and Jaime, not only to make sure they were both doing okay, but to thank them for all their help in such a critical situation. I also checked in with Arturo and his niece.

By the time I finished, Willy had found me and ushered me back to Marine One.

Before long, we'd taken seats across from each other and buckled up and prepared for takeoff. Once we were airborne and had leveled off, I engaged Willy in conversation.

"You think people change, Willy?"

"What do you mean?" he replied.

"What do you mean, 'what do I mean?' Isn't it a straightforward question?"

"It is, for sure. I guess I meant, why are you asking me that now? Of all questions. I mean, after everything that's just happened."

I shrugged. "I guess because it's on my mind. I didn't really think it was possible. You know, a man changing. I figured most men were set in their ways. Like Ortiz, for instance, the infamous Butcher of Baja. Once bad, always bad, right?"

Willy nodded.

"But take Juan Manuel Delgado," I continued, "he apparently changed for the better, didn't he? At least it looks that way now. He changed his name to Jimmy D, started a foundation that only wanted to better the situation for his people, he resisted the cartels, shunning all his former connections in the process. He's a real-life example of change."

I paused and waited to see if Willy responded. He said, "I guess that's right. He did change in the end."

I watched Willy pull his duffel bag onto his lap. He unzipped it and started rifling through its contents. "Whatcha looking for?" I asked.

"I have one of those neck pillows I like to use."

"Got it."

"Can't seem to find it," he said. "Guess I didn't bring it."

"Right. So, you agree, people can change then?"

"Yeah, I think so. Sure, why not?"

"You know the problem with that question, though?"

Willy sighed. "What do you mean? Problem with what question?"

"Whether people change or not," I said. "It's an age-old question: Can or do people change? There's an inherent problem with that question, however."

"Okay, and what's that, Mr. Chase?"

"The assumption with that question when asked is that we always mean change for the better."

"What are you getting at?"

"People also change for the worse, Willy. People change and get bad. It's not a one-way street. Take you, for example."

As I paused, he tensed.

"I mean you're perfect," I continued, "a perfect example, aren't you? A real-life example that a person can change for the bad. Isn't that right?"

Willy Blanco's Adam's apple bobbed, and his forehead suddenly creased with tension. Since his hand was still inside the duffel bag, I said, "You don't really need a neck pillow, do you, Willy? There's a perfectly comfortable headrest behind you."

He clumsily pulled out a pistol and stretched it toward me.

"An Obregón," I noted. "Not surprising, Willy."

Jabbing the gun at me, he asked, "When did you know?"

"Not until recently, very recently, in fact."

He blew out a breath and shook his head. "What, may I ask, tipped you off?"

I gave a short, hearty laugh. "My mother, actually. She tipped me off about you. Inadvertently, albeit."

"Your mother? How?"

"She told me about an older man and his great-granddaughter that worked in the tunnel. That those two had mysteriously vanished hours ago. But they weren't in the basin with everyone else. And they weren't murdered on the surface either. The man's name was Javi, but they also called him Mr. White. Which probably wasn't a random name. After all, it's not like he was a white man. But blanco is Spanish for white, so I imagine Javi's full name is Javier Blanco, and my guess is he's your grandpa and Sylvia is probably your niece."

Willy held a long blink.

"I get it, Willy, obviously I do. I mean they kidnapped my mother to get me to kill Jimmy D. Ortiz used your grandpa and niece to get you to do his bidding. Right?"

His gun arm shook as it stayed outstretched. "Alpha and Omega, that's what Ortiz called his plan."

"Beginning and end?" I questioned. "Why that?"

"Grandpa was the oldest, Sylvia the youngest. Beginning and end of the Blanco family. A not-so-subtle threat if I didn't follow his orders."

I nodded. "And what was your exact connection with Ortiz, anyway?"

Willy didn't respond right away. Instead, he wrestled with pulling the trigger. I could see it on his face.

I held my hands up, palms toward him, and said, "Tell me how I assume a good man like yourself turned so bad, Mr. Blanco. At least clear your conscience before pulling that trigger."

After a tense, quiet moment, Willy eased his arm back. He rested his elbow on his lap, but kept the gun leveled at my chest.

"We're from the same area, the northeast," he said. "That's our connection. Ortiz was always a very powerful man in the Coahuila state. Before the president appointed me her chief of staff, I was the CEO of a Fortune 500 company. But I needed lots of schooling to get to that position. Ortiz had taken a special interest in me once I gained citizenship in the States. He helped with my education. It's incredibly expensive attending an Ivy League school for an MBA. Anyway, I foolishly let him help finance my education, thinking his support came from a good place. That he only wanted to see a boy from Coahuila succeed in the US."

He gripped the gun's stock too tightly. I could tell because the pistol shook, and his knuckles were all white. When he calmed himself, he said, "Anyway, a couple of months ago, he came to collect. That was how he phrased it. That *cabrón*." After shaking his head, Willy continued, "When I turned him down and said I couldn't do what he asked, he kidnapped Javi and Sylvia. And forced my hand."

"And he wanted you to dupe the president, I imagine."

He nodded. "My job was to get her on board with taking out Juan Manuel Delgado. At first, I didn't know why Ortiz wanted Delgado dead so badly. But I eventually pieced it together."

"So, you knew that Ortiz was the Butcher, and that he was trying to pin that identity on Delgado?"

He sighed, and subtly nodded. "Like I said, I pieced it together."

"Was it also true that Ortiz was fed up with Sinaloa's demands on Operation Crossroads and was looking for an out?"

"From what I understand, yes. In the northeast, there's a small cartel called El Hombres. Ortiz has deep connections with them. The cartel has slowly been moving west along the border and expanding. Ortiz wanted to work with them because he could cut a much better deal than the one he had with Sinaloa. And, of course, he trusted those men more."

When Willy paused, I took over. "So, Ortiz orchestrates the killing of his partner, framing Jalisco as the perpetrator. Sinaloa then claims that Jalisco is trying to move in on their area. Jalisco, in turn, becomes enraged because they're accused of doing something they clearly didn't do."

"Right," Willy said, nodding. "A war ensues. Now Ortiz has the perfect excuse for getting out, saying he doesn't trust either major cartel, so he cuts a deal with the cartel he trusts, El Hombres."

"Therein lies my problem."

"Your problem? What's that?"

"Why not use El Hombres to do the job on Jimmy? Why try to bring in SEAL Team Six, or eventually me, to do that job?"

"Listen, I'm certainly glad that Ortiz is dead, so I'm not extolling his virtues here, but you have to give the man credit. He was a criminal genius, and the biggest manipulator of men I know. He always had reasons for doing things and stayed two steps ahead of everyone. To be honest, bringing America into this was what the plan was all about. And it was ingenious."

"How so?"

"He could've used El Hombres, absolutely. But he wanted the Delgado hit to be flawless, to be untraceable. He didn't want it to lead back to El Hombres or himself. Ever. And he felt the US was most equipped for that particular task."

"And he had you in his back pocket to get the president on board to make it all happen. He'd been grooming you for years."

"He dangled the carrot of killing the notorious Butcher of Baja, which he knew Henrietta couldn't resist. She'd send her absolute best to get the job done right."

I sighed.

Willy kept going. "The US finally gets their most wanted man, or at least who they thought was the Butcher. They get vindication and justice for the murdered and maimed American businessmen. And Ortiz's secret is buried with Delgado's body. A win-win. See what I mean? Brilliant."

I didn't nod in agreement, though I certainly saw the merits of Ortiz's plan.

"There's more, though," Willy said. "Something you had no idea about."

I leaned forward.

He jabbed the Obregón at me. "Settle back, Mr. Chase."

When I did, he continued. "Like I said, Ortiz was always two steps ahead. He had a contingency plan in case something went wrong. He's big into using drones these days if you didn't know. During the late afternoon of the planned hit on Delgado, he had a drone in the air recording everything. You would've never spotted it or heard it, but it definitely saw and recorded you on the cliffside."

While I was thinking about what that meant, Willy filled me in. "If you would've killed Delgado, Ortiz would've had footage of America's responsibility for the hit. Of course, he wouldn't have used it unless he absolutely needed to. But boy, think about the leverage he'd have with this president, or any future president. Unbelievable power, right? And if he ever got heat from one of the major cartels accusing him of starting the war, he could use the footage and prove that America was the true source, not him."

I shifted forward in my seat.

He jabbed the gun a second time. "I told you to settle back."

But I didn't budge since I was seething at this point. "You sit there bragging about his plans. Bragging about this terrible man. And you're still so naïve to his ways."

Willy scoffed. "Naïve?"

"You think a man like Ortiz wouldn't use leverage like that? Leverage that you helped him acquire, by the way. No wonder you respect him since you're so stupid."

Willy took my anger and ran with it. He unbuckled and stood and pointed the gun between my eyes. Six feet away at most. "First of all, Mr. Chase, we're talking about what could have happened. None of his plans actually came to fruition, just as a reminder."

"Think I don't know that? Boy, you're dumber than you look. I was the one who didn't pull the trigger if you recall. I stopped all this." I jabbed my finger toward him. "And you set this all in motion. And if his plan had come to fruition, two hundred innocent women would be buried alive."

He lunged at me, stopping just short of arm's reach. "I had no idea, no part—none—when it came to those women and what was going on, and what Ortiz ultimately had planned for them."

It was my turn to scoff. "Save it, Willy. Please. The president came to me with her directive because she believed she had a leak in her administration. Someone who may have leaked the Nogales operation. That was you, wasn't it?"

"Hell no," he said.

"That was you and Ortiz, admit it. You're responsible for the dead soldiers."

"No way," he said through clenched teeth. "That was the Jalisco cartel getting to one member of the American team, no more than that. Think about the fallout from Nogales. Ortiz wouldn't want that, would he? We already had the SEAL Team Six in place to carry out Ortiz's plan. We didn't need you to do it. Nogales threw everything into chaos, which caused the president to go it alone and approach you. I had to play catch-up and figure out what she was doing. No, I had nothing to do with Nogales and neither did Ortiz."

He actually made a good point. "So you had no knowledge of the Nogales leak and of Ortiz drugging and selling women to the States? You expect me to believe that?"

"No clue. None whatsoever."

"Maybe you're right about Nogales, just maybe, but don't feign innocence about the women. The president told me she'd delegated responsibility for Crossroads. You were in charge, weren't you? You oversaw the operation. And don't you dare claim it was simply an oversight that two hundred women went missing from your program."

He shook his head like a young child. "No idea about the women. No idea what Ortiz was up to."

"Even if I believed you, which I don't, you and Ortiz were copartners in this massive conspiracy and cover-up. Don't ever forget that."

"I had to." He gritted his teeth. "Was forced to by Ortiz. What would you have done if you were in my position?"

"A million things differently," I replied.

"Like what?"

"I would've figured something out, that's for sure."

"Ha!" he scoffed. "Much easier said than done."

"Maybe for a man with your pea-sized brain."

He tried to blink away the rage in his eyes. "You're the stupid one here. I'm the one holding a gun to your face."

"And what are you going do now? What's your plan? I can tell by your tense trigger finger that it's to kill me."

"You better believe it."

"Then what? Huh, genius?"

When he hesitated to respond, I kept at it. "Meet up with the military vehicle, I bet. Kill me, then put a gun to the pilot's head and command him to land at the rendezvous site? I imagine before Ortiz took his swan dive, he sent your grandpa and niece off in the military vehicle."

"Something like that," Willy responded.

"But then you must kill the pilot and copilot, then get rid of the most famous helicopter in the world. It will never end. You won't cover this up, not a chance."

"There's definitely a chance."

"Drop the weapon," I said. "Do something right, Willy. Turn this whole situation around."

He shook his head. "I can't."

"You can. Be a better man."

Willy thought about it for a moment, but only a moment. "I can't."

"Change, Willy. Make a good choice. Now's your chance."

His creased brow started dripping sweat into his eyes. He wiped it away with his left hand. When he returned to his shooting position, he looked resolved to fire.

"Don't do it," I said. "And I'll tell you why, why it's an absolutely horrible idea."

"Shut up!" He jabbed the gun. "Shut your blabbering mouth."

"The president knows everything," I blurted. "Everything, Willy."

"No, no, you're a liar," he replied.

"There's no point in killing me and the pilots. None. It's over, Willy."

"*Liar!*" he shouted.

"Henrietta and I spoke earlier, we set this all up."

"Not a chance, you haven't spoken with her. No way."

"How do you think I knew about your grandpa and niece? The president confirmed it."

"You guessed!" he shouted back, stabbing the gun at me. "A total guess."

"Nope, no guessing here. Days ago, when waiting for Henrietta to text me back, I had a thought. How did POTUS acquire her burner phone? It's not like she could waltz into a Best Buy or gas station and buy a burner cell with cash. She'd use someone in her inner circle get her a burner."

"Speculation." He nodded to himself. "You're speculating now."

"Again, nope. I asked Henrietta who was responsible. She confirmed it was you. You control all her communication, don't you? What'd you do? Swap the SIM card in her burner? That way when I finally texted her back, she didn't get the message."

Willy's eyes were wide as his mind raced. He wasn't looking at me. Since I was getting into his head, I kept going. "You had her original burner SIM, so you popped it into your phone and sent me those three texts tonight. Right? That way it looked like she finally texted me back. Yet you set me up to die and coordinated that with Thiago and his men."

He looked back at me. "Not that it matters, but she doesn't pay attention to details, so I didn't even need to switch SIM cards. I just replaced her burner phone with an identical-looking burner. She never memorized any phone numbers, so swapping out burners, which obviously would mean different numbers, wasn't a risky move. But you could've guessed all this, couldn't you?"

"But I didn't, Willy, and I'm giving you an out here. The president knows everything. No point in continuing. It's over. Put the gun down."

He didn't. Instead, he approached me, quite calmly, in fact. Stretching out the gun, so it was a few feet from my head, he said. "You're manipulating me to save yourself. I won't fall for it. I've been manipulated enough."

"I'm not, Willy. I promise."

This time he replied in a cold, calculated voice. "Yes, Garrison Chase, you are. You definitely are."

Then he pulled the trigger.

CHAPTER FIFTY-THREE

CLICK.

Willy Blanco pulled the trigger again. Another click. In a confused rage, he pulled again and again and again. *Nothing. Nothing. Nothing.*

While he pointed and pulled, I calmly unbuckled and stood. He followed my movements with his gun arm, the whole time continuing to pull the trigger.

"I tried to tell you, Willy. I gave you an out. Gave you a chance to at least do one thing right. Just one thing."

Finally realizing his gun was empty, Willy lunged at me with both arms outstretched, gunning for my throat. Since I had a much longer reach, I caught him by the underside of his wrists and pushed his arms up, then kneed him hard in the groin as his momentum carried him forward. As he doubled over, I walloped him with a right-handed uppercut. It connected square with his mouth and broke several teeth.

Willy Blanco flopped backward and fell to the side, right by the helicopter's rear side door. He curled up into a ball and moaned. I took the moment to pick up the pistol.

"Pilots did a good job. And, yes, both were in on this, along with the president." I extracted the magazine and glanced at it. It was taped at the top to contain the sand inside. Sand was approximately the same weight as a full magazine.

"The president and I knew you'd do anything and everything in your power to stop me from speaking or getting to her. When you left Marine One to come back and get me, the pilots rummaged through your duffel bag and found the Obregón. I told the president if the pilots found a weapon to empty it and fill it with sand."

I tore off the tape and poured the sand onto Willy, who was curled up in the fetal position whining about his bloodied face and missing teeth.

"Your face and teeth are the least of your worries, Willy. The least."

Willy crawled to his knees, but he stayed in a tight ball. Just as I was about to address him again, the man lunged toward me. In my periphery, I caught the glint of a blade. But it was a late catch, so I didn't move my leg fast enough. The bastard had a knife hidden in his boot top. The inside of my right calf took a direct hit.

The plunging knife felt like a hundred hot razors penetrating at once. Before I collapsed to the ground in excruciating pain, I managed to kick Willy off me with my left foot.

He tried to pull the knife with him as he fell backward, but he failed. All four inches of the blade was deep inside my leg. The knife tip, no doubt, had wedged into bone. I bent over and examined it and tried to extract it. Just touching the handle sent shock waves up my body, though.

Better, I figured, to leave it in so I didn't bleed out.

When I turned my attention to Willy, I noticed he was on his knees pushing on the side door, preparing to open it. The long end of the nearest seat belt had been wrapped around his right wrist twice. He kicked against the door until it opened. The collapsible five stairs and railing opened into midair. The whole structure almost ripped off its hinges from the wind outside.

Alarm bells started blaring inside the helicopter.

There wasn't a huge suck of air after the door opened, but the rush certainly pulled me toward the rectangular opening. I scrambled to grab anything I could. Unfortunately, I was between seats, so nothing was around to hold. I slid toward the opening. With my long reach, I managed to grab the seatbelt strap, just above the spot where Willy's wrist was wrapped.

"Off me!" Willy screamed. "*Off!*"

We were chest down, nearly on top of each other, with two-thirds of our bodies outside the helicopter on the shaking stairs. I felt the helicopter starting to slow.

Willy was locked in by his wrist and going nowhere. I could see the man's hand turning purple from the cinching belt. He used his free hand and pulled on my shirt and shoulder with all his might. I couldn't fight back very well because my left hand was my free hand, and it was weak from my bicep wound.

When I felt my right hand slipping, I knew I had only moments to spare. My Kershaw folding knife came to mind but opening it one-handed would be time consuming. Using my core muscles, I brought my injured leg up, then gripped the knife's handle with my left hand and ripped out the blade.

Willy pulled and tugged and tried everything to loosen my grip.

But I was laser focused on the seatbelt strap, on the inch-long spot separating our hands. It took me two saw-like motions to cut the belt just above Willy's wrist. But I didn't slice all the way through. A centimeter or so from the end, the weight of Willy's body tore the final piece of belt away.

And Willy Blanco bumped down the steps, then slipped into the dark night. A terrible scream echoed behind him.

I didn't pay a moment of attention to him, though. Instead, I fought to hang on. With the bloody knife in my left hand, I stabbed it into the floor as hard as I could to keep me from sliding down the stairs and to my death. Closing my eyes, I held on with everything I had.

Moments later, I felt a pair of hands grasp my forearms.

"I got you," the copilot said. "I got you."

After yanking me in and wrestling with the door, the copilot rushed away. I stayed on my forearms and knees, fighting to get my breath back. Between breaths, I managed a thank-you at the retreating pilot.

At this point, my head was low enough that I could get a close look at the knife I'd stuck into the floor. "El Hombres" was carved into one side of the handle. After pulling it from the floor, I collapsed against the closed door and turned over the knife.

The name "Thiago" was carved into the handle's other side.

Unbelievable. That blade had stabbed my dog, now me. And Willy must've climbed down to Thiago's location and taken it from his dead body.

Suddenly the copilot swept in carrying an emergency medical kit. "That was close," he said.

"Too close," I replied. "Way too close."

While he began bandaging my wound, he handed me a cell. "The president is on hold for you."

The pain in my leg was fierce, so all I could muster was, "Ma'am."

"Garrison, are you all right? What happened? What's happening with Willy?"

I took a moment before responding. "You're gonna need a new chief of staff, Madam President. Sorry about that."

She paused longer than I did.

I broke the silence. "He's dead, ma'am, and I'm responsible for that."

"Understood. Everything will be fine, Garrison."

"Ma'am, I'm responsible for a few more bodies, in fact. This is shaping up to be quite an international incident. I may need a pardon from you."

More awkward silence, then the president said, "I'm just glad you're okay, Garrison, so glad. And that's the main thing."

I thought about that. "No, Madam President, the main thing is that you're not involved." I breathed a huge sigh of relief. "That's what I'm glad about. That two hundred women and my mother are still alive, and that you're not a traitor."

"I'm so glad the women are alive. I'll make sure they all get citizenship if that's what they want. I'm also very glad you don't think I'm a traitor, Garrison."

"Me too. I had my doubts, ma'am, I must be honest. But I feel better about you now."

"Glad to hear."

Feeling loopy from the pain, I said, "Ma'am, I may even vote for you again."

She responded with, "Well, that's something."

I cleared my throat. "I have one more request, if that's all right."

"Anything you want, Garrison. Absolutely anything."

"Can we make a detour before crossing the border? One quick stop."

"Sure. Where?"

"Tecate."

"Tecate? Why on earth do you want to stop there?"

"My dog, ma'am. We have to pick up my dog."

CHAPTER FIFTY-FOUR

One month later

Karla and I held hands while leaning against the fence. Since walking was still difficult after being stabbed in the calf, I'd spent most of the party leaning against the fence. On a positive note, my bicep wound had healed nicely.

Ranger was to my left, sitting on the dusty ground watching the festivities. The sun was currently setting across the desert. Orange and yellow hues lit up the dry, arid land before us.

We stood on Javier Blanco's property in northeastern Mexico. He'd arranged a celebratory festival on his beautiful ranch land. Mariachi music filled the air. The intoxicating aroma of roasted meat on a spit wafted our way. Javi and my mother were laughing and talking while working the pit area together.

Moments later, Javi looked over. "Meat's ready." He stepped away from the barbecue area and approached us. "Time to eat."

Karla squeezed my hand. She gestured toward Simon, who was off to our right playing soccer with a slew of other children. "I'll fix him a plate."

As Javi took position where Karla had been, I said, "This is some beautiful property, Javi, just beautiful."

"It is. What makes it even more beautiful are the people."

As we stood together in silence, my eyes darted around at the guests. "You're right," I said, breaking the silence. Pointing to a group of men to my left, I said, "The men you worked with, Raoul and Jaime, we wouldn't be here without them, without their sacrifice. And from what I understand, your niece Sylvia, too. And Arturo and Mariana"—I gestured toward them— "they did anything I asked, without hesitation or question."

I met Javi's gaze.

He nodded and said, "Salt of the earth. Honesty, goodness, sacrifice, even if it means your life. All these people exhibited those traits. We need more of them in our world, Garrison. These are the people who will preserve our world."

"Agreed."

A moment later, I sighed and said, "Speaking of honesty, Javi, I . . ."

"What?" He put his hand on my shoulder. "What is it?"

After clearing my throat, I said, "I need to come clean. I need to tell you the truth."

While I paused, he tapped me on the shoulder. "Go ahead. I can take it."

"I feel compelled, Javi, to tell you the whole story. You deserve it. But it's hard, and I'm not sure I'm doing the right thing. It may be better for you not to know."

He looked off in the distance for a moment, then said, "If it helps, I think I know what this is about. For the record, I don't buy Washington's story. I know my grandson Willy. His ambition was blinding. I doubt that he took his own life. And if he did, it wouldn't be from him thinking Sylvia and I were dead. It would be from him trying to cover up his involvement."

Naturally, the White House had spun the story, which did not sit well with me. News outlets reported that the president's chief of staff took his own life after it had been falsely reported that his granddad and niece had been buried alive in the tunnel.

"I confronted him in Marine One, Javi, about his involvement. I gave him an out, a chance to do something right. Like you said, he chose to cover up his involvement instead."

Javi blinked a few times. I noticed his eyes were glistening.

"He planned to rendezvous with the military vehicle," I continued, "to come get you and Sylvia. He did a lot to save you two, but he also planned to kill me and the pilots and dispose of the helicopter."

Javi looked up into the orangey-red sky and shook his head. "Willy, Willy, Willy," he repeated.

"The president and I had no plans or intentions of killing him, just so you know. None whatsoever."

"I know," Javi replied. "And I know my Willy. He didn't go down easy. Did he?"

"No, he certainly did not."

Eventually, Javi looked over. "Were you the one that . . ."

I pushed a long breath through my nose and finally said, "I was."

Javi stepped forward and placed both his hands on my shoulders. I had no idea what he was prepared to say or do. He looked me dead in the eye. "For everything you did to save us, for your truthfulness, even though it was hard for you to admit and hard for me to hear, I thank you. Like the others, you are truly the salt of the earth, Garrison Chase, truly."

I was too choked up to reply.

"Now let's celebrate," Javi said. "To life and to the triumph of the human spirit." He walked toward the pit and waved me over. "Come on, that's what this evening is about."

"Be right there," I said.

Bending down, I stroked Ranger's head and took a moment to compose myself.

Karla saw me by myself and walked over. I'd told her on the trip down that I had to come clean with Javi. She leaned against the fence and said, "How'd it go?"

"Better than expected. Much better."

"Good," she replied. "One down, one to go."

I furrowed my brow. "One to go. What do you mean?"

"Slim," she said. "You promised me you'd come clean with Slim, too. About the Valen Jackson story and your job. And why you're hesitant to become his partner."

"Right. I did, didn't I?"

She grabbed my hand and pulled me away from the fence. Slipping her arm around my waist, she said, "When are you going to tell him?"

As I limped toward the food line, I said, "Too bad he's not here now."

"Classic Chase. Avoiding the question, like you do best."

"Me? No."

She kept at it. "When?"

I hesitated to respond.

"Garrison Chase, you have a problem committing, so I want to hear you commit to a time and place right now."

"Ouch," I said, laughing. "Fair enough. As long as you're talking about Slim and nothing else."

She slugged me on the shoulder.

"Okay," I said. "How about I call him on the drive back? We have a long ride home."

She squeezed my side. "Deal. And I'll hold you to it, you know?"

I squeezed her back. "I know you will, Karla. I know you will."

AUTHOR'S NOTE

Dear Reader,

Thank you for taking the time to read my book. I hope you enjoyed THE BAJA DIRECTIVE. If you did, I'd be grateful if you'd consider leaving a review on Amazon.com and/or Goodreads.com. Reviews are extremely helpful!

If you'd like to learn more about me, the Garrison Chase thriller series, or sign up for my newsletter, please visit my website at:

craignhooper.com

I'm also giving away a free ebook to all my fans! FALLOUT, the prequel to the Garrison Chase series, is FREE when you sign up for my newsletter. Please visit my website to get your free copy.

If you have any questions or comments, please don't hesitate to reach out at craig@craignhooper.com. I absolutely love hearing from fans!

Thanks for being a reader.

ALSO BY CRAIG N. HOOPER

Fallout (FREE!)

The Greatest Good

A Thin Line

All the Good Men

The Garrison Chase Series (Books 1-3)

Made in the USA
Coppell, TX
03 May 2022

77347734R10162